THE 95,000 WORD SUICIDE NOTE

More books by the same author:

EMAIL FROM A VAMPIRE

SOPHIA

BOY

S.U.N.D.S

THE SOUND OF CRYING

DIGITAL ROMANCE DISORDER

THE KILLING OF EMILY CHANDLER

THE 95,000 WORD SUICIDE NOTE
Nigel Cooper

Generic Pool Publishing

First published in Great Britain in 2020 by Generic Pool Publishing

ISBN: 978-0-9573307-5-7

Cover design by Nigel Cooper
Cover photo: Self portrait by Nigel Cooper

Typeset in Garamond 12.5/14.75 pt.
by the author

This novel is also available for Kindle, details of which
are available on the author's website at:

www.nigelcooperauthor.co.uk

"Write something, even if it's just a suicide note." ~ Gore Vidal

"We cannot tear out a single page of our life, but we can throw the whole book in the fire." ~ George Sand

"Death is life's way of telling you you're fired. Suicide is your way of telling life you quit." ~ Anonymous

Prologue

By the time you read this I'll be dead – or at least I hope so. The story I'm about to unfold will categorically shock, inform, educate and evoke a multitude of emotions as I peel away the sugar coated topping and various rosy layers from the world that most people – in the so-called civilised western world at least – live in, to reveal *my* world, a world that is beyond most people's comprehension. But, it's not all doom and gloom. Throughout this rather unorthodox, and quite often emotional, rollercoaster of a story you'll laugh, you'll cry, you'll sympathise and, at times, you might even hate me, momentarily at least, and wonder what the hell's going through my mind. But, as the late Seattle grunge rock singer, Kurt Cobain, once said, 'I'd rather be hated for who I am, then loved for who I am not'.

Over the years I've become something of an existential nihilist, but that does not mean I don't enjoy or appreciate life, I do, or at least I used to, many moons ago, before I was born. However, my intelligence, unorthodox customs, unique ways of looking at life, many proven theories and life experiences have given me deep wisdom that has landed me in a place, a world, an environment, that I find much more painful than pleasurable.

My friends say I have OCD; Ok, I'll admit to that. I'll also admit that I have most of the traits of a person with bipolar disorder, though I've never actually been medically diagnosed as such. My personality can be somewhat volatile at times; this is usually brought on by the words or actions of another human being/beings. I also suffer from manic depression and I sit on a unique spectrum that is yet to be given a medical name. Sigmund Freud once said, 'Before you diagnose yourself with depression or low self-esteem, first make sure you are not, in fact, surrounded by assholes.' I must admit, for the most part, it is usually another human being that is responsible for my depression, or tipping me over the edge or triggering one of my emotional meltdowns or igniting my volatile nature. Although when I steer clear of people I'm generally ok, there is still something that lurks deep in my soul that prevents me from living anything that could be considered a normal or content lifestyle.

I'm intelligent (my IQ is 148), I'm introspective and I daydream a lot. I often see things in ways that leave others scratching their heads.

Sometimes I wish I could find a brain surgeon that would be willing to perform some sort of partial lobotomy on me, in the hope it would allow me to go about my life in ignorant bliss, like the lower IQ members of the great unwashed, so I didn't have to know the things that I know, that I didn't have the insights that I have, that I didn't have to see the world for what it really is – the 'real' word that sits underneath the sugar coated topping that most people live in.

I think everybody should take a good 'existential' look at life once in a while – with a side helping of nihilism.

I'm angry and disappointed in society. Humanity, ironically, has no humanity anymore and, as I sit in a dark corner every night and cry, the pain, loneliness and hate seeps out of my every pore like a fever-induced sweat.

I wasn't always like this. Once, I was a balanced person swimming in a warm pool of equilibrium – right up until the moment that truck swerved to avoid hitting a cat and, instead, slammed into my parents and 5-year old sister right in front of my eyes, killing them all, when I was just six years old. What happened during the next couple of years would change my life, forever, in ways I could never have imagined.

Chapter 1

My mother and father, like pretty much every other set of parents in the world, were a pair of selfish bastards. They weren't selfish bastards generally, you understand, but when it came to their own selfish child-wantingness reasons, they were. They procreated and had children for their own self-interest, that and the ever-present ticking biological clock that most women possess. The fact is most parents don't give any thought or consideration as to how their precious beloved little newborn baby's life will turn out when they're older. I mean, how many parents say, 'Let's have a baby, we're affluent, educated and our baby can grow up to have a wonderful life, a private education, go to university and perhaps they can become a lawyer or a doctor, see the wonders of the world and buy a nice 5-bedroomed detached house in the suburbs and marry a rich and educated woman and start a happy family of their own and go on lovely family holidays twice a year,' and so on and so forth. They don't. Most couples say something along the lines of, 'Let's have a baby, that would be nice,' or 'Let's start a family,' or how about this selfish self-seeking example, 'Let's have some children so they can look after us when we're old and decrepit,' yeah right, don't count on that one.

Couples have children for all kinds of reasons and, from what I can glean, most of the reasons are selfish ones. In all the years I've been around, 42 years now, I don't ever recall asking anybody the question of why they chose to have a baby, or babies, and getting any sort of tangible answer that comes from the said child's viewpoint or interest.

Like most people – well, all of them actually – on this planet, I did not ask to be born and I unreservedly resent, even hate, my parents for putting forth the time and effort it took them to create me. During the three years (yes, three years, I found this out later in life) that they tried to conceive me they did not give a second thought to any of the thoughts or feelings that I might have on the matter, not even a first thought actually. They just knew that they wanted children and they were going to have them, come hell or high water. I don't know why it took them so long to get pregnant with me. Perhaps there was a bug or a glitch in my mother's gynaecological workshop or perhaps a low sperm count on my fathers part, or both, who knows? All I know is that, eventually, they managed it and I can only imagine that they had a whole bundle of lovemaking fun along the way – but my life would turn out to be anything but fun.

Let's skip forward 42 years from my 'unrequested' birth to where I find myself today and we'll take it from there.

Chapter 2

My name's Marion Redwood, but the few friends that I have (if you can call them that), call me Red. For the record, I'm a man, in case you were wondering. Marion does actually sound like a woman's name, but, believe it or not, it is in fact a unisex name and I can prove it. Remember the American actor, John Wayne, from back in the 60s and 70s? Well, his birth name was Marion Morrison, John Wayne was his alias. There was also an American NFL football player called Marion Rushing and a Brazilian footballer called Marion Silva Fernandes.

From my understanding, Marion is a French diminutive form of Marie, which is derived from the Hebrew name Miryam, which means 'sea of bitterness' or 'sea of sorrow'. They certainly got that right in my case: sorrow by name, sorrow by nature. Though something tells me that my parents had no idea of the name meaning when they picked it. Like most parents, they probably picked the name based on some famous person from the time, favourite actor or singer perhaps, or maybe they just liked the way the name sounded, who knows?

I detest my name, and the two people who assigned

it to me when I was born 42 years ago, and I hate it when people use it to address me. I got a lot of stick for having a 'girl's' name when I was at school and I was damned if I was going to allow that crap to follow me through life into adulthood so, these days, I always introduce myself to new people as Red. The nickname, short for Redwood, my family name, in case you hadn't guessed, was not my idea. The name Red was first allocated to me back in 1988 (I was only 12 back then) by my, then, friend, Brian. His parents were going out for the evening and they'd asked me if I wanted to come around to watch a movie with him. Brian was the same age as me and while a large proportion of parents didn't have a problem leaving a 12-year old at home alone while they went out for the evening, Brian's parents didn't quite trust him not to get up to no good. They figured if they invited me around and left us food and a rented VHS movie all would be good. Hmmm, what were they thinking? I mean, Brian was always getting into some sort of trouble, both at school and at home. He often truanted from school and, when he did, I was usually with him. In fact, I was often the one who instigated the truancy. Don't get me wrong, I value education these days and I did back then too, but there were some classes that had absolutely zero appeal to me: History and Religion to name two. Julius Caesar didn't float my boat, and God, his son (and questionable mother), and that bearded guy who carved mandates into stone slabs certainly didn't. Even at the tender age of 12 I was rational and intelligent enough to know that God didn't exist any more than Santa clause, the tooth fairy or little flying pixies at the bottom of the garden. Once, during assembly, I had to read a passage from the New Testament (after doing a quick rehearsal in the headmasters office), as all the kids did. Every morning a different kid would read a different passage of Chinese Whispers and lies from the New Testament. After I stepped off the stage I vowed never to do it again, and I didn't.

Luckily for me, both history and religious studies fell on the same day, along with PE (Physical Education, as it was known back then). The only other class I had that day was Science, which I actually enjoyed so, sometimes, I'd nip back into school for that one, as it was the last lesson of the day.

So, Brian's parents headed off to the dinner party they'd been invited to and left Brian and me with a load of finger-food, snacks, fizzy drinks and a VHS copy of *Big*, starring Tom Hanks, which Brian's dad had picked out for us from the local video rental store. Brian's parents tried their level best to bring their only son up well, which included limiting his movie viewing activities to PG rated films, at best. However, Brian's dad had forgot to take the movie back that he'd rented to watch with Brian's mum the night before. So, Brian and I now had a choice of two films, *Big* with the rather child-like Tom Hanks, or *Midnight Run*, with the rather manly and very cool Robert De Niro. Hmmm, Brian and I decided this was an easy choice. *Midnight Run* it was, especially given that this movie had a little red BBFC circle in the bottom right hand corner with an eye-opening '18' rating written in the centre of it. There was bound to be sex, swearing or violence in it, or maybe even all three!

So, back to how I got the handle, Red. During the aforementioned movie there was a scene where Bob De Niro and Charles Grodin were doing a con in a bar called Red's Corner Bar and owner of the bar was called Red. Grodin's character asked him why he was called Red and asked if it was because he died his hair. The owner said it was short for Redwood. With my surname also being Redwood, Brian looked at me and said, 'You want another sausage roll, Red?' smiling, and that was it, it stuck. I liked my new handle; in fact, I loved it, especially when the only other choice was Marion. Brian knew I hated my first name so, from that day forth, he called me Red and he always introduced me to any of his friends as Red and I also introduced myself to any new friends as Red too. Of course, the older kids and bully boys at school always stuck it to me and continued the insults for having a girl's name, but inside, deep inside, where they could not see, I was Red, with a capital R.

These days I work as a driving instructor. I say 'these days' as I haven't always taught people how to drive for a living. Back in 1998 I was a concert pianist, for eight years, a talented one too, a virtuoso, right up until the time that I got a little out of it after smoking a couple of joints at my friend's house. I hardly ever smoked dope, but I was going through a bout of depression at the time, brought about by my beautiful, but unfaithful, wife, and I did something rather silly that resulted in me severing a tendon and losing the ability to move my third finger (that's third finger in pianistic terms) on my left hand with any real conviction so, in the blink of an eye, or rather, the slip of a knife, my virtuoso concert pianist days were over.

For as far back as I could remember I'd always drifted in and out of depression and on that particular evening I was particularly depressed. In fact 'depressed', as a word, just didn't really sum up how I felt that evening. It's a long story, one that you'll learn about later on, but for now, let's just say I was low, really low. I was spiralling down into a vortex that I'd created and I was been sucked in, deeper and deeper, down into a hell-like place where there was no hope and no absolution. It was 2006, I was 30 years old and my Decree Absolute had just arrived in the post. I'd been married for five years and I thought my wife, Melanie, and I were going to be together forever, until she decided to sleep with one of her colleagues at her company's Xmas party. Well, she didn't really *sleep* with him; more fucked him up against a filing cabinet.

I had my suspicions, so one evening, while giving my wife's friend a lift home after she'd been over to our place for a chat and a few glasses of wine, I blagged it. Made out I knew and said, 'So, what's the name of the guy Melanie's been fucking at work?' to which she replied, 'Oh, you know about that?' to which I replied,

'I do now'.

All she could say was, 'Oops, Marion, I'm really sorry.'

Amanda was Melanie's best friend; they'd known each other since school and I knew they had their little secrets, what best friends don't? And I knew that most of them were harmless, except this one. Amanda always called me Red, except when she was tipsy, or out-and-out shit-faced, then, for some, very annoying, reason, she called me Marion, emphasising every syllable, usually with a stupid drunken smile on her face.

Anyway, during that 10-minute journey back to Amanda's house she spilled the beans and told me everything: how it started, how long it had been going on behind my back, et cetera. Unbeknownst to me, it turned out that Amanda had a bit of a soft spot for me.

'Marion, you're a lovely guy. I know what you went through when you were just a kid and I think it's amazing that you turned out so well. You're a real gentleman, you're kind, caring, selfless and…' She started to sob and reached into her handbag for a packet of tissues, 'You deserve to be with somebody more … loyal. Oh, Marion, I'm so sorry. It's not the first time either.'

'What isn't the first time?' I asked.

'Melanie, she's done it before.'

'Done what before?' I said, but I knew what she meant.

'Been unfaithful. Two years ago she had a brief affair with Colin. It didn't last long, about six or seven weeks.'

'Who's Colin?' I enquired.

'Colin from Corfu.'

'Wh– wait, you mean Colin as in Colin and Tara, the couple we met on holiday?

'Yes.'

'Fuck, I knew we shouldn't have stayed in touch with them. That's the thing with people you meet on holiday, they say, "We must keep in touch", and they do.'

'I'm so sorry, Marion,' she said, blowing her nose into a fresh tissue.

'Wait a minute, they were trying for a baby,' I said.

'I know, that's men for you,' she said, 'present company excluded, of course.'

'Where were they doing–' I had to cut myself off.

'At his place, when his wife was at work. Melanie would go to his place during her lunch hour.'

'Of course, he was an architect; he worked at home from a small office drawing up plans for extensions all day. Christ, why didn't I see it?'

'You're too nice, Marion, you see the best in people, that's all.'

So, there it was. My beautiful wife had been unfaithful to me, twice, that I know of. So I figured she didn't love me and love had to be a two-way thing, so I confronted her and asked for a divorce. She didn't argue or put up a fight and she didn't try to deny it. But she was a domineering woman, a force to be reckoned with, so when she said she'd fight me through the courts for the house I'd simply said, 'No you won't.'

'Yes, I will. You'll see, I'm not going anywhere. I'm keeping this house.'

'No, you misunderstand, you won't be fighting anybody in court because I'm not going to be there,' I said.

'You have to be there, first thing in the morning. I'm getting a solicitor.'

'You can do whatever you want, but you'll be wasting your money.'

'Not only am I keeping the house, but you're not going to get a penny from it,' she said, angry now and up for a fight, in her usual confrontational way. She had a tone that suggested this was all my fault; maybe it was my fault that some guy had slipped, fallen on top my wife and got his dick accidently stuck in her vagina.

'I'm aware of that, Melanie,' I said.

'What?' she said, slightly taken aback.

'You can keep it,' I said, separating my car key from the house keys on my keyring and tossing them onto the coffee table.

'What are you talking about?' she said.

'It's yours, all yours, you can keep it, Melanie,' I said, walking over to *my* Hi-Fi and disconnecting the cables. She could keep the house but I'd be dammed if she was staking a claim on my beloved Hi-Fi and vinyl record collection. This wasn't just a 'stereo system' (as she used to call it), this was quality Hi-Fi: Linn, Naim, Nakamichi, top notch equipment that audiophiles appreciated and Melanie was no audiophile. She liked Michael Bolton and Whitney Houston for crying out loud.

'I'm taking my Hi-Fi, my records and my clothes. The rest is yours, including the house,' I said, while carefully removing the metal platter from my LP12 turntable.

'Are you serious?' she said, suspicion in her voice.

'Melanie, you can have the house, ok. Just have your solicitor send me whatever papers I need to sign and I'll sign them. I'll be staying with Mathieu,' I said.

Mathieu was a good friend who I met when I was 19 after I responded to an advert in the NME (New Musical Express). Mathieu was a singer and his rock/ funk fusion band needed a bass player. I liked his band and their influences, who were Red Hot Chilli Peppers, Nine Inch Nails, Faith No More, Primus and Living Colour, with a bit of Led Zeppelin thrown in, all the stuff I was into, especially Living Colour as their bass lines were really funky and awesome.

I'd recently added 'slap' to my bass playing technique, rather than just using my fingers or a pick. So by the time the audition came around for Mathieu's band I was confident I'd nail it. Mathieu and I had met up in a local pub, where he'd given me a copy of his bands demo tape. Of course, CD was out at the time, but Mathieu still liked to record the bands demo's using a Fostex 4-track tape recorder and then transfer it onto a regular audio cassette. There were ten songs on the tape, which I learnt and played over and over again until I had them down. The bass lines were fairly simple, AC/DC simple. So I figured I'd 'funk' them up a little. I worked out some variations to the bass lines that had been laid down, making them a little more complex, with the odd slap and pop here and there.

Back then I lived in Camden Town in North London, so Mathieu had arranged for me to come along to one of their rehearsals at a rehearsal studio in Chalk Farm. The audition was amazing, the drummer and I connected, musically speaking, immediately – we were tight. He loved the way I played and followed his kick drum, which he held down with metronomic precision. The guitarist was pretty damn good too. He was a big fan of Joe Satriani and Steve Via and he could fly up and down the fret board with similar speed and dexterity with the occasional Eddie Van Halen style tapping technique whenever a solo opportunity presented itself. Mathieu and the band loved what I'd done with the bass lines that Mathieu and the guitarist had written. After we'd been through the ten songs, we messed around with a few other songs that they were working on and I was amazed with myself at how easy it was for me to listen to the chord progressions and drum beat and drop a funky/rock bass line into it. I'd never had to come up with original bass lines for somebody else's songs before as I'd only ever played along to CDs that I'd bought in record shops.

Afterwards we went to the pub and we all got on really well and they informed me that I was the new bass player for 'Nine Yards of Dead Cats'. Hmmm, not the best band name, I admit, which probably explains why we never got any record company interest. Still, we managed to do a bunch of gigs in and around London at the time; the usual, pubs, small clubs and the like, and it was great. I loved been on stage and, back then, I had no shortage of friends, or girls. Mathieu was not only French with a seriously sexy French accent; he was a good-looking guy too, with seductive, almost hypnotic, big brown eyes. The way he toyed, suggestively, with the microphone stand practically had the girls in the audience throwing their knickers onto the stage. It's the same story with most bands, the singer gets most of the attention, especially a good looking singer like Mathieu. However, there was usually a smattering of young women left over to entertain the rest of the band members. Mathieu, being a lady's man – and something of a womaniser back then – played on his accent and good looks and was having sex with different girls every week, sometimes two different girls in a week and sometimes two different girls at the same time. In hindsight, he was playing Russian roulette with his dick with all the unprotected sex he was having. He's mellowed these days, but he was incredibly lucky to get away with it. As for me, I was aware that HIV, although not rife, was certainly a big consideration, as were the other nasty STI's that were going around so I was a more careful, and selective. Truth be told, even back then, when I was only 19, I was looking for something more serious out of a relationship, something meaningful, something that could, potentially at least, develop into a long-term relationship. If I suspected that a girl just wanted to have a bit of fun for the night, or more to the point, if I suspected that she was promiscuous, I'd politely decline.

Mathieu lived in a three-bedroomed house in Muswell Hill with his girlfriend, Shari. He'd been with her for three years now. Since the days of his band, Nine Yards Of Dead Cats, Mathieu had moved out of his shared 2-bed flat, built up his own business and got a mortgage on a place of his own. He'd done rather well for himself, running his own organic health food shop. It's doing so well he doesn't even have to be there much as he's got a trustworthy manager and two sales assistants who practically run the shop for him.

I knew his lodger had recently moved out so – as I drove over to his house, my car laden with Hi-Fi equipment, vinyl records and clothes – I was confident he'd put me up for a while. Shari liked me, so I doubted she'd object.

Mathieu and Shari often shared some marijuana in the evening and it was during my first evening with them, as I sat there all depressed and feeling sorry for myself, that Shari proffered me a joint. She could see that I was a little anxious and upset and she thought a puff or two would calm me down a little: it did, perhaps too much.

As the evening progressed I started to loosen up as we chatted and reminisced about the band, back in the day, omitting Mathieu's womanising activities of course. I had no idea if Shari knew exactly how many girls Mathieu had slept with and I was not about to ask her. The TV was on and the movie *Aliens* was airing. By the time Bishop's famous knife game came around, I was out of it enough to think that I could pull off the same stunt with a similar degree of speed and accuracy.

Mathieu, being French, was into his French sticks of bread and various cheeses and there was usually a breadboard with such edibles on the coffee table in front of the sofa in his lounge, especially if he and Shari were having a smoke. So, I reached forward and picked up the cheese knife – which had not one, but two, lethally sharp points at the end – and placed my left hand flat on the large wooden bread board, between a triangle of Brie and some spreadable Torta Dolcelatte.

'Hey, hey, hey, Red, I don't think that's a good idea,' said Mathieu, getting up and leaning forward to take the knife from me: too late. I raised my right fist up in the air, clenching the said knife and brought it down with the intention of stabbing the breadboard through the gap between my thumb and first finger; I was off, way off. I stabbed myself in the middle finger, one of the curved points of the knife slicing through the edge of my finger, hitting the bone at the same time. I almost cut the damn thing off on the first strike. Shari screamed as blood jetted out of my severed finger, spattering all over Mathieu's cheese like some sort of exotic crimson sauce.

'Merde, merde, merde, Shari, call an ambulance!' he yelled as he ran into the kitchen and grabbed a tea towel. By now, the site of all the blood and the effects of the dope were making me feel rather queasy, to say the least. Mathieu struggled to wrap the tea towel around my finger and hand, the blood just would not let up. Meanwhile Shari was yelling the address down the phone. If Mathieu and Shari were chickens, they'd just been beheaded – they were frenetic.

And that was that, in the blink of an eye, one stupid moment in time, one little slip of a cheese knife, and my concert pianist days came to an abrupt end. And they say TV doesn't influence people.

I was the bass player in Mathieu's band for just one incredibly enjoyable year, until the band broke up, and it was during that time that I discovered the piano, classical piano. I'd bought a book on bass guitar techniques and in this book was the left hand part to Bach's prelude number 2 in C minor, from the 48. I was so intrigued by it that I wanted to know what the right hand part did so I bought the sheet music for it. But I didn't have a piano, not even an electronic keyboard, so I phoned a local piano teacher and off I went to my very first piano lesson. Of course, when I handed her book one of Bach's 48 Preludes & Fugues and told her I'd never had a lesson but wanted to learn the C minor prelude, well, she almost fell off her piano stool in fits of laughter. At the time I had no idea that Bach's preludes and fugues were seriously difficult and very technical. She informed me that I'd have to 'work up to it'. She started me off with a book by James Bastien called The Older Beginner Piano Course. I questioned it, saying I was only 20, but she said I was not 7 and did not need a beginner book that had pictures of large green frogs on every other page.

I took to the piano like a duck to water and I flew

though Mr Bastien's book in no time at all, with flying colours too. My piano teacher recognised my talent immediately and had me looking at the Associated Board's Grade 1 pieces after just a handful of lessons. I already knew how to read music notation – the bass clef at least – because of my bass playing. The treble clef caused no problem for me, neither did reading them and playing both hands together. I'd bought a second hand Yamaha DX27 keyboard. It was hardly ideal, but would have to do for now. I astounded my teacher when I returned a week later having learned, and committed to memory, all three of the grade 1 pieces. By now I'd only had eight lessons with her and I'd got through the Bastien book and had committed to memory the three grade 1 pieces, along with scales and arpeggios, in preparation for taking my first music exam. I passed, with distinction. I was so keen to crack on that I purchased the sheet music for the grade 2 pieces from my local music shop on my way home from the exam and a week later I'd already learned two of them. And this is how it went. To cut a long story short, it took me just three years to do all eight grades (attaining distinctions on all but one), along with theory for each grade too. Along the way I also won the North London Piano festival competition and at the end of the third year I attained the Trinity College Performance Certificate. I was 24 years old when Decca records signed me up and during the next six years I'd make eight CD recordings of works by Bach, Beethoven and Liszt. I also gave several concerts, not only in the UK, but in Europe and America too.

I was doing pretty damn well for myself but I did not buy a house until I met Melanie. We moved in together and got married soon after. It was a beautiful 3-bed semi in Islington, not far from Camden Passage.

I refer to my years from the age of 24 to 29 as 'The Piano Years'. Not only were these five years the best years of my life (along with the year that I spent playing the bass in Nine Yards Of Dead Cats), they were, in fact, the *only* good years of my life. Not because I was with my wife, Melanie, during that time, but because of the piano, classical music, and how that ignited my soul and made me feel incredible inside. Melanie was not a creative type, she didn't have a creative bone in her body; her idea of being creative was making a Victoria sponge cake. She worked for an accountancy firm, smoked Kensitas cigarettes, drank Liebfraumilch by the gallon and lived for Eastenders, Home and Away, Footballer's Wives and cheap holidays in the sun. But, I loved her and she loved me, or so I thought. We had good times together and I was really into my music. When I touched the piano keys and played, the music touched me right back. Before I joined Mathieu's band and after the finger-stabbing incident that ended my piano-playing career, my life was not good, not good at all.

Freddie Mercury once said something about one year of love being better than a lifetime alone. Well, I'd had five years of love, with a Bösendorfer 6 foot grand piano and Beethoven. What is the ratio for happy/sad (or Lustig und Traurig as Beethoven would say) in life? Are people happy most of the time or do they just sit somewhere in-between happy and sad – 'contentment' for example. Picture, if you can, the temperature gauge on your car's instrument display. It sits in the blue (cold) part when you first start the engine and stays there for a couple of miles. After the car has warmed up the temperature gauge sits steadily in the middle at about 90 degrees, but if the engine develops a problem and overheats the gauge will go up into the red. I suspect – if blue is sadness and depression and red is euphoric happiness and dead centre is contentment – that most people sit bang slap in the middle, or thereabouts. Me, I sit in the blue (depression and sadness) area most of the time. Occasionally I might creep up into the mid, contentment, section and on rare occasions I might even hit the red, but only briefly, and like a car engine, once it is turned off I soon descend back down into the blue again. During 'the piano years' I was in the red every time my fingers touched the keyboard, but those days are long gone.

Chapter 3

Monday morning was the worst morning of the week for me. Not because it was Monday and I had to go back to work. Being a self-employed driving instructor meant that the weekends were the busiest time for me. That's when most people, young people who wanted to learn to drive, were off work and could fit in driving lessons. Monday was crap because I had to get up at the crack of dawn and drive from Waterbeach (about a five miles north of Cambridge city centre), where I lived, down to Haverhill to pick up a young girl for her 2-hour lesson, which started at 6:30 a.m..

I'd spent almost a year living with Mathieu and Shari when I'd decided I didn't really want to live in London anymore. I wanted something a little less stressful and not so manic (not to mention the sheer volume of rude buggers who lived in London), but somewhere that still had some sort of city. Cambridge seemed to fit the bill perfectly. It's peaceful and, unlike London, is not all hustle and bustle. I lived in a village called Waterbeach, just a few miles north of Cambridge, in a 2-bed end of terrace house.

I lived an isolated life for the most part, in solitude. I was single and had been since divorcing Melanie twelve years ago. Of course, I'd had relationships during that time, but none of them really stuck. I think, with age, I'd got a little fussier in regard to whom I wanted to have a relationship with, spend time with, maybe live with and develop a meaningful long-term relationship with. I always thought that after Melanie I'd lost the ability to fall in love, that something inside me just died, stopped functioning correctly. I'd had several failed short-term relationships post Melanie. After a few short months – or even weeks in many instances – into any of these relationships, it soon became apparent that not only was I not falling in love with any of these women, but I wasn't developing any sort of feelings towards them either. I had spoken to Mathieu's girlfriend, Shari, about my concerns about love and emotions towards romantic interests and she'd said, 'Don't be silly, of course you have the ability to fall in love. You just haven't met the right woman yet; but when you do it will be amazing.' Well, that conversation took place when I was 35, seven years ago, and I was still waiting.

I'm not entirely sure if it's me who picks unsuitable women, or if unsuitable women pick me, but I just can't seem to meet a woman that I, how do they say it, connect with, click with, have synergy with, spark, attraction et cetera. It's always the same old story: meet up, have coffee, meet up, go to restaurant, meet at her (or my) place, have sex (sometimes great, sometimes average, sometimes downright lacklustre), have more sex, try and get to know each other better, then, a few weeks later it all just fizzles out like a damp touch paper on a wet and miserable Guy Fawkes Night.

Hanna was 18 years old and I'd been teaching her to drive for eight months. She'd put in for, and failed, her driving test six times so far. This reflected badly on me but, unfortunately, Hanna was not a born driver. In fact, she had absolutely zero observational skills, no awareness as to what was going on around her and no ability to plan ahead or anticipate any given situation on the road. Her bay parking was a disaster and she couldn't grasp the fact that when going around roundabouts you have to stay in your own lane and not drift sideways into the other lanes, and, in turn, other vehicles. Basically, she was a disaster and I didn't think she stood a hope of ever passing her driving test, but both Hanna and her parents, with whom she lived, were adamant that she learnt to drive and got a car so she didn't have to get the bus from Haverhill up to Cambridge to work every day.

I got out of my Vauxhall Corsa and jumped into the passenger side. Hanna looked out of her living room window and smiled and gave me a wave, as she usually does. I had to give it to her; she was incredibly enthusiastic and happy about her driving lessons, even after 38 2-hour driving lessons and six failed attempts at her test; usually because of something major – correction, 'always' because of something major. If it was me, I'd be losing the will to live, but out of her front door she skipped with the usual spring in her step and a beaming great smile revealing her pristine white teeth.

'Hi, Red,' she said, jumping into the driver's seat.

'Hello, Hanna, how are you this morning?' I said, not quite matching her enthusiasm due to the fact that although I was here in physical presence, my brain was still asleep in bed back home.

'Absolutely fantasmagorical and raring to go,' she said, all bright-eyed and bushy-tailed. How was it possible that somebody could look so damn good at such an unearthly hour in the morning? Youth is wasted on young people. I wonder if she'll be this chirpy and enthusiastic about life when she's pushing 40 with a couple of kids and a midriff of stretch marks?

'Ok, you know the routine. We'll take the usual route up to the test centre at Cowley Road and then we'll go around the usual test route up the A10 and through Impington.'

'Ok,' she said, adjusting the seat, steering wheel and mirrors and going through her cockpit drill.

It usually took less than two minutes into the lesson before Hanna made her first mistake, usually a major one. She was happily driving along the main road, keeping to the 40mph speed limit, when a car coming out of a side turning on the left decided it was not necessary to look right when pulling out thus she pulled out right in front of Hanna, who slammed on the brakes, at the last possible minute.

'Stupid fuckin' woman,' yelled Hanna, who looked like butter wouldn't melt in her mouth but if another driver did something wrong Hanna's colourful language came out in spades.

'Hanna, remember what we talked about? The road is no place for rage and anger.'

'Red, that's why they call it road rage, duh,' she retorted. Hanna's problem was that she didn't listen; she was too contrary and argumentative.

'How many times have we talked about "Anticipation", Hanna?'

'Too many,' she groaned.

'Exactly, if you listened and paid attention I wouldn't have to keep repeating myself would I?'

'But that stupid fuckin' woman just pulled out in front of me. She didn't even look! It was *her* fault,' she argued.

'No, Hanna, it was your fault.'

'What? That's so not fair! You saw what she did. She just pulled out in front of me. Stupid fuckin' woman, shouldn't be allowed on the road.'

'Hanna, can you please stop swearing and pull over and park on the left.' She huffed, indicated and pulled over, without checking her nearside mirror or looking over her shoulder for any early-morning cyclists who might be passing on the inside. I sighed, internally, and ignored the horn beep and rude gesture from the driver that overtook us.

'Ok, here's the facts, Hanna. If you'd done that on your driving test you would have failed bec–'

'But I didn't do any–'

'Hanna, stop talking, you have two ears a–'

'And one mouth for a reason, I know,' she interrupted, 'it's one of your favourite lines.'

'Ok, good, so put that little gem of knowledge to good use for the next few minutes while I explain something too you. If you'd done that on a test you'd have failed because of your lack of observation and anticipation. Yes, she pulled out without looking, but you should have anticipated it. As she approached the main road she was looking left in the other direction and she was showing no signs of slowing down at the give way line so you should have seen this and anticipated that she was going to pull out without stopping. You should have taken your foot off the accelerator and let the car coast down to a slower speed, which would have given her time to pull out and move away, rendering your emergency stop unnecessary. The man behind in that black BMW almost crashed into the back of us, Hanna.'

'Well, he shouldn't have been driving so close then, should he? Serves him right.'

'Hanna, you've failed your test six times now and if you continue with this attitude you'll fail it another six times. Please, can you just listen to what I tell you and pay attention? I'm here to teach you to drive, Hanna, so you can pass your test, get a licence and become a safe and responsible driver. Please?' I pleaded.

She must have detected the pleading desperation in my voice. 'Ok, you're right, Red, you're always right.'

'Ok, continue, and remember, always assume that other drivers are going to do stupid things because a lot of the time they will, try to anticipate that,' I said, gesturing for her to move off in her own time.

We made it all the way to Cambridge without a hitch, not major ones anyway. I wouldn't go as far as saying it was a miracle as the A1307 was just one long straight, slightly winding road all the way up to the Cambridge. She even managed to drive to Cowley Road test centre without too much shouting and swearing at other early morning city drivers. From the test centre I instructed Hanna to go around the 'usual' test route, in preparation for her seventh upcoming driving test.

A minute after leaving the test centre we approached the elongated multi lane roundabout that crossed over the A14, which always filled me with dread and trepidation. This particular roundabout has four sets of traffic lights on it and on the straight sections it has two lanes, which expand into three lanes on the bends.

'Ok, we're going to go around the roundabout three times, as usual, so take care to stay in your own lane and be aware of the cars either side and behind you as you go around the corners.' Nothing. 'Hanna, did you hear me?'

'Ok, ok, I got it,' she said.

I always got Hanna to loop this roundabout three times in succession so she could get used to changing lanes on her way around and, more importantly, looking over both shoulders, using her mirrors and signalling, and definitely *not* drifting sideways without looking or indicating and potentially slamming into another vehicle.

Hanna was positioned in the right lane, correctly, when we approached the first set of lights, which were red, giving her time to work things out in her head. The lights changed and we pulled away smoothly and without issue. Well, my car was automatic so there weren't going to be any stalling problems. We headed along the short straight and up to the next set of lights, which were green this time. Hanna went through them and instead of moving over to the middle lane she stayed in the left one so, as always, I had to intervene.

'Ok, we really need to be in the middle lane as we're going around the roundabout again. If you stay here we'll be forced down the slip road onto the A14.'

'I know, I know, you don't have to keep telling me,' she said.

Boy did I wish that were the case. The thing is, I did have to keep telling her because she never bloody listened. So, the usual thing happened, as she approached the next set of lights – which were green – in the wrong lane, she drifted across into the middle lane as she went around the bend. She didn't look over her shoulder, or in her mirror and she didn't bother signalling either, even though I'd explained the drill regarding looking over shoulder, checking mirrors and signalling, what felt like a thousand times. I grabbed the steering wheel and pulled it hard, towards me, to prevent imminent side impact into a shiny new Jaguar, the owner of which pushed on his horn and held it there for a good five seconds to make sure we felt his anger.

'What are you doing?' she yelled, as I yanked the steering wheel to get the car back into our lane.

'Hanna, just concentrate and stay in this lane and drive straight ahead,' I said, heading back towards the test centre. I'd had enough roundabout stress for one day. She parked up just along the road from the test centre, where I instructed her to turn the engine off, which she did, with a huff.

'Hanna, I've got to be honest with you, I really don't know if I'm the right instructor for you, perha–'

'No, don't say that. I like you, Red, you're a great driving instructor. I don't want anybody else. Please, please don't do this, Red, I beg you,' she said. Her hands were trembling and she was almost in tears. I'd never seen her this way before. The thought of me recommending she find another driving instructor had traumatised her and brought her to tears.

'Hanna, I just don't think you're meant to drive. Seriously, you're dangerous. You have no observational skills, no awareness, no judgment and no ability to anticipate what other road users will do. You came close to passing your test just once out of six attempts and I'm sure, if you play the numbers game, that eventually you'll get lucky one day and not make a major mistake on your test and you'll pass and that scares me Hanna. I'd worry that within a few days of passing you'd have a serious accident and hurt yourself, maybe worse. Hanna, you can't even get through a 2-hour lesson without serious incident and a whole amalgamation of smaller ones. You always fail your test, usually with at least one major fault, sometimes as many as three. Think about it, Hanna. After all this time and all these lessons, if you can't even drive for 20 minutes without almost having a major incident what chance will you stand being able to drive every day, day in day out, all year round?'

Her eyes were well and truly red, tears flowing down both cheeks now. I felt genuinely sorry for her and I was concerned that she'd have an accident if let loose on the road alone. Fact is, during every single lesson I'd ever given her, I'd had to grab the steering wheel to prevent her hitting a parked car, or slamming sideways into another car on a roundabout and, on one occasion, to prevent her from driving straight over a 'Keep Left' beacon on a central reservation. And, lord knows how many times I'd had to use my dual controls, the rubbers were wearing out more on my side than they were on the driver's side.

'Please, Red, I'll try much harder, I promise,' she pleaded.

'Hanna, it's not about trying. It's about listening to what I say, my instruction, and paying attention. This isn't a game. You could kill somebody, or yourself.'

'Ok, I promise, I'll listen to what you say and pay more attention from now on, but please don't give up on me,' she said, wiping her snotty nose with a tissue she'd grabbed from her bag on the back seat.

I'd never give up on anybody but I was seriously concerned for Hanna's safety and wellbeing. I actually liked the gobby little thing and I felt protective towards her, which is why I secretly wished she'd give up this driving thing and stick with public transport or taxis.

'Ok, Hanna, but if I don't see a marked improvement in not only your driving, but your attitude, you'll leave me no choice but to–'

'Thank you, thank you, thank you,' she said, leaning over and kissing my cheek, which made me uncomfortable to say the least. I was relieved that there were no passers by to see her emotional appreciation.

We finished up the lesson, by way of some nice easy straight roads, before driving to her place of work in Cambridge, where she started at 8:30am. She thanked me again, got out and skipped off to work. I got into the driver's side and headed off to a local café to get a much-needed cappuccino and sausage roll before my next lesson. Boy was Hanna hungry work.

Chapter 4

I pulled up at the BP petrol station on Newmarket Road and lined my beloved red Audi TT MK2 Quattro S Line up with the 'Ultimate' 99 octane rated unleaded pump. Surely you didn't think I drove around in the little Corsa that I taught people to drive in did you? I'm six foot one and can barely fit behind the wheel of the damn thing. The only saving grace was that, when I was teaching people to drive in it, I got to sit in the passenger side where there's at least a bit more leg room when the seat is pushed all the way back. But the main reason I didn't use it for my personal car was because it's just too damn slow. I liked to put my foot down and use Cambridgeshire's B-roads as my own personal racetrack, when they were quiet and the opportunity was there. Don't get me wrong, I'm not a boy-racer and I'm certainly not a dangerous, or reckless, driver. In fact, I'm a brilliant driver. I know, I know, most guys say that, but in my case it happens to be true. I passed my driving test first time and then I went on to do an advance-driving test, which I also passed first time. I even got some training from a retired police driving instructor on chasing/pursuing techniques and, to top it off, I also had several track-day driving lessons which covered many really cool techniques such as handbrake turns, doughnuts, drifting and the like. Of course, I also did my ADI driving instructor training. Turned out that I was a natural born driver and the retired police driving instructor, who gave me some driver training, told me that if I ever decided to go that way, I'd make a damn fine getaway driver. So, I drive fast, but accurately and safely. I just like to have a bit of fun in my Audi TT around the winding roads of Cambridgeshire – it's one of the few pleasures I get out of my, otherwise, miserable life.

My first TT came off the back of some early royalty payments for the classical Decca CD recordings I'd made. My first recording – Beethoven's Pathetique sonata, Waldstein sonata and 32 variations in C minor – for Decca records sold really well, by classical CD standards. It got some good airplay on Classic FM and shot up the classical charts. The money I made from that recording alone was enough for me to go out and buy a 10-month old ex demonstrator TT from a local dealership. It was the MK1 back then, but when the MK2 came out I sold my MK1 and upgraded, but not straight away, I was never wealthy enough to afford a brand new car, especially an Audi. It was three years after the MK2 came out that I bought a used one with 50,000 miles on the clock and what I paid for it was a good few grand less than what most people would pay for a new Ford Focus.

There are several reasons that I choose to go to this particular BP petrol station to fill up. First, it has a Marks & Spencer mini mart and a Wild Bean café inside, which saves me having to drive to the M&S in Cambridge, which was a royal pain in the proverbial as it meant parking up in the underground car park and having to walk through the Grand Arcade shopping centre and out into the busy square, which was too much like hard work. Of course, I could go to the other M&S in the Beehive Retail Park but the reason I'm reluctant to do that is because it's in a 'retail park'. I was not a fan of retail parks, or commercial retail commerce in general. I can't stand shopping. The car parks are always full, there are too many people at those places and the whole experience is just too damn depressing.

The Newmarket Road BP was only 6 miles down the road from my house – if I took the direct route, avoiding the A10 and A14, which was the way my satnav always wanted to take me – and if I put my foot down and had a little bit of driving fun I could make it in under ten minutes.

So, the BP petrol station was nice and convenient, nice and quiet and the M&S inside sold everything I needed in terms of my bodily requirements: vitamins, minerals, nutrients, protein and fluids. Besides, I hated shopping at large supermarkets, all pretending to be the caring avuncular arm around your shoulder with their stupid strapped-family-friendly slogans while all they really care about are their bottom lines while trying to screw you out of what little money you had with their cleverly calculated 3-for-2 offers or their so-called buy-1-get-1-half-price horseshit deals. What they really mean is every little you spend helps turn us into even bigger and fatter cats.

Sometimes I put £40 of fuel in my car and sometimes I filled it up until the nozzle automatically cut off. Today I was doing the latter, with the aid of an old plastic fuel filler cap. This I must explain. Back in the good old days you didn't have to stand around physically holding and squeezing the lever on the pump to fill up, there used to be a clip that you could flick into place, leaving your hands free to do other things such as empty rubbish from your car into the bin. But, for some stupid reason, some dickweed decided that we should have to stand there and physically hold the pump, which made no sense whatsoever. The damn pump automatically cuts off the fuel whether you were holding it by hand or if it was held by the clip, so WTF did they ever change it? My TT had a 'capless' system, meaning it had no filler cap, so I bought a cheap plastic filler cap off eBay and whenever I fill the tank I squeeze the lever on the nozzle and then wedge the plastic cap into the gap where my fingers would usually have to hold the lever in place. Usually I don't have any rubbish that needs clearing from my car into the conveniently located bin next to the pump, but I do like to stand there, hands-free. I also got a great sense of satisfaction knowing that the twat – or twats – that decided to decommission the auto-holding clips had not got one over on me. I don't mind admitting that I'm somewhat anti-establishment and something of an anarchist. I have a somewhat rebellious side, especially when it comes to idiotic laws and stupid bureaucratic decisions like so-called health and safety petrol pump one.

In this instance I did, however, take the opportunity to remove the maple 'helicopter' seed leaf that had somehow managed to jam itself under the passenger side windscreen wiper. It had been annoying me while driving down here. It was a nice sunny day, no sign of rain, but just seeing it there had induced an irritable itch on my brain and, like the helicopter seed leaf, an itch I could not reach to scratch. The resilient little bugger would not budge, no matter how fast I drove to try and get the wind turbulence to shift it, and jetting mists of water onto the windscreen resulted in an annoying streak across the screen.

So, after removing the annoying leaf I also took the opportunity to examine the front grills for stuck leaves and other debris. All good.

The fuel automatically cut off – as I knew it would – when the tank was full, so I removed my plastic cap before moving my car over to a proper parking space. Next, I headed inside where I chose my usual groceries, which consisted of various ready packed salad-based meals such as Super Wholefood Salad with creamy lemon & mint dressing and Honey Smoked Salmon & Lentil salad with creamy lemon dressing. I also quite like their Super Bean, Lentil & Barley soup. These (according to the ingredients labels) appear to be pretty healthy and should provide my body with the relevant vitamins, minerals, nutrients and protein that it needs. I also bought some full fat goat's milk, sparkling water and a few other bits before heading over to the checkout.

'Hi, Red, how you doing?' said Ross.

'Peachy. How about you, Ross?' I said.

Ross was about 30 years old and appeared to work the day shift. He was a stocky guy with a few artistic tattoos on his chunky, Popeye-like, forearms and he wore those silly earrings – the black plastic disc things that, when inserted, reveal a massive gaping hole that you could push a medium sized Cuban cigar through – a somewhat primitive look that would be more fitting to members of an Amazonian tribe than a modern English guy living in Cambridge.

'I'm good. Not sure if I'd say "peachy", but I'm good. I'm still lovin' that car of yours,' he said, looking out the window in admiration.

'Me too, Ross, me too. It's one of the few things that puts a smile on my face every time I put my foot down in it.'

'I bet. What's the brake on that thing, anyway?'

'208.'

'Not bad! Nought to sixty?' he asked.

'5.6 seconds, according to the book, but it feels quicker.'

'Nice!' he nodded, ringing up my groceries. I asked him to add a mocha to the bill, from the Wild Bean Café at the other end of the counter.

The card machine bleeped to inform me that my

contactless card had been accepted. I grabbed the bag and waited for another guy to make my mocha before heading off.

'Later, Ross.'

'Have a good one, Red, enjoy the drive home,' he smiled.

'You bet.'

I pulled out of the BP station onto Newmarket Road and put my foot down a little and listened to the sweet sound of the engine, happy in the knowledge that the quality fuel I choose to put in it was not doing any damage. I only ever use 'decent' fuel from the likes of BP, Shell or Esso. I never use supermarket fuel, not under *any* circumstances. I remember this one time when I was almost out of fuel. The warning light had come on and I'd reset the trip computer to zero and I'd covered 41 miles and, from experience, my car could manage about 45 miles post the petrol warning light coming on. There was a Morrison's that had a petrol station about a mile up the road, which I would have made. According to my Satnav the nearest 'decent' petrol station was 11 miles away, which I knew I would not make. So, not wanting to let the car run out of fuel entirely – knowing this can be bad for a car – I pulled over and phoned a cab from my mobile and got the driver to take me to the Shell petrol station 11 miles away, where I bought a petrol canister, filled it with fuel and took the cab back to my waiting car. I'd rather pay £30 for a cab and £5 for a canister than put crap supermarket fuel in my car.

I know, you're probably thinking that it all comes out of the same refinery, which it probably does, but EU regulations state that a minimum amount of additives, lubricants and cleaners be added to the fuel and the supermarkets generally only add the 'minimum' legal requirement. Why? Because it costs money to add these engine lubricants and cleaning agents. Companies like Shell, BP and Esso, for example, go above and beyond these 'minimum' guidelines. The end result, my precious car engine is lubricated and cleaned properly via the fuel I choose to put into it so it won't get all coked up or suffer from untold amounts of internal damage as the miles clock up. Also, my car runs smoother, quieter and more efficiently with decent fuel. Most people – the masses, great unwashed, hoi polloi – only think about the pennies they can save or the points they can gain on their silly loyalty cards, they don't see the bigger picture. So, they might, on average, save £25 per year on fuel but their mpg won't be as good due to lack of additives – cancelling out any saving – and they might well have to spend £3,000 on an engine rebuild five or six years down the line if they drive a 'regular' make/model car that is, way more for top marques cars such as BMW, Audi or Jaguar for example.

Back home, I park my car in the garage that I rent just 50 yards from my house (the Corsa sits in the parking space outside the front of my house), unpack my groceries and make a drink. By make a drink, I mean pour half of the mocha I just bought from the BP garage out into a mug, to half fill it, then top it up with goat's milk and stick it in the microwave for 60 seconds. Wild Bean's mochas are pretty good, but they're too damn strong for me. Adding a goodly amount of milk tailors things to my taste buds' satisfaction. I put the plastic lid back onto the take-out mocha so I can have another cup later: two cups for the price of one.

I check my watch, 4:35 p.m.. I don't have another pupil until 7 – Jason, age 21 – so between now and then I'll have something to eat with my heavily modified mocha while listening to my new Tom Waits album, on vinyl. Well, I say new; it's actually a re-issue of the 1978 album, 'Blue Valentine'. I'm a massive Hi-Fi connoisseur and I love my vinyl records, they just sound so much better than CD. No, shut up, they just do.

I'm usually sceptical about re-issue vinyl records but in this case the sticker on the cover read 'Newly Remastered with Waits/Brennan' so I figured if the rather fussy, Mr Waits had a hand in it, then it must be ok; it was and I approved.

While I listened to Tom's deep gravel-seasoned raspy voice I checked out the news on my BBC News app: Coronavirus this, Covid-19 that, NHS the other, today's confirmed cases and death figures and stories of people being sent to prison for coughing at police officers. The so-called government being all secretive about the plans for coming out of the lock-down, playing God when they are supposed to be serving the people. More lies, more spin, more corruption, evil corporations, more lying bureaucrats, more dick-swinging and more pissing contests as the Labour party have yet another pop at the Conservative party for getting it all so badly wrong – sour grapes.

Do any of these parties or politicians actually give a crap about the country? Actually, I know the answer to that one. Deflated by the state of the so-called civilized western world I closed the app and dropped my phone onto the couch next to me. I looked around my living room: the 55-inch TV, the Hi-Fi, the 'manly-themed' framed images hanging on the walls – nothing feminine, no sign of a woman living here and certainly no sign of children. If anything, my living room walls looked more like the walls in the Hard Rock Café in London.

The place where I lived in Waterbeach is a 2-bed, end of terrace house, which I rent from a private landlord who has several similar properties on his portfolio. I like the fact that my landlord is a 'proper' landlord with multiple properties and not just somebody who bought a second property to let because at least I know that when his daughter leaves home he won't be giving me notice to move out so she can move in. The few friends I do have suggested that I should buy somewhere, that the money I'm spending on rent each month is money down the toilet. I've been living in my current house for ten years now, since moving out of Mathieu's place in London. I don't even want to work out how much rent I've paid during that time and, more importantly, I don't really care. I'd already bought and left a really nice house to my ex-wife and I don't fancy doing it again any time soon. Sceptical, I know, but, truth be told, I don't have kids, my immediate family are all dead and I don't have anybody so close to me that I'd feel compelled to write up a will to leave them my house and worldly possessions. I know, it could be an investment to secure my future, but I don't think I have one of those either. Actually, I know I don't.

I love dogs and have had a couple in the past. I remember there being a small black mongrel in the family when I was five and then I had another when I was with my ex-wife, which sadly died prematurely. I sometimes think about getting another dog, a small one, a Japanese Chin or King Charles's Spaniel perhaps, a loving 'therapeutic' lap dog with no agenda. But if I did, I'd be forced to stick around in this miserable godforsaken world for another ten years or so until the dog eventually passed away; something that I have no intention of doing.

I've already started clearing out some of the unnecessary items in my house in preparation for my departing this world. I'm not talking about my TV, Blu-ray DVD collection, Hi-Fi or vinyl records, these things give me pleasure and make my miserable life somewhat tolerable, to some small degree. I'm talking about all the other things, the stuff I don't love or use. I have this theory that if you don't love, or use, something, why bother owning it? Get rid of it and, if in doubt, throw it out, or, in my case, stick it up for sale on Gumtree or eBay. You'd be amazed how much money people will bid for all your old shit. I heaved a bunch of crap out of my garage, pulled more junk down from the loft and then scanned my living room, bedroom and office for anything else that I didn't use on a regular basis – or love – and stuck it all up on eBay with no reserve and just a 99p starting price. I figured, at the very least, it would save me phoning the council and paying them to come and take it all away. To my shock and utter amazement, 10 days later all my old crap from up in the loft and in the garage sold for over £2,500, (less eBay's extortionate commission fees of course): go figure. For other more valuable items, where I know for sure what I could get for them, I'll advertise on Gumtree because it's free and there is no commission on the sales. I only ever used eBay when I had no idea what any given item would sell for.

The last thing I wanted was for Mathieu and Shari to have to drive up from London to wade through all my crap after I'm gone. Sorting, putting stuff in bin bags to throw out or take to the recycling centre, deciding what to keep, what to sell, what's sentimental et cetera. No, I wanted this to be as easy as possible for him, especially when it comes to my funeral. I didn't want anything complicated, or expensive. If it wasn't a health hazard and I thought I could get away with it I'd instruct Mathieu to simply toss my corpse onto the nearest skip (yup, that would upset the bugger who hired the skip for sure), or a landfill site so it can biodegrade with potato peelings and all those soiled nappies, or perhaps he could fly-tip me into the undergrowth alongside the A428 for the local wildlife to feed on.

For me, being an atheist, my body would be nothing more than a 195 lb inconvenience that would have to be disposed of before it started to go rotten and stink up the place. I figured cremation would be the simplest, and cheapest, option.

Although I had not written up yet, I figured when I got around to it I'd leave Mathieu in charge of dealing with all that horrible deathly stuff, funeral, paperwork etc. As for my earthly belongings, when the time drew closer, I'd sell, or give away to my few friends, all of my belongings: Hi-Fi, computer, mobile devices, TV, record and DVD collection and white goods. I'll also sell both my cars and give that money to a couple of my friends who I know need it. Mathieu is financially affluent; his income from his health food shop in London keeps him and Shari in exotic holidays, nice restaurants and a nice new car every three years.

Right now my house was actually looking better than it ever had and I felt quite liberated after clearing out all the crap. As the saying goes, the things you own end up owning you, and I didn't want to be beholden to this world for any longer than was necessary. But, like all good plans, my suicide had to be organised and worked out. My affairs (no, not the romantic ones, I don't have any of those anymore anyway) had to be put in order.

Apart from the 'piano years', my life has been pretty shit, to say the least. It didn't start out well and it continued to go from bad to worse. Like I said earlier, my parents spent three years trying to get pregnant with me; it was as if I just wasn't meant to be. Even before I existed I'm sure I would have been protesting not to come into existence, but three years and nine months later – regardless of my pre-conception objections – I popped out, reluctantly. I learned later in life that my birth was a difficult one (just like my life would prove to be). I wanted to come out sideways and the midwife struggled for ages to try and get me to point in the right direction and even when they did manage to get my head facing downward my broad shoulders proved problematic, resulting in vaginal tearing and rivers of blood.

Less than six months later my mother was pregnant again, with a girl. My sister, Jennifer, didn't get very far in life; she died when she was only five, along with my mother and father. I remember it, vividly. We were all standing at a bus stop waiting to go into town (We lived in Hertford, Hertfordshire – where I was born – back then) when a lorry driver had to swerve to avoid hitting a cat that had run out into the road. The driver lost control and the lorry careered into the bus stop, killing my mum, dad and sister, along with an elderly couple who were also waiting. I'd escaped the carnage, as I'd momentarily run 20 yards back along the path to retrieve a football that I'd spotted under the hedgerow. My mum shouted after me to come back when she saw me run off.

'I'm just getting this ball, mum,' I yelled, as I crouched down to retrieve it.

'Marion, come back, right now,' she yelled after me.

'Got it,' I said, all proud, holding up the black and white football, which wasn't even punctured as I thought it might be. I started to run back to my family and that's when I heard the screech of tyres against tarmac. I looked to the right and saw the big, out of control, truck skidding, at speed, towards the bus stop. It ploughed straight through my family and the elderly couple, taking out the bus stop at the same time. I dropped the ball and froze to the spot. I remember the sensation of warm urine pouring down the inside of both legs as I stood there, in total shock, frozen to the spot in horror. My world ended in an instant. I vacated this world and took up residence in a very dark cave in the furthest corner of my mind before blowing up the entrance to create my own mental tomb, where I stayed. I was only six.

Chapter 5

Jason was 21-years old and lived in Ely. Unlike the contrary and argumentative Hanna, Jason was polite, quiet and laid back. He only ever spoke when he had a specific question relating to his driving lesson. He paid attention and followed my instructions to the latter and, unlike Hanna, he was progressing rapidly. He didn't argue, retort, or question anything I said. His driving and road manners were courteous, he had great awareness and he predicted and anticipated the road ahead with a skill and maturity that belied his age. Jason was the perfect pupil. This was only his sixth lesson and the lad was coming on in leaps and bounds. In fact, I'd asked Jason if he'd be kind enough to be my pupil during my upcoming ADI Standards Check, which is something that all driving instructors have to do every four years to assess their ability to teach. Jason was such a model pupil I'd anticipated a stress-free ADI check that should go seamlessly and without issue.

I got out of my Corsa and rang the bell. Jason shared a house with two other young men, students I assumed. Jason had just started an MA in Creative Writing at Anglia Ruskin University, for all the good it will do him.

Still, being an ex concert pianist, I respected creativity. These days everybody wanted to be a fashion designer, a photographer, a writer, web site designer, movie director, or some other creative or exotic job. There are too many people on the planet and not enough of these glamorous jobs to go around. I remember speaking to the director for one of the classical DVDs that Decca had arranged for me to record back in the day. He told me that there were approximately 60,000 jobs in the entire British television industry. Yet 62,000 media students graduate each year – not a hope. To get one of those jobs you'd have to put your name down at birth, preferably during conception. If a young person asked me for careers advice today I'd tell them to go and do a two-year plumbing course, be it a young man *or* woman. Not an electrician, you can get a nasty shock doing that. The worst thing that will happen in a plumbing disaster is you'll get a bit wet. I've known a couple of self-employed plumbers who were pulling in £500 a day on some contracts. They have nice houses, nice cars, go on nice holidays and always seem to have plenty of money in the bank. You can't say that about out-of-work actors and actresses – as they live on crumbs from the occasional extra, walk-on or television commercial – writers or poets, that's for sure.

'Hello, Red, I'll be right out,' said Jason, opening his front door.

I headed back to the Corsa and got in the passenger side. Jason strutted down the path from his house and got in the driver's side.

'How are you doing today?' I enquired.

'Ok,' he said, adjusting the seat and steering wheel.

'You still ok for my ADI check next week?'

'Yeah, of course, it's a free lesson, right?' he laughed.

'Ok, I think we should do a little work on your reversing around a corner first. You ok with that?'

'Sounds good to me,' he said, in his typical easy-going tones as he adjusted the mirrors.

'Ok. When you're ready, you can pull away and follow the road straight ahead.'

Jason put his seat belt on, put the car in drive, checked his mirrors, looked over his right shoulder, indicated and pulled out safely: textbook.

The Corsa was an automatic car, which meant I only taught pupils who wanted to learn in an automatic. People often ask me if I get much work teaching only automatic, suspecting that most people wanted to learn in a manual car. Truth be told, there are not that many automatic driving instructors around (for this very reason) so, although there are less pupils wanting to learn in an automatic, there are hardly any automatic instructors to teach them so I pretty much have the 20-mile radius north of Cambridge all to myself. It's a psychology thing, where most people will naturally go after the big market. But if you actually analyse it in a different way, flip the coin and look at what's on the other side, I'm the one who has the bigger market.

There are only two other automatic instructors in this area, but, like me, they are usually fully booked for two or three months ahead at any given time. Also, more and more cars are automatic these days, especially from top marques such as Audi, BMW and Mercedes.

Jason had a good head on his shoulders. He told me that he wanted to buy an automatic car when he passed his test and that he only ever intended to own and drive automatic cars, so why bother making life difficult for himself by learning in a manual. 'Besides,' he said, 'once I've been driving for a year or two and become an experienced driver I can always go back and take a manual test if I choose, and it will be a whole lot easier because I won't have to worry about all the other stuff as it will be second nature by then. I'll have done all the manoeuvres a thousand times over and I'll be familiar with the road and signs so I can concentrate on the gears, clutch and biting point.'

I wish more young people had Jason's way of thinking things through, such wisdom and ability to see things objectively. Jason was unique in that, like me, he wasn't a lemming or a sheep and he certainly didn't 'go with the flow'. I hate that saying, why on earth would anybody want to go with the flow, isn't that what sheep do? I want to go *my* way.

Jason thought for himself, he questioned things, flipped the coin and took a good look at the other side. That's a rare thing with today's youth. It would be fair to say that I liked Jason; he just oozed politeness and kindness and he wouldn't hurt a fly. Don't get me wrong; I like all my pupils, even though some of them can be bloody annoying at times. I have one young lad who thinks that picking his nose in the presence of others is perfectly acceptable. I have a young girl who leaves as much foundation on my steering wheel as she has on her face. I have another young man who has some sort of gland problem. He's overweight and his pores seem to emit the most disgusting, profuse miasma you ever smelled, and he sweats like a man who'd just won the Californian 'Death Valley Fire Stoker Championship', in July. I had anti-bacterial wet-wipes to rid the steering wheel, gear selector, door mirror switches – and other 'touchable' parts of my car – of sweat, bogies and foundation, and lord knows what else that my pupils fingers had come into contact with prior to getting into my car for their lesson.

Fact is, my pupils gave me some sort of purpose in life, something to live for. At least, they used to when I first trained to be a driving instructor. But as the years rolled along, I couldn't really care one way or another anymore and teaching people to drive just doesn't seem to be enough of a reason for me to stick around.

When I was recording classical CDs for Decca records things were great, sort of. I suffered from depression back then, like I have most of my life for as far back as I can remember. But I was making CD recordings and giving concerts and the thought of people buying my CDs and getting 70 or so minutes of listening pleasure in return for a small financial outlay made me feel really good inside. They were getting pleasure out of my CD recordings, pleasure that I had brought into their homes. This gave me purpose, evoking emotions in others via my music. When people came to see me perform, the feeling was even better. There's nothing quite like sitting at a 9-foot Steinway grand piano on stage, on your own, the absolute focus and centre of attention, in front of 2,900 people at a sold-out Festival Hall concert. I had this thing that I loved doing during concerts. After walking out onto the stage and taking a bow, I'd sit down, adjust the position of the stool, compose myself, take a breath with my eyes closed then I'd slowly raise my hands and position them half an inch above the keys, but I would not start to play at that point. The audience were silent with anticipation and I'd enjoy that moment, make them wait. I'd delay playing for 30 seconds, which doesn't sound much, but in that situation it feels like a dog's age. I'd count the seconds out in my head while feeling the intense atmosphere emitting from the audience and when I struck that first note to break the silence, it was electrifying.

I've been accused of being co-dependent in the past, 'Same old Red, always helping damsels in distress' one friend had said, laughing. But it wasn't just women I helped. I liked to help anybody who needed it or appreciated it. I just enjoyed helping people, doing things for people, giving up my time for people. While I genuinely liked living this way, I'm also aware that my selfless ways takes my mind away from my own depressing life, so I guess you could say that it is some form of co-dependency, who knows. Perhaps the psychotherapist that I've set up an appointment with next week will have some insights on this front, and other fronts, hopefully.

Jason successfully carried out his reversing around a corner manoeuvre three times in succession, each one as perfect as the last. The only part of today's lesson that needed a little work was his emergency stop.

'Ok, I want you to drive along this road, obeying the speed limit. What's the speed limit here?'

'30,' he replied.

'Good. So when you pull out and get up to speed, I'm going to bring my hand down and tap the dashboard and - when I do that - I want you to carry out an emergency stop, ok?'

'Ok.'

'When you're ready.'

Jason pulled out and got up to speed. I waited, to build up the anticipation, like I used to before playing that first note when giving concerts. I subtly checked the rear view mirror, which was clear, then, in a flash, I struck the dash with the palm of my hand. Jason braked and came to a standstill.

'Ok, that was similar to the one we did last week, still a bit slow. You're breaking progressively, but a little too carefully. It was a little too tentative, too nice, just like you,' I joked. He laughed, knowing exactly what I meant. 'So we're going to do it again only this time when I slap the dashboard I want you to imagine a young girl has just run out in front of the car and you only have a few meters to stop before you hit her. The car won't skid, it has anti-lock brakes, so I want you to stamp on that brake pedal like you mean it, con fuoco!'

'Sorry?'

'Oh, sorry, it's an Italian musical term, it means with fire, with passion and vehement energy.'

With this, Jason's facial expression took on a more serious look.

'Ok, you ready?'

'Yes,' he said, intensity written all over his face now.

I checked the mirror for traffic behind as he built up speed again. It was a quiet road that I use for this routine a lot, and it's long enough to carry out the emergency stop routine about three times in a row – if needed – without having to turn around.

Out of the corner of my eye I could see that although Jason was relaxed, there was a certain degree of intensity in his eyes as he focused on that imaginary little girl up ahead.

I slammed the palm of my hand down on the dash and before the nerve endings in my fingertips had time to register the mild pain Jason had stamped his right foot into the break – con fuoco – bringing the car to an efficient standstill.

'Great. If you do it like that on your test you'll nail it, if they ask you to that is, which they may or may not. Ok, well done, straight ahead,' I instructed.

Jason let out a little sigh of relief, but looked rather pleased with himself. After the lesson, Jason drove back to his house, I swapped seats and headed off home, not that there was anything, or anyone, to head home for.

I turned the hallway light on and cranked the heating up to 24 degrees then headed into the kitchen, filled the kettle with fresh water and turned it on. While it boiled, I went to the bathroom and washed my hands and face and then changed into something a little more comfortable: soft lounge pants and an old Queens of the Stone Age T-shirt. Although I studied classical piano, for my listening pleasure I preferred something with a bit more muscle – like the sort of stuff I used to play when I was bassist with Nine Yards Of Dead Cats. Every time I think of that band name, twenty odd years later, in hindsight, I still almost piss my pants laughing. And whenever I mention that I was in a band when I was younger and the familiar question of 'what were they called,' came up, the asker of the question would usually half-choke on their drink, or fall about the place in hysterics.

This evening I felt like something a bit laid back, hypnotic even. So I dug out the Younger Brother album, 'The Last Days of Gravity', which I knew would do the job while I sat down on the sofa to eat my M&S Honey Smoked Salmon & Lentil Salad with my mug of tea.

As I sat and ate my food I mentally reminisced with myself (is that even possible?), about how life would have been if I'd had kids. Although, in recent years, I'd done a good job of convincing myself that I'd chosen the creative path in life, not the domesticated one. Truth is, I would have loved to have had a child, a girl. Possibly for all the wrong reasons, those 'selfish' self-satisfying reasons, in my case a substitute for my sister, Jennifer, who's untimely death still hurts – and haunts – me, even after all these years. In hindsight it would have been amazing to have had a little girl, who I could have loved, cherished, and protected. I'd have spoilt her rotten every chance I got, given her everything she wanted. Lord knows her adult life would probably have become just as shit as everybody else's: work, rush hour traffic, bills, taxes, speeding tickets, extortionate parking costs, post office queues, mortgage payments, HP payments on some overpriced sofa and chairs, struggles, bad times and not quite enough good times to balance out the bad – a cruel and unfair ratio. I would have made sure that she had the best childhood ever, unlike my own bleak and miserable childhood. No, my daughter would have had a wonderful and magical childhood, being doted on and given a safe and loving environment, not brought up by a mean and horrible foster family who abused you mentally, physically and sexually – every single day for years on end, years that feel like they will never come to an end.

My ex-wife did fall pregnant; but only briefly, she miscarried after just eight weeks. In hindsight, it was probably a blessing in disguise. Now I'm 42, the days for me having a child are well and truly over. Sure, people have said, 'Don't be silly, Red, you're still young, you can still have children, look at Simon Cowell, he was 53 when he had his first child and Hugh Grant was 52. Mick Jagger was 56 for crying out loud.' This may be true, but there are in fact a couple of reasons I would not want to entertain having a child now. First, even if I met a woman next week and we fell in love the week after and six month later she was pregnant, I'd be heading towards my 44th birthday by the time the baby arrived and three years of sleepless nights at 44 would probably kill me and if that didn't, playing football with my 12 year old son (if it was a boy) at the ripe old age of 56 certainly would. The other reason, well, make of this what you will, the world is coming to an end, let's face it. I don't mean in a biblical way and I don't mean it in a the-sun-is-going-to-burn-out-and-the-earth-will-die sort of way either, that's about five billion years from now if you believe what you read on the Internet: how the hell did they work that one out? No, I'm talking about issues that are more imminent than that. Try the year 2040. The government have announced that all new petrol and diesel cars would be banned in the UK as of 2040, or is it 2030 now, the cretins (who we see fit to vote in) keep changing their minds on this one. They claim that this is to help tackle emissions and air pollution, but who knows what the real reason is: money? Probably. I know one thing; the governments of the world don't give a flying fuck about the planet, pollution, global warming or anything else. The only person who – on the surface at least – seems to give any sort of crap is that nauseating little Swedish adolescent halfwit. Poor little girl doesn't have the first idea what's going on the 'real' world. I have to side with Donald Trump on this one, what the hell were Time magazine thinking when they named her Person of the Year? Once upon a time you had to actually 'achieve' something or do something of note to be put on that list.

The fact is, the world is coming to an end for a whole plethora of other reasons: oil will soon run out, there isn't an endless supply. Then there are other factors like crops that are depleted of all but a bare minimum of nutrients due to the excessive growing of vegetables over the years so the carrots, radishes, beets and turnips have little to no nutritional value anymore – at least not the mass-produced ones found in certain evil corporate supermarkets chains – and it's only going to get worse. By the time oil runs out, possibly sooner, the world's population will have grown from the current 7.6 billion to going on 10 billion and God (if that's what works for you) isn't making any more food to feed all those extra people and the so-called World Health Organisation trying to come up with a diet of nuts, chickpeas and lentils just isn't going to cut it somehow. So, with no oil, no fossil fuel, electricity in rations, no heating and not enough food to go around, it doesn't bode well for the future of a child being born right about now, as for that child's children, well, let's be honest here, they're fucked. I won't be around to see what sort of post-apocalyptic world that those who are still around will be living in post 2060 and I certainly would not want my kids (if I had any) to be around to live in such hell.

Most people just live day-to-day and don't give too much thought to the future, Christmas being about as far into the future as most families care to look, and even that seems such a long way away to most people, who complain that greedy supermarket chains are stocking Christmas crap before they've even got Bonfire night and all the firework stuff out of the way. Sooner or later people are going to have to start thinking about what sort of lives their children are going to have when they grow up and reach retirement age. Would you really want to die knowing that when your kids reach 80 some savage barbarians could break into their home and club them to death for the last remaining tomato plant that they had growing in their greenhouse out back? No, me neither. Food for thought, pun intended. If I did have children, I'd make sure that I taught them how to make a bow and arrow and kill a deer with it and start a fire using two pieces of wood because fifty years from now they'll probably need skills like that, unless WW3 or some global airborne virus takes out at least two thirds of the world's population before then – either way the future looks grim. Mind you, the current modern world is hardly a great place to live in; it appears, from my experience, to be one big hoax anyway.

Chapter 6

I'd found Shannon MacNamara after doing a Google search for 'psychotherapists in my area'. She was a Doctor, but in the PhD sense, not the medical one. She was registered with all the relevant governing bodies and a member of a couple of counselling associations. She seemed to have all the right qualifications, skills and – because of her age (50, I found out after doing more searches on her name) – experience. Listed under her set of expertise were: depression, low mood, anxiety, post-traumatic stress and relationship difficulties, to name a few. Shannon appeared to have an excellent reputation and she was nice and local on Cherry Hinton Road in Cambridge. I'd ploughed through loads of therapists before I stumbled upon Shannon. I'd phoned four therapists before her but none of them inspired me with any confidence. However, when I spoke to Shannon, I knew that she was the one, that she was the one who could, maybe, save my life and actually *give* me a life. At least that was the hope.

I parked on her drive, as she'd instructed me to do on the phone, and walked down the side of the house where I knocked on the door to the extension, again, as per her instructions.

'Hello, Red?' she said, in a cheery tuneful southern Irish accent – Cork, perhaps – that had dulled ever so slightly by many years living in England, I suspected.

'Yes.'

'I'm Shannon, pleased to meet you. Come on in,' she said, leading the way into her therapy room. Having never been to a therapist or counsellor before I had no idea what to expect. I'd built up a cliché picture – based on therapists offices I'd seen in movies and on television – of a moody dimly lit room with some sort of large comfortable chaise lounge and an antique leather oxblood Chesterfield chair for the therapist to sit in with perhaps a couple of plants, a coffee table with a jug of water, a glass, and mandatory box of tissues while a clock ticks away, hypnotically, on the wall.

'Have a seat and make yourself comfortable,' she said, gesturing to the large comfortable sofa. Not quite a chaise lounge, but close. Shannon sat down in her leather armchair, again, not quite an antique Chesterfield, but heading that way.

'Would you like a tea or coffee or anything?'

'No thank you, I'm good,' I said, getting myself comfortable on the incredibly comfortable sofa. It felt like I was never going to stop sinking into it. The back was high enough for me to rest my head, which also started to sink into the soft velvet-like material. Couple the comfy sofa with the toasty warm room temperature and the subdued lighting and I started to suspect that I might fall asleep before the hour was up.

'Ok, we only spoke briefly on the phone and you

told me that this was quite a unique situation,' she said. I noticed an A4 pad and pen on the small round wooden table next to her. I suspected, depending on how my opening sentence went, that she would probably be picking it up and taking notes at some point during the session.

'Yes,' I said.

'Ok, would you like to tell me about it?' she said, more a demand than a question.

I could see no point in wasting time building up to it, after all, Shannon was charging me £45 for the one-hour session, so I just came out with it, matter of fact.

'Ok, I have to ask you something first, about your confidentiality code. I'm aware that anything we talk about in this room stays in this room and is in the strictest confidence, right?'

'That's right.'

'But I'm also aware that there might be an exception to that, if you suspected a patient were in imminent danger, could hurt themselves or others, correct?'

'Well, it depends on the specific set of circumstances, there are many factors to be taken into consideration, with many other varying factors.'

'If I told you I was planning to end my life exactly three months from now and that you were my only hope of preventing my impending suicide would that A: give you reason to make a phone call and have some men in white coats come and drag me away to the local nuthouse and B: would you be comfortable with the notion of taking on such a client?'

Shannon didn't hesitate with her response, said, 'No, I wouldn't be calling any men in white coats and I'd be happy to take on such a client. So, is this a hypothetical question or is this something you're actually planning?'

'It's something I'm planning, well, planned actually. I've already made a start,' I said.

'How do you mean?'

'I've started selling things in my house, kind of a clear out. I'm starting to, how do they say in the medical world, get my affairs in order.'

'I see,' she said, picking up her pen and pad. 'So you plan to take your own life three months from now?'

'Yes, well, depending on how these sessions go. I'd like to see you once a week, for the next twelve weeks. If you can fit me in that is?'

'Yes, I can fit you in. Red, you said. 'You said, "depending" on how these sessions go?'

'Yes. I'm aware that it's not your job to give me a reason to live (although, secretly, I was kind of hoping that she would) and given your profession I know that you're not going to sit there and sing me lots of pretty platitudes as to the many reasons to go on living: pretty sunsets, birds twittering, *love*, and so on and so forth.'

'No, Red, I won't be doing that. I noticed you emphasised the word "love" with a hint or sarcasm, or regret?'

I'm glad she added 'regret' to the end of that sentence as I'm not sarcastic, never have been, never will be. For me, sarcasm is the lowest form of wit and it does not constitute comedy or being funny. In fact, incessant sarcasm borders on belittling and the twats who choose to converse with an abundance of sarcasm are not funny at all; they think they are, but they aren't. Any silly twat can come out with sarcastic remarks, as it requires no real skill or thought process, which is why stand-up comedians are not sarcastic. It's for this reason that I've always steered clear of women whose dating profiles on websites say things along the lines of 'love a bit of banter' or 'love sarcasm'. I can just imagine these dullards engaged in their tedious sarcastic banter. I'd rather have a prize marrow or a deformed pineapple inserted into my rectum and pushed half way around my colon before attempting to push it out in an attempt get an idea of what childbirth feels like.

'Yeah, I don't believe in love. Well, it's not that I don't believe in it, it's just that love doesn't believe in me, not anymore anyway.'

'Ok, we'll come back to that, carry on,' she said.

'I'm 42 years old and this is my last ditch attempt to start my life, I don't mean start over, I mean, "start", period.'

'How do you mean?'

'Frankly, my life has been shit, and I *do* mean shit. I know that a lot of people aren't happy with the way their lives turned out and lots of people say their lives are shit, but mine never really got going. After a few brief happy infant years, my life was abruptly switched off and it all became rather dark and grim. From the age of six I've lived in the darkest corner of my mind, in a constant state of anxiety and depression, with life-long feelings of hopelessness. My only company being a large, aging, black dog of depression that follows me everywhere, like the faithful companion that he is. He sprawls across my lap at home, weighing down on me like a constant reminder.'

'So there's no joy in your life at all?'

'No, well, perhaps a few smatterings here and there, but the joy/depression ratio is far from balanced and there's certainly not enough of those "joy" moments to justify my being here, living in the dark in a near constant state of misery and depression.'

'Have you ever felt joy and happiness in your life?'

'Yes, for a few years, what I refer to as "The Piano Years".

'Tell me about those.'

'I started learning the piano when I was 20 and, it turned out, I was pretty good at it. "Gifted" is what my piano teacher had said. It only took me a few years to do all eight grades and get a Performers Certificate in classical piano and when I was 24 Decca records signed me up to their classical label. My career as a concert pianist lasted just six years until I was 30.'

'What happened?'

'I severed a tendon in my middle finger so it doesn't function properly anymore,' I said, holding up my left hand while trying to wiggle my middle finger. 'I mean, I can move it up and down a little and it doesn't really stop me doing day-to-day things, but it doesn't function well enough to be a virtuoso concert pianist anymore, so my career ended.'

'Can I ask how you got the injury?'

'It was a stupid accident, with a knife.'

Shannon noticed me looking down at my hand and didn't press for more information, not just yet anyway.

'Ok, so you had, what, six years of joy while you were a concert pianist?' she enquired.

'Yes, music was my life; I put my heart and soul into the piano. It was the best form of escapism, a way for me to get away from the world.'

'Red, I can't begin to imagine how awful it must have been, losing that incredible connection that you had with the piano.'

She was right; it was like a connection, a total connection that nothing else could compare to and there was no replacement. I'd connected more with the piano and the music of Bach, Beethoven, Liszt and Chopin than I had with any living human being. When I played, I went somewhere else; I was in my own private bubble and nobody else could get in.

'After I lost the ability to play the piano, well, with any degree of virtuosity that is, it was like any remaining part of my soul had been yanked right out of my body. I'd found out that my wife was being unfaithful so I told her I wanted a divorce and I moved out and went to stay with a friend; it was on that day that I had the *accident* with the knife. So I lost what I thought was the love of my life, and then I lost what I *knew* was the love of my life.'

'The latter love being the piano,' she said, correctly.

'Yes.'

'How old were you when this happened?'

'30, twelve years ago.'

'And since then?'

'Several things happened that day, physically and emotionally. The surgeon tried his best to stitch my finger back together. I'd almost sliced the damn thing off. I was informed that the tendon was severed so severely that I'd almost certainly lose the ability to straighten it out fully or move it like I could before. But it scarred me more mentally than it did physically. Having my music taken away from me like that was harder to come to terms with than losing my wife. I eventually moved on regarding my wife, but I can never move on from losing my ability to lose myself at the piano.'

'Are you with anybody right now?'

'How do you mean?'

'A girlfriend, partner?'

'No, nobody.'

'Not since your ex-wife?'

'Oh, yes, of course, lots of times. But they're usually quite brief, they never work out.'

'Why's that?'

'I don't know, I can't put my finger on it, not this one anyway,' I joked, holding up my left middle finger. 'It's like I've lost the ability to fall in love. Almost like there's a little switch buried deep in my chest somewhere with the words "Emotions On/Off" written on it and when I was 30 it got switched off somehow and I have no idea where that switch is anymore to be able to turn it back on.'

'How many relationships have you had since you got divorced?'

'Loads, too many to recall, fifteen, twenty, perhaps, maybe more.'

I could see Shannon doing the mental arithmetic, I did the same: about two per year.

'But I've had loads of dates on top of that, many of which resulted in very short term flings that lasted maybe a few days to a few weeks.'

'How many times has that happened?'

'Oh god, I don't know, twenty, maybe more.'

'So during the past 12 years you've had maybe 20 relationships plus about another 20 short-term flings?'

'Sounds about right.'

'So how long did the relationships last, on average? Excluding the short flings.'

'Two to four months.'

'So what usually happens?'

'I end them.'

'Why?'

'Various reasons, but the same reason is always firmly rooted right at the centre.'

'And what's that?'

'No feelings. Ha, like the Sex Pistols' song,' I joked.

'Can you elaborate?'

'On the Pistols' song?' I joked. Shannon smiled, briefly. I coughed and got back to the topic in hand.

'I don't seem to have the ability to fall in love anymore; I don't develop any feelings for these women. I care for them and their wellbeing, but that's about it, there's just something missing and I know the problem lies with me and my screwed up emotions. I'm desperate to fall in love so I can develop a long-term meaningful relationship with somebody, move in together and grow old with them, but I'm dead inside. The idea of growing old alone scares the shit out of me. I think, as we get older, we get fussier about what we want, we don't want to *settle* for just anybody, well I don't anyway. She has to be right, perfect, and I have to be perfect for her too but I just can't seem to find it so I've given up. There are too many variables and we've complicated the hell out of relationships these days.'

'Ok, we'll revisit this at another time, Red. I'd like you to tell me what happened when you were six, the event that caused you to set up residence in that dark cave in the corner of your mind.'

I told Shannon all about the accident at the bus stop, my family being ploughed down by an out-of-control lorry, right in front of me. She took lots of notes and gave me lots of sympathetic looks. I could see the pain on her face as I described the incident, in detail.

'After that, I was put into a children's home, temporarily, for a couple of months until they found a foster family for me. I stayed with my new foster family until I was 10, for four long years, but I couldn't stay there anymore because of what was happening to me. The authorities took me out of that placement and put me into a so-called care home again, until they found another foster family for me. I stayed in the care home for about three months this time, before they found me a new foster family placement in Hertfordshire.'

'How long did you remain with the second family?'

'Until I was 16. I wasn't really happy there either, or so I thought.'

'What do you mean?'

'I think, in hindsight, it was because I just wasn't happy in myself, but I guess I projected it onto the family, blamed them.'

'Where did you go when you were 16?'

'My social worker arranged a flat share for me and I got a job.'

'Let's just go back to the first foster family. You said you had to be taken out of there because of things that were happening to you?'

'Yes.'

'Can you tell me a little bit more about that?' she said, softly.

I paused, composed myself. She noticed me fidgeting, uncomfortably, on the sofa.

'Red, it's ok, this is a safe environment for you,' she said. She sounded so reassuring and I actually did feel safe in the room with her. I didn't hear any noises coming from any other part of the house and wondered if she had any family of her own: husband, kids.

'Red?'

'Well, what can I say? It was brutal. The family were horrible and I have no idea how they managed to get on the fostering register to start with. These days an animal shelter will visit your home and scrutinise you before letting you adopt one of their mutts. I suppose back then things were a little different. Anyway, it was the worst kind of abuse you could imagine: mental, physical and sexual,' I said. I didn't take my eyes off Shannon's; she looked down and scribbled on her pad.

'Can you tell me what sort of things happened?'

'*She* was the worst. Well, they were all bad, but it's her face that remains so vivid in my mind's eye if I choose to think about it, which I don't. They were a married couple with a son of their own. He was two years older than me, a nasty little piece of work.'

'So you were six and he was eight?' she confirmed.

'Yes. He bullied me, hit me, teased me and tormented me, insistently, every single day I was there. I hated him and fantasised about smothering him to death with a pillow while he was asleep. I would have actually done it too, if I'd known for sure he would not wake up and fight me off. He was bigger and stronger than me. He was a disgusting kid, the worst kind of bully boy you could imagine and he hated me being part of *his* family.'

'What about the parents?'

'The father was brutal. He used to call me a "worthless little good-for-nothing shite" and he'd beat me too.'

'What would he do?'

'He liked his black leather belt. He'd take it off, fold it in half and whip me with it. That was about as good as it got from him, he did much worse. He used to slap me around the head, really hard, to the point that it left ringing in my ears for the rest of the day. And if I ever did anything wrong or anything that displeased him, he'd grab me by the hair and drag me across the floor and out of the room and take me to the garden shed and lock me in there, leaving me there for hours on end. I'd look out of the glass window of the shed up the garden and see his disgusting son pulling faces at me from the kitchen window.'

'What about the mother?'

I had to pause again; this was not going to be easy. I looked down at my hands as I was embarrassed to look Shannon in the eye for this part.

'It's ok, take your time,' she said, reassuringly. Her softly spoken, soothing Irish tones managed to open me up a crack, just enough for me to speak.

'Well, she's where the sexual abuse came from,' I said. 'It started one day when I was off school sick. I remember having an upset stomach and I felt nauseous, like I was going to vomit. Anyway, her son was at school and her husband was at work. She came into my room where I was in bed and she told me that we should try harder, try to be friends. She was smiling; I'll never forget that smile. At the time, I was pleased as she sat on the bed and gently put her hand on my shoulder. This was the first time she'd ever shown my any sort of love or affection and I drank it all up. Well, I'd been starved of any sort of love and I was desperate for somebody to be kind to me, to love me.

"Would you like to be friends with me, Marion?" she

said, gently stroking my hair now. I said yes and smiled at her. Her horrible son and drunken violent husband were not there and, although she used to shout and scream at me all the time, she'd never beaten me. That was the domain of her husband and son. Sure, she'd slapped me a few times, but nothing excessive like what her husband used to do. So it felt like bliss, and for a moment I was in heaven.

"When two people are friends and like each other they do nice things for each other. Would you like that?" she said. Naturally I said yes, enthusiastically. "And after we've done something nice for each other, you can have ice-cream, how does that sound?" she said, warmth and tenderness in her voice. "Ok then, I'll go first, I'll do something nice for you, then you can do something nice for me, yes?" she said.

I agreed, with enthusiasm, even though I felt sick – anything for a bit of love and kindness. Anyway, she reached under the blanket and touched me through my pyjama bottoms, over them at first, then she put her hand inside and started to stroke me and play with me. I didn't know what to think. I was only six and I didn't understand what was going on. I can't even remember what sort of reaction I had, if any. I just liked that she was being nice to me, for once. Well, for the first time actually. Anyway, after a few minutes she stopped and then said it was my turn. She made me lick her at first, you know, *there*; and then she handed me a dildo and showed me how to use it on her, insisting that I lick her at the same time. I remember hating it. She tasted

75

disgusting and I felt like I was going to be sick. That was the first of many. Whenever her husband and son were not there, she always took the opportunity to get me to do things to her, as friends. Those were the only times she was kind to me, so I obliged.'

Shannon didn't say anything; she just took notes, lots of them, and looked up with a sympathetic, and horrified, expression.

'Red, when you first came in here you said you were going to end your life twelve weeks from now. I need to ask, what is it, exactly, that you expect from me?'

'Honestly, I'd like you to give me a reason not to do it. Well, maybe not give me a reason, but to help me unravel all this shit so I can at least try and find one for myself. I've never really had a life, Shannon. I'm 42 years old, I live alone in a 2-bed end of terraced rented house and I work as a driving instructor. I've been diagnosed with clinical depression, I have most of the traits of somebody who has bipolar, I have OCD and I sit at home most evenings in the corner with the lights off and cry while the pain and loneliness seeps out of my pores. Sometimes I don't know the difference between being asleep and being awake; they merge into one dark and surreal space and I see no reason to carry on. You know what my favourite time of the day is?'

'When?' she asked.

'It lasts for a few seconds, those brief moments just before you fall asleep, you know, that time when you're laying in bed and you're just about to fall asleep and it feels like you're about to fall and you suddenly catch yourself. You ever felt that?'

'Yes, yes I have.'

'Well, during the few moments after catching myself I say to myself, "Maybe tonight I'll have a peaceful 8-hour sleep with no dreams", or rather, no nightmares as the case would be. For a few moments before I fall asleep I'm happy with the notion that I might not dream, that I'll be at peace for at least a few hours, blissfully unaware of the fact that I exist, until I awake again the next morning.

'Thing is, Shannon (I was feeling comfortable enough to address her by her first name now, as she'd used my name often enough to make me feel comfortable about this), I have nightmares pretty much every night, horrible, disgusting vivid ones. And when I'm not having nightmares, my dreams are always full of anxiety, where I can sense something horrible looming in the dark corners of the dream. I read that if you have nightmares all the time it's a sign of an unsettled and tortured man. I think I'd agree with that. I'm an atheist, I don't believe in God or any sort of afterlife. I believe that when we die it's lights out, an eternal sleep, with no dreams ... that sounds like bliss to me. You see, every morning I always wake up to another nightmare, my real life.'

'Red, there's quite a lot of work for us to do here, but I'm confident I can help you,' she said, smiling, confidently.

'Really?'

'Yes, so don't go selling any more of your stuff just

yet. I'd hate for you to have to go out and buy it all again three months from now,' she said, smiling. 'Look, Red, there's a lot to unravel here and we're going to have to dig deep, very deep. You've suffered and you're still suffering from post-traumatic stress disorder and not just because of witnessing your family die right in front of you, but the horrible foster placement and severing the tendon in your finger and having your career as a concert pianist taken away, and I suspect more too.'

'What? PTSD? Even after all this time?'

'Yes, even after all this time. You never healed from what happened to you as a child and your ensuing boyhood years and then you got slammed with two more sledgehammers when you were 30, an emotional one and a physical one. It sounds to me like you never got any professional help either. I'm confident I can help you, Red, and at the very least I can promise you that, after a few more sessions, you're going to start feeling a whole lot better about things as you start to get all this stuff out, and it has to come out, Red. I know you walked into a very long and very dark tunnel, Red, a tunnel that's been blocked off at the end for quite some time. But I'm going to blast the end of that tunnel away so you can see the light at the end of it. Then I'm going to guide you through it so you can live a real life, a life that has meaning, joy and happiness, maybe even love.'

'You sound pretty confident.'

'Red, I've never failed any of my clients and I'm not

going to fail you,' she said.

I'm not sure why, but I took comfort in that, momentarily at least, but I was still going to move forward with my plan nonetheless, as I was not entirely convinced that Shannon could really change my thoughts and ideas about life, even if she could untangle all the mess and mental infestations that had become sitting tenants in my mind, body and soul, for so many years I didn't have the mental energy to try and evict them anymore. Shannon would have to be some sort of miracle worker to fix me to the point that I'd want to stick around. If Shannon could not help me I still had suicide to fall back on.

As I got into my car and pulled out of Shannon's drive onto the main road to join life's stream of traffic I figured there would be nothing Shannon could say or do that could change the world or the people in it to make it a place I'd want to live in and I very much doubted she'd be able to change my view of it, even if she could untangle the emotional junkyard in my mind before banishing the dark demons from it while opening up my heart to the possibility of love.

Chapter 7

I got home from my last driving lesson of the evening with a young man called Teal, like the colour, or the duck. Yes, that's what I thought, an unusual name for a young man. As usual, I had sweet FA to do. No plans, nobody to go and visit, nothing: zilch, zip, nada, diddlysquat. As I hung my coat by the front door, kicked off my shoes and tossed my wallet and keys onto the kitchen work surface, I came back down to earth as I was reminded of my solitary life in my small, quiet, 2-bed end of terrace house in a small quiet village just out of town.

My evening routine, after getting in from work, was the same every day. I'd put fresh water in the kettle and flick the switch on and while the water steadily worked its way up to 100 degrees I'd change into some comfortable lounge pants, have a wash, then put on a T-shirt. I'd take my cup of tea (weak, plenty of full-fat milk, but no sugar) into the lounge and quickly scroll through the 'Top Stories' on the BBC news app on my iPhone. I say 'quickly' because most of the time it was the same old dirge: Coronavirus, Brexit (which has been somewhat overshadowed by the former), Trump, some MP getting a speeding ticket, a black footballer being racially abused by a group of extreme right wing chanting football fans, another sexual abuse case (usually involving an 80's TV personality and a 12-year old boy), a teenage stabbing in London, or, heaven forbid, some nauseating boy band's manager announcing that they are breaking up and every teenage girl on the planet is about to slit their wrists as a result. Whatever happened to good old-fashioned *quality* journalism that involved at least some degree of research and effort?

I feel that the art of investigative journalism has all but died. For me, BBC journalists are nothing more than a vehicle for the government to distribute its press releases – there is no investigative journalism whatsoever, just a so-called news reporter verbalising a re-hashed press release handed to him/her by their boss. The ownership and governance of most mainstream media has been brought inside the pillars of the state, all but eliminating the supposed 'freedom of press'. Today's so-called news stories follow a barrage of the same old nothingness over a quick newsflash of the day, never actually exploring the roots with good old-fashioned investigative journalism to ascertain the actual 'truth', before flipping on to the next headline.

I have scant regard for modern mainstream media journalists as, from what I can gather, most of them have been duped in the same hypnotic trance as the mainstream of the public. If this were not the case, why do they keep regurgitating the messages of their employers and those of the state? The latter so-called news pieces often loaded with 'nudge theory' influence to keep the masses in their place and to 'nudge' their thought processes in whatever direction the government dictates. In my opinion there hasn't been a decent investigative journalist since the days of Roger Cook.

After spending all of 30 seconds sighing my way through these futile, spinned, smoke up my arse, news pieces, I'd quit the app and open the Sky Sports app instead. Like the BBC news app, the Sky Sports app is also about winners and losers - only not in love and war - in football. Those guys were all multi-millionaires who didn't have to worry about where their next square meal was coming from and, from what I can gather, they all had pretty Barbie doll blonde bombshell wives sitting around, just waiting to give blowjobs on demand in exchange for a fake plastic money-driven lifestyle.

Spurs are my team, or at least they used to be. I didn't get into football until I was in my early teens (14 to be exact) and I only really got into it because of my school friend, Brian, who was a big Spurs fan. I guess it was because we both lived in Hertford and Spurs were the nearest team, well, nearest decent team anyway. I mean, Hertford Town had a football club but they are so far down the league tier system if they got any lower they'd drop off the coupon, as Brian's dad used to say. So Brian had settled on Spurs, and so had I. It was Brian's dad who took me to my first football game at White Hart Lane. I remember it vividly, an FA Cup third round match, 7:30 evening kick off on a

Wednesday. It was an incredible experience for me and I was hooked from that moment. It was a hairy game because Spurs were losing 2-0 at half time, but they came back to win 3-2 in the second half – phew!

When I turned 15 my foster parents would let Brian and me go to matches on our own. It was amazing; we used to go to most of the home games together and a few, more local, away ones too. Between the age of 16 and 18 I probably only missed about three home matches and I went to about half the away games during the same period. In hindsight, I'm not sure why I was so into Spurs. Maybe it was the feeling of 'belonging' as 30,000 fans all chanted, sung and shouted for the same thing. When the Spurs fans got going – especially against rivals, Arsenal – the atmosphere was electric, and being a part of that made me feel like I belonged to something, that I was a part of something, that I fitted in.

But as my teenage years came and went I realised that I didn't fit in at all. I didn't belong and that I was part of nothing and I never really had been. I had no circle of friends, at least not a circle that I felt that I 'belonged' to and there didn't appear to be any niche little circle, demographic, kind, race, tribe, community or group that I felt particularly comfortable in. Sure, I could 'chameleonise' myself if you put me into a room full of people. You can take me anywhere, so to speak, and although I'm there in physical presence – and will usually be the life of the party with my quick wit and impromptu stand-up comedy routines based on the snippets of information that I grab during conversations – I simply am not there. I don't fit in, I don't belong, I never have and I never will. It's like I flew into this world on the tail of a comet and just never really settled or found my true place, my meaning. I never *really* belonged.

So, back to football, I don't go to see matches anymore and I haven't for 24 years. These days, when I watch Tottenham on TV, I see a corporation, corporate boxes, money, so much money; I just wish I owned the club. Apart from 22 multimillionaires kicking a ball from one end of the pitch to the other in an attempt to kick said stitched piece of cow's hide (or whatever they make footballs out of these days) into the opposing teams net, all I see is a board of directors and overpaid players. The so-called 'beautiful' game is ruined and it has been for quite a few years now.

Once upon a time, the players would sit on the same trains as the traveling fans, boots hanging around their necks via their knotted laces, and they'd drink in the same pubs after the game. There was an interaction where *everybody* felt like they were members of the club, part of the team. I mean, the very definition of the word 'club' means belonging to, a group of people with something in common. These days there is no such interaction. After the match, the 'working man' will walk from the ground and get the train home, hopefully in time for sausage and mash and a cold beer, while the player leaves, some time later, after taking a shower and donning their designer cloths,

£40,000 earrings, clasping on a £50,000 watch and then jumping into a gleaming white £175,0000 top of the range 4x4 or bright red sports car and speeding off to their £8 million house (getting a speeding ticket en-route, which they won't get any points for as they will pay some top solicitor a stack of money to find a loop hole to get them off) to get a blowjob from their ever-willing high-maintenance supermodel wives. It was all bullshit and those top premier league clubs take the gullible fans – and all their money – for granted. But not mine, not anymore.

I still showed some interest in football but I was hanging onto that little bit of interest by my fingernails. I'd recently cancelled my Sky Spots and BT Sports subscriptions, having decided that I didn't want to put any more money into the already overpaid player's pockets. Sky and BT Sports have to pay premier league clubs obscene amounts of money to air their matches and that money (along with other revenue) goes towards paying the players colossal salaries. This fact used to leave a sour taste in my mouth so, instead, I now choose to watch Match Of The Day and listen to what Gary Lineker, Allen Shearer and Ian Wright have to say about things on a Saturday night. That was about the extent of my football involvement, but, like everything else in my life, that would be coming to an end in twelve weeks time too.

I used to have another app on my phone that I would peruse and it would take me a lot longer than the sports app, and hell of a lot longer than the news app: it was a dating app. Some evenings I'd spend hours on it, reading through the profiles of hundreds of women, going through every intricate detail of each and every one of them with a fine-toothed comb, trying to find that elusive 'perfect' woman. But I've long since given up all hope of finding her, or any kind of romantic interest, perfect or otherwise. In the modern world people just didn't seem to know how to form or maintain a relationship or live, love, or be loved anymore; it's all got screwed up and crazy. George Sand would be seriously disappointed with the lack of anything deep and meaningful, the rarity of real romance and a lack of unconditional love in today's so-called civilised western society. Most of the profiles I used to read on the dating app read more like a list of demands, a shopping list, than anything else: He must have a house, a car, be affluent, have a good job, wear nice clothes, be this way, be that way, love me, love my children, we come as a package, and so on and so forth. No mention of romance, love, purity, poetry or anything that's deep or meaningful, or anything that could even evoke a single human emotion. The thing is, shallow superficial people that are obsessed with e-commerce shopping and expensive gaudy accessories were of no interest to me: they never had been and never will be. I just can't understand people who worship 'brands' like they are Gods. 'Look at me, I've got a Louis Vuitton shoulder bag and it was only £1,695.' Seriously, honey, who gives a monkey's left bollock.

I wanted intelligence and an organic purity that simply didn't seem to exist on these dating sites, probably outside of them too.

These days I spend more time looking at my banking app to check the financial incomings and outgoings of my life than I do on any dating app for potential romantic incomings and outgoings in my life.

People just don't know how to communicate on dating (or any other) sites and it was spilling out into the real world too. I find it incredibly ironic that with all this amazing 'communication' technology – email, text, WhatsApp, instant messenger, Facebook messaging and so on and so forth – people aren't really talking anymore, not in any real sense of the word anyway.

I have, or at least had, a handful of small pleasures in life that made it sort of worthwhile. Well, bearable at least. But those small pleasures have become less and less as the years rolled along; football being a prime example, for the reasons outlined previously. I was into photography once and, I don't mind blowing my own trumpet a little here, I was pretty damn good at it too. For me, there are three vital ingredients that make up a good photograph: subject matter, composition and lighting. If you nail these three the rest is down to your own creative flare, which I had in spades. I had decent equipment too: Nikon 35mm cameras and lenses, Hasselblad medium format equipment and a decent Gitzo tripod, and I knew how to get the best out of it. Although I took many excellent photographs

a

– landscapes, nature, portraiture and journalism – I decided that there was no point in me documenting anything anymore. After all, I didn't have any kids who would grow up to appreciate them. So, one day, during a melancholy moment, I got quite despondent and decided to sell all my expensive photographic equipment.

I really don't want to come across all doom and gloom but my life, for the most part, had been a grim and depressing affair. Pre and post my 'piano years', it was like life had personally greased the pole that was sliding me into a bucket of shit.

Nobody really cares about anything anymore. Companies are producing crap quality products that the masses are happy to spend their hard-earned money on. Politicians line their own pockets and chain store CEOs feather their own nests in the year leading up to the company going into liquidation, while in the background some bank is getting a multi-million pound bailout from the government at the expense of the tax payer because some greedy fat cat scooped off too much cream.

Yet, when we watch this stuff on the so-called news, we just sigh and say, 'Oh well, what can you do...' before switching over to watch the latest action movie from the aging Stallone, Schwarzenegger or Willis. In an instant it's forgotten about and we're all heading off to bed to prepare for yet another futile and meaningless day that we think we're in control of. We all think that we're free and that we have choices but the truth of the matter is we don't have any more freedom than the folk in North Korea. We're living under a dictatorship too; only it's all wrapped up in cotton wool by our 'nanny state' government with a nice pink sugar coated topping. Everything we do is controlled, all our choices are already chosen for us, all our decisions are already decided for us. Choosing to do your shopping at Tesco, Sainsbury, Aldi or Morrison's isn't a choice; we only tell ourselves it is, when in reality there's just a different logo in a different colour on that little plastic bullshit 'loyalty' card that we all subscribe to. Choosing to bank with Barclays, NatWest, Nationwide or Santander isn't a choice either. And anybody who thinks these are choices is already doomed. No, we don't make any choices at all, we only think we do, as we all run around living lives that are indistinguishable from everybody else's. Living in brand new cul-de-sac house with 2.4 children, trips to the retail park on a Saturday and washing the car on a Sunday. All beavering away so we can buy a bunch of materialistic crap that we're conditioned to believe that we should have and own; and then at the end of it some shallow superficial twat will come along and pat you on the shoulder and tell you how great you are once you've got it all. It's just an illusion of choice and it's all bullshit. Did I say I suffered from depression? ;)

So, like every other depressed single guy out there, living a bachelor-style life, I looked at the pile of recently purchased DVDs lined up on the shelf under my TV, picked one out (Denzel Washington's latest in this case), popped it in the Blu-ray player and while the disc span up to locate the home menu I went into the kitchen, turned the oven on at 180 degrees, set my digital timer for 33 minutes (3 minutes added time to allow for the oven to heat up, no, I didn't bother heating the oven first, is there really any point?) and popped a ready meal onto a tray, pierced the film lid 'several times' and put it onto the middle shelf. I don't even bother reading the cooking (cooking, that's a joke, it's hardly cooking) instructions anymore. They were all typically 25 to 35 minutes at somewhere between 180 and 200 anyway. I grabbed the small digital timer and took it to the living room with me. I'd made the mistake of leaving the timer in the kitchen once before – *once*. I was watching an action movie and the sound system and subwoofer had masked the gentle digital pips of the timer, but – good as the sound system was that I had hooked up to my TV – it didn't quite drown out the sound of the smoke alarm in the kitchen. Since then I always take the timer with, plonked on the coffee table right in front of the couch, in direct line of sight to the TV.

So, in comfy lounge pants and a T-shirt, I settled back to watch Denzel kick some ass for the next ninety minutes or so. I was barely five minutes into the movie when my phone rang; it was Mathieu, calling to see how I was I expect. I paused the movie and studied the pores and other high definition detail in Denzel's close-up as he looked off screen to the left, while I listened to Mathieu talk.

Mathieu was aware that I didn't have many friends, especially since moving out of London to Cambridgeshire. A house move (even one of just 60 miles) can have a detrimental effect on your friend count. Of course, you stay in touch with your friends for a while and you go to visit them a few times, and vice-versa, but a year later everybody has moved on. Mathieu, on the other hand, had stayed a good friend and had been for the past 22 years, since the days of Nine Yards Of Dead Cats. Amazingly, he was still with Shari. They were not married, but loved each other and didn't need a piece of paper to remind them of that fact. I liked that about Mathieu and Shari. They both had a 'pure' attitude towards life, love and their relationship. In fact, it is only their relationship that had inspired me and given me hope of a loving romance myself over the years. Mathieu never takes Shari out on Valentine's Day. He says it's a farce, totally fake and crap. He says if a man only takes his wife out when he's reminded to do so by some commercial fake day in the calendar then he doesn't truly love his wife. Shari agrees with him, so do I. She said she'd be embarrassed if Mathieu ever took her out to a restaurant on Valentine's Day just to sit there with all the other unlucky women who only get taken out on rare occasions such as Valentine's Day by their superficial partners who they are not 'in' love with anymore, they only convince themselves that they are. Mathieu will take Shari out when *he* chooses, because he loves her and will suddenly be consumed with an urge to take her out because of the overwhelming feelings inside him, not because society, or some superficial date in the calendar dictates to him that he should.

We chatted on the phone for 10 minutes or so. Well, let's face it, do guys need any more than that? He said he and Shari would like to come up and see me at the weekend, if I was not too busy with driving lessons. Weekends were my busiest time, typically, but this particular Saturday I only had a few in the morning. Some of my pupils were away and a few others had cancelled, leaving my Saturday afternoon and evening free. So Mathieu said he and Shari would be at mine at about 1 p.m. and that I'd better know a 'decent' place for us to go out and eat.

I was about halfway through the movie, Denzel was kicking ass for the third time (and it was a great scene too), when the phone rang again, my landline this time. That reminded me, put a note in calendar to call BT and cancel phone/broadband package, but not for another seven weeks. I paused the movie and answered it. I rarely ignore the phone in case it's an enquiry about driving lessons; it was.

'Hello?' I said, my professional, but polite voice.

'Oh, hello, can I speak to Red?'

'Speaking.'

'I'm calling about driving lessons and wondered if you had any spaces at the moment?' said the female voice.

'Yes I do, I have one space available at the moment and, test-permitting tomorrow, I'm confident I'll have another space freed up,' I said. What the hell was I thinking? I'm supposed to be winding down my lessons in preparation for my departure from this planet in less than twelve weeks.

'Oh, that's super. What day and time would they be?'

'The one I have available at the moment is on a Tuesday at 7 p.m. and, if my pupil passes his test tomorrow, I'll have another one free on Sundays at eleven in the morning.'

'Tuesday at seven sounds ideal. Can I book that?'

'Of course. Who's it for?'

'Me,' she said.

She didn't sound young, not 17 or 18 young anyway. I know it can be hard to define the age of a woman, purely by her voice on the phone, but you can generally tell a very young woman or a very old woman. But anywhere between 30 and 55 women are generally ageless in their voices. I'd guessed (having spoken to lots of parents calling on behalf of their teenage children) that this woman was old enough to have children, and I thought she could be calling about lessons for a son or daughter perhaps – not in this case.

'Ok. Let me take some details. Can I take your name?'

'Gina,' she said, offering no surname.

I didn't ask. It wasn't necessary at this time and I certainly didn't ask her age either; I'd consider that rude. I figured I'd be able to hazard a guess during the first lesson anyway, not that it's an important factor when learning to drive.

'And your address?'

She gave me her full address, including postcode. Great, she was relatively local in a village called Longstanton, which was only about a 20-minute drive (12 miles) from where I lived.

'Ok, Gina, when would you like to start?'

'Straight away. How about this Tuesday?'

'Of course. Do you know my rates?'

'Yes, I've seen your website,' she said.

'Super. Do you mind if I ask how you heard about me?'

'You taught my friend's daughter, Kristen, about a year ago.'

'Kristen? Kristen. Oh yes, she lives in Longstanton too, right?'

'Yes.'

'Ok. Well, I've got you booked in the diary so I'll be around to pick you up at seven on Tuesday.'

'Great, I'll look forward to it,' she said, sounding all enthusiastic.

'Ok. You have a good evening,' I said.

'You too, see you Tuesday,' she said.

I released Denzel from pause to allow him to continue his altruistic endeavours. For some strange reason, I couldn't quite concentrate on the movie anymore; the sound of Gina's voice still lingered in my ears.

Chapter 8

It was the day of my ADI Standards Check test and, unlike the last time around, I was not feeling anxious in the least. In fact, I don't really know why I'm bothering with it as I'm not going to be around much longer, but, I am hanging onto a glimmer of hope from my therapist, Shannon.

This time around I had a star pupil, Jason, who would make me look good, so I'd probably breeze through it. We arrived at the test centre, Jason driving, and although I'd already explained to Jason what it would entail I went over it again.

'Ok. So as far as you're concerned I'm just going to be giving you a normal driving lesson. The only difference is there'll be a man sitting in the back who will be examining me by monitoring how I'm teaching you. He's not interested in you; it's me he's here to check on. Make sense?'

'Course. Don't worry, Red, I'll make you look good,' he said. I headed into the building while Jason waited in the car.

The test went swimmingly and Jason was the perfect pupil, as I knew he would be. He only made a couple of tiny errors, which I corrected him on while clearly explaining his errors in a comprehensible manner, which impressed my examiner. After the lesson was over the examiner spent fifteen minutes discussing the test with me. He was impressed in all areas: my lesson planning, risk management, and teaching and learning skills. He said I was a 'text book' driving instructor and even suggested I consider taking up one of the examiner positions – he could put in a very good word for me. I got a grade A and scored 50, which is just 1 shy of the maximum mark you can attain on this test. Knowing this particular examiner's reputation for being strict, I'd take that score all day long.

The drive from the test centre in Cambridge back up to Jason's house in Ely was an uncomplicated one, straight up the A10, nothing challenging. Jason had done it a few times before. I didn't have time for any manoeuvres or anything else with Jason as I had to get over to Shannon's place for my therapy session. But I didn't feel guilty; Jason had just had a free lesson during the course of my test.

'I was thinking, after I pass my test, of getting one of those electric cars. Not a hybrid, one of those all-electric cars, a Nissan Leaf,' said Jason, as he drove up the A10 towards Ely.

'Bad idea,' I said.

'Why? They're the future, they're good for the environment and you save loads of money on petrol and stuff,' he said.

'If only that were true, Jason.'

'What do you mean?'

'Well, there's a chance they could be the future, but I'm not entirely convinced about that. And they're certainly no good for the environment and you don't save loads of money on petrol either. Actually, they actually cost you a lot more than petrol cars in the long run, if you do the math.'

'That doesn't compute,' said Jason.

That's the thing with young people these days, everything has to compute. Nobody really questions things anymore or actually does any thought-out research to check things for themselves. I could imagine Jason walking into a Nissan dealership and listening to some salesman spoon-feed him a bunch of crap about the environment and huge savings in running costs and Jason lapping it all up. Jason came across as a pretty smart kid, but, like the majority of the car-buying public he just didn't do anywhere near enough research into any given car and the long-term running costs of it. Even when they do most people will only look at one side of the coin and convince themselves they are making the right choice, rather than looking at the bigger picture.

'Ok, tell me what you know about EVs?' I said.

'EVs?'

'Electric Vehicles,' I said.

'Oh, right. Well they don't run on petrol so you save tons of money there. Also, you don't have to pay road tax either and there are no congestion charges for when you drive into the centre of London. Oh, servicing and repairs are cheaper too,' he said, happy with his answer.

'That's it?'

'What else is there? Isn't that enough?' he said.

'Ok, so what happens when you flip the coin over and take a look at the other side?'

'There is no other side, not that I can see,' he said.

I took a deep breath. 'Ok, let me try and unwrap this for you. Firstly, the average price of a new Nissan Leaf with a couple of basic options added is about £30,000, whereas a mid-range Nissan Micra petrol car with similar specs comes in at around £15,000, that's half the price. So, your electric Leaf has already put you £15,000 out of pocket before you've even driven the car out the showroom.'

'Ah, but you'll get all that back in petrol savings,' he said, chuffed.

'Not even close. Do you think electricity is free? Let's just say you do the national average of 10,000 miles per year. That means you'll have to plug your Leaf in and charge it pretty much every day, every other day at best. You'll also want to keep it topped up, knowing that you've got the maximum range at all times. When you do that do you really think your domestic electric bills are going to stay at £40 per month? Not a hope. They'll go through the roof and even if you do have one of those super-fast chargers installed it will suck up super amounts of electricity. Don't think just because you're charging the car with a rapid-charger that it's still only taking a small "trickle charge" from the national grid. No, your electricity meter wheel will be spinning around in nuclear power station mode. Thing is, Jason, even if it only cost £5 per charge, that's still going to add … at say, four charges per week … about £80 per month onto your household electric bill, at least. So goodbye £40 per month electric bills and hello new £120 per month bills.'

'That's still a saving on petrol though isn't it?' he asked, not so confident now.

'No, a Nissan Micra petrol car with a 1 litre engine will return close to 60 miles per gallon and at the current fuel prices, based on you driving 10,000 miles per year, that's slightly north of 800 miles per month. That's about £75 per month in fuel costs, £5 less than your electric car could cost you in electricity bills.'

'Yes, but you still save on annual car tax and the London congestion charges,' said Jason.

'Maybe, but at £150 a year for road tax on a Micra how many years do you think it's going to take you to break even on the £15,000 extra that you laid out to buy the Leaf in the first place?'

'Hmm, not sure,' said Jason.

'Well, I'd say somewhere in the region of about 100 years. That's if you keep the car that long of course,' I said. He laughed. 'But there's more to it than that, Jason.'

'More? How can there be more?'

'The batteries. They're lithium ion battery cells, the latest and most advanced ones you can get.'

'That's a good thing, right?' he said.

'Yes, but even though lithium ion batteries are the most advanced they're still pretty crap in the grand scheme of things. They're the same cells that are in a Samsung Galaxy or your iPad. Ever noticed how after a year or two your phone doesn't hold as much charge as it did when it was new?'

'Oh yeah, my Sony Xperia's only a year old and I have to charge it every day, sometimes twice if I use it a lot. When I first got it it was good for two days. Now it's less than half that.'

'Exactly. That's because over time the cells die and lose their efficiency, slowly, but surely. They're only any good for about 800 charges and discharges. After that they just don't hold their charge very well, so your Nissan Leaf might be good for 140 miles of real world driving when it's brand new, but don't expect to get anywhere near that range five years down the line. And when that happens you'll be stumping up about £5,000 to have that dud battery pack swapped out for a new one.'

'What! five grand?' he exclaimed.

'Well, it's not like popping down to the Apple store to have them change a battery on an iPhone. The battery in that car takes up the entire floor space under the seats, front and back, and they're not cheap, nor is the labour to do it.'

'Hang on, so if you have to change the battery every five years to maintain the same range as when the car was new that would be costing you a grand a year,' he said.

'Now you're starting to see the bigger picture.'

'And if the petrol cost £75 per month on a regular car …' he paused and did some mental math, 'wow, the petrol costs less way less than that,' he said.

'Yup, and I hope you haven't forgotten that you paid £15,000 extra for the privilege to begin with, over a petrol car. And for your information servicing costs are not cheap either. Oh yeah, just because they're electric, doesn't mean they don't need servicing. It still costs between £150 and £200 per year to service a Leaf.'

'No!'

'Yup. Call Nissan and ask them they'll tell you the same thing.'

'Wow, you know, I just wouldn't have thought of half that stuff. So in the real world an electric car could cost me double, over time,' said Jason.

'It could cost you double just to buy it. As for the environment, anybody who tells you that battery cars are better for the environment is ill-informed, or just hasn't looked behind the scenes.'

'How do you mean?'

'It's a story that will take longer than the two minutes it's gonna take to get back to your house, Jason, but I'm sure you know how to use Google, right?'

'Course.'

We arrived at Jason's house and he jumped out. I hopped into the driver's side and headed over to Shannon's house for my second therapy session.

'Hello, Red, come on in,' said Shannon, in her usual cheery Irish tones. I took up my usual position on the couch and asked Shannon if there was any chance of a coffee.

'Of course. What would you like?' she replied, walking over and tapping a rather expensive looking coffee machine with a large digital display on the front.

'Can that thing make a decent cappuccino?'

'You betcha. How do you like it?' she said, tapping away at the screen and putting a cup in place.

'Milky with one sugar, please.'

'So, how's your week been?' she enquired, while frothing up some milk.

'You know, same old, same old,' I sighed.

'And what would the same old be?' she asked.

'Living in a world that I don't fit into, surrounded by people who comfort themselves with self-deception on a daily basis.'

'Do you ever remember a time when you felt like you fitted in, Red?'

'No. Well I might have once when I was a child, before my family died. You don't really remember anything before the age of three or four anyway and as I was six when the accident happened I can only really recall a few short years of memories from back then.'

'We haven't gone into the time you spent with foster carers in any detail, Red, and we will, but right now I'd like you to skip forward into your adult life – the last ten years. Why do you feel you don't fit in?' she asked, putting the cappuccino on the table in front of me.

'What can I say? I'm not like other people. I'm kind of a lone wolf, Shannon.'

'Is that through choice or circumstances?'

'A bit of both, I guess. But I think the balance is

tipped in the favour of choice.'

'Why do you make that choice? To live in solitude and not mix with people?'

'I wish it wasn't this way, I really do. But the fact is, I'm different. I'm just not like everybody else. I'm too quirky and unorthodox, Shannon, and I've just never managed to find any group of people that I felt totally comfortable with. Well, I did, briefly, when I was in a band. Whenever I find myself in any sort of group situation, a party or anything like that, I usually can't wait to get out of there. I just don't feel like I fit into the scheme of things where people are concerned. I'm not even convinced I really like humans that much if I'm totally honest, they always seem to disappoint.'

'Explain your feelings, the thoughts that go through your mind when you're in a room with a group of people,' she said.

'It's always the same. I listen to the conversations going on around me and I even participate in some of them. I look at the people around me, their clothes, their deportment, the expressions on their faces, the way they hold themselves and I hate it. If they're not shallow and superficial they're talking about what I consider to be futile subject matter that are of no interest to me.'

'Such as?'

'I don't know - usually their jobs: accountants, project managers, construction engineers, health and safety, stuff like that. I know that their jobs are important to them and they could talk about their occupations for hours, but it's of no interest to me. Their conversations have no soul, no meaning, no real point; they're just talking for the sake of it. These people get up at six in the morning and sit in rush hour traffic for hours on end, work all day in an office, sit in more rush hour traffic, go home, have dinner, watch TV for an hour, take a shower then go to bed. And then they get up and do it all over again the next day and then the weekend comes and they all converge in the nearest retail park. Then on Sunday they do something else that's equally as futile and meaningless like wash the car or visit the in-laws. Then on Sunday night they shag their wives, if they're lucky, or if their wives are lucky, depending on the relationship, before repeating the seven day ritual all over again come 6:30 a.m. on Monday morning.'

'Red, two thirds of the world's population would consider that to be a slice of heaven,' she said.

'That may be, but to me it's hell. It's meaningless and none of it has any real purpose in the grand scheme of things. They're hurtling towards retirement without giving a second thought to "life". Then in retirement they'll sit around for another ten years waiting to be scooped up by the grim reaper and that will be that; lights out, an eternal sleep with no dreams. And what would it all have been for, Shannon? That's not what life's supposed to be.'

'How would you have them live their lives?' she asked.

'Honestly, I wouldn't want them to change a thing; I wouldn't want everybody else to be like me, to think like me. I'd hate that.'

'Why?'

'It's like what Groucho said, I wouldn't want to belong to any club that would have me.'

'Elaborate.'

'I don't like conforming, living my life like I'm on some sort of conveyor belt, steadily rolling along towards my grave. It's worse in America, but only slightly. I mean we're just 20 miles away from European shores, a land of great beauty and culture, yet we take our lead from those superficial arseholes three and a half thousand bloody miles away just because they speak English. What's all that all about? I mean, over there, they have their whole lives mapped out pretty much from birth. Within hours of popping out in the delivery room some nurse sticks a needle in their backside containing all sorts of questionable vaccinations to enable them to go to school in the first place. Because without those certificates showing the babies have been vaccinated, they can't even get into school. Then the school is structured and regimented in such a way that if you step out of line there'll be somebody there to nudge you back into place again, telling you that you can't do that, you can't be individual or creative. Christ! The girls start planning their weddings from the age of thirteen for crying out loud. Then they leave school and marry a guy called Chuck, work hard and have a bunch of kids so they can grow up and keep the pointlessness perpetuating along for even more generations of easily brainwashed dullards.'

'Nothing means anything anymore. Nobody knows how to live or love anymore. Everything's just one big commercial and materialistic farce. I've got more respect for aborigines living hundreds of miles from civilisation with no electricity. At least they haven't lost their souls and their lives actually have some meaning.'

'What about your ex-wife?'

'What about her?'

'Did you have chemistry with her, connection?'

'In hindsight, she just annoyed me less than anybody else on the planet, and I was happy with that. I was in love with her but thinking about it now there was no *real* chemistry there and certainly no connection, not my type of connection at least. I was 25 when I got married. I think I was probably infatuated with her more than anything but over time my love for her grew more and more. Unfortunately, she didn't feel the same way.'

'When did you find that out?'

'When I found out she'd been unfaithful to me, twice. If somebody does that to you they don't love you, simple as that. Well, I mean, they might love you but they're not *in* love with you, know what I mean?'

'Yes, and you're right, Red. If she were in love with you she wouldn't have done that. Getting back to your comment about everybody else comforting themselves with … self-deception, did you say?'

'Yes.'

'How do you compare to that?'

'I live in the real world, at least I try to, but it's difficult when you're surrounded by idiots who fool themselves on a daily basis by subscribing to organised living. I'm not under any illusions and I'm not deluded. I'm alone in my own world, Shannon, but at least my life is pure, honest and organic with no superficial bullshit. I don't confirm and I don't "go with the flow" as people like to say. I'm true to myself. You know, in a way, I'm glad I never had children.'

'Why's that?'

'The struggle. I don't mean the struggle of bringing them up, but the struggle of trying to shield them from all the shallow superficial crap that their peers at school would be into: games, iPads, retail parks, fast food, Britain's Got Talent. Christ! How could I ever prevent my daughter from being infected with all that crap? And I could just imagine how the meeting would go where I visit the school to insist that she doesn't sit in assembly, sing hymns or be infected by any of that religious crap. I would never have anybody groom or infect my daughter with any of that religious nonsense.'

'You said "daughter". Would you have liked a daughter, Red?'

'Maybe, but only because I miss my sister. It would have been nice to have had a little girl that I could have loved and cherished, you know…'

'Yes, I know,' she said, softly. 'We'll come back to that, Red,' she said, scribbling a few notes on her pad. I finished my cappuccino while she wrote; it was almost cold now.

Shannon asked me more questions; some quite

specific, some more general. I went into detail on various other things that had happened in my life, most of them grim or downright wretched and depressing.

'Red, if you had to describe yourself in two words, could you do it?'

I thought for a moment, said, 'Existential nihilist, but a depressed one.'

Shannon wrote on her pad and then looked up at me. 'We'll explore that in another session, but not today. Time's up.'

Shannon showed me out and I drove home, where a ready meal and aging Clint Eastwood was waiting for me – 'The Mule', on Blu-ray.

Chapter 9

I'm not sure why but as I started the Corsa and pulled away from my house I felt a little bit anxious, or was it something else? A small cluster of tiny butterflies were making their presence known, gently fluttering in my stomach, as I drove over to Longstanton to pick Gina up for her first driving lesson. *Stupid, stupid, stupid,* I told myself. I had no idea how old this woman was and I had absolutely no idea what she even looked like. I'd only spoken to her for a few minutes on the phone when she called to enquire about driving lessons. I was pretty sure she wasn't in her late teens or even twenties. She didn't sound old either, not *really* old. There's something about a woman's voice as she moves through the decades, just little subtleties, which make it easier to hazard a guess as to her age upon hearing her voice. I suspected that Gina was somewhere between 30 and 50, but I couldn't be sure. I don't know any man who possesses the ability to judge how attractive/tall/heavy a woman is based on her voice over the telephone. This was ridiculous, I was acting like an infatuated schoolboy – building up fantasies in my head – over a woman I'd never even met and knew nothing about, including her age. *Get a grip, Red, you're going to give her a driving lesson, that's all.*

As I neared Longstanton I'd managed convince the butterflies to bugger off but Gina was still on my mind and for unexplained reasons I was actually a bit nervous. I shouldn't be feeling like this as I'd given up on love years ago and even when I was in the dating game I didn't seem to have the ability to develop any sort of feelings for anybody, well, apart from sexually, but that was a physical need, not an emotional one.

Since I'd spoken to Gina on the phone I'd attempted to build up a mental image of what she might look like, what sort of person she might be and so on and so forth, based on her alluring voice. There was something about her voice that resonated with me. Not what she said, but the timbre, the speed, the delivery, the inflections and nuances. Her voice was kind, smooth, rich and warm. It was like listening to Jacqueline du Pré playing Bach's cello suites, only with warm melted milk chocolate poured on top. With her tonal qualities there was a mystery in Gina's voice and I found it mildly hypnotic.

I had about three minutes to shake these silly thoughts out of my head, for several reasons, namely my impending suicide. But I knew nothing about this woman. She was probably married with kids and even if she weren't she probably wouldn't be my type anyway. More to the point, I'm probably not hers. Lord knows I'd been through enough women since my ex-wife. Why would Gina be any different? I'd given up trying to find that elusive 'perfect' woman quite some time ago.

Since my ex-wife had decided it would be fun to sleep around with other guys behind my back I'd kind of lost a little faith in the female species. I always thought it was only guys who did that sort of thing: lie, cheat… However, I'm rational and intelligent enough to realise that you can't tar everybody with the same brush so after spending nearly a year licking my wounds while living in Mathieu's spare room in London I got into the dating scene after his girlfriend, Shari, talked me into it. She'd set up an account on a dating site and she even wrote up my profile for me. I was surprised. She wrote up a very accurate 'character profile' on me and, if I say so myself, I sounded like a pretty good prospect for all those single women out there. She took a few flattering photographs of me using her mobile phone, taking time over composition, the lighting and angles, and they looked pretty damn good considering she wasn't a professional photographer. I usually hate having my photograph taken as I don't photograph well and my facial expressions always look weird. Shari knew how to make me laugh and smile so I looked happy and natural, which made a refreshing change from my usual demented facial expressions in photos, where I usually look more like a wretched gargoyle that's been looking out over a grim rainy cityscape from high up on an equally grim grey sixteenth century church for the past 300 odd years.

Being a keen photographer in the past I knew a thing or two about a good photo and how to achieve one and

Shari had done a pretty decent job. However, although Shari was excited – playing the matchmaker – about my first date, I didn't really share her enthusiasm. She'd picked out a young woman who she thought would be a good match for me and although she was pretty enough there were a few things in her profile that rang alarm bells in my head. However, Shari convinced me to send her a message, she even helped me compose it. The next thing I knew I had a date, or at least an initial meet up. We'd arranged to meet in a pub in Crouch End, not too far from where the romantic interest lived. As I suspected, it didn't work out. She drove me nuts with her incessant verbal diarrhoea, which I wouldn't have minded if she actually had anything of interest to say, or if any of her dull stories had a point – 'empty vessels make the most noise' as the saying goes.

'Don't be too despondent, Red, you've gotta get back in the saddle,' Shari had said.

I did get back in the saddle, several more times over the years. Since leaving my ex-wife twelve years ago I'd probably been on at least 50 dates (probably more - I'd lost count), which had resulted in about 20 *very* brief flings that had lasted anywhere between one night and a few weeks. On top of these brief flings I'd had about a dozen relationships that had lasted somewhere between two and four months – on average. I was always the common denominator, I know that, and I was always the one who brought the proceedings to an abrupt end. The thing is, I have this set of criteria that my 'perfect' woman needed to have for a relationship to work and sometimes it took me a few weeks, or months, to figure out that she didn't possess them, not all of them anyway. As soon as I could see that she was not *truly* the one – my kindred spirit, the woman I connected with on a multitude of levels (some deep, some shallow), the woman I had synergy with, connection, spark, energy, passion, love (*real* love), the ability to practically read each other's minds, the ability to not speak as our silence and gaze said so much more than words, the woman who completed me and who I completed in return – I broke it off because I didn't want to waste her time or mine. When you know there is no future in a relationship there's just no point in dragging it out for a few years when both you and the other person could be spending that time looking for somebody more suitable. At the end of the day you can't change people so just go out and find somebody who is already built how you want them to be and hope you're built exactly how they want you to be too. If you want to drive a cool red sporty looking car that goes like stink you'd go out and buy a red sports car that does 0-60 in 4.7 seconds, you would not go out and buy a white Ford Fiesta and then start adding large spoilers and a body kit to make it look cool, or attempt to shoehorn a V6 twin turbo-charged engine into the tiny engine bay or paint it red, it will still be white underneath, always was, always will be.

Modern love is not a complicated thing, or rather, it's a fucked up thing, big time, but it shouldn't be, we've just made it that way. I think we've lost the ability to form any sort of meaningful relationship, let alone fall in love, I mean *really* fall in love, unconditionally and without agenda. Most of the profiles I've read on dating sites over the years read more like a list of demands, a shopping list of wants with little mention by way of what that person actually has to offer themselves. Lots of the profiles read like they were written by greedy selfish people who are in it for their own gain, thinking purely about themselves and what they can get out of the relationship: he must be this, that, and the other, 'I'm looking for somebody to fill the gap in *my* life,' for example. Really? I don't want to be a person who merely fills a gap in somebody else's life, what about my life? I mean, they make it sound like I'd be a little rubber ball that they'd keep in their pocket and every now and then they'd take me out and bounce me up and down for a while – no thank you. Or how about this one, 'I have three beautiful, darling, little children who I love and who are my life, and any man who comes into our lives must realise that my children will always come first.' Hmm, this is a fairly obvious statement and guys aren't so stupid that they don't know this. Most guys don't want this fact shoving down their throats three lines into a dating profile. It's so off-putting and what guy, in his right mind, would want to be a mere 'extra' in this woman's busy domesticated life with kids? A backseat passenger in somebody else's life?

Then there's the 'I live a busy and active life. I work long hours and play hard with the little bit of free time that I do have. I travel a lot and love to participate in sports and outdoor activities.' Well this sounds like I'd be nothing more than a leaf in this woman's whirlwind of a life – no thanks.

So if it isn't a selfish woman demanding – via her very long list of demands outlined on her dating profile – that the man owns a house, a car, has a good job, is affluent, dresses nicely, shaves every day, cleans up after himself, helps out with the chores, does DIY, helps with the shopping, treats her like a princess and takes her out a lot, you're left with being a back seat passenger in somebody else's life where you 'fill the gap': take, take, take. No mention of love, poetry, romance, spirituality, nature, purity, nothing of meaning, just shallow, superficial fakeness in abundance. Half of these dating profiles read like job applications, the suitable candidate must… but there is no salary at the end of each month, just PMT and a shit load of misery.

I'd given up wasting my time and had resigned myself to being alone for the rest of my life. It doesn't bode well in the loneliness department and it certainly doesn't help with my depression while I desperately try – or should I say 'tried' – to maintain the will to live.

I scanned the numbers on the doors as I drove along Gina's street – having reminded myself why I gave up dating and had long given up all hope of ever finding a woman, along with the fact that I had less than three months remaining on this miserable planet – and then I spotted the correct door number. I parked right outside, got out and went to ring the doorbell but before I got to the door it opened and Gina – at least I assumed it was Gina – stepped out.

'Red? Hi,' she said.

'Gina?'

'That's me. I didn't really know what to wear, are these ok?' she said, looking down.

My god, she looked amazing. She was so beautiful. I don't mean stunning or supermodel beautiful, but *my* kind of beautiful. She was the perfect height, for me, about 5' 8", with long dark hair (nearly black, but not quite), a beautiful pale porcelain complexion with some cute subtle freckles around her little nose, lovely brown eyes and she was super slim.

'Err, well, there isn't really any sort of dress code. Nobody's ever asked me that before, but if they did, I'd suggest they just wear comfortable clothing,' I said.

'I was talking about my shoes, silly,' she said, laughing. Already she was joking around and being friendly.

'Oh, sorry. I see, yes, they're perfect,' I said, noting her red Converse All Star basketball trainers.

She closed her front door and walked to the car with me. Even though she was wearing jeans and trainers she still walked with grace and elegance. Now that I'd seen her close up, I'd say she was somewhere between 36 and 40 – she looked perfect. Remember that movie, Weird Science? From the 80s, about those two teenage boys who designed a woman with computer software and she actually came to life? The result being Kelly LeBrock. Well, if I could design a woman – from a physical perspective at least – it would be Gina.

'Ok. How does this work?' she said.

'Well, I know a nice long quiet street, not far from here, so I'll drive us there and then you can hop into the driver's seat and we'll start with the basics. You've never driven before, right?'

'No, never.'

'And you've never had a lesson before either?'

'No.'

'Ok. Let's go,' I said, opening the passenger door for her, which she seemed to appreciate.

'Thank you,' she said, getting in.

I drove Gina a few miles away to a quiet street that I was familiar with, the ideal spot to teach a beginner. Being an automatic car I didn't have to worry about teaching clutch control, biting point and the like. It was simply a case of foot on the break, D for drive, handbrake off, mirror, signal, manoeuvre. As I drove I was aware that Gina was looking at the dashboard and the various controls of the car: the steering wheel, gear selector, indicator lever, handbrake etc. Momentarily, just momentarily, that fantasy wormed its way back into my mind, the one where she checked out my thigh muscles (not that I was some sort of athlete, I'm actually quite slim, but I had the right amount of muscle in all the right places) and forearms while she checked out the car's controls. I shook the thought from my head as I pulled up on the left and I tried not to think about Gina's legs, in tight-fitting jeans, which I was more than aware of in my peripheral vision.

I briefed Gina with the controls of the car, explained all the relevant things and went over a few rules as well as explaining what the duel-controls were for, which I'd already told her to be careful not to accidently step on during the drive over here.

We swapped seats and I explained the importance of a comfortable driving position and that she should take her time with the height of the seat and distance from the pedals as well as the rake and reach of the steering wheel. She did what a lot of women do and moved the seat way too close to the steering wheel to the point that her arms were too bent while holding it and her right knee had to come right up to push the brake pedal. I also explained that her chest was so close to the steering wheel that in the event of an accident the airbag could cause injury or potentially even kill her.

'Oh, really! How?' she asked.

'I notice you have a pencil in your blouse pocket,' I said.

'Oh yes. I thought I might need to take notes. I have a pad in my handbag on the back seat.'

'Ok. But in the event of an accident the airbag could deploy and with you sitting that close and with the seatbelt right across that pencil there's a tiny chance it could snap in half and penetrate your heart or lung.'

'Oh my god! I wouldn't have thought of that,' she said, removing the pencil from her blouse pocket.

I got out of the car and went around to her side and opened the door and then had her make some adjustments to the seat until her arms had only a slight bend at the elbow when she was holding the steering wheel at 10 and 2 o'clock and her right leg had only a slight bend in it when the brake pedal was depressed all the way down.

'How does that feel?'

'Comfortable, like I'm not right on top of the steering wheel and dashboard. But it feels like I'm too far away.'

'Trust me, that's the perfect driving position for you, you'll get used to it,' I said, shutting the door (while, inadvertently, checking out her thigh in my peripheral vision) and getting back into the passenger side.

'Ok. Let's make a small adjustment to the steering wheel for you,' I said, reaching across and pulling rake/reach lever to allow for adjustment. 'Move the steering wheel down towards your legs a little,' I said, she did. 'How does that feel?' I said, locking the lever back in place.

'Oh, that's much better. That feels great,' she said.

Up until now Gina had not seemed in the least bit nervous, quite the opposite. She'd been quite chatty, but not overly so. After we'd covered the basics, done the cockpit drill and she'd put her seatbelt on, adjusted the mirrors and prepared herself, I asked her to start the engine and that's when I noticed the first little signs of nerves kicking in. Gina turned the key and started the engine, as I'd instructed. The way she tentatively turned the key anybody would have thought she was expecting the car to be wired up to a bomb or something. She winced ever so slightly as the engine turned over. Gina's expression turned to one of relief.

She smiled, pleased with herself for taking this first step.

I went through the procedure for pulling away and she followed my instructions to perfection: foot on brake, selector into D for drive, handbrake off, check mirrors, look over shoulder, indicate, look over shoulder again and gently pull away. I'd typically have a new learner drive about fifty yards and then pull back over to the left. Gina did it almost perfectly, removing her foot from the brake and gently – perhaps a little too gently – pulling away. I had her gently build up speed to just 20mph, then drive for a further 50 yards before instructing her to indicate, gently slow down and pull over to the left, my hand ready to grab the steering wheel in case she potentially kerbed the front nearside wheel. She didn't. I'd already explained that she should look at the kerb and line it up about half way along the bottom of the windscreen. She managed to straighten the car up before gently bringing it to a standstill. She was so excited that I had to remind her that she hadn't completed the manoeuvre yet, she still had to pull the handbrake on and put the selector in park and then take her foot off the brake.

Gina was ecstatic. I found her quite endearing and her smile was warm, friendly and radiant all at the same time. I had an incredibly acute sixth sense, gut instinct and ability to figure people out very quickly and I could see that Gina was a woman of love, compassion and kindness. Gina would not hurt a fly and I doubted there was an evil bone – cell, amoeba or microscopic sample of DNA – in her entire body.

I'd never felt like this, emotionally speaking, giving a driving lesson to anybody before. Gina and I had a good rapport during the lesson; the connection and understanding, the way I gave instruction and the way she received it – it was natural.

Gina listened and spoke at just the right times and I could imagine us having a conversation outside of a driving lesson, a conversation that had ebb and flow, harmony. One listened and paid full attention while the other spoke, and vice-versa.

As the lesson drew to a close I had to remind myself that Gina was not an option for me. I'd been in situations like this before where somebody was all happy, smiley and chatty, and appeared to really like you. Then I'd asked them out on a date and had received a look of either perplexity or shock. Realistically, I probably wasn't Gina's type and I suspected – if I got to know her – that she would not be mine either. I was her driving instructor and I had to be professional – besides, she was probably married, and let's not forget the little matter of my imminent departure from this world. I'd already decided that Gina would be the last pupil I'd take on. Although, on average, by my standards, it generally takes me around 30 to 35 lessons to get a pupil to a standard that they could take their test, I knew I wouldn't be able to achieve this with Gina, not within the 3-month timeframe I'd given myself to live. But, after her first lesson, I was confident I'd be able to get her most of the way there, then I'd pass her – along with the few other remaining pupils I'd have when that time arrived – onto one of the other automatic driving instructors in the area.

I had to forget about this silly fantasy with Gina – and that's all it was, nothing more. I was not about to cancel my own suicide plans just so I could become infatuated with somebody only to be disappointed and let down by yet another futile relationship two or three months down the line. It's always the same, you get to know somebody a little and then you have sex, and it's at that point that it all starts turning to shit – 9½ Weeks syndrome. Let me explain. Like in the movie, 9½ Weeks syndrome is something that was carefully worked out, after a survey. Turns out that nine and a half weeks is the average amount of time it takes most people to lose interest with their new partner after having sex with them for the very first time. So, a tad over two months after meeting a new partner and having sex with them it all starts to fizzle out and become rather domesticated. If I were to get involved with Gina (even if she was available and even if she did like me) I'd only be delaying the inevitable and subjecting myself to further unnecessary misery. There was no way on earth that I was going to allow that to happen.

Chapter 10

'Hi. Red?' said a rather gruff and thickset man as I opened my front door.

'Richard?' I asked.

'Yes.'

'Come on in, the table's just here,' I said, leading him through to the kitchen. Richard had come to buy the dining table and chairs that I had on Gumtree (along with a whole load of other items). I'd already cleared a load of stuff out of the loft and a few bits from the garage, along with some unwanted items that I didn't really use anymore, and got almost £2,500 for them on Gumtree and eBay. In the past, whenever I've had any unwanted items to sell, I always put them on Gumtree first and given them a couple of weeks. If they didn't sell in that time I'd move over to eBay as a last resort. Gumtree is free while eBay fuck you harder than a freight train with their extortionate selling and final valuation fees and to add insult to injury the greedy buggers even take a percentage of the postage costs, even though you don't make anything from the postage.

'Very nice,' said Richard, walking around the table and chairs and touching the wooden top. 'The photos don't do it justice. It's in amazing condition, hardly looks like it's been used,' he said. So I assume he won't be haggling on the price then. 'It's perfect. Did you say the legs come off easily?'

'Yes, just a large bolt on each corner. I've got the right size socket spanner right here,' I said, pointing.

'Great! Well, I'll see if it fits in the back of my car without taking the legs off first, and if it doesn't I'll quickly whip them off,' he said. 'I know you were asking £150, but would you take £100?'

Cheeky git. It was already a bargain, the damn thing cost me nearly £500 new and it had hardly been used. The guy loved it yet he was still taking the micky with a silly offer. I mean, I knew I was not going to need the money where I was going but there were a few people I knew who were not what I'd call affluent, who I intended to help out before I departed this world – buy a few things for this one, that one, leave a few items for some and leave money to others – and I knew that they would really appreciate the money and various items I was planning to give them.

'Sorry, it cost nearly £500 new and, as you can see, it's hardly been used. £140 is the lowest I'll go,' I said.

'Why are you selling all this stuff? I noticed you've got quite a lot of things up for sale on Gumtree,' he enquired.

'I'm not going to need it where I'm going,' I said.

'Oh, emigrating are you?'

'Something like that.'

I must have said this in a certain tone, with a certain

facial expression, as Richard just gave me a 'look' and didn't pursue it. I wasn't about to start informing buyers that they were buying items from a man who was preparing for his own suicide. Instead he just took the cash out of his pocket, counted it out, and handed it to me.

'Can you give me a hand out to the car with it?'

'Of course.'

With all the back seats folded down in his Ford Galaxy, along with the high roof, the legs didn't even have to come off after all. The chairs stacked in there too, with a few inches to spare.

Just as Richard was pulling away another car pulled up into his vacated space. I suspected this was Mike and his wife, coming to check out my massive mirrored wardrobe. She loved it. He was concerned about having to hire a van, take it all apart and then assemble it again. I was with him on that one, as I'd had to assemble it when I bought it new and it was bitch, it took me all afternoon. She gave me a cash deposit and said they would arrange to come back and get it within the next week.

It was all happening today. As Mike and his wife drove off I saw Mathieu's 'Chronos grey' Audi Q3 ambling down my street. I remember ribbing him about the 'miserable-wet-bank-holiday-grey' colour. He was quick to correct me, 'Chronos grey, if you please.' He was adamant that this was no 'ordinary' grey. I guess if I'd just spent £35,000 on a brand new 'grey' car, I'd want to convince myself that it was a special sort of grey too.

'Hey, Red, how you doing?' he called to me out of the open window as he slowed. Mathieu and Shari were supposed to have come down last Saturday but they'd had to cancel the evening before due to their shop manager having a family emergency, which led to him having to take Saturday off. 'Hey, man, so sorry about last Saturday. Had to spend the day in the shop myself,' he said, closing the car door and coming over to shake my hand.

'Hi, Red,' said Shari.

'Hi, Shari. How are you?' I said, kissing her on the cheek.

'I'm good. You're looking pretty good yourself, isn't he, Matty?' she said.

'Yeah, there is a certain sparkle in his eyes. Maybe there's a woman in his life,' said Mathieu, joking around.

'Get outta here,' I said, leading them into the house.

'Oh, I almost forgot, I've got you something,' said Shari. 'Open the car, Matty.' Mathieu popped the locks from his key fob and Shari went into the boot and came out with a rather large green houseplant of some sort, a cheese plant perhaps. Shari struggled to see where she was going with said plant blocking half her view. 'We thought you might like this, didn't we, Matty,' she said. 'It's good to have something living in your house and you won't get a dog so I thought you could nurture this. You won't have to do much, just water it once every two weeks,' she said.

Great, I was supposed to be getting crap out of my

house, not introducing new things into it, especially a houseplant – the damn things always died on me within a couple of months anyway.

'Thanks, Shari, that's thoughtful,' I said, trying to sound happy about it.

Mathieu and Shari had been up to Cambridge to visit me quite a few times since I moved here 11 years ago so I didn't have to give them any sort of grand tour. Instead, Mathieu headed straight for the bathroom, announcing that his bladder was about to explode. When he returned he said, 'Ok, where's this pub then? I'm starving.'

'Not far. 10 minutes.'

'We go in my car?' he said.

'Unless one of you wants to be squashed into the back of my Corsa,' I joked.

We all piled into Mathieu's *grey* Q3 and headed to the pub. Shari had asked me if I could find somewhere that had a nice beer garden, which I had, but such pubs fill me with trepidation.

Mathieu pulled up into the large gravel car park and, as I had suspected, the place was packed. The car park was packed with 4x4s and people carriers and beyond that the large pub garden was packed too, with families and loads of shouty/screamy little children – great.

Inside it was pretty busy but at least there were tables available. I'd spotted one that was next to an elderly couple and on the other side was an internal wall, a relatively safe enough distance from any loud, boisterous, or generally nauseating families with 2.4

children. Don't get me wrong, I've got nothing against families but I hate the way that they seem to have taken over pubs. It wouldn't be so bad if they were civilized, well-mannered families with parents who knew how to take charge of their unruly brats, or better still, parents who brought their kids up well so they would behave appropriately in public places.

'How about that table over there,' I said, hoping upon hope that Shari would go for it.

'Well, it's a nice day, how about we find a table outside? I'll go and check and see if there's a free one. I'll have my usual, please' she said to Mathieu, trotting off.

It was an unusually nice day - the sun was beating down, but it wasn't really hot – but you know how us Brits can be. The first sign of sun and the tops on the convertible cars come down and everybody heads off to their nearest beer garden. The next thing you know, what was once a peaceful adult-only domain becomes a noisy bloody crèche. Damn, she'd found one and was beckoning us over from the door to the garden.

Outside it was bonkers. Families everywhere - babies, toddlers, kids, kids and more kids! What a bloody godforsaken racket. I doubted we'd be able to hear each other think let alone have any sort of conversation at a reasonably private volume level. We'd probably have to shout as loud as the singer from Napalm Death. As Mathieu and I walked over to the table that Shari had managed to find a little kid, about 2-foot tall, came running right across my path, screaming some incoherent gibberish, without even looking where he was going. I had to make an emergency stop to prevent the reckless little brat slamming into my leg, potentially taking out my beverage in the process.

'Watch where you're going, Jack!' shouted its mother, from about fifty bloody yards away. I glanced over at her. No sign of an apology; in fact she shot me a dirty look like it was my bloody fault. *Twat*.

We sat down and I assessed the situation to make sure I was safe and was not going to get hit by a stray ball, projectile toy, or speeding uncoordinated toddler...

'You ok, Red?' asked Shari.

I wasn't doing a very good job of hiding my utter annoyance. 'Yeah, don't worry, I'm good,' I said, faux smile.

'So, what's new?' asked Mathieu.

'Same old. Nothing new or exciting to report,' I said, taking a sip of my drink.

'You're ok though, right?' he queried, mild concern in his voice.

I wasn't about to tell Mathieu and Shari about my suicide plan. I'd been thinking about it for a while before I eventually set myself a 3-month deadline and thus, I was used to the idea now, resigned to it, looking forward to it even. I'd got to the point that I was actually comfortable with it. My suicide plan had become the norm; it was a part of my life now. So much so that I didn't think there was anything in my tone when I spoke to Mathieu and Shari that would make me come across any different than usual. Mathieu and Shari knew about my depression and they'd witnessed my 'lows'. They'd worried about me whenever I'd sank into those dark places, where I would reside for a couple of days.

'Mathieu, I'm fine,' I said.

He smiled a little smile and, although we chatted away, ordered food and had a few more drinks, there was a look of concern sitting behind Mathieu's eyes.

A screaming little girl, running away from her loud boisterous brother, bumped into our table, causing my fresh glass of soda water and blackcurrant juice to slop over the top and onto the wooden bench. Again, no apology from said child, or parents, wherever the hell they were.

'How the hell did all this happen?' I said, annoyed.

'What?' said Mathieu.

'This! Kids running the damn country. I mean what idiot in parliament decided it would be a good idea to give children power for crying out loud. We're all expected to bow down to the little sods these days. Creepy little fuckers, they should stay in horror movies where they belong,' I said, *half* joking.

'They're hardly running the country, Red,' said Shari.

'I know, but you know what I'm talking about. Once upon a time a pub would be a safe haven for an adult to come and enjoy a peaceful and relaxing drink. At one point you had to be 18 just to enter a pub. If you go back to the 50s, 60s, even 70s–'

'I didn't realize you were that old, Red,' joked Mathieu.

'Shut up, you tart,' I joked. 'Seriously, back in those

days pubs like this would be full of working men. The working man would be out toiling hard all day and after a long hard shift the last thing he'd want to do is go home and have to deal with the kid's tea and bath time and all that goes with it. No, he'd want a bit of bloody peace and quiet after a hard day down the mines. So after work he'd go to the pub with other working men for a few pints and a bit of peace and quiet, to have a catch up with his buddies, a game of darts or dominoes perhaps. But then some bloody landlord somewhere decided it would be a good idea – probably a profitable one too – to allow children into the beer garden and because they wouldn't actually be inside the pub they could get away with it, just as long as the parents didn't buy the kids any alcoholic beverages. It wasn't long after that all these kiddies found their way into the pubs themselves. Then they became known as "family pubs". What a joke that is! Crèches more like, and lined up under the optics of whisky, vodka and rum, they now have rows upon rows of Fruit Shoots for fuck's sake.'

Why oh why do parents fall for all that Fruit Shoot crap anyway? They see the words 'Apple & Blackcurrant' on the label with a pretty picture of apples and black currents across a lush green grassy meadow insinuating that the drink is actually full of 'goodness' for said child. If the so-called *caring* parents actually read the ingredients on the back they'd quickly learn that there's next to no nutritional value in those stupid drinks. When a company advertises that a product has no added sugar on the front of a *sweet* tasting drink it does make one wonder what chemicals and crap they put in them to compensate.

'These little kids have invaded the adult world and there's no peace and quiet anymore and there's nowhere you can go to escape it now. You know I won't go into Cambridge shopping at the weekend; I go into town mid-morning during the week instead, when I can go into a Costa and have a cappuccino in peace and quiet without families and little kids stinking up my day. I swear to god, coffee shops and pubs become crèches at the weekend.'

'Something tells me you don't like children very much, Red,' said Shari.

I wasn't sure if she was joking or not.

'It's not that, Shari. Truth be told, I don't mind kids but just a certain kind of kid, a well-balanced well-behaved kid that's brought up right, brought up to realise that he/she isn't the most important person in the family, that the adults are, that the world doesn't revolve around them and that they have to just fit into the world that's already here, that was here for millions of years before they arrived. I mean it's not like this in other European countries, only here.'

'Isn't it?' asked Shari.

'No. Come on, Mathieu, back me up here, kids don't run around like this in France, chaotic, noisy, out of control, with all this power, demanding everything and getting it.'

'Yeah, I got to admit things are a little different in

France,' he agreed.

'Besides, what sort of example is this setting? You've got little kids aged four and five standing at the bar watching daddy order a pint of Guinness and a glass of red for his wife, while other punters are ordering Vodka and Scotch from the optics. And then they're stepping out onto the patio for a smoke, or vape, and the kids are watching all this drinking and smoking activity. So what's gonna happen? They'll grow up to do exactly the same thing. Most of these parents are too thick and ignorant to see that.'

Mathieu and Shari looked around, then at each other, not quite sure if they should agree with my reasoning or not. They knew that I was an intelligent guy and that I had a unique way of looking at things and I'd previously left them dumbfounded by some of my theories in the past, theories which had since been proved right – in most instances anyway.

'How are the driving lessons going?' said Shari.

'Yeah, good,' I said, going with her as she steered the conversation in the direction of something a little more cheerful.

'You busy?' said Mathieu.

'Yeah, very. It's really easy getting pupils as I'm one of only three automatic driving instructors in the area; we're all really busy, all the time. The other two work more hours than me. I could work more if I wanted to but I take a few mornings and afternoons off during the week. I still want time for myself, don't want my life to be all about work,' I said.

'You got that right,' said Mathieu, taking a swig of his San Miguel.

'Any hint of romance, a woman perhaps?' enquired Shari.

'No … well … no, nobody,' I said, correcting myself.

'Ooooh, that didn't sound like a no to me,' she said.

'No, really, you know I gave up all hope on that front a few years back.'

'I'm not buying it, Red. You said "well" as if you were going to say something,' she said, probing.

'Really, it was a stupid fleeting fantasy that lasted all of a few minutes, until I got my head back in gear. So no, there isn't anybody and there won't be either.'

'Red, come on! I'm not gonna let you off the hook that easily! You've built it up too much now, so you have to tell me the story behind the "well" thing,' she said, making little air quotes with her fingers. Knowing Shari as I did, I knew I had little choice but to tell her, or she'd just keep banging on about it.

'It's nothing, Shari. Just a new pupil I took on recently, but it's nothing.'

'I knew it,' she teased. 'Tell me more. How old is she? Is she pretty? Does she live locally?'

'I don't know how old she is for sure, 35 to 40 I suspect.'

'But she's beautiful, right?' said Mathieu, with a wry smile.

'Well, she is beautiful, yes, she's perfect and she lives only a few miles away.'

'So what's the problem, Red? You should go for it,'

said Shari.

'No! No way,' I stated.

'Why?' said Shari, detecting my adamant tone.

'Because she's a pupil. It would be unprofessional and for all I know she's married … with kids,' I said, gesturing to the infant mayhem going on around me.

'Yeah, but she might not be. She might be single,' said Mathieu.

'Guys, forget it. It's never gonna happen, ok. I'm her driving instructor and that's as far as it's ever gonna go,' I said, taking another sip of my drink.

They both stared at me, intently, but with comical smiles on their faces.

'What?' I said. They both laughed.

'You're gonna marry this woman,' said Shari, smiling.

'Get the fuck outta here,' I said.

Just at that moment a mother walked past and clasped her hands other her little girl's ears while shooting me a filthy look – good. *It's a pub, take your kid to the damn park if you don't want to hear my expletives.*

'Who's for coffee?' said Mathieu. Damn, we were going to have to stay in this place of horror for another thirty minutes now. 'Red, you still make a mean coffee?' he said. Thank Christ for that, we can leave.

'Damn right I do,' I said, standing up to leave.

We made our way across the battlefield of a beer garden, trying to avoid all kinds of kiddy shells, toddler landmines and other fast moving infant shrapnel, and out to the car park and safe refuge of Mathieu's Q3. His grey car had never looked so inviting. Shari gave me one of her 'I'm right' smiles as we all got into the car.

Chapter 11

Shannon was kind enough to allow me to shift my therapy session to a different time – an hour later – due to it clashing with Hanna's (seventh) driving test. As I predicted, Hanna failed, miserably. Several scattered minor faults within the first 10 minutes alone, then two serious ones, before a third 'dangerous' one, which led to the examiner instructing Hanna to stop the car so he could take over and drive back to the test centre himself. Actually, there were two consecutive dangerous faults. The first one happened on the elongated roundabout that crossed over the A14 and heads up the A10 – the one that I'd had Hanna drive around four or five times in a row, on several occasions, so she could nail her roundabout issues. She'd done her usual party trick of swerving sideways while going around one of the bends without checking her mirrors, looking over her shoulder or indicating. She almost careered, sideways, into a white Range Rover. Christ, Range Rovers are hardly bloody Sinclair C5's! I mean, I know this one was the same colour as a C5, but come on! The Range Rover is a massive beast of a car. But, Hanna has bugger all in the way of observational skills and she has absolutely no idea what's going on around her at any given time. She drives with blinkers on, concentrating only on that tiny little patch right in front of her.

Within 5 minutes of her first serious fault she almost had a head-on collision with a white van, almost crashed into a parked car and nearly killed a cyclist, all at the same bloody time: WTF. The examiner had explained that she was driving up a narrow street and up ahead there were cars parked on both sides. There was a white transit van driving towards them and instead of slowing down to allow time for the white van to clear the parked cars (there was only enough room for one vehicle to get through) Hanna thought it would be a good idea to test the physics of space and time. She'd got it into her head that the two inches of space between the white van and the wing mirrors of the parked cars was more than enough for her to squeeze my Corsa through. At the last minute she had second thoughts and made an abrasive move over to the left – to prevent a head-on collision with said van – without checking her left mirror and did not notice the rather speedy lycra-clad cyclist coming up on her inside. The cyclist yelled out some colourful language as his front wheel hit the curb. The examiner yelled too – though not quite as colourfully as the cyclist – as he stamped on the duel control pedals and yelled for Hanna to stop. To say the examiner was angry and annoyed would be a serious understatement. Hanna later told me that his cheeks had turned red and his forehead had become quite shiny.

There was a delay getting back to the test centre as

the examiner had to speak with the cyclist, whose front wheel was scuffed, but he was ok. Luckily for Hanna the cyclist was sympathetic to her and decided not to press charges for dangerous driving.

When I saw the examiner driving into the test centre car park I knew it wasn't good. Examiners don't take over the driving unless they have a very good reason to. Hanna had given him several. He was annoyed with me for putting her in for the test in the first place and, yes, I should have known better, but Hanna - and her parents - had been putting such a lot of pressure on me and even though I'd explained to them that Hanna was nowhere near ready she'd put in for the test on her own and just paid for my time and car for the day of the test.

'Hanna, I'm so sorry.'

'That's ok, I'll try again,' she said.

'No, you misunderstand. I'm afraid I can't teach you anymore,' I said.

'What! But why?' she pleaded.

'Hanna, you're just not a born driver; you don't possess the basic human instincts to drive. You have no awareness of what's going on around you, you've no observational skills, you don't anticipate anything, your judgement is diabolical and, frankly, you're a danger to yourself and other road users. I'm sorry, Hanna, but as I've already explained to you one day you might get lucky on your test and pass. Then you'll go out and have accidents in abundance and you might even have a fatal crash and be left crippled or even dead. Hanna,

I implore you to give up the idea of driving. It's not all bad you know. There are actually loads of advantages in not driving.'

'Like what?'

'Well, you'll save about £300 per month for a start. That gets you a hell of a lot of cabs, trains and buses, Hanna.'

'You mean it costs £300 a month to run a car?' she asked, shocked.

'For most people, yes, but more for you.'

'How do you mean?'

'Ok. If you add up the insurance, tax, petrol, mot, servicing and general things that require changing over the years such as tyres, brakes, exhaust, that sort of stuff, most people will be paying around £300 a month for all that. But in your case the insurance isn't going to be £350 a year, it will be at least double that, possibly more, for a few years, until you reach the age of 20 and start to build up your no claims.'

'Oh, wow, I hadn't thought of that,' she said, despondent.

'And I haven't included the price of buying a car to start with either. Even if you buy a used one on finance you'll have monthly payments for that too so you could be paying around £700 a month all in all. Then there's parking fees, which aren't cheap these days and of course speeding tickets and a whole bundle of other things.'

'Oh my god, Red, you make it sound like one huge expense.'

'It is, Hanna. Most people drive a car out of necessity and they accept, reluctantly, all the expense and hassle that goes with it. A car's nothing more than a hole in the road that you pour all your money into. Honestly, I'd always advise anybody the same thing. If you can get by without owning a car, then do. Quite a lot of people in cities like Cambridge, and especially London, don't own cars.'

'Hanna, I imagine your monthly bus pass cost a fraction of what it would cost you to run a car.'

'Yeah, I pay £96 a month for my bus pass.'

'There you go then. That leaves you well over £200 for taxis and other forms of transport, if you need it. Also, by not owning a car you don't have to worry about accidents, claims, having to clean your car or worry about it getting keyed or dinged in supermarkets. The list of advantages is endless, Hanna. You won't have to worry about any of that stuff. Just live like a lady of leisure and have taxis drive you around on the weekend, or a boyfriend maybe. It will be more pleasurable taking taxis and buses and it'll be a lot safer too, and cheaper. Think about it, Hanna. You can read a book or something too. You can't do that while you're driving,' I said.

'Yeah, I do read my Kindle on the bus to work every day.'

'There you go.'

Hanna smiled and was warming to the idea as I drove her home. Later that evening Hanna's mother phoned me and thanked me for all my efforts. She thanked me for the post driving test conversation I'd had with Hanna – the advantages of not owning a car or driving – and she really appreciated it. She said that Hanna was happy about not driving now and had not looked at it that way before. So it all worked out in the end and I wouldn't have to worry about Hanna having a fatal car accident any time soon – not during the few months I have left anyway.

I arrived at Shannon's house, an hour later than usual as we'd agreed.

'So how's things been since our last session?' she said.

'Nothing's changed,' I said.

'Well, you look well. Radiant in fact,' she said.

Strange. I didn't particularly feel any different and there was no reason for me to be emitting any sort of radiance.

'Oh, thank you. I wasn't aware of being radiant. I'll do my best to cancel that out and get back to being clinically depressed,' I joked.

'Well, trust me, you look much better today. You sure nothing's happened or changed since last week?'

'Nope, nothing,' I said. Just then my phone pinged.

'Sorry, forgot to silence it,' I said, taking it out of my pocket and flicking the mute switch on. Typically in situations like this I'd leave my phone in the glove compartment of my car but I bring it into the session in case Shannon needs to schedule a different time, or date, allowing me to enter the session into my iCal app.

I glanced at the screen as I put the phone on mute, and sighed.

'Everything ok?' she asked, as I put the phone on the coffee table next to the box of tissues.

'Yeah, just another bloody text message alerting me to the fact that "smart meter" installers are in my area – again – next week and it's not too late to have one installed. I mean, are the masses really that stupid that they actually fall for all that rubbish?'

'How do you mean?' she said, not in a general 'chit chat' kind of way, but in her 'analysing' sort of way. Shannon was good, really good. She would use any old topic, including general chit chat about the weather or smart meter installers, as a means to analyse me, get a handle on me, figure me out, see what makes me tick, dig deep into my mind and devour it.

'Some electricity board called me about smart meters a couple of months back. Some guy told me it will make my life easier, more convenient, that I won't have to go outside and take readings off the meter on the outside wall anymore and that smart meters are so much better and, best of all, they're free to have installed. Well, as soon as he said "free" I hung up the phone. There's no such thing as a free lunch, especially in the modern world where everybody's out to scam everybody else or take every last little bit of excess money that you might have. But everybody falls for all this crap and the funny thing is they actually believe that some huge multi billion pound monopolising corporation is going to spend hundreds of thousands of pounds, possibly millions, rolling out "free" smart meters just to make our lives a little easier. Yeah, right, and why would they want to do that? There's always a flip side to the coin and there's certainly a flip side to this one and I'd bet anything that it's a costly flip side too. Somehow, by hook or by crook – and they are crooks by the way – the customer will end up paying extra for the privilege, probably in more ways than one.'

'You really think so?'

'Of course, it's obvious. These huge corporations are in the business of getting richer, not doing the customer favours for free and at their expense. Just look at those television adverts for EE, you know the ones with Kevin Bacon?'

'Yes, I've seen them. There was one recently with him, something about an iPhone deal,' said Shannon.

'Exactly, offering all sorts of so-called amazing deals if you sign up with EE and get the latest iPhone. I mean how could anybody possibly believe that there's a deal to be had when EE have to pay Mr Bacon obscene amounts of money to do the adverts in the first place, let alone stump up for a multi-million pound television advertising campaign to broadcast the things and they have to organise some sort of deal with Apple, let's face it, Apple aren't going to give EE their phones out of compassion and kindness. I mean, who the hell's gonna pay for all that? EE? I doubt it! The customer, the sucker who actually signs up to an 18-month prison sentence to get a "must have" iPhone, that's who. I'd never do that. Christ, bloody iPhones. Every time they bring out a new one they have this massive cult following that are ready to queue around the block for a day and a half just to own some overpriced piece of shit that cost about £30 to make in China. Lemmings, the lot of them. You know I was gonna develop an app for the iPhone,' I said.

'Really? What?'

'An anal thermometer. So all the iPhone owners can stick their phones where they belong,' I joked. Shannon laughed.

'What do you do?' said Shannon, 'I mean, if you don't get a phone contract?'

'I usually buy an insurance replacement, or mint condition phone, off eBay, which is basically new, only half the price, and I have a sim-only contract that costs me £14 a month. If you walk into an EE store and get a new iPhone on an 18-month contract there's a reason it costs £50 a month but people don't question these things and they certainly don't break that £50 down and look at where that money's going.'

'You certainly strike me as somebody who does their research, Red, looks at the other side of the coin and leaves no stone unturned.'

'Yeah, you have to, or you get shafted over and over. I mean, I don't research things like an investigative journalist on speed to avoid getting stung. I do it because it's just something that's built into me. It's just how I work I guess.'

'Red, I'd like to revisit your relationships.'

'Relationships?'

NIGEL COOPER

'Yes, as in the romantic variety, girlfriends.'

'Oh, those,' I said. 'Can I grab a cappuccino?'

'Sure, I'll make you one.'

'No, don't get up, I'll do it. Your machine looks pretty self-explanatory,' I said, getting up.

'Just flick that switch on the side and then tap what you want on the display. There are cups just there on the right.'

'Thanks,' I said, flicking the switch and putting a cup in place. 'Continue,' I said.

'You left your wife when you were 30, 12 years ago, right?' she said, checking her notes.

'Yes,' I said, turning back to the machine and tapping the single shot cappuccino icon.

'When was the last time you were in a relationship?'

'You mean one that lasted more than a few days?'

'Yes.'

'About two years ago.'

'And how long did that one last?'

'Two or three months, something like that, can't really recall.'

'Why did it end?'

'She wasn't right for me.'

'Why?'

'Oh, I don't really remember, the usual stuff, we were just different.'

'Can you define *usual* stuff?'

'I just couldn't gel with her, didn't feel entirely comfortable, no real connection or understanding between us and, as usual, I always had to dumb myself

146

down to converse on her level but she could never come up to meet me on mine. You know that's a lonely place to be, Shannon.'

'How do you mean?'

'When you have to switch your intellect off momentarily, leaving just enough brain cells firing so you can talk about your partner's futile crap, stuff that's of no interest whatsoever. Their boring jobs, the conversation they had with their mother the previous evening, so-and-so's upcoming birthday party, the usual kitchen sink drama. But whenever I want to talk about anything I'm into, it just goes over their heads and all I get is a perplexed look.'

'Does this happen all the time with your partners?'

'Not quite, but a good ninety per cent of the time.'

'What do you want to talk about with them?'

'Anything other than bloody work, shopping trips, hairdresser's appointments, clothing brands, TV soaps and regurgitated conversations they've already had with other dullards.'

'Example?'

'I don't know. Something meaningful; poetry, nature, a good book, a worthwhile project. I just can't get enthused about the every-day stuff that most people want to talk about – "where ya goin' on ya 'ollidays",' I said, in my best Essex girl hairdresser accent.

'What about love?'

'Love's a joke. Love's supposed to be simple and pure and with meaning, but we've complicated the hell out of it. The risk/reward ratio of being in a modern relationship is just too unbalanced; the gulf is far too great. It's all risk and hardly any reward.'

'What kind of women do you go for, Red?'

'Mentally or physically?' I asked.

'Both.'

'Well, all of my ex's were attractive. Well, there were maybe a couple of misjudged exceptions. Thing is, there are pretty women everywhere. Such critical matters are nice of course and one has to have that initial physical attraction but intelligence and passion born out of living and the ability to move and be moved, emotionally, by subtleties of the mind and spirit are what really count, at least as far as I'm concerned. This kind of purity just doesn't exist in the modern so-called civilised western world. This is why I find most modern woman unattractive, regardless of their exterior beauty. It's not just younger women either – who haven't lived long enough to have developed or possess the kind of qualities that I'm interested in – it's woman of my own age group too. Dating sites are full of women in their late thirties and early forties who haven't got the first clue how to go about dating or forming the beginnings of a meaningful relationship. Either that or they've simply forgotten. They've all been swept along with the teenage way of doing things, taking their lead from the iPod generation for crying out loud – bloody aimless millennials. The McDonaldization of mankind has spilled out into our love lives and relationships. I want – or at least wanted – a woman with passion and intelligence, somebody with a soul and a heart that's

overflowing with love, not some shallow superficial …
starfucker.'

'Starfucker? I haven't heard that one before,' said
Shannon.

'Ah! Yeah, somebody who's obsessed with celebrities,
seeks interrelation with them for no other reason
than the fact that they're celebrities, name-dropping
celebrities all the time as if that somehow makes them
cool and famous by association. These people are just
shallow and superficial, more concerned about owning
a Prada handbag than owning a soul and having that
soul ignited by witnessing the sun rise while standing
on an old wooden veranda of a romantic 19th century
house in Tuscany. I mean, come on, Shannon, what the
hell's all that Prada or Gucci handbag nonsense about?
I don't understand why any intelligent or rational
woman would ever consider spending £3,000 on
something that's, essentially, a piece of dead cows arse
hide that's been dyed pink with some shiny material
sewn to the inside and a big gaudy gold badge stating
the company brand for the whole world to see, and
seemingly be impressed by. I mean, Christ, the damn
things can't cost more than £10 in raw materials. It's
all fake and superficial and a thousand years from now
nobody's going to give a shit. These women seem to
think that other women will be impressed because they
have a leather bag over their shoulder with a "word"
written on it in big gold letters. I'm not in the least
bit interested in those women, but these superficial
dullards seem to be in the majority.'

'I agree, I don't think I've ever spent more than £75 on a handbag,' she smiled.

Shannon continued to probe and analyse while asking me many more questions, not only on the subject of women and relationships, but other subjects too.

'You know, your question shouldn't have been what sort of women do I go for, but what sort of women go for me,' I said.

'Ok, what sort of women go for you, Red?' she asked.

'Scorpions, poisonous snakes and venomous spiders. They trap me in their dark web of deceit, manipulation and conniving antics, eat me up and then spit me out before moving onto their next victim.'

'Why do you think you attract women like that?'

'I don't know, one of life's mysteries I guess.'

We were out of time, Shannon brought the proceedings to an end and I left. I decided to pop into Waterstone's in town on my way home to see if I could pick out a decent novel to help take my mind off 'life' for the several hours or so it would take me to read it. Oh, and I needed to swing by M&S in the BP petrol station as I didn't have a ready meal for tonight. Suicide is going make my life so much easier.

Chapter 12

I was ten minutes early when I pulled up outside Gina's house for her second driving lesson. I shut the engine off and decided to check my lesson plan along with my emails in case I'd had any new enquiries about the items I had advertised for sale on Gumtree. I'd put both my mobile number and email address on the adverts, as some people prefer to email about stuff – millennials, God forbid they actually have to dial a number and speak with an actual human being on the phone. It wouldn't surprise me if some of this generation wanted me to email them my unwanted garage storage unit so they wouldn't have to leave the house and meet me in person.

The ten minutes must have shot by, as I didn't notice Gina exit her house and tap on the passenger side window. I gestured for her to get in and put my phone away.

'Hi, sorry about that, just checking emails,' I said.

'That's ok, I saw you out the window.'

'You ready for your second lesson?' I asked, starting the engine.

'Yes, I've been looking forward to it,' she said. Just then the CD player automatically came on, that I'd been listening to on the way over here.

'Oops, sorry about that,' I said, reaching forward and turning it off.

'Liszt,' she said, just as the music shut off.

'You know that piece?' I said, very surprised.

'Of course. The piano sonata in B minor,' she said.

'Wow, I'm impressed,' I said, and I was, considering Gina had only heard three or four notes from a single bar to recognise it, and not an obviously recognisable bar at that, not even for a classical – or Romantic, in this case – music aficionado.

'I love classical music,' she said.

'Yes, but Liszt, it takes a certain kind of person to be into Liszt. Especially his solo piano works. Not for your average person that's for sure.'

'Well, I guess I'm not your *average* person,' she said, as I pulled away and headed towards our quiet street.

'I guess not,' I said. 'Most people opt for Beethoven, Mozart, Grieg, Tchaikovsky, Vivaldi. You know, the usual favourites.'

'I like some of their works too,' she said.

'Who are your favourite composers?' I asked.

'Depends on my mood. For chamber music, Schubert, all day long but for orchestral, I'm partial to Beethoven and Brahms. I really love Handel and Bach too, especially those slow romantic movements. I know they weren't from the romantic period, but there's just something wonderfully romantic about some of those slow baroque movements, you know what I mean?' she said.

'I'm with you on that one,' I said, and I was. Slow baroque movements were incredibly moving.

'For the piano, I like Chopin and Liszt, but I also love certain movements from some of Beethoven and Mozart's piano sonatas, but not all. I'm not overly keen on Beethoven's earlier works. I think it took him a little while to get going. I'm not a fan of his later works either, but those in the middle were sublime. As for Mozart, a lot of what he did was a little bit on the *light* side for me, too child-like, but some of his works are capable of evoking such emotion and depth. Every now and then the odd movement will just jump out and get me, right here,' she said, patting her heart.

'Well, Gina, I'm seriously impressed with your taste in classical music and your knowledge of it,' I said, and I was. Gina appeared to love all the same composers and styles that I did. If she'd asked me the same question, I'd be answering along the same lines.

'How about you, who do you like?' she asked.

I didn't want to share the fact that I was an ex-concert pianist with Gina. I wasn't sure why exactly, just didn't seem appropriate, too personal perhaps, talking about things I used to do. Going into the past like that with a pupil wasn't really the thing to do – I liked to keep things professional.

'Believe it or not, the same. I'm a Beethoven man, for sure. For the piano, Beethoven, Bach, Liszt and Chopin, a few odd movements from various Mozart sonatas here and there, so long as they're in minor keys, dark and emotional but for the most part Mozart's a little light and tentative for me too. You've probably guessed that I love Liszt's sonata in B minor, that's just an incredible feat of solo piano composition. It's my favourite solo piano work, ever,' I said.

'Why?' she asked, in a tone that suggested she didn't mean in a general way, but in a 'what does it mean to you' sort of way.

'It just has everything, all kinds of energy, emotion and passion. It evokes pretty much every emotion we have: joy, sorrow, fear, surprise, love and romance. At times, there's even an eeriness about it, an underlying darkness, but the sun's never far away. I just love that it's one continuous movement and, once it starts, it doesn't stop until the end. Sure, I know it can be broken down, but you know what I mean.'

'Some musical analysts claim that sonata's superimposed over four movements, all rolled into one of course,' she said.

'You continue to astound me with your knowledge on such things, Gina. Do you play?'

'Oh no, I've never played any musical instrument. Well, that's not entirely true. I did play the flute when I was in my early teens for a while, got as far as grade five and then, well, you know how it is; you get a bit older and leave music behind. I just love listening to music these days and I have a real passion for it.'

'Perhaps you should take up the flute again. I bet you were really good,' I said.

'I got a distinction at grade five,' she said.

'That's impressive, Gina, getting a distinction at any

grade's not easy. Ok. We're here,' I said, pulling up in the same quiet street we'd started on last week.

Gina and I swapped seats and Gina adjusted the driver's seat, steering wheel and mirrors and got herself comfortable.

'Ok. You remember everything from last week?' I said.

'Yes, everything.'

'Super! Did you download the Highway Code app I told you about?'

'Yes, and I've been working on it every day. Did you bring the theory test practice DVD?' she asked.

'Yes, it's in the glove box. What computer do you have?'

'I've got an iMac,' she said.

A woman after my own heart, iMac, iPhone, (which I knew she had as I'd told her to download the Highway Code app and she'd taken her phone out while in the car to double-check with me that she was downloading the right one) great. Why people struggle with those ghastly bug-ridden Windows computers I'll never know – a virus with an interface, as I call them. I had Windows machines to start with donkey's years ago but when I moved over to Apple it was like getting my sight back after being blind for ten years and, from what I've heard from people who use the latest Windows OS, things haven't improved much over the years either. I don't know why but I was pleased that Gina owned a Mac, knowing that she was having an easy, intuitive and crash-free computing experience, and not pulling her hair out with computer problems, comforted me. I'd also bet the iMac was her choice too.

I just got the feeling that Gina was the kind of woman who researched things, questioned things, looked into things for herself, rather than simply asking a friend for advice.

'Ok. When you're ready you can pull away and drive straight ahead unless I direct you otherwise,' I said.

Gina started the engine, did her observations, signalled, checked her mirrors again then looked over her right shoulder as she pulled out and built up speed: textbook. The previous week we'd practiced pulling out like this several times and Gina had picked it up pretty quickly and today she was continuing exactly where we'd left off. I suspected that Gina wasn't going to have any problems with her driving, as she seemed to have a natural awareness.

As the lesson progressed Gina's road positioning improved as she fine-tuned her position by checking her distance from the kerb and the centre line by using both wing mirrors, just as I'd taught her. As she drove I could see that she had excellent all round awareness and she was constantly checking her mirrors, not just the rear view for cars behind, but also the wing mirrors to keep her road positioning in check. After a while her road positioning would become second nature and she wouldn't have to check the mirrors for this anymore, once she'd judged the width of the car and the fact that she was not sitting in the middle of the car but on the right side of it.

Gina was getting the hang of driving pretty quickly and doing everything right, for the most part. There were a few little things, here and there, but hey, this was only her second lesson. One thing she was getting wrong was something that most pupils got wrong at the beginning and that was after making a turn – from a main road and turning left into a side road, for example, she would wait until the car was straight and aiming directly down the road before straightening up the steering wheel, causing the car to head towards the kerb, or a parked car. When this happened Gina would have to straighten up the wheel rather quickly, then turn back out slightly towards the centre of her road again to compensate. I explained that she had to start straightening up the steering wheel slightly before the car was pointing straight down the road so the car would line up in a timely manner after straightening up in advance; kind of like making a manoeuvre on a boat in advance due to the sheer latency of boat-on-water. Gina got this comparison and tried it at the next turn. It was much better, but not quite perfect. A few turns later she was getting the hang of it.

'Do you feel confident enough to drive back to your house?' I asked, as we neared the end of the hour's lesson.

'Yes, I think so. What do you think?'

'Well, the roads back to your house aren't much different to the ones we've been driving on for the past hour. They're all quiet B-roads and back roads between here and your house,' I said.

'Ok. Let's do it,' she said, enthusiastically.

'Great! Straight ahead and turn right at the end of the road,' I instructed.

When we got back to Gina's house I gave her the theory test practice DVD on loan – not that I'd be needing it back – so she could get up to speed for the theory test.

'The same time next week still ok for you?' I asked.

'Yes, but I was thinking, is there any chance we can do two hours instead of just one?' she said.

'Yes, of course,' I said.

A beautiful warm smile settled on Gina's face. I knew I didn't have another lesson after Gina so I didn't have to check my diary. I was pleased about this as it meant I'd be able to get her closer to test-ready with two-hour lessons before my … exodus. Twenty more hours might not quite be enough tuition time but given what I'd seen of Gina's driving ability so far, I wouldn't be surprised if it was.

'Great,' she said.

'Ok. I'll see you at the same time next week, only for a two-hour lesson,' I said.

'Thank you,' she said.

'Not a problem.'

'No, I mean, thank you. I didn't know if I'd be able to do this, didn't think I'd have the confidence. I mean, my husband's always been the driver so I never really had any need and I never bothered learning to drive when I was younger, I couldn't really afford it at the time. Anyway, you're making it easy for me, Red, I feel really comfortable with you, so thank you.'

'You're welcome, Gina. Ok. Until next week,' I said, keen for her to get out so I could get home. Not that I had anything exciting waiting for me at home, except a cold loneliness and my faithful black dog of depression.

Idiot, you idiot, I thought to myself as I drove away from Gina's house. She was married, just like I'd suspected she was. I'd fantasised about Gina – in more ways than one, I don't mind admitting – several times since giving her that first lesson, even though I knew I shouldn't. After all, I'm not going to be around in, what, just over nine weeks. Still, I couldn't quite manage to shake Gina from my thoughts and just now I'd gone from a warm fuzzy feeling in the pit of my stomach – at the thought of being in the car with her for two-hours instead of one – to having that feeling yanked away in the blink of an eye at the knowledge of her being married. Just another sad reminder of how miserable – no, shit – life is and how love and romance sucks. Like everything good that's happened up to this point in my wretched life, it's there for but a brief moment in time, like a carrot being dangled, momentarily, in front of my face before being yanked away by the cruel hand of life.

I've just never had any luck with love and happiness in life; no crumbs ever fell off God's table and landed on my lap. I know, I know, I'm an atheist, but I can't think of a better analogy right now. I've worked hard and tried, boy have I tried, but everything gets taken away from me in the end: my wife, my piano career, just about every decent thing I can remember, only, unlike my wife and piano career, things are usually yanked away from me a hell of a lot quicker. If I were to be buried (which I won't be, I've decided on that) a fitting epitaph would read something along the lines of: HERE LIES A MAN WHO TRIED SO HARD IN LIFE, BUT NEVER ATTAINED HAPPINESS, ONLY MISERY, LONELINESS, SOLITUDE AND INNER DARKNESS, and that would pretty much sum up my life. How could I have been so stupid to allow the idea of a woman to creep into my head like that, after all I'd been through with women. I was annoyed with myself, angry with myself, for allowing that tiny remaining part of my heart and soul that still worked – just, hanging on by a thread – to be punched like that, by a bloody woman. Hadn't I learned anything from my so-called relationships and other female endeavours? They'd all ended in pain and misery – they always did and probably always would.

I could feel my anxiety creeping up on me and I could literally hear the blood rushing in my ears. I was worked up and stressed and had to calm down. I hit the steering wheel with the palm of my hand, incensed that I could let something like this happen. Even if Gina hadn't been married she'd probably be just like all the rest of the women who'd snared me in their traps over the years. It was always the same, I don't really know if I pick them or if they pick me, and then prey on me. It's like they're venomous spiders with elaborate webs and I'm this little innocent fly that lands right in the middle of it. They play around with me, bite me and send venom through my veins, chew me up and then spit me out when they're done. Well, not all the time, most of the time I break it off as soon as I realise they're not suitable for me (and vice-versa), but I've had my fair share of venomous spiders and scorpions too, or maybe that's just how I interpret it. Amid all the confusion, smoke and subterfuge of what modern love is I've kind of forgotten what it's supposed to be about, or at least everybody else has. It's all too damn complicated these days and thus I've lost the plot with love and relationships and I have no desire to ever try and figure it out again. As for Gina - she's a pupil, that's all she ever was and that's all she'll ever be. That's it, end of verse, chapter and story.

Chapter 13

I'd just finished a lesson in town and I still had about ninety minutes before my therapy session with Shannon so – while in the vicinity – I decided to pop into the Grand Arcade shopping centre, more specifically, the Apple Store, to have them swap the battery out in my iPhone as it was only holding charge for about six hours these days. The saleswoman made me a Genius Bar appointment, which was 35 minutes off, so rather than hang around in there with the masses I decided a coffee would go down well so I popped along to Costa. I'm not a fan of coffee shops in town, especially chains like Costa, Starbucks and Nero. I can't see the point in paying £2.50 for a cappuccino – typically with beans that are past their best that leave a bitter after-taste in your mouth – when I can make a better one (and mine are way better) at home for 50p, not to mention all the other negatives that come with drinking coffee in these places.

As I stood in the queue waiting for my turn I perused the various sweet and sticky offerings and asked myself if any of these items actually contained anything of nutritional value: vitamins, minerals, nutrients, protein. I doubted it - cancer-inducing sugar and e-numbers most likely - yet the place was full of people buying this crap for their children, oblivious to the health issues their children could suffer later in life as a result of such an unhealthy diet.

I ordered my usual (usual for the rare occasions that I found myself in such establishments), a small cappuccino made with just one shot. Well, the coffee beans rarely taste like they were roasted within the past 30 days, usually having an edge of bitterness in the aftertaste. Anybody who knows anything about coffee knows that the beans have to be roasted, ground and consumed within 30 days of the 'roast' date and definitely *not* the 'sell by' date. Coffee beans aren't like regular food products, they are complex and the moisture and aroma are a science. Sell by dates are stuck on packs of coffee for idiots, not coffee connoisseurs. Once roasted the beans should sit for three to four days, then be consumed no later than day 30, leaving a window of about 26 days for grinding and consumption. I once asked the manager at a Costa branch to check the sack of beans and tell me the roasted date. It was two months ago, already way past usability – at least if you possess working taste buds that is – and should have been thrown in the bin a month ago. I looked around at the other customers. What a lacklustre ensemble, collectively gibbering away in dull tones like some hootenanny. People watching is of no interest to me and I don't understand people who participate in this dull and futile pastime. I consider people watching to be the lowest form of voyeurism and it can only be of interest to dullards, those with a low IQ and with no originality or creativity whatsoever.

How can one human being be so fascinated with the 'looks' of another human being? A fleeting glance at the coffee shop congregation is about all I can stand with regard to the fascinations of other human beings. That's more than enough to get a general idea of the demographic that frequent such places. As for how attractive or unattractive they are and what they're wearing, I simply don't care and I don't understand people that do.

'That's £2.55, please,' said a 14-year old looking girl with tattoos on both forearms. Such a shame, a pretty little thing who would otherwise have grown up to be a very attractive woman if it weren't for the dirty looking ink she'd seen fit to desecrate her, otherwise, perfect skin with. And why was her hair vibrant purple? I presented my debit card to the contactless machine as I pondered these things, for all of the two seconds it took the machine to bleep in acceptance of my.

Even though it was mid-week and still within working hours Costa was pretty busy. I spotted an elderly couple getting up to leave so I went over and loitered with intent. The old woman smiled at me, said, 'Sorry, darling, I'm not as quick as I used to be.'

'That's ok. Take your time, I'm in no hurry,' I said, smiling back at her. Her husband – I assumed – was struggling to find the second arm hole in his corduroy jacket so I grabbed the shoulder of it and pulled it up to meet his searching hand.

'Oh, thank you,' he laughed, appreciating my help.

I was helping him out of good manners and kindness, not because I wanted the old couple to get a shift on. In this country we don't exactly look after the elderly and we don't have much in the way of respect for them, let alone patience, which is tragic on so many levels. We really need to take a leaf out of Japan's book on this front. Here, we just ditch them into some old people's home where they can live out their later years being lonely, miserable, abused and mistreated by so-called 'care' workers, the thought of which angers me beyond words.

'Thank you,' said the man.

'Goodbye,' said the lady.

'You two have a lovely evening,' I said, smiling, which they seemed to appreciate. I expect elderly couples like this don't receive too many smiles from strangers these days.

Like me, the lovely old couple were obsolete in today's modern world. As they walked away and I sat down I actually felt a little envious of them. They only have a few more years to put up with this and they would have lived through some great times, times when folk got together to support and help each other in times of need. They would have danced their way through the 50's and still been young enough to enjoy a Beatles concert in the 60's while running around naked and being free and happy, and then discovering the delights of Robert Plant's vocals and Jimmy Page's guitar work in the 70's. But what do they have to live for now that the good times have long gone? The McDonaldization of mankind, the iPod generation, the aimless millennials, where everybody is walking around with their face wedged into some small digital screen, all living their lives in pixel-vision, not seeing the 'real' world around them and not caring about it either. Living in the digital domain of Facebook, Twitter, Instagram and the like while they push things around a screen with their finger. They might as well just have their spinal cords connected up to a machine and submerge themselves into a sealed glass tub of some sort of formaldehyde substance like those chaps in The Matrix, and be done with it. These people don't seem to care about watching the sun set over some rolling hills in Tuscany or standing on a lake shore in the Lake District and looking out over a placid tarn at the reflection of a large, bright, full moon in the clear sky above. Why would these walking corpses care about what that experience would actually 'feel' like and what emotions they would evoke when they can watch it on YouTube? (or PooTube as I like to call it, because people send all sorts of crap down it).

I took one of my napkins and brushed away the crumbs from the table – not left behind from the old couple, they only had drinks – which some uncivilised family had probably left behind. I did the same for the floor around my feet by kicking away a few lumps of dropped blueberry muffin and some other unidentifiable snacks. *What a disgusting place,* I thought, nothing pleasurable about it at all. Sitting at a crumb infested table drinking bitter coffee with numerous pieces of cake around your feet.

There was a woman at the next table with a toddler perched on her knee. He was reaching out desperately trying to grab the lemon tart she had in front of her. Lord knows what that nuclear green coloured substance with a straw sticking out of it was, and she was about to put that into her little child's precious body? She started by trying to cut small pieces from the lemon tart to feed to said child but he just kept clambering to take it himself; he was going to feed himself, come hell or high water. Eventually, the woman gave in to his little grabbing hands and just let him take the entire tart. With a look of ecstatic happiness – child 1 mother 0 – the child proceeded to take a bite out of the sugar-loaded treat. Why people call them 'treats' is beyond me when all these sugar-loaded cakes do is encourage the growth of cancer cells and cause obesity and other illnesses. If anybody ever bought me a cake on my birthday I'd sue them for attempting to cause my body physical harm.

My god, the child was probably only 18-months old and already this woman was feeding it all sorts of toxins and chemicals, before the poor little bugger's life had even got going. At least wait until his little organs have finished growing and are fully developed to the point that they can break down, filter out and deal with such sugar and e-number infested crap. If I had a kid, or kids, I'd do my utmost to keep them as far away from sweets and junk food for as long as possible to give their little developing bodies and immune systems the best possible chance in life. Then, when they became teenagers, at least I could say that I'd kept them toxin and poison free for at least a decade. The last thing a child's developing body needs is cakes, sweets and other artificial crap. These same parents are probably wrecking their car engines too by putting inferior quality supermarket fuel into their brand new PCP-financed cars as well.

As I drank my cappuccino I studied the queue of people at the counter. It was non-stop, a never ending supply of income for Costa, people who are more than happy to spend £2.50 on a coffee that cost all of 15p for the shop to make and another £1.95 on a muffin that probably cost just 15p to produce. The profit margins must be mammoth.

Having nothing better to do I checked the time on my watch and counted the customers over a 15-minute period, figuring each one was spending, on average, £5 (coffee and cake, coffee and toasted sandwich et cetera). I multiplied it by 4 to come up with an hour's gross takings, then multiplied that figure by 9, the daily opening hours, then I multiplied that figure by 7 (days of the week) and then again by 52 (weeks in the year) and the gross figure I came up with was £350,000 per year, give or take. I figured after paying the rent, council tax, staff wages (of which there were four, none of whom could possibly be on more than £15,000 a year), bills and stock costs they were doing pretty damn well. So the £2.34 profit from my cappuccino went towards paying landlords, utility companies, staff wages, suppliers, the council and lord knows what else. It made me feel like a little cog in a very large machine, keeping the whole commercial world turning – I hated it.

Mingling, in such close proximity, with the public in places like this was my idea of hell as it only served as another reminder of just how shit everything had become. We aren't living anymore; we're just on a long conveyor belt heading to the finish line as our lives are dictated to by evil empires and the government. Boy was I going to need Shannon after this.

I ambled back along to the Apple Store, paid them for the new battery installation and then headed down to the car park.

'Hello, Red, come on in,' said Shannon. 'Oops, you've got some fluff on ya',' she said, brushing my chin with her thumb. 'There you go,' she said, dropping the red mass of fluff that had snagged itself in my stubble.

'Ah, damn towels,' I said. 'How many times do you have to wash new towels before they stop depositing bits of fluff all over your body every time you get out the shower?' I joked, 'I mean, I've washed these new ones four times now and they're still showing no sign of letting up with the shedding.'

'They can be a real pain can't they?' she sympathised.

'I never used to have this problem with towels. Everything's going cheap and crap and I expect

Dunelm, like everybody else, are subscribing to it by sourcing their towels from crap suppliers who are making inferior products on the cheap these days.'

'Sounds like you need a coffee, Red,' she said.

'I'm good, actually, just had one half an hour ago, in town, if you can call it coffee. Tell you what though, I'll have a glass of water if that's ok?' I said, leaning forward and pouring one from the waiting jug and clean glass on the coffee table.

'Help yourself,' she said, picking up her A4 pad and pen, which she studied for a moment.

Perhaps Shannon was thinking the same thing that I was. This was my fourth session and I was sure she'd done the math. I'd been seeing her a month now, only two more to go before I depart this world.

'Red, I'd like to revisit your childhood and the accident,' she said.

'Ok,' I said. I didn't mind talking about that, it was a long time ago and I'm over it. Sure, I missed my sister and not having a mum and dad around for support but it was 36 years ago and the effects of such had well and truly diluted over the years.

Shannon asked me about my childhood before the accident. I explained to her that I was six when the accident happened and that I only had a few vague memories from perhaps a year or two before that. Well, we don't really remember anything before the age of about three or four. She asked about my mum and dad. I told her that my mum always seemed to be buzzing around doing something or another while my father was a man of few words, the polar-opposite, he'd generally sit in the comfy armchair in the corner gazing out the window with a thoughtful dreamlike expression on his face as if pondering the dreams that would never come to fruition due to 'family' circumstances and all that went with it.

I had a very close relationship with my father and sister. My father and I had a great connection. We didn't have to exchange many words and we generally didn't. We didn't really have to; we just knew what the other was thinking or feeling. There was something magical about our relationship and the special bond we had. As for my sister, we had an amazing relationship too. I loved her so much and she loved me too. We shared everything and we had our own little secrets in that way that children do. My mother was a different story. She didn't really have a maternal bone in her body and sometimes I felt like she resented Jennifer and me. It was like we were nothing more than inconvenient obstacles getting in the way of her life. I don't even think she loved dad and I think dad probably knew it, but he stuck around anyway – sacrificing his own dreams – for us. I think, had they not been killed by that truck that day, that mum would have, at some point, left us all and gone on to pursue her own dreams – whatever they were.

Shannon asked me to tell her about the accident, in more detail this time. I did, detailing the horror of the situation, a horror that is still as clear and vivid in my mind's eye today as it was when it happened 36 years ago – if I chose to think about it hard enough, which I generally didn't.

Shannon then moved things forward a little to what happened after my parents and sister died that day.

'I remember a uniformed policeman sitting with me on a bench on the green, about hundred yards away from the bus stop where the accident happened. He was a really nice man, sympathetic and, although authority figures like that scared me when I was a child, this man comforted me the best he could, given the circumstances. In hindsight, I think he must have been a family man with kids about my age.

'I was taken to the police station where I received more sympathy and compassion and was given food and drink, not that I felt like eating or drinking. I guess the treatment I received at the police station that day was of a different kind to their usual detainees. After a while a nice lady from social services came to take me away. I was placed in a children's home, temporarily, while they tried to find suitable foster parents for me,' I said.

'How long were you in the children's home before they found you foster parents?' she asked.

'I can't be sure. It felt like a long time but I'm sure it was only a couple of months.'

'What was it like? The children's home?'

'It wasn't great; you know how those places can be, especially back then. It wasn't a big place, just a large converted 5-bed detached house. There were about fourteen children there. I shared a room with three other boys. It was horrible.'

'Can you elaborate?'

'They were all screwed up, from dysfunctional families. Boisterous bullies, you know the type. I hated the place and everybody in it. The staff were not much better either. They dished out cruel and unusual punishments for the most trivial of misdemeanours.'

'Can you tell me more about that,' she said, pen poised.

'Well, there were beatings, but well thought-out beatings that would not leave any bruises for visiting social workers to see. They'd lock you in the storage room in the dark for hours on end and they'd constantly belittle you.'

'Was there any sexual abuse?'

'No, just mental and physical.'

'Ok. We've touched on the first set of foster parents that you were living with … until you were 10?' she said, checking her notes.

'Yes.'

'Can we talk about the next foster placement you had?'

'Sure.'

'You were with the second foster family from the age of 10 to 16 right?' she said.

'Yes.'

'Can you tell me how that was?'

'Sure,' I said.

I'd already covered the brutality and sexual abuse from the first set of foster parents and their disgusting son that I'd had to endure from the age of 6 to 10. This was going to be easier as there was no sexual abuse and they had no children of their own so there were no jealous or bullying siblings. I covered my years with these foster parents relatively quickly as there were no instances of abuse: mental, physical or sexual. However, I did explain to Shannon that there was no real love or affection either. It was like they didn't really know what to do or how to engage with a 10-year old boy. They were much older than my real mum and dad. Sure, they fed me, let me watch my favourite programmes on television, took me out and bought me nice presents on my birthday and at Christmas, but there were never any heart-felt hugs or any connection with them. The man would sometimes ruff up my hair for a few seconds in a playful manner and that was about as far as his expression of love would go. The woman didn't go much further than saying that I was 'such a sweet and tender boy'.

Chapter 14

'Red, how you doing?' said Ross, as I walked up to the counter in my local BP petrol station/M&S minimart.

'Not bad, thanks, you?' I said. *Not bad, if only,* I thought. Still, what was one supposed to say to the familiar faces who served you petrol and M&S ready meals, who I'd come to be on a first-name terms with, such as Ross.

'Fantastic,' he said, and he sounded like me meant it.

Secretly, I hated Ross. Well, 'hate' was probably the wrong word; 'envy' was probably a better choice. Yes, I'd say I envied the lucky bastard. Sometimes when the petrol station was quiet – and it often was at the time of day I chose to shop there – Ross and I would have a little chat. At first it was just the usual general pleasantries: nice weather, miserable weather, doing anything nice at the weekend, the usual futile crap that people feel the need to say, but sometimes Ross went into a little more detail about his own life. He had a girlfriend (his 'hinny', as he often referred to her), on a part time basis, he once told me, 'wink, wink, nudge, nudge,' he'd joke, winking at me with a wry smile, or was it a sinister grin? 'Well, I go to her place a couple of times a week for a hot meal and a shag, if I'm honest,' he'd said. You've got to admire the truth in it and the odd thing about it was, his girlfriend was happy with the arrangement too, apparently. Well, Ross had told me, 'she has her needs too, it's not just us guys that need a regular shag,' he'd said, in his strong Geordie accent. I'd always found people from Newcastle to be refreshingly honest – they tend to say what other folk only think.

Ross lived in the smallest 1-bed flat in Cambridge with barely enough room to swing a cat. 'If I did own a cat it would have to wear a bloody crash helmet, mind,' he'd said, insinuating it would crack its furry head open on one of the nearby walls during said cat-swinging activity. His job couldn't pay that much, minimum wage, perhaps a trifle more. He drove a shitty 10-year old Honda Civic with 140,000 miles on the clock but it went like the 'stink' according to Ross. He had a small handful of friends and he went to visit his dad (his only remaining living parent) every Sunday over in Bury St Edmunds. In his spare time he played snooker at a club in Cambridge, loved football and a pint: well, he was a Geordie after all. That's about it. Ross's life encapsulated in one neat paragraph (or a five-minute conversation at the counter of the BP station while I was waiting for my mocha to be made by his colleague), yet he was the happiest son of a bitch this side of the nuthouse. Like I said, the lucky bastard. How could he be so content and so happy with so little in his life? As for me, since giving up on women, love and romance, I needed, well, I didn't really know what I needed to make me happy anymore. I guess it didn't really matter anyway because in eight weeks' time my miserable life would be well and truly in life's terminal rear view mirror – permanently – as I drove into a pitch black exit-less tunnel while watching the little white dot in the rear view mirror get smaller and smaller, until it was no longer there, like the little fading white dot on old cathode ray tube television sets from years gone by after they'd been switched off.

'Filling up the Corsa for a busy lesson schedule?' asked Ross, nodding towards my little white car at pump number 3.

'Yup. One of the advantages of teaching in an automatic, Ross, is there's hardly any of us around so I get most of the business all to myself.'

'Is that why you decided to teach in an automatic car then?' he said.

'Uh huh,' I said.

'That's grand, man – good idea,' he said.

'No food today?' he asked.

'Nope, just the fuel, Ross. New Blu-ray arrived in the post this morning so I think I'll order a Chinese to go with.'

'Ah, good idea, what movie?'

'Dragged Across Concrete.'

'Oh yeah, that's that new Mel Gibson one, right?'

'Yup, trailer looked pretty damn good too. Can't beat a good Mel Gibson action flick for a bit of escapism.'

'Wey aye, man,' he said. Which I took to mean, yes, I agree.

Damn, I thought, as I drove out of the BP petrol station. My cars, I had to sell my two cars. That was going to require some careful timing. I didn't want to have to spend my last days on this earth walking everywhere like Caine in the old Kung Fu TV series. I'd advertise the Audi TT straight away. It was a popular car and it was in pristine condition with full service history and it had just passed its MOT (with no advisories) last month so it should sell pretty quickly.

After 10 minutes on the A14 I was forced off due to part of it being closed for roadworks. I had an emergency appointment with my dentist, who was based in St Ives. Every time I had to make this 20-mile journey (every six months for my routine check-up) I tell myself that I should register with a dentist locally, but I'd gone with this one based on good reviews online. But today – due to the bloody on-going A14 roadworks – I was been forced through loads of little villages: Boxworth, Elsworth, Hilton. It was just as I was exiting the latter that I saw a delivery van up ahead almost hit a dog, or maybe it was the dog that almost hit the van. Either way, the van driver didn't stop. As I approached I spotted the dog running back across the road, right in front of me. I hit the brakes, not quite an emergency stop, but close, as the canine continued to play Russian roulette with the traffic. I watched the dog for a moment, a border collie, as it ran into the field by the side of the road. Then it ran back across the road again, barking, hysterically, and so on and so forth. I figured if I left the dog like this it would surely get hit by a passing car, eventually and, unlike cats, they didn't have nine lives. There were only three houses; about a hundred yards back down the road, maybe it belonged to somebody that lived in one of them. Could be a farm dog but I didn't see a farm, just lots of fields and open land.

Unlike the van diver who nearly hit the dog before speeding away I'm actually a huge animal lover and I couldn't just drive off knowing that this dog could get hit so I pulled over and figured I'd go and check the dog's collar for a phone number or address.

'Come 'ere, boy,' I shouted, in my best friendly dog tone, getting down on my haunches and patting my knees. The dog just barked at me and glared, cautious and defensive. Then it started to run up and down while looking at me with a 'catch me if you can' thing going on. 'You're not gonna make this easy for me, are you?' I said. The dog started to bark more, still cautious and backing away more as I continued to approach it. 'Come on, boy,' I said, softer this time and back down on haunches so as not to seem so big and intimidating. The dog was adamant, just stood there, staring me down and barking, slobber flying from its mouth as it protested vocally.

I started to creep, slowly, towards the dog in a none-threatening manner. It barked more incessantly as I got closer, but it was not backing away anymore. As I got closer the dog's barks turned into a steady low evil growl, teeth bared. 'Come on, boy, don't give me this shit, I've got to be somewhere,' I said, still creeping forward. The dog was not letting up with its teeth bared and that intimidating evil growl. I was giving serious through to just getting up and heading back to my car before this thing decided to chew my face off, but I couldn't, and I'd come this far. I was less than ten feet from the dog. The closer I got the more it looked like some sort of vicious wolf from a horror movie. *What the hell are you doing, Red?* I thought. I thought I'd try another tactic so I lowered my head and started making sad little whimpering noises, like a puppy that had hurt its leg. The Border collie's growls slowed and then stopped completely as its chops came down to cover its fangs. I continued my faux whimpering dog sounds; head low to the ground. I became aware of the dog moving, slowly, towards me. It sniffed my head, which I slowly lifted up.

'Hey, boy,' I said, in a slow soft tone as I reached up and gently massaged behind the dog's ears with both hands (I'd read somewhere once that that's how you calm a dog down). After a moment the dog settled, trust had been established. While continuing the massage treatment with one hand I gently turned its leather collar with the other, bingo, a name and phone number engraved into a metal disc.

'Sadie, so you're a girl? Well, sorry about all that "boy" stuff, but it's kind of your fault, you weren't exactly acting like a lady now where you? Mind you, in the modern world…' I said. I took out my mobile and called the number on the dog's collar, which promptly answered by a woman.

'Hi, I have your dog.'

'I'm sorry?'

'I found her running around on the road playing with the traffic,' I said, light heartedly.

'Oh no! Has she escaped through the fence again?'

'It would appear so. I don't know where your house is but I've just come out of Hilton, heading in the direction of St Ives.'

'Oh, I'm the first house on the right as you come back into the village, if you hang on I'll come out and find you,' she said, hanging up.

I looked back down the road and about a hundred yards away I saw a woman come out onto the narrow path that ran alongside the road. Keeping hold of Sadie's collar I walked back down towards her.

'Thank you,' she said. 'She's always escaping through the fence, aren't you, Sadie?'

If she's always escaping through the damn fence why don't you get it fixed? was the first thought to enter my mind and I was amazed that the woman hadn't considered this.

'She was playing Frogger with the traffic,' I said.

'Playing what?' she said. The reference to the old arcade game went over her head.

'She was running back and forth across the road. A van ahead of me missed her by a few feet and when I came along she ran right in front of my car too. She seems to enjoy dodging moving vehicles, like a game. I'd suggest getting the fence fixed because next time you might have to come out here and scrape her up off the road. You wouldn't want her to end up like one of those foxes or rabbits or any other number of road kill, would you?' I said this in a friendly way but I also wanted the woman to have a vivid image of Sadie, dead in the road like a large bloody road kill. It worked; she looked horrified at the thought.

'Oh, dear, no! No I wouldn't want that,' she said, looking very thoughtful and concerned now.

'Ok, ma'am, you have a lovely day,' I said, heading back up to my car while checking my watch to see if I could still make my dentist appointment. I could, just.

'Thank you,' she cried after me.

My dentist informed me that I needed a tiny filling in the lower back tooth, the one that had been causing me pain and sensitivity recently. Because it was only a tiny hole no numbing injections were required, thank god. Not that I had any more lessons today – giving driving lessons sounding like a drunken Sylvester Stallone probably wouldn't help – and, as usual, I wouldn't be seeing, or talking to, anybody this evening. Still, it made drinking a cup of tea difficult and one usually ended up biting one's inner cheek while trying to eat within a few hours of having numbing injections in the gums. My dentist escorted me back through the reception area to the exit.

'Ok, Red, enjoy your evening and I'll see you next month,' she said.

'Next month?' I said.

'Yes, I noticed you're booked in for a routine appointment on the 23rd,' she said.

'Oh, that won't be necessary,' I said. As I heard my words scurry across the air molecules towards my dentist's ears, I instantly regretted it and immediately tried to come up with an answer for her imminent question.

'Red, I know you're not a fan of coming here. Trust me, none of my patients are, but you really must have routine check-ups every six months,' she said.

Phew, no explaining required. 'Yes, of course,' I said.

I wouldn't just leave it until they eventually read my obituary in the local paper, not that there would be one. I'd call and tell them I was emigrating or something, so they could free up my appointment for somebody else, as well as freeing up a patient place.

Final chore of the day, I had to swing by Ely on my way home as I'd sold two Dimplex convector heaters to a chap who lived up there. I'd bought them when I first moved into the house I'm in now as the landlord explained that he was in the middle of having the broken combi boiler replaced but it was going to be a couple of weeks before that happened and, as it was winter when I moved in, I figured I'd need some sort of heating. They'd sat in the loft for ages but were now part of my house clearance. The man in Ely didn't drive but said he'd pay me for my petrol.

I was about half way there, heading along the B1381, when I saw a fully-grown swan flapping about in obvious distress in the road ahead.

'Oh Christ, not again.'

I slowed down and as I got closer I could see that

the swan was injured. Both its wings were splayed out. One looked a little lame and crooked and the animal was also limping, causing it to just flap around in circles, unable to move in a straight line and certainly unable to take off. The B1381 was not the busiest road in Cambridgeshire but cars passed along here every minute, even during quiet periods, so I couldn't help wondering how many drivers had simply slowed down and swerved around the injured bird, not wanting to be inconvenienced in any way as they made their way to their destinations. I know I moan and groan about life – mostly for good reason – and I've come to hate the world and pretty much everybody in it, but that's people, not animals. I could never leave an animal in distress like this.

I pulled over on the left, literally a few yards away from the swan, onto the grass verges so that my Corsa was mostly off the road, to allow space on the narrow road for other vehicles to pass safely. Cars often zipped along this narrow B-road at anywhere between 60 and 80mph. I've sometimes been overtaken by the odd lunatic doing close to a 100mph and, trust me on this, on the B1381 the overtaking car's wheels would almost be skimming the grass verges on the other side of the road, that's how narrow it is.

I knew I had to do something or the swan would get hit by a car and probably die. Also, the temperature was dropping and although it was nowhere near freezing it was only 8 degrees Celsius and the weather forecast said it was going to drop to as low as 4 later. Ok. First things first, I had to get the distressed/injured swan off the road. I figured if I put the bird across the back seat of my Corsa it would be out of harm's way while I looked up a number for the RCPCA on my iPhone. It would also be warmer for the injured bird too.

That was my plan anyway. I mean, how hard could it be to lift an injured swan into a car? Hmmm.

As soon as I got out of my car and made a few steps in the direction of the swan it started hissing at me. I didn't know swans hissed, this thing was hissing like a Spitting Cobra that had just had root canal – and the anaesthetic was earing off – and was just as scary. This was not going to be easy. I grabbed my Reefer jacket off the back seat, returned to the hissing swan and threw the coat over its head and neck. I figured if the swan's head was in the dark and it could not see, its stress levels – and hissing – might give a little; it worked. I gently folded the splayed wing into its body and felt across the ridge and bone structure of the other lame one before gently folding that in too, while listening and watching for any 'winces' from the bird, in case a wing was broken. I figured the bird had been hit by a car and had been left for dead, or maybe some heartless twat knew the bird was injured and in agonising pain and just left it to freeze to death and die during the night.

I managed to carefully lift the bird, which was way heavier than I'd imagined swans to be – it must have been all of 10 kg. I got to the back of my car and, as I took one arm away from the swan to open the back door, its head and neck escaped my coat, along with one of its wings. It started flapping and hissing wildly in protest while its long conger-eel-like neck jabbed forward as it proceeded to try and bite my face off with its pecking orange (or was it deep yellow? To be perfectly honest it's kind of hard to tell when one is trying to peck your face off from such close range) beak. It was at that point that I realised that although swans don't have teeth their beaks do have small jagged serrated edges along them which I suppose help them grip weed while they pull it from the river bed, only – right now – they were being used to try and grip my nose to yank it right off my face.

'Stop, I'm trying to save your life you ungrateful son of a bitch,' I yelled, while struggling to get my coat back over its head with my free hand. Whatever way you slice it this swan wasn't keen to know what the inside of my Corsa looked like; it had been quite clear about that.

'Ok, ok, we'll just stay out here on the road, where it's nice and bloody cold,' I protested.

I placed the swan down on the grass verge behind my car with my jacket over it and ran back to get my mobile from the car. During the seconds it took me to do that the swan remained (head and neck included) under my coat.

'Ok, Google, do your stuff,' I said, as I waited for the results to come up on the screen for my 'RSPCA phone number' search. There was some faffing about as I was given another number by the person who answered, then put on hold while I was transferred to somebody else who, eventually, told me (after I'd explained the situation) that the closest person who could help was in Norwich dealing with something else and it would be about three hours before she could drive down to me: about an hour or so for her to finish up, then the 65 mile journey to where the swan and I were. Great, this was going to be a long (and very cold) evening. The grass (and mud under it) was cold so I lifted the swan across my lap – at the expense of suffering a cold arse myself – and allowed its head to poke out from under my heavy (but warm) Reefer coat. I was sure to keep a gentle hold on its neck just in case it tried any funny business, which it didn't. I think the swan and I were starting to connect a little, well, perhaps 'connect' was a little strong but I at least felt that the swan was gaining a little trust in me now as it had calmed down and ceased trying to strip the skin off my face with its serrated edge beak in an attempt to sculpt it into something that resembled Freddy Krueger.

The temperature was dropping and boy was I feeling it. My backside was numb and I was sure the cold ground was inducing haemorrhoids, or was that an old wives tale? Right now it didn't feel like it.

Eventually a small white van with a blue RSPCA logo on the side pulled up in front of my car on the grass verges and a woman, about 30, hopped out and ambled over to me.

'Hello, you must be Red?' she enquired.

'Yes. Thanks for coming,' I said, relieved.

'Sorry it took me so long to get to you. They explained the situation to me. You just found the swan in distress on the road?' she said, getting down on her haunches and removing my coat from said bird.

'Yes, I saw it flapping around. Its left wing looked a little lame and it was stumbling about in circles limping. I think it was hit by a car,' I said.

The woman gave the swan a brief examination, expanding its wings and feeling the various bones, as I'd done, only more expertly. She felt all around the bird and checked it over thoroughly.

'It seems quite happy for you to carry out this examination, the thing was going mental with me earlier,' I said.

'Ah, it's a woman thing,' she smiled, 'we have an understanding.'

'It's a female? How do you know?' I asked. I mean, I didn't see her check its genitalia.

'There are a few ways you can tell, but you see this black knob on top of the beak? It's called a blackberry. The female's is much smaller than the male's. Also, the female's neck is more slender and its beak is more vibrant and a little darker – the female's is more yellow than orange,' she said.

'So, what's the verdict?'

'Well, the good news is, there are no broken bones. I'm pretty sure about that, just a few bruises here and there.'

'Looks like she had a lucky escape then. I mean, cars zip along here really fast. I would have thought that the impact with a speeding car would have killed it outright,' I said.

'I doubt she was hit by a car,' she said.

'Oh?'

'No, what's happened here isn't uncommon. This little road has no road marking, no centre lines and no verge lines either, so from the sky it looks like a river. The swan would have come down to land on it and put its feet out in preparation to make its skate landing and when they came into contact with the tarmac it would have bumbled over several times, which has caused the bruising and pain.'

'Oh, that's fascinating. Well, not for the swan, I'm sure. It's ironic that this road runs parallel to a river, that's five times wider,' I said. 'Looks like you didn't choose your river wisely, girl.'

'She certainly didn't. Anyway, I'll take her back up to Norwich and get her x-rayed and checked out and then, if all's well, I'll bring her back down here and release her in the morning.'

'Well, thanks again,' I said, getting up, now the swan was in her arms being carried – without protest – away to her van. My backside had gone to sleep and I had to stand for a moment and wait for my legs to start working again.

'Would you like me to call you, keep you posted?' she offered.

'Yes, please, that would be nice,' I said.

'Ok, I've got your number already. I'll call you tomorrow,' she said, shutting the van door, having placed the swan inside.

She headed off while I tried to get some feeling back in my backside by turning the heater on in the car, to no avail, as it had been a good few hours since the car's engine was up to temperature. If I were in my Audi right now the heated seat would be on and set to maximum. Still, I felt good that I'd helped the bird as I headed up to Ely to drop the heaters off with the buyer, who I had to apologise to for being nearly three hours late, but he enjoyed my swan-saving story and said I should get my nose looked at. 'Looks like you've been in a fight with a cheese greater,' he joked. The swan had got a few good pecks in on my face and nose during our little tango but I was sure it wasn't that bad, having checked it out in my car's rear view mirror.

The RSPCA woman was true to her word. The next day she called me to tell me that, as suspected, it was just superficial bruising and the swan could now walk and extend its wings without difficulty. She'd driven the swan back to the location where it was injured and let it go next to the river, not the road, and waited around for a little while to make sure it was ok. It wasn't long before the swan executed a river take off and was on its way. The thought of that kept my depression at bay and lit me up inside (that and saving the dog from becoming road kill earlier the same day), though for how long I'd be able to sustain that feel-good factor was another matter – probably not long.

Chapter 15

I got to Gina's ten minutes early so, like last week, I sat there and checked my emails on my iPhone. There was a slight difference this week. I didn't have any butterflies in my stomach and I wasn't glancing over at her window every five seconds for a glimpse of her as she moved the curtains to check if I were outside her house. I'd dismissed the silly fantasy I'd had about her at the beginning, which *was* silly. I mean, one can't be having fantasies about every beautiful woman one sees and when I say 'fantasies' I'm not talking sexual – well, some are – I'm talking more along the lines of fantasising about a relationship with somebody, a life with them, the whole nine yards. It was all a stupid idea, I knew that could never happen, lord knows I'd tried and being disappointed time and time again. Gina was married and in seven and a half weeks I'd be dead: good riddance to this stinking world, everybody in it and everything it stands for.

Gina knocked at the car window and I gestured for her to get in.

'Hi, how are you?' she said.

'I'm good. How do you feel about driving from the off today?' I said, getting straight to the point, the job in hand.

'From here?' she asked.

'Yes. Last week you drove back here without so much as a hiccup so I figured you'd be fine driving away from here too?'

'Erm, yeah, sure. I can do that,' she said.

'Super. You'd better hop in this side then,' I said, getting out. I was aware that Gina was looking at me as I walked around the front of the car, the opposite direction (on purpose) to the route she took, around the back of the car.

'Are you ok?' she asked, making adjustments to her seat.

'Yes, I'm fine,' I said, in the most naturally forced faux tone I could muster up.

'You seem a little … distant,' she said.

'I'm fine,' I said. 'So, you ready?'

'Yes, I'm ready,' she said, making a little adjustment to the nearside mirror.

'Ok then. As usual, straight ahead unless I direct you otherwise. We're going to head over to the street where you had your first lesson, to do your first manoeuvre, a turn in the road.'

'What's that,' she asked.

'3-point turn?'

'Oh, yes,' she said.

'They call it a turn in the road now,' I said.

'Why's that? Was there something not quite politically correct enough about the old 3-point turn name?'

'Ha,' I laughed. 'I think it was probably because people took it literally and felt they had to do the turn in three moves – forward, back, then forward again – when the truth of the matter is on some narrow roads it sometimes takes five moves to complete the turn, hence the new term, turn in the road,' I said.

'Makes sense,' she said, pulling out and building up speed.

As Gina drove I explained to her that although the DVSA had dropped the turn in the road manoeuvre from the driving test it was still going to be good practice as it would get her used to manoeuvring the car, feeding the steering wheel through her hands and shifting the selector from drive to reverse while using her all round observations.

A few minutes later we arrived at said quiet side road. I got Gina to pull over where there were no parked cars and then I explained – and demonstrated – the procedure for the turn in the road manoeuvre. She seemed to grasp it, especially the part where I told her if a wheel touched a kerb it would have gone against her on the old test because the overhang of the car could, potentially, hit a pedestrian.

'That makes sense,' she said and, full of enthusiasm, went about the manoeuvre, pulling out and heading towards the kerb on the other side of the road. She stopped, with a few feet to spare, pulled on the handbrake, like I'd showed her, put the car into reverse, started to move after releasing the handbrake, turned the steering wheel in the opposite direction and then, just as she was slowing down the rear wheel butted up against the kerb with a slight bump.

'Damn,' she said, 'I hit the kerb didn't I?

'Yes, but don't worry, it was your first attempt and you only touched it lightly. You just need to stop a few feet before that point. Ok. Let's complete this manoeuvre anyway, then we'll do it again,' I said.

Gina completed the manoeuvre and then I asked her to pull up on the left.

'Ok. Same again. What you did was really good. I like the way you're feeding the steering wheel, quickly, while not moving the car too fast. Ok this time let's avoid hitting the kerb during the reverse part,' I said, encouragingly.

Gina paused for a moment and then, totally out of the blue, she burst into tears – I mean big time. Not just a few 'I can't do this' tears, but full on emotional meltdown tears.

'Oh god,' she cried, her face dropping into the palms of her hands as the tears flowed. I was seriously concerned; Gina was in a terrible state, something wasn't right.

'Gina, it's ok. Trust me, you're doing really well. Honestly, you're the best student I've ever had, you're—'

'It's not the driving,' she said, through choked sobs and tears. 'I'm sorry,' she managed. Of course, I knew it wasn't the driving, nobody could be this upset over a driving lesson, but I had to eliminate it anyway.

'Gina, what is it?' I asked, in a kind, genuine and

gentle tone.

She reached for her handbag on the back seat and took out some tissues, blew her nose, took out another, pulled down the visor and opened the mirror and dabbed her eyes gently, trying not to smudge her make-up any more than it already was.

'Look at me! My eyes look terrible,' she said.

'No, don't be silly. You have beautiful eyes,' I said.

'I meant, my make up,' she said, looking at me and managing a small muted laugh.

'Oh, sorry, I didn't mean—'

'It's my sister, well, her daughter … my husband … everything … oh god, what am I going to do?' she said, going back into an emotional meltdown.

She seemed inconsolable and I wasn't one for platitudes.

'Gina, is there anything I can do?' I said, softly, and I meant it.

I'd never seen such intense pain and anguish on a woman's face before; something was upsetting Gina, deeply, very deeply. I recognised the pain Gina was feeling, I could see all the signs. I'd felt pain like that before myself, but I'd never seen it emotionally expressed by another person before, and not this close up.

'I wish there was, Red, I really do.'

'Would you like me to drive you home, we can reschedule this for another time, if you like,' I said.

'No, I don't want to go back to that empty house. I've been cooped up in there all alone for nearly two years now. I can't bear it anymore; something's got to change. I've got to force a change or I'll die. I can't live like this anymore, it's not a life, I'm here in physical presence only,' she said. Holy shit, I knew exactly what she meant.

Cooped up in there all on my own, she'd said.

'What about your husband, is he away?' I asked, genuinely concerned for Gina and wanting to know that she had a supportive husband or other support network while she's going through whatever it is she's going through. She'd said two years, even a military man would not be away that long.

'He's dead,' she said. 'He died nearly two years ago.'

'I'm so sorry, Gina,' I said.

It must have sounded heart-felt (which it was) because Gina turned to face me, looked into my eyes for a moment before saying, 'Thank you, Red,' in softer tones now, sobbing subsided. 'Do you fancy a coffee?' she asked.

'Erm, yes, sure,' I said, shocked. It was the last thing I expected her to say.

'Ok. I know somewhere not far from here. You'd better drive though,' she said.

In no time at all we arrived at The White Horse Inn and, to my surprise, they did a half decent cappuccino. But I was more concerned about Gina than the taste of the pub's coffee.

'I'm sorry, I don't usually drink,' she said, taking a gulp of brandy. She'd ordered a coffee too, but she obviously needed a shot of something to help with what she was going through. I'd already decided that I would not charge Gina for this lesson, before she said she'd pay me for my time as she realised that I could be giving this lesson time to another pupil.

'Don't be silly. It's ok, we'll just reschedule,' I insisted.

'No, that's not fair. Not only am I taking up your time but you bought the drinks too.' Which I had, I'd insisted.

'Gina, it's no big deal, really,' I said.

I'm not sure what it was - my sympathetic smile, my soft tones - but Gina appreciated it and I got the impression that she needed somebody to talk to right now – about what I still didn't really know, though I was getting the impression it could have something to do with her being a widow – and I was happy to lend her a sympathetic ear. It was becoming apparent that Gina had bottled a lot of things up during the past two years, lots of emotions, and she had to talk to somebody, to get it out. It just happened that it had all come to a head in the middle of her driving lesson with me.

'You're a good man, Red,' she said, smiling through mascara-smudged eyes. 'God, look at me, I look like Robert Smith,' she said, checking her face in her tiny hand mirror.

'I actually quite like Robert Smith, and his looks,' I said, with a slight laugh as I tried to cheer her up. Again, Gina impressed me; she was familiar with The Cure and their frontman, Robert Smith, and his, often, heavily made up panda/gothic eyes.

She laughed and put her mirror back in her handbag and took another sip of brandy.

'So, what's your favourite album,' I said.

'Sorry?' she said, momentarily perplexed.

'The Cure? I'm assuming you know the band enough to get my Robert Smith reference?'

'Oh, right,' she said, laughing. 'Bloodflowers.'

'You're kidding?' I said.

'No, why?'

'That's my favourite album,' I said.

'No kidding.'

'No kidding,' I confirmed.

'Ok, what's your second favourite album?' she said, with a faux suspicious tone.

'I'll go one better, second favourite album, Disintegration, and the third, Pornography,' I said.

'I think they're Robert's top three favourite albums too,' she said, 'can't remember where I read that.'

'I think you're right. Have you seen the Trilogy DVD, live in Berlin?'

'Seen it, I own it on Blu-ray,' she said.

'Ha, that's quite something,' I said. The fact that Gina had said 'Blu-ray' and not 'DVD' hadn't escaped me. She obviously recognised the fact that there's a difference and appreciates the added quality that Blu-ray brings to the table, as I did.

'How are you feeling?' I asked, as she knocked back another gulp of brandy.

'A bit better. Look, I'm really sorry about that. You must have wondered what the hell had got into me,' she said.

'No, not at all. I wasn't sure what it was at first but it soon became apparent that you were in real emotional pain, the deep kind, the kind that tends to stick around and keep you company for a long time,' I said.

'You're very perceptive, Red,' she said, looking at me, intently.

'Gina, I hardly know you and you don't know me from Adam but I'm a good listener and I'm mature enough to know that talking about something, getting it out, can help, even if the listener doesn't say anything, just listens. You know what I mean?'

'I know exactly what you mean. Funny, I kind of feel like I know you, even though I don't,' she said, looking down at her coffee now. After a moment she took a sip and then spoke. 'My husband died just under two years ago, in a road traffic accident. He was cycling when he got hit by a lorry,' she said.

I just looked at her and paid full attention, without interruption, which she seemed to appreciate. I didn't need to give her any platitudes, I wasn't that sort of man, and I think Gina knew, and valued, that.

'It was horrible. After his death I was inconsolable, heartbroken, it felt like a part of me died with him that day. But then things got worse,' she said, looking up at me again. 'My sister helped me a lot, did everything she could to comfort and support me during my time of need, but then, three weeks after my husband died, my sister died too.'

'Oh my god,' I said, at least I think I said it; I think

it must have been a barely audible whisper. I just sat there, shocked, looking at Gina as she continued.

'Another traffic accident, only she was driving. She'd been out for the evening with her husband. She was driving as her husband had had a few drinks. The police told me that there was some sort of spillage on the road. The car had skidded across it and my sister had lost control of the car. It ran off the road and went down a verge and landed upside down in a river. One of the windows had broken while it rolled down the verge and the car filled up with water in seconds. They both drowned.'

I was speechless. I mean, her husband and her sister dying in tragic accidents in the space of a month. That's not bad luck. Bad luck is when you're team get knocked out of the FA Cup semi-final, bad luck is when you step in dog's doings in the park, bad luck is when the carrier bag splits in the car park and your groceries fall out the bottom and the eggs break. No, this was not bad luck. I don't know what the hell you would call what happened to Gina, but 'bad luck' just didn't seem to do it somehow.

'That's not quite the end of it. They left behind their 4-year old daughter,' she said. She looked up at me, right into my eyes. 'That's why I lost it in the car just now. I had a phone call from social services about an hour before you arrived. They want me to consider looking after her, being her legal guardian,' she said.

She continued to look at me, searching, as if wanting me to tell her what to do. This felt a little unorthodox,

I mean, I was her driving instructor and this had come out of nowhere during our third lesson. I didn't know Gina at all yet in an unexplainable way I kind of felt like I did, even though I'd only spent a trifle under three hours in her company, and a few minutes on the phone at the beginning. She obviously trusted me enough and felt that I was the kind of man she could talk to about this.

'She's my niece; I'm the closest family she has. Not long after she was born my sister and her husband had a will written up naming me as the one to take her and look after her should anything ever happen to them. Naturally I said all the usual stuff, "Don't be silly, nothing's going to happen to you," to which she'd said, "Gina, please, take this seriously, I need to know that you'd be happy to have Kaylen if anything ever happens to us". I loved the little girl to bits so I said yes without even consulting my husband, though I knew he'd be fine with it.'

'Why didn't you take her?' I asked.

'Well, for the first year after my husband and sister died I was locked in, couldn't function. I couldn't even look after myself never mind a 4-year old child. She went into the care of the local authorities. I was so torn up. It was like everything just went black inside me. I stopped living, I all but died inside. I was here in physical presence only, you know what I mean?' she said.

'Yes, yes I do,' I said.

'I couldn't even eat. I lost a lot of weight during the

first three months, turned into a stick insect because I was already slim. I looked ill. I was living off protein milk shakes for the first few months because I could hardly even chew food, let alone keep it down. I was messed up, emotionally, physically and mentally. After a year I got a phone call from the social worker. She knew what I'd been going through but a year had passed and she wanted me to reconsider taking Kaylen, so I agreed to a meeting and she came to visit me. Then she came to visit me again, only this time she brought Kaylen with her. She was five by then and had been with some temporary foster parents during that time. I looked into her eyes and saw my sister and broke down on the spot. Everything came flooding back. I couldn't handle it. I told her to leave. It was a horrible scene. The social worker took Kaylen and left. I went to the window and saw Kaylen crying as the social worker fastened up her seatbelt in the car. She looked over at me, red-eyed as the car drove away. I closed the curtains and dropped to the floor and cried until there were no more tears left. I don't know how long I stayed down there on the floor, a day, maybe two. I just lay there, hoping to die so the pain would finally come to an end.

'My god, Gina … there are no words,' I said, so softly.

'Hell of a story, huh,' she said, gulping down the last of her brandy before picking up her coffee. She elaborated on the story and told me more about her husband and her sister. I really did feel sorry for Gina because, like me, she didn't have much in the way of family and, like me, she was existing, at best, not living.

Her husband and sister been taken away from her long before their time. Her father – who Gina had had an amazing and loving relationship with – died of cancer in his late 60s while her mother – who she didn't have such a great relationship with – left her father a long time ago and moved to the USA to be with another man when she was 55. Gina was 23 at the time and, like her father, she was shocked and disgusted by her mother's behaviour. Like me, Gina just had a few cousins scattered here and there, none of whom she was in contact with, in any real capacity anyway – Christmas cards, that sort of thing.

As I drove Gina back to her house she seemed to be feeling a little better, relieved – in fact, she told me so – that she'd got this out. Apparently, I was the first person she'd spoken to about it since it all happened. She'd, for all intents and purposes, been in emotional exile, evicted from her own life and living in a dark and lonely place for the past two years.

'Oh dear, we've gone way over my allocated two-hour slot. Red, please, let me pay you,' she said, unclipping the fastener on her handbag.

'Absolutely not,' I said, putting my hand over her handbag to prevent her reaching into it for her purse.

'But I don't want you to be out of pock—'

'Gina, please,' I said, softly, while giving her an understanding look. I could see in her eyes that Gina realised that offering me money for my time was the right thing to do, but she also realised that it was not the right thing to do, all things considered.

'You're a good man, Red,' she said, putting her hand on top of mine. She meant it too and this was the second time she'd told me that I was a good man in the space of a few hours. 'Are you ok?' she asked. She must have noticed my slight intake (or was it outtake) of breath and my slight physical wince as she placed her hand on mine. She'd only put her hand on mine as a friendly thank-you-for-listening-to-me gesture, but there was something in her touch that sent a bolt of electricity from every peripheral nerve ending in my hand and fingers, straight up my arm and across my chest. Her touch, quite literally, had a physical effect on me. It was a wince, but a good one. The air in my lungs escaped momentarily while my heart did a quick summersault.

'Yeah, yes, I'm good,' I said. My words came out strangely, as if my diaphragm and lungs were not quite as inflated as I thought they were. I had to take a breath. Gina had quite literally taken my breath away with her touch. It had just kind of leaked out of me while her soft warm hand lay over mine momentarily. Of all the senses, touch is by far the most underrated.

'You're sure I can't give you anything? I'm … I'm sorry,' she said, realising it was a silly thing to say.

'It's ok. Besides, if I were to charge for counselling sessions they'd be free.'

'Well, that wouldn't be right. I mean, you're really good, Red. You're an amazing listener. Not many people have that quality. Most people only ever listen with the intent to reply,' she said, and I knew what she meant. 'You'd be able to charge a fortune,' she smiled.

'Well, that's just it.'

'How do you mean?' she said, smiling, but a little puzzled.

'Liszt never used to charge any of his pupils for piano lessons, did you know that?'

'No, no I didn't,' she said. 'Why was that?'

'He said if he charged for lessons he'd be judged on his fees. Liszt figured that his lessons were priceless so he didn't charge anything,' I said, smiling. Gina smiled and got my funny analogy. I paused for a moment, changed my tone to a more serious, but gentle, one, said. 'Gina, I don't usually give people advice, unless they ask for it, but, with your permission I'd like to offer you my thoughts … regarding Kaylen … if that's ok.'

She paused for a moment and looked right into my eyes, 'Yes, I'd like that.'

'Ok, I'm not going to say that you've been looking at that situation in the wrong way, but there is another way of looking at it. I mean, if you could shift your thought process, just momentarily, onto a slightly different axis, just tilt it a little.' I paused for a beat before continuing. 'Seeing your sister in Kaylen's eyes isn't a bad thing, the fact that Kaylen brings back memories of your sister. In fact, it's a good thing, a very good thing. Kaylen *is* your sister; she came from her, your sister made her. She's made up of your sister's DNA, which makes her a part of you too, Gina. Kaylen is as close to your sister, or even your own daughter, as you could possibly get. Everything you miss and loved about your sister you can have again, through Kaylen. You can still see your sister every day, through Kaylen. You can love your sister every day, through Kaylen. You can nurture that little girl and watch her grow up into a fine young woman, just like your sister.'

Gina's eyes welled up and she gently wept, but in a good way. As she turned to look into the middle distance through the windscreen, I realised that not only had she put her hand back on top of mine but her fingers were tentatively stroking mine, almost involuntarily.

'Thank you, Red,' she said, looking up at me. 'So, I guess we should reschedule my driving lesson,' she said, caught half way between the emotional conversation and a more practical one.

'Of course,' I said. 'Same time next week?'

'No, I feel like I'm on a roll with this and if I stop now I fear I'll step back into a place I'm trying to get out of,' she said. I understood this only too well. 'I don't suppose you can do tomorrow, can you?' she asked.

I gently went to slide my hand back from under Gina's to reach for my diary.

'Oh, sorry,' she laughed, letting me have my hand back, not realising she was still holding it.

'I can't tomorrow but I can do the following day?' I said.

'Yes, that's ok. Can you do a two-hour slot?' she asked, hopefully.

'Of course. How's 10:30 in the morning?'

'Perfect.'

'Ok, until then,' I said.

'Until then,' she said.

Gina got out of the car and walked up to her front door. I watched and waited until she was inside. She put her key in the door and pushed it open and stepped across the threshold. She turned, paused, and looked at me for a moment, then she put her hand up, not a goodbye wave, more a 'thank you' wave. I put my hand up too, in acknowledgement. She smiled and slowly closed the door, breaking our eye contact. I sat there for a moment before starting the engine.

Chapter 16

I'd finished my driving lessons for the day and headed back to the depressing solitude that is my home. I'd had my dinner, an M&S sausage and mash ready meal that Ross at the petrol station had recommended, which I'd modified by taking it out of the oven 10 minutes before the 25-minute suggested cooking time so I could mix in some butter and chuck some greeted cheese over the mash in an attempt to make it a bit more palatable. Well, unless it's home made (preferably by me and with a ton of pasture-fed butter mixed in), mash is bland at the best of times so the added butter and melted cheese helps give it some texture and flavour. Up until I took the decision to terminate my own life I'd been making a big effort with food; trying to eat more healthily, but now, well, it really doesn't matter anymore. So I'd reverted back to eating all that crap that isn't really all that good for you: frozen pizzas and ready meals.

I tossed the plastic container in the bin, having eaten my evening meal straight from the pack, leaving just a knife and fork to wash up, which I did so, promptly. I could never understand those people who just throw everything in the sink and leave it for later, or the next day, so all the food could cement itself to the cutlery and various pieces of crockery.

I sat down at my trusty iMac – *oh shit, my iMac, I mustn't forget to put it up for sale too* – and drafted an advert for my cherished non-work car:

Audi TTS MK2 Quattro S Line, immaculate metallic red paintwork, 19-inch alloy wheels, automatic, heated seats, satnav, cruise control, 2 owners from new, low mileage, full service history. 208 bhp version that does 0-60 in just 5.6 seconds. This is my pride and joy and I'm going to be sad to see it go.

That last part was true. When my beloved TTS went I'd be even more depressed than I already am, but it would only be for a short while if I timed the sale right.

The conversation – or rather her talking and me listening – I'd had with Gina yesterday was still on my mind but all that fantasy stuff was not. Even though I was sure she was single (I doubted she'd been on the dating scene since her husband had died so tragically and suddenly), I had my own terminal plans to think about, which would be finalised in a tad over seven weeks. I'd gone over all this Gina stuff in my head. I'd thought about it, how we seemed to just connect, how I just felt so comfortable and 'at one' in her presence, how I felt like I could be vulnerable around her, safe in the knowledge that nothing would ever happen if I, mentally and emotionally, exposed myself. Then there was her incredible knowledge of classical music, and

The Cure. I'd be willing to bet that Gina and I had way more common ground than these little things, but I'd never know as I'd made up my mind not to go there, not to take that chance: correction - risk. I'd lost faith, not only in women, but in the human race in general.

Many years back when I lived in London a friend once told me that if he had to think about something for too long he dumped the thought out of his mind and did not go with it. If he was in a shop and had an item in his hand but he couldn't quite decide if he should buy it or not, he'd give himself about 10 seconds thinking time and if he couldn't make up his mind during that time he'd put it back and forget about it. For him it had to be clear cut and obvious. I pondered, contemplated and considered, and even fantasied some more after Gina and I spoke in The White Horse Inn yesterday. I took a lot longer than my old friend's recommended 10-second 'thinking' time limit and in the end I decided to stick to my guns – my plan. At the end of the day Gina would not change anything. I might fall in love with her and she might even fall in love with me. We might even have great sex but like all good things, they come to an end, eventually, after the so-called 'honeymoon period' comes to an end and the relationship slowly, but surely, turns to one of tedium monotony and once-a-month sex, if that.

Having made my emotional executive decision I felt comfortable with the notion again and went about listing my TTS on Gumtree, along with some pretty good photographs I'd taken of it. Although I didn't have any quality Nikon camera equipment anymore my iPhone took a pretty decent snap, certainly good enough for the purposes of photographing items to list for sale via the online classifieds.

Just as I was in the middle of creating the listing my mobile rang – Gina. I kept all my pupil's names and numbers on my mobile.

'Hello,' I said.

Even though I knew it was Gina, for some reason I didn't feel I could announce that fact during my greeting.

'Hi, Red, it's Gina.'

'Hi, Gina, is everything ok?' I said.

'Yes, everything's good. I was just wondering, is there any chance we can put tomorrow's lesson back 30 minutes to 11 o'clock?' she asked.

'One sec, let me just check what time my next lesson is after you,' I said, reaching for my diary. 'Yes, I can do that. You still want two hours?'

'Yes, two hours. I was thinking about what you said yesterday, about Kaylen. I slept on it and thought about it some more this morning and then I called the social worker. I told her I'd like to speak with her again about becoming Kaylen's legal guardian.'

'That's wonderful, Gina,' I said, sincerely happy for her.

'She was thrilled to hear from me and she's coming to see me in the morning at 10 a.m.'

'Are you sure you won't need more than an hour?'

'Possibly, but she has another appointment at 11:30 that she has to get to. She said she'd have to leave mine by eleven. She said we might need longer but she was so happy that I'd been re-thinking things she wanted to come and see me as soon

as possible.'

'Ok. Well I'll get to your house for eleven but I'll just wait outside. I won't knock on the door in case you run a little late,' I said.

'Super. I'll see you then … oh, and Red?'

'Yes?'

'Thank you.'

'Anytime,' I said.

'No, really, I mean it, thank you. It was because of our conversation and you taking the time to let me pour it all out and your incredible words of wisdom about Kaylen when you dropped me home that got me thinking again. You know, I took my iPad out of the cupboard this morning to look at some of her pictures. I had to charge it up as it had gone flat. Up until we spoke yesterday I hadn't wanted to look at any of her photos. It's always been too painful so I put the iPad away in the cupboard and I guess I put the memories of her into an even darker cupboard in some far corner of my mind. Thing is, when I looked at her pictures this morning, for the first time since the accident I didn't feel sad. Quite the opposite in fact, I felt a little bit of sunshine in my heart. I hadn't felt that for a long time, Red, and it's all thanks to you.'

'That's wonderful, Gina. I'm so pleased for you,' I said, sincerely, 'but please, don't give me too much credit.'

'You're so altruistic, Red. I'll see you tomorrow,' she said.

'See you tomorrow, Gina,' I said, and hung up.

I immediately got back to my Audi advert, which I listed quickly and efficiently. I'd had a lot of practice listing various items on Gumtree and eBay recently.

While I was in the 'selling stuff' mood I wrote up some other descriptions for various other items, but not everything as I'd planned to give some household items away to my friends. It was gone eleven by the time I'd written up the adverts and listed some more items. I'd even worked out a schedule of dates that certain items would have to be listed, some of which would sell quickly and some which might take a little longer (bed and wardrobe for example, which I'd listed immediately as they could take some time). I could enjoy my TV and Hi-Fi equipment until the last minute as I'd planned to give these away to a couple of friends. Most of my other belongings I'd start listing during the next seven days. I would have to work it so everything was sold, paid for and collected, at least three of four days before my suicide date, the details of which still had to be worked out, but I had a couple of ideas that would almost certainly get the job done. I'd hate to end up with severe liver damage, or being paralysed from the waist down, should something go wrong, as often the case with those who attempt suicide – I'd read some real horror stories about failed suicide attempts online. I'd actually Googled 'painless ways to kill yourself' only to find that the first thing to come up in the search results is a 'NEED HELP' Samaritans 24-hour seven days a week telephone helpline, followed by a similar NHS page on suicide, with more helpline numbers, followed by even more helpful 'DON'T DO IT' websites and then just when I thought I'd found a helpful site – a site that listed several 'painless' ways to end your life, covering the top 10 most common ways that people kill themselves: overdose, poisoning, jumping off a building, to name a few – it turned out to be yet another of those 'DON'T DO IT' sites, dressed up as something else. Like lots of sites on the web, I felt like I'd been scammed. Bastards, they're even trying to con me out of suicide by attempting to take away your free will.

This particular article stated that for every one successful suicide there were 33 unsuccessful ones with many people having either short term, or long-term, health implications as a result, and many who jump off buildings and bridges end up crippled for life, in no real physical position to be able to make a second attempt.

Funny thing was, when I re-opened my web browser (Safari on my iMac) Google didn't remember my 'painless ways to kill yourself' search. Usually if I just click in the Google search box it comes up with my most recent searches – furniture for sale, cars for sale, how to photograph deer, for example – in case I want to scroll down and simply select one of my recent searches rather than having to type it in again. My browser, and Google, remembers my recent searches, but not this time. I chuckled to myself when I went to type it in again. When I typed 'painless ways to kill' and left the 'yourself' bit off the end, Google auto-filled the remainder of the sentence with 'a rat', 'a hamster', and 'a fish', but not 'yourself'. I guess rats, hamsters and fish are expendable, though I can think of quite a lot of people who I'd consider to be more expendable than some poor guppy with a severe case of fin rot.

What I had in mind for my own suicide would not fail. It would get the job done, and even if I did survive it would only be brief, *very* brief, to the point that I'd last about as long as a snowflake in Hell, a fire engulfed Hell on the night that Hell was celebrating 'Hell Fire Night' having previously stocked up on chlorine trifluoride, acetone and gasoline especially for the occasion. I was more than confident that my own suicide would be, without a shadow of doubt, a successful one.

Chapter 17

I arrived at Gina's for her driving lesson even earlier than usual on account of making an extended detour via Cambourne to drop off the iron and ironing board I'd advertised, not that I ironed much, if ever. I wasn't a fan of ironing and had only bought the iron for the few formal shirts that I own for those rare occasions that I did get invited to something that required such attire. I certainly didn't intend ironing anything during the time I had left so I figured these two items could go straight away.

The buyer had asked me if I could deliver them to her, not even offering to give me an extra fiver to cover my petrol. What is it with people? Don't they realise that, on average, it costs between 30 and 40p per mile to run a car (and that doesn't include wear and tear either). My little detour to drop the iron and ironing board off (which I was selling for just £20 in total) was going to be 16 miles out of my way. Even in my little Corsa that was going to cut into that £20. I'd agreed, just to get them out of the cupboard and it was two less things I'd have to worry about. When I got to the buyer's house I noticed not one, but two cars parked on the drive outside: a Nissan Qashqai and a BMW 5 series. Although it was a woman I'd spoken to on the phone it was her husband, I assumed, who answered the door.

'Darling, it's the iron man,' he yelled over his shoulder. 'She'll be right with you,' he said, before darting back into a side room to get back to whatever urgent business he was tending to before being so rudely interrupted by the 'iron man'. I looked down at my shirt and trousers to double check that I wasn't wearing a titanium 'Hot rod red' flying suit.

'Oh, thank you,' said a rather snooty woman coming to the front door. 'Darling,' she yelled into the side room, 'do you have £20 to give the man?'

Christ, she knew I was on my way over! Why didn't she have a £20 note at the ready? Her husband came out of said side room and went into another room and returned with the cash, which he handed to her so she could hand it to me. She thanked me, no eye contact – in the tone that one would when thanking a delivery person after signing for a parcel – before promptly shutting the door in my face. I shook my head in utter astonishment as I walked back into my car.

While I waited outside Gina's house I killed some time by scanning the Top Stories on the BBC News app, not that world (or UK in this instance) news was of any interest to me these days. I didn't really know why I bothered with the news. I'm not entirely sure why I *ever* did – most of it's propaganda, smoke, spin, bullshit, lies or advertisements and press releases dressed up as news stories.

I closed the app and opened up the Sky Sports app instead to check the footie fixtures, more out of habit than anything else, that and trying to kill time while I waited for Gina to emerge from her house. Spurs were playing Arsenal this weekend, the good old north London derby, the game of the season that all Spurs fans penned into their diaries. Although this match – along with most other Spurs fixtures – used to be a big deal to me and it was something I used to get excited about, these days football had lost its appeal. I really didn't give a crap anymore. Not just because of my imminent departure from this world, but because football, on the whole, had all become very corporate and money-driven. If I'm honest with myself, the so-called 'beautiful' game died many years ago and I'd been hanging on to the enjoyment of it out of pure desperation, along with the few other hobbies and mildly enjoyable distractions I had from life, which had also turned to shit in recent years.

I didn't even bother reading the team news. Harry Kane might be playing after his recent injury, or he might not be; I really couldn't give a monkey's left bollock anymore. He could be spending Friday night living it up with a bunch of drunken nymphomaniac groupies in a fancy London hotel for all I cared, because I won't be watching it, much as it could be fun watching Harry trying to run around scoring goals on weakened legs after spending the entire night with no sleep, scoring other sorts of goals.

I looked up and sighed. *How did it all come to this?* I

thought. Then I noticed Gina's front door open and a woman, about Gina's age, smiling, came out. Gina saw me over the woman's shoulder as she shook her hand. The woman headed to her car and Gina gave me a quick wave, putting one finger up to indicate she'd be out in a minute. I put my phone on silent and slotted it into its cradle.

As Gina came out and locked her front door I got out of the car and said, 'Would you like to drive off from here?' Not quite sure how her emotional state would be in after her visit from the social worker.

'Yes,' she said, smiling, with a new-found spring in her step.

She got in and I got in the passenger side. She didn't say anything about her social worker visit, just made her adjustments to the driver's seat, steering wheel and mirrors and prepared for her 2-hour lesson.

'Ok, I'm ready,' she said, looking at me, all enthused and smiling, just like she was on her first lesson a couple of weeks back.

'Ok then. As usual, straight ahead unless I direct you otherwise.'

We drove around some quiet roads for about thirty minutes and then I turned on the satnav and typed in the destination for that quiet road where I'd first let her drive. I explained to Gina that the new driving test involved having to follow a satnav for part of the test, without the instructor giving any sort of direction. She was excited at the prospect of following the instructions from the TomTom that was fixed to the dash.

Gina followed the satnav with ease and managed to keep good road positioning while being aware of her surroundings, checking her mirrors and indicating at the right times. When we arrived at the quiet side road I demonstrated how to carry out the parallel park manoeuvre. By the third attempt she'd pretty much nailed it so I asked her if she wanted to try bay parking next.

'Oh yes,' she said, enthusiastically.

I directed Gina to a local car park that I often used to teach pupils how to carry out the bay-parking manoeuvre. It was quiet during the day; only half full so there were plenty of spaces to carry out the manoeuvre.

We switched places so I could demonstrate the correct way to perform the manoeuvre before Gina had a go. I had to intervene to make a few tiny corrections to the steering wheel due to some slight oversteer and then not straightening the car up quickly enough. Without my intervention she would have reversed over the painted white line. I'd picked a spot where there were no cars parked for three spaces so she could try and park in the middle one, with no cars in the bays either side to accidently hit. It took a few attempts before Gina understood the dynamics of the car's movements while reversing and steering into a bay, but after five attempts she was getting the hang of it. After the bay-parking practice we drove around for another fifteen minutes or so before heading back to her house – using the satnav again, for practice. The two-hour lesson had passed quickly and I was relieved that we (or should I say I) were back on instructor/ pupil terms with no emotions or feelings involved, on my part at least.

'Do you have time for a quick coffee?' she asked, as she turned the engine off outside her house.

That was unexpected and a little unwelcome. I was steaming ahead with my plan and I'd been over this in my head a hundred times and had made my decision. The fact that I'd previously fantasied about Gina inviting me in for 'coffee' after one of our lessons didn't help my thought process at all and I was struggling to stop those thoughts from reigniting themselves.

'Erm, well,' I said, not quite sure how to say no. I mean, just two days ago I'd spent three hours listening to her in the pub, being sympathetic and even offering her some pearls of wisdom and now I was about to say no to her coffee invitation and leave her to it. I wanted to be supportive to Gina if she asked me, but I didn't want any of those 'emotions' coming to the surface either. I didn't want, or need, any complications at this precise point of my life.

'I'd like to tell you about my meeting with the social worker, but if you've got another lesson to get to I'll understand,' she said. She had a pleading and hopeful tone in her voice, even slightly anxious and sad at the thought of me not having the time for her to tell me about her meeting. Well, I guess that was my fault for giving up my time for her in the pub, along with my pearls of wisdom. I couldn't just ditch her at this stage of the proceedings and leave her to struggle with whatever emotions she must be struggling with right now regarding her deceased sister's daughter. She obviously wanted to run things by me, for feedback, advice, I expect.

'Ok, sure,' I said, forcing a little smile.

I was anxious about entering Gina's house. It felt like I was crossing some sort of instructor/pupil line. I was aware that instructors are informed that if they engage in any kind of sexual relations with 16 or 17 year olds it would be seen as exploitation and they could be punished, and rightly so. Well, at 42 I would never entertain such a thing anyway, but I wasn't entirely sure of the ethics of starting a relationship with a pupil in your own age group. Anyway, I'd dismissed those thoughts after our last lesson and I was only going to lend her my ears, be it in her house, while she told me about her social worker meeting.

Gina's house wasn't how I expected it to be. It wasn't all feminine with an abundance of unnecessary 'decorative' cushions all over the sofa, pretty ornaments on display, frilly curtains and light pastel abstract paintings in white frames donning the walls. Instead, Gina's living room was, although quite minimalist, tasteful and artsy in a neutral gender-free style – I approved.

'Tea or coffee?' she asked, having told me to make myself comfortable on the sofa in her living room.

'Tea, white, no sugar, not too strong, thank you,' I said.

Gina headed off to the kitchen and returned a few moments later and put my tea on a coffee coaster on the coffee table in front of me; it was the perfect colour too – the tea that is, not the coffee table.

'So,' she said, sitting down with her own cup of tea, 'the meeting went well, better than well, actually. I've met her before a few times, when she came to visit me previously to talk about me becoming Kaylen's legal guardian. We had a good talk; she asked me how I was these days and what I'd been up to. You know, the usual chit-chat. She told me how Kaylen was doing and where she'd been these past two years. After the accident she was put into the care of the local authorities, which I knew about because they'd contacted me first because I was named on my sister's will as her benefactor. She was in a care home for a few months and then they found her a foster family, but that only lasted fourteen months and for the past six months she's been back at the children's care home,' she said.

I took a sip of tea and couldn't help wondering why the little girl's foster placement had ended and was filled with dread at the thought that it could have ended for the same reasons mine had with my first foster placement all those years ago.

'Why didn't her foster family placement work out?' I enquired.

'Oh, it was quite sad. The woman had a stroke and her husband had to look after his wife on a full-time basis. They could no longer manage to look after Kaylen.'

'Oh,' I said, relieved. 'That's good … I mean, good that it wasn't for another reason, you know,' I said.

'Ho— how do you mean?' she said.

'Well, you know, it's not uncommon for children to be abused while in foster placements and care homes. Though probably not quite so much these days,' I said, looking down into my tea.

'Oh, yes… but it was nothing like that,' she said.

I could feel her looking at me so I took a sip of tea and looked back at her over the rim of the cup. She paused briefly and then continued to tell me about the rest of the meeting with the social worker. She went on to tell me that the social worker had been ecstatic that Gina was now considering having Kaylen, permanently. She was going to arrange for Gina to visit the little girl at the children's home, which was a forty-minute drive away.

'You know I could never have children of my own so, in hindsight and with your insightful thoughts on the matter, I think this could be a blessing in disguise … what do you think?' she asked.

I wasn't entirely sure why Gina had asked me what I thought about it, she spoke with the kind of tone you'd speak to with your husband, as a couple, when making an important decision together.

'I think you're right, Gina. I think she is a blessing in disguise and I think she'll be really good for you – you'll be good for each other,' I said.

She smiled, 'Yes, yes, so do I. I have you to thank for this, Red.'

'Don't be silly, I haven't done anything.'

'Yes you have, not just the listening and your advice,

but … I don't know, there's just something about you, Red, that's helped me see things a differently, with a clarity I never had before. Just a month ago I still wasn't in any kind of place to entertain this. If I'm honest I've been in quite a dark place for nearly two years. It's like you've switched a light on for me and I see things with more clarity now.'

'Well, I wouldn't want to take quite so much credit for it, but I'm glad I could help in some small way.'

'It wasn't a *small* way, Red. It was a *big* way. You listened to me while I got it all off my chest. I haven't spoken to anybody about it, haven't been able to get my thoughts out and release my feelings and emotions, but when I spoke to you the other day in the pub you listened, I mean, you *really* listened. That was huge for me, Red, it really helped me, more than you'll ever know. I have tried speaking to a few people about it in the past, but they just keep cutting in with banalities and unwanted advice, they frustrated me, so I gave up and locked it all away, supressed it. As for your insightful advice, that was special. I appreciated it and I thank you for that.'

'You're more than welcome,' I said.

'You know, I'm really looking forward to seeing her again now.

'That's good, Gina, and she'll be in a much better place here with you, a proper family home where she'll be nurtured and loved,' I said, looking down into my tea again while drifting in and out of the terrible memories of my own time with foster families and horrible children's homes.

'Red, are you ok?'

'Oh, yes, I'm fine,' I said, snapping out of it.

'You seemed to be somewhere else there, for a moment,' she said.

I laughed it off, 'No, really, I'm fine,' I said, taking another sip of tea, which was now borderline cold.

Gina studied me for a moment. I felt like she had some sort of special ability to read my thoughts, see right into my soul, read my every emotion like she was reading it straight off the page of a freshly printed large print book.

'So... your next lesson? Would you like to revert back to your usual date and time?' I said, to break the mind-reading I could feel going on.

'Oh, er,' she said, shaking her head as if to find the quadrant of her brain where the driving lesson stuff was stored. 'Can we stick with the morning slot, 10:30, like we'd planned before I had to put it back thirty minutes? I kind of like the morning time, it's quieter,' she said.

'Of course,' I said. 'I left my diary in the car but I'll pencil it in for you.'

'Ok, great,' she said.

'Right then, I'd better be on my way, another lesson,' I said, getting up and checking my watch.

I did have another lesson, that was not an excuse, but I was glad of the lesson, as I would not want to lie to Gina and make up an excuse to leave. Not sure why, but I'd consider that disrespectful to a woman like her, not that I lie often, but I have told a few white lies in the past. Besides, Gina would see right through it anyway, just like she appears to be able to see right into my soul.

Chapter 18

I arrived at Shannon's house for my weekly therapy session having no idea what we were going to discuss this week, what she was going to analyse or how deep she was going to dig. We'd covered my family's premature, tragic, and horrific deaths along with my grim childhood, which was riddled with misery and abuse. She'd touched on my adult life too, which wasn't much better, divorcing my unfaithful wife, the knife incident that put paid to my concert pianist career and then the multitude of women I'd been with during the past ten years. It would appear that women are lying, cheating, money-grabbing, conniving, devious and manipulating bitches – at least the ones I pick – or do they pick me? Actually, in hindsight, most of the women in my life – post divorce – had actually sought me out, at least the evil praying mantises that had homed in on me and taken advantage of my kind, generous and loving nature, only to use me for a while before stinging me. They weren't all bad, just the majority. Not all were praying mantises, you understand, I've had my fair share of poisonous spiders too, whose web I'd accidentally landed in, sticking around long enough for them to tangle me in a web of emotional confusion before chewing me up and spitting me back out onto the dating scene again. As for the good ones, they've been so few and far between I can barely even recall them, perhaps two.

'So, how's your week been,' asked Shannon, as I settled on the couch.

'Good,' I said, reaching forward and pouring a glass of water from the freshly filled jug.

'Well, I say *good*. What I mean is, good and bad.'

'Ok. Well how about we start with the good,' she said.

Shannon seemed overly cheerful and I suspected she'd had a good day, thus far, and wanted to try and carry on that 'good day' feeling a little longer. I figured she had about ten minutes, tops, before I brought her feel good factor crashing down.

'Erm, well, I don't really think it was that much of a big deal really.'

'Why don't you tell me anyway?'

'It was just something I did for one of my pupils. Well, I didn't really do anything, I just listened to her, I guess. She had something of an emotional meltdown followed by an equally emotional dilemma. I lent her my ears while she got it off her chest, that's all,' I said. I took a swig of water then settled back into the comfy sofa, thinking that would be the end of that conversation and Shannon would move on to other things; she didn't.

'So what happened?'

I went on to tell Shannon the story about Gina and the whole terrible ordeal regarding the death of her husband, sister and sister's husband in the space of just four weeks and her emotional dilemma regarding Kaylen, who was currently residing in a children's home but could be getting out soon to go and live with Gina on a full time basis. How Gina and I spent a few hours in a pub instead of having a driving lesson, where I listened to her and offered her my thoughts on her situation when I dropped her back home.

'Getting out? You make it sound like Kaylen's in prison,' she said.

'Well, let's face it, children's homes are pretty fucking horrible places to be at the best of times, aren't they?' I stated.

Shannon detected my annoyance and knowing my history she decided to tread carefully.

'They certainly can be,' she said. 'You know, Red, I think what you did was quite something. It sounds like she just needed to talk, get it off her chest, and you were her outlet and, from the sounds of it, you did a miraculous job … I couldn't have done it better myself,' she said. I looked at her, was she throwing me a platitude?

'I mean it, Red. You were in the right place at the right time and now, thanks to you, that woman's life looks like it's about to make a huge turn, for the better,' she said.

'So how long have you been giving Gina driving lessons?'

'Not long, four or five weeks now.'

'Good,' she said, smiling. *Don't even go there, Shannon,*

I thought. She maintained eye contact for a moment, still smiling, then she reached for her pad and pen and scribbled a few notes down, though I got the impression she just wanted to let the thought linger in my mind a moment longer – what thought? Damn, she'd planted it there again. The last thing I wanted was for my therapist to start playing the psychological matchmaker without having to actually say or do anything.

'So, you wanna hear my bad news for the week?' I said, moving swiftly away from the subject of Gina.

'Sure,' she said, looking up from her pad with a satisfied look on her face. Shannon knew that, in the past at least, I'd been desperate for a woman, the right sort of woman, the stuff that dreams are made of, but that I'd totally and unreservedly given up on that idea quite some time ago, hence she wasn't about to start forcing any such issue right now. Being a smart and professional woman, Shannon knew just what to say, how to say it and when to cut the subject off.

'I've fallen out with Shari,' I said.

'Shari?'

'My friend, Mathieu, in London, his girlfriend.'

'Mathieu that you were in a band with in your early 20s?'

'The very one.'

'Oh, you're close to them, though,' she stated. I'd gone into a bit of detail about Mathieu when I'd told Shannon about leaving my ex-wife and moving into his spare room; told her what good friends Mathieu and Shari had been and that I still saw them quite a lot, even though it was a 130-mile round trip to their house in London – and vice-versa. 'So what happened?'

'Shari was doing a sponsored parachute jump for some charity or another. She'd phoned me up to ask if she could count on my sponsoring her. I said no and she was dumbfounded and later, according to Mathieu, very upset. I explained my reasons but she wasn't having it, said that I should make an exception because she was a close friend.'

'So what were your reasons for saying no?' she asked, more than curious as to why somebody would refuse to sponsor a *good* friend who was doing something for *charity*.

'I don't believe in charities,' I said.

'Don't believe in them?' she said.

'Well, it's not that I don't believe in them. I just don't like them or anything that they all stand for. Most charities are nothing more than legalised theft, a big con, a façade, a front for making a small board of directors very affluent, without doing a damn thing for the very people they're supposed to be collecting money for in the first place.'

'How do you mean?'

'Come on, Shannon, you're an intelligent woman. Once upon a time, about fifty years ago, a guaranteed percentage of the money charities collected would go directly to the cause, leaving just enough money for the charity to carry out administrative duties and a few other expenses. Then, as the years rolled along, that amount became less and less, to the point that it was probably so little it was hardly even worth writing the cheque. I think most charities are corrupt these days, just like everything else in this shitty world.'

'You think?'

'I know.'

'How do you know this, Red?' she asked, genuinely, not challengingly.

'I knew somebody who worked for a spinal injuries charity back when I was married. She said they'd often get phone calls from some poor bugger who'd been in a car accident, spent a year in physio undergoing rehabilitation, and in desperate need of a wheelchair or mobility scooter and she always had to tell them the same thing, that they had no money left that year and that she was sorry. She told me how much that charity took in each year and the figures were staggering, Shannon. After they'd paid the rent, office staff and admin there was a small fortune left over.'

'So what happened to that money if they weren't giving to people who needed it?'

'A small, but very fat and greedy, board of directors, that's what. They all drove brand new Mercedes, Jags and other big fancy cars that only did fifteen miles to the gallon – company cars of course. And pretty much every month they had meetings, but they didn't use one of the empty rooms in their offices for these meeting. Oh no, they hired a fancy hotel in the country, the kind of place that had a spa, several masseuses, a gym, a swimming pool. You know, the kind of place where you get a dollop of caviar on the side of whatever fancy finger food they're serving up. Anyway, these four directors, one of whom was a woman by the way, would go away for these luxury "meetings" on Friday evening and stay until Sunday afternoon. My friend told me that the bills for these extravagant weekend away meetings would come in at around £10,000, about £2,500 each, and they were doing this pretty much every month. Oh, expensive luxury cars and expensive weekends away were just the beginning for these fat cats. They made sure that if it did look like there was going to be any money left come the end of the year, they'd would find something to spend it on.'

'That's disgusting,' said Shannon.

'No Shannon, it's perfectly normal. Like I've said before, people are inherently evil and if they can take more and get away with more they generally will. Don't even get me going on bloody so-called charity shops and Sue Ryder. Fact is, most charities operate in the same way, take, take, take, and little to no giving back.'

'So what did your friend … Shari?'

'Yes.'

'What did she say when you explained all this to her?'

'She said the charity she was doing her parachute jump for were not like that, they were a good charity. I said she was wet behind the ears and didn't have the faintest idea how the *real* world worked. I told her that underneath the pink sugar-coated world that she lived in there was another world, the *real* world.'

'How did she take that?'

'She didn't, she called me an arsehole and slammed

the phone down on me.'

'When was this?'

'Oh, I don't know. Three or four days ago now.'

'What about Mathieu? Have you spoken to him since?'

'Nope. I think he has to be seen to be siding with his girlfriend. Anyway, I'll never give money to a charity again, friend or no. There's always some bastard trying to take what little money you've got for some phony cause. As for Shari, well, fuck it, none of this will matter soon … it's just another sad reminder,' I said, taking another gulp of water.

'You said you'd never give money to a charity *again*, suggesting that you have in the past,' she said, while giving me a searching look.

I looked up at her over the rim of my glass of water and said nothing. I wasn't always like this, such a misery guts, such a moaner, complainer, a pessimist living in my own cynical world where I hated pretty much everything and everybody. A world that I hated so much I sometimes wished it would just implode in on itself and become just another dead planet floating around in a never-ending universe. I can't remember the exact moment I crossed over from being a relatively content guy to what I am now. That's what I was hoping Shannon might be able to figure out but thus far she hasn't been able to shed any light on it or blast away the end of that long dark tunnel that I've been trapped in for years or, if she had, she wasn't saying anything.

'Red, I'd like to talk a bit more about your marriage, if that's ok?' she said, moving on, for now at least.

'Of course,' I said.

Shannon proceeded to delve into my marriage; how old we were when we met, how we met, how long we'd been together when we got married and so on and so forth. She asked the usual questions about what kind of relationship we had, mentally, emotionally, sexually and how we spent our free time together. She said that my ex-wife sounded very domineering; she wasn't wrong there. She also suggested that the relationship probably wasn't quite right for me, that it was a little one-sided, and that I wasn't getting out of it what I really needed, on many levels.

She then got back to the numerous other failed relationships that I'd had since I divorced Melanie. Shannon wanted to analyse them, the pattern and the reasons that I'd ended them all after such a short space of time. She took lots of notes and asked me lots of questions, some of which I didn't feel were relevant, but I'm sure there was a methodology behind Shannon asking them.

'Ok, Red, we're out of time,' she said, glancing up at the clock on the wall.

That was it. I didn't feel any different, or better, after this session than I did after the first one five weeks ago. Shannon, as far as I could tell, was still no nearer to figuring out how I'd arrived where I was at this point in my life, how I'd ended up seeing the world the way that I did, with such revulsion, loathing and with such a cynical view. She didn't have any psychological or emotional insights or any objective conclusions about my life and how it had spiralled down into such unhealthy depths of depression and solitude; or if she did, she wasn't giving anything away. She'd hinted that I'd been on a path of self-destruction for quite some time now and, based on the knowledgebase that she'd built up of me so far, she was not surprised that I was the only passenger on my own private out-of-control train, with no driver, hurtling directly towards the last 'terminal' station, where I would disembark – permanently.

Chapter 19

Gina's fifth driving lesson went well and she was coming along swimmingly. In fact, considering she wasn't doing any practice in-between lessons she was doing amazingly well and she was retaining every bit of information that I was imparting during our 2-hour lessons. She was also cracking on with her theory practice, studying the Highway Code and practicing the theory test DVD I'd loaned her. It was with the latter that she'd asked for my help, as she was having an issue with the exact point that she should be clicking the mouse during the hazard perception part of the test on the DVD. She'd asked, if she paid me extra, if I could spend an additional 30 minutes, after our scheduled two-hour driving lesson, going over things on the DVD on her computer.

'Ok. This is one of the ones I'm struggling with,' she said, as the video example started to play on her computer screen. 'Right. This white car pulling out from the right is only a *potential* hazard, so I don't click for this one, right?'

'That's right,' I said.

'And this white van coming up to the main road from this side street,' she said, pointing, 'that's also just a potential hazard, so I don't click on that one either, right?'

'Yup,' I agreed again.

'Ok. This is the one I struggle with. That light blue car speeding up to the main road from this side street,' she said, pointing, 'I can see that it's a developing hazard because it shoots over the stop lines but I'm not sure at which point I'm supposed to click,' she said.

'Ok. Let's run the clip again and you click when you think you should and I'll tell you if you're too early or too late,' I said.

Gina ran the clip, clicked, but was too late.

'Ok. What they expect you to do is click when you become aware that there's a developing hazard. What you're doing is clicking once the hazard has occurred; you have to click earlier to show that you've seen it, but not too soon. You have to wait until it becomes a developing hazard. Make sense?'

'I think so. I just figured I had to click to acknowledge it once it had happened, to show that I'd seen it. Let me try it again,' she said, playing the clip through again. This time she clicked a little earlier, at the right time.

'Now,' she said, as she clicked.

'Perfect,' I said.

'And that white van on the left… I don't click for that, right?'

'That's right. It's stationary, something you have to be aware of, but no need to click for it,' I said.

'Great. I think I'll start getting higher marks now that I know at what point I should be clicking. I think I was clicking when it was already at the danger point, rather than during the developing point; thanks for clearing that one up,' she said.

I glanced at my watch; we were about 25 minutes into Gina's allocated 30-minute spot.

'Can I ask you something?' she said.

'Sure.'

'Well, don't take this the wrong way, but you seem like an intelligent guy so how did you end up doing this? Not that there's anything wrong with being a driving instructor, but you seem to have a brain that's, how should I say, beyond this. So what did you do before this? I mean, I find it hard to believe you've always been a driving instructor,' she said.

'What makes you so sure I haven't always done this?' I said.

'Ha, no way! I'd bet all my earthly possessions on it. So, come on, what did you do before? Something creative, I bet.'

'Ok. You're right. I did a couple of things before this, and yes, all creative. I used to be a concert pianist immediately before I trained to be a driving instructor.'

'I knew it!' she said, excited. 'I thought you seemed knowledgeable on the subject the other week when you were playing the Liszt piano sonata in your car.'

'Yes, but there are many classical music lovers who can't play a note, who just love listening to it,' I said.

'This is true, but there was something about the way you described that sonata, with such passion, like you knew it intimately. Can you play it?'

'I could… not anymore,' I said.

'I bet you were pretty damn good.'

'I was. I got signed up by Decca records and made a bunch of CD recordings.'

'What was your speciality? Wait let me guess ... not the romantic period ... though I bet you play Liszt and Chopin really well. I'll go with the classical period. Beethoven – I remember you telling me you liked Beethoven,' she said, smiling.

'Yeah, you're right,' I laughed. 'I made recordings of works by Bach, Beethoven and Liszt, but Beethoven was always my favourite composer. A lot of pianists say Bach was the main man and, up to a point, I agree, but for me Beethoven was the one. He's a *man's* composer. You could take any single work by Beethoven, or any single movement from any one of his works, and that alone would prove his genius. Not only that but you could take any 8-bar section from any of Beethoven's works and those eight bars alone would be more complex, more technical and with more emotional depth than the entire Beatle's back catalogue,' I said.

'I think you're right. I love the Egmont Overture, it's so quintessentially Beethoven.'

'Wow, you know that piece?'

'Yes, I love classical music, but only from the baroque, classical and romantic eras. I don't do early music and I certainly don't do contemporary. As for Schoenberg and his 12-tone row, he can keep it.' We both laughed.

'I had no idea, Gina,' I said, looking at her, impressed with her knowledge of classical music.

'So what happened, Red? You speak in the past tense about your concert pianist days. You don't do recordings anymore, nor do you give concerts. I figured that bit out already. So how did you get from that to this?'

'Oh, it's a long story; the abridged version is that I severed a tendon in my third finger on my left hand. The surgeon stitched it back up the best he could but I don't have full movement or control in that finger anymore,' I said, holding my left hand up and pointing out the scar on my middle finger.'

Gina took hold of my hand and turned it slightly while moving the neighbouring finger out of the way to get a better look at the little scar. She was gentle and her warm hand felt good as she delicately turned my hand in hers as she examined my hand and finger. That bolt of lightning fired off inside me again, triggered by her touch. The nerves in my fingertips (well, not the injured third finger) and hand shot straight up my arm and enveloped my chest with a beautiful warm sensation, one that I'd be happy to sustain for as long as possible. When Gina touched me, even though in this instance it was not sensual – though it felt like it was and something deep in my mind told me that perhaps she did too – I felt like I was home, home after being away, in exile, for a very long time, like an astronaut who'd spent five years getting to his destination, spending five years there, then another five years getting back home. As her fingers touched mine it felt like a warm evening July sun sending heat into my chest – only from the inside out.

'That's so tragic,' she said, in the softest, caring, compassionate, loving tone. I could have sworn I saw her eyes well up a little.

'Well, shit happens,' I said, thinking about my wife, her sleeping around, my leaving that night and smoking too much marijuana at Mathieu's house and stabbing myself in the fucking hand with his cheese knife. Although I'd never thought of it, Mathieu and Shari had both told me that my wife was indirectly responsible for my concert pianist career coming to an end, that she'd had a hand in it. Gina sensed my sadness, and anger, and that there was more to this story than the abridged version I'd just given her.

'I also worked as an investigative photojournalist too,' I said, changing the subject to something a little less painful.

'Oh?' she said, keen to hear about it, and gently releasing my left hand.

'Yeah, before I got signed up with Decca records. It was quite a long time ago. In fact, I wanted to be a professional photographer from quite an early age. I was 16 when I got my first professional SLR with a zoom lens. I also got into medium and large format cameras too but I ended up setting on the 35mm format as it allowed me to do the sort of photography that I had a passion for. I was using a Nikon F4 back then. It was an amazing camera, a real workhorse. I had a whole range of prime and zoom lenses with it. I loved traveling around, researching, getting stories and taking great photographs to accompany them,' I said.

'What kind of stuff did you shoot?' she asked.

'Various things, stories for newspapers and magazines, anything people commissioned me to do,' I said.

'You had stuff published?'

'Yeah, loads of times. Stories, news pieces and articles that I'd researched and investigated for various newspapers and magazines,' I said.

'Wow! So you were a professional,' she stated.

'Yes, for a while at least.'

'I'd love to see some of your work, if you don't mind?' she asked.

'Yeah, sure,' I said.

'Will you bring something for me to see next week?' she asked, genuinely interested.

'Ok. I'll bring my laptop. I've got a bunch of photos on it that you can look at.'

'So how did you end up a driving instructor?' she smiled, still wanting to know.

'Oh, well, it wasn't my idea. I found myself at a loose end and I had a friend who used to train driving instructors. He was like a regular driving instructor, only he taught driving instructors. He offered to teach me for nothing, so I figured what the hell? The rest, as they say, is history,' I smiled. 'What about you, what do you do?' I was a little curious as I got the impression that Gina was at home a lot of the time.

'I haven't done anything for the past two years. Well, I haven't been in a good place.'

'I can understand that,' I said.

'I used to be a magazine editor,' she said.

'Wow! One that I might have heard of?'

'Maybe. I was the section editor for BBC Wildlife magazine,' she said.

'Wow! I'm impressed. I never had anything published in that magazine, but I didn't do much wildlife photography,' I said. 'Did you enjoy it?'

'Yes, yes I did. I found it rewarding, having a hand in the creative side of things and then seeing it come to fruition every month on the shelves of WHSmith.'

'Would you like to get back to that, at some point?' I asked.

'Maybe. I don't know... we'll see. I'm in the fortunate position that I don't have to work. I didn't tell you the whole story behind my husband's death. I told you that he was cycling and got hit by a lorry, but it was a delivery lorry for a big well-known supermarket chain ... I can't even say the name out loud, I can't even shop there anymore, it's too painful.' She paused to compose herself. 'Anyway, turned out that the lorry driver was drunk and over the limit and on top of that he'd been banned for drink-driving and was actually on his ban at the time he hit my husband so he shouldn't have even been behind the wheel in the first place. His employer's didn't bother to check his driving licence when they hired him. I got quite a large payout from them,' she said.

It was obvious that Gina was still hurting. Who wouldn't be after something like that? I guess you never truly get over something like that – you never 'move on' you simply 'move forward' best you can, learn to adapt. I know I didn't, even though I kid myself that I locked away those memories into a vault in some dark corner of my mind before throwing away the key. Gina would never move on from what had happened to her but, in time, she'd learn to move forward and evolve somehow. At least, I hoped she would … that she'd learn to *live* again – not like me.

Chapter 20

My doorbell rang. I suspected it was the chap who'd called me last night about my Audi.

'Red?' said the man as I opened my front door.

'Justin?'

'Yes,' he said.

'The car's in the garage around the corner,' I said, grabbing the keys and locking my front door behind me.

'Am I ok parked there?' he said, pointing to a massive gleaming silver brand new Audi A8 on the other side of the road.

'Oh, yeah, it's fine there,' I said, envious.

'That's the family car, but I've always wanted a TTS, just for a bit of fun at the weekends,' he said. He was older than me; 50 would be my guess. Maybe he was going through some sort of midlife crisis, but then I always thought a Porsche Boxter S or maybe even a Harley Davidson motorcycle were the traditional male mid-life crisis weapons of choice.

As we walked around the corner to my garage I glanced over my shoulder and checked the registration plate on his A8. As I suspected, it was brand new. Judging by how showroom pristine it looked it probably hadn't even covered 3000 miles yet. How the hell do people afford cars like that? I mean a brand new A8 has a starting price of about £68,000, and that's with no options. Justin was wearing white Dunlop squash trainers, jeans (not even a brand from what I could see, there certainly wasn't a little red tab stitched to the edge of the back right-hand pocket) and an ill-fitting blue t-shirt that had seen better days. He was quite well spoken, admittedly, but his hair resembled what I could only imagine Donald Trump's to look like after a group of angry feminists had tried to separate his head from his torso. What the hell did this guy do for a living to be able to afford a brand new A8? Let alone come and give me £9,850 (at least that's what I'd advertised it for, or nearest offer) for my car, just so he could have a bit of fun driving it at the weekend.

'Ok. Here she is,' I said, lifting the garage door up.

'Oh, wow, it looks great!' said Justin.

'Let me bring it out for you, so you can look over it properly,' I said, jumping in and firing up the engine, the bass note of which sounded incredible in the enclosed acoustics of my tiny rented garage. *Oh yes, that reminds me, cancel garage rental,* I thought.

I could see Justin smiling from ear to ear as I drove the car out into the daylight. He walked around it and had a good look, getting down on his haunches to look at the condition of the inner wheel arches and under the sills. He wouldn't find any rust, not even a speck. I knew for a fact there was no hint of rust anywhere. Although the car was a few years old now, it was as close to showroom condition as he would find. I'd loved and cherished this car and, as soon as I'd found any tiny little issue, I'd got it sorted, professionally, and usually at some expense. I also carried out most of the preventative maintenance myself: oil, oil filter, air filter, pollen filter, spark plugs, coil packs, brake discs and pads. I was quite the enthusiastic DIY car mechanic, and I was pretty good at it – probably much better than a lot of working mechanics. My DIY car maintenance endeavours had started within a year of my passing my driving test. Back then I'd buy cheap cars, sometimes from auction, and they quite often had problems. I used to take my cars to various mechanics with varying degrees of success but, in the end, I got sick and tired of paying them to screw up my car and not fix it properly I decided I might as well screw it up myself and not pay for it. I remember buying my first Haynes car maintenance manual for a used Saab that I owned at the time and I successfully fixed several things on it, rather well. Turned out that I was a dab hand at it – I never looked back. These days I wouldn't trust any car mechanic as I would not be confident that they would be using the correct grade of oil, or a quality one at that, or decent plugs, coil packs, filters and the like. I'm sure there are many reputable car mechanics out there, but they are probably outnumbered by those who choose to fit the cheapest parts and lubricants possible.

'Can you pop the bonnet?' he asked. He continued to examine the engine before asking me if he could take it for a test drive. I said yes, but I went along with him. Not that I thought he'd steal my car. After all, his £70,000 A8 was parked outside my house. I just didn't want him to mistreat my car by thrashing the engine too hard, especially before it had reached the optimum engine temperature (90 degrees Celsius) or driving over speed humps too fast, knocking the wheel alignment out or damaging a CV joint in the meantime.

Justin didn't rag it during the test drive. In fact, he treated the car with respect. He did put his foot down a little when we got out onto a nice quiet stretch of straight B-road, but no more (in fact, considerably less) than I would when having fun in it. He loved it, commenting on how quick it was compared to his A8.

'Well, I won't have any problem overtaking other cars in this bad boy,' he said, still smiling ear to ear.

We headed back and he declared that he loved the car and wanted to buy it. He haggled, as expected, a little, but I only let him get away with knocking £350 off my £9,850 asking price. If he'd pulled up in a 12-year old Ford Focus (with rusty sills and wheel arches) I would have let him knock me down to nine grand, but he hadn't, so I didn't. We did the paperwork and he asked if he could leave it in my garage and pop back later that evening when he could get his friend to drive him over.

He did a bank transfer, which I confirmed on my banking app on my iPhone, and he took the paperwork, but left the keys, fearing he might forget them later. Besides, I'd have to unlock the garage to let him get the car out anyway.

I watched as Justin got into his massive Audi A8 and drove away. It appeared that pretty much everybody on the road had a better car than me. I know I had – or had – an Audi TTS, but it was far from new and only worth £10,000, it was only £24,000 when I bought it as an ex-dealer demonstrator. These days, everywhere I looked people were driving brand new top marques cars: Audi, BMW, Mercedes, Jag, not to mention those big 4x4 things from the likes of Range Rover. I'd grown tired of seeing all these £80,000 cars in front of, behind, and to the sides of me, everywhere I drove. I know that 99 per cent of all brand new cars were financed these days, but still, some of them had to cost around £1,500 per month for the repayments, and that's over five years. Christ knows what their mortgages must be if they can afford huge payments on a financed car; what the hell did some of these people do for a living?

Personally, even if I did earn, or have, that sort of money, there'd be no way on earth I'd buy a brand new car. Spending £85,000 on a brand new BMW 7 series, only to discover that it's only worth £60,000 a few short months later, and for it to be worth about half its new price a year after that, no thanks. Besides, I believe that lots of new cars have built in obsolescence these days. Call me a conspiracy theorist, but I'm convinced that many car makers want their cars to break down – especially the top marques – so they can sting you time and again on extortionate hourly labour costs and overpriced parts once the 3-year warrantee has expired; kind of like how inkjet printer manufacturers sell you their printers for peanuts then sting you for a silly little overpriced plastic cube with a few teaspoons of ink in them. It's ink, for fuck's sake, not Horseshoe Crab Blood.

Not much is going to go wrong with these big expensive fancy cars during the manufacturers initial 3-year warranty period, but it's when the company who originally bought these cars replace them every three years and the poor second owner takes it on that all those dashboard warning lights start to light up like the Blackpool illuminations and all hell brakes lose as, sensors and lord knows what else start to go wrong and in the case of some top marques cars it will usually be expensive, very expensive. I find it ironic how Range Rover are one of the most unreliable car makers on the planet yet, compared to much more reliable cars such as Ford and Vauxhall, they cost way more (three times more in some instances) to buy in the first place. But Ford and Vauxhall don't have snobby 'star fucker' badges on the front so who, with more money than sense, is going to buy one of those?

Anyway, my TTS was sold and later that evening it would be gone and, like my ex-wife, out of my life, though unlike my ex-wife my TTS proved to be incredibly reliable. So, that was it, now that my beloved TTS was sold there was definitely no turning back – it was conclusive, I'd passed the point of no return. I only had five weeks left to continue getting my affairs in order, just five weeks to put up with driving around in my tiny little Corsa, which I would also be advertising for sale imminently.

I arrived at Shannon's for my seventh therapy session. Last week was pretty much like the week before, and the week before that. I was starting to wonder why I was paying good money for these sessions when I could be saving it up in preparation for giving it away to some of my needy friends, who would appreciate it a lot more than Shannon, who, by comparison, was doing much better than my small handful of friends were. Still, I only had five more sessions to go and I did promise myself that I'd give Shannon every chance to help me find the root cause/causes of my current path of self-destruction, mental state and the cynical – resentful and even hateful – way in which I viewed the world and all those in it.

'It doesn't matter, Shannon. None of it matters. It's shit. Everything's fucking shit. The world's a disgusting place and so are most of the people in it. Humanity is at rock bottom and I can't deal with it anymore. There's nothing good in this world and I can't even remember when anything was ever any good, seems like a distant memory from many moons ago. To be honest, I think you'd have to go back to the days before electricity and technology, before I was even born. Those fuckers, Tesla and Edison, have got a lot to answer for. The sooner I'm out of it the better,' I said, voice raised now as she was starting to piss me off with her analytical, and futile, line of questioning. I can understand those people who say you might as well just talk to a friend down the pub, for all the bloody good therapists do.

My childhood this, my childhood that, my childhood the other, my dysfunctional teenage years, my one-way-love marriage, my injury that led to my concert pianist days coming to an abrupt end. She just kept banging on about all this historical shit and I was in no mood to talk about any of it as it all added up to one massive tangled ball of emotional twine with a couple of thick layers of PTSD to hold it all together. I'd waved goodbye to my beloved Audi TTS and, right now, I was not in the mood for Shannon's fucking analogies. Ok, I admit it, I was upset that I'd parted company with my TTS *and* I was hungry. Oh yeah, I turn into a real bitch when I'm hungry.

'What about all the amazing things we've built and created, technology, the arts, the satellites sent we've sent into space, Wordsworth, Mozart, da Vinci?'

'Dust, inconsequential specks of dust, in the grand scheme of things. Good dust maybe, but it's just a way of escaping what's really pushing us along deep down inside.'

'What would that be, Red?'

'I don't know. Like everybody else in the so-called civilised western world I forgot a long time ago. We make out that we're so damn superior, like we're so much better than any other species in the animal kingdom, but we aren't. If you want to get all fundamental about it we're all eating a giant shit sandwich and in the grand scheme of things we're no more valid, important, or evolved than family of dung beetles who spend their days moving little balls of shit from one point to another. We're all sailing on the same boat here, heading out to wherever it is we're all going, which is nowhere, and that's just the way it is; at least that's how I see it. Thing is, people just can't accept that. Idiots! You know why they believe in God, aliens, haunted houses, tunnels of light, the fucking Loch Ness monster?'

'Why?' she said.

'Because they want to believe that there's more to life than the shit they got stuck with, that there's something else after death, but the cold truth is, there isn't. These fools have to realise that all they have to look forward to after death is an eternal sleep with no dreams. Christ, we didn't exist before we were born so why is it so fucking hard for people to get it into their heads that we won't exist after we die?'

'When you say we're heading nowhere, you're talking about death presumably?'

'Of course.'

'Well, I know you're an atheist, Red, and I remember you saying something along the lines of an eternal sleep with no dreams after you die previously.'

'That's right.'

'You don't believe there's anything after death?'

'Of course not. We're just like the dinosaurs, the animals in Africa – the hunters and the hunted – the nicely packed fillet steaks we buy in the supermarkets. Humans are no different from any other animal species. We're nothing more than pieces of meat and one day, whether you like it or not, we'll all be dead meat. The only difference is they won't slice us up and put us into nice little plastic packets with little labels on them saying "Scottish Prime Human Fillet Steak". Or who knows, maybe they will at some point in the future, or maybe they'll do something else with our remains after we die, like in that movie, Solent Green,' I said, half joking.

'The idea of nothingness after we die is just too hard for most people to comprehend so they invent some imaginary guy in the sky for the same reasons we invented Santa Clause... for comfort. The only difference is that Santa Clause is for children and God and Jesus are for adults. Religion is nothing more than gullibility on a mass scale, a result of grooming children from a young age with all that religious mumbo jumbo. Fucking vicars and priests, sanctimonious prigs, the lot of them, child molesting prigs at that. Standing on their pulpits on a Sunday morning spouting lies while the gullible great unwashed put their hard-earned cash in the collection bowl, cash they can't afford. Honestly, Shannon, I can't understand how any rational or intelligent human being could buy into all that crap, especially when most religions are just so damn toxic and destructive – they do more harm than good. And it's not just religion that attracts the gullible great unwashed either; every science has its corresponding pseudoscience, psychology has parapsychology, medicine has acupuncture and homeopathy, while astronomy has astrology, and each and every one of them has hordes of fanatics who attach themselves to all this shit.'

'Red, you seem quite passionate today. Angry even. Has something happened?' she asked.

'I sold my car,' I said, 'and I'm hungry, I haven't eaten yet.'

'You sold your car?' she asked, with a tone that suggested that couldn't possibly be the reason for my current volatile state.

'Well, I had two. A Corsa that I use for my driving lessons and a *really* nice Audi TTS, which I just sold. He's already paid me and he's coming back to pick it up later this evening,' I said.

'This is all part of your preparations, selling all your earthly possessions?'

'Yeah,' I said. Shannon checked her notes; probably to see how many sessions – and time – we still had before…

Then, out of the blue, she said, 'Are you still giving Gina driving lessons?'

'Why bring her up all of a sudden?' I said.

'Well, I think there's something there worth visiting,' she said.

'There's nothing there worth visiting, so drop it,' I said, sternly.

'Red, the way you spoke about Gina during our previous session—'

'Yes, Shannon, like you said, "previous" session. Gina's not relevant anymore, nothing's relevant anymore, so please, just drop all this Gina shit.'

Shannon did drop it, she wrote something on her pad. I didn't know if she was doodling to buy time while she tried to figure out what direction she should go, or if she was writing something of great significance: *Red gets angry and agitated when I mention Gina*, perhaps.

The fact is I was trying my level best to keep up some sort of pretence during my remaining weeks on this godforsaken planet and giving driving lessons, including Gina's, was doing nothing more than help pass the time. Leading up to my ultimate decision to end it all I'd done a little research and read a couple of books on the subject of suicide. More often than not neighbours and friends typically say something along the lines of, 'I was shocked. I mean, he seemed perfectly happy to me.' Nobody ever really sees it coming because once somebody decides to take their own life and starts preparing for it they become resigned to it, they get used to the idea, to the point that it becomes normal to them and a part of their life.

Like all the suicides before me, mine would be no different as I was used to the idea now, to the point that I'd worked out, down to every last detail, how I was going to do it and on what day and at what time. From what I'd read in the books on suicide that I'd read, people generally killed themselves during the day, usually the evening, very rarely in the morning when they've just got up. I'd even given the time of day careful consideration. Until that day I'd plod along, seemingly happy and ok with life, while I wound down my driving lessons, sold off my remaining possessions, wrote a few letters that would be left to my friends with my money that would be divided up, having worked out who would get what amount. Then, lights out, an eternal sleep with no dreams – bliss.

Chapter 21

I arrived at Gina's house for her driving lesson, got out of the car, plonked myself into the passenger seat and waited for her to come out. She didn't expect me to knock on the door anymore; she usually kept an eye out of her window for me and came out when it was exactly 10:30. While I waited I deleted the classified adverts on Gumtree that had sold. My house was starting to take on something of a minimalistic look as more and more items were being sold off. When I looked around the rooms of my house and thought about the items that had now gone it saddened me, momentarily, like remembering old friends who were no longer in your life. However, they were only inanimate objects and emotions and sentimental feelings should not come into it. Having said that, a child can get incredibly attached to an inanimate object. I felt the same way about a few of my possessions, especially my TTS. I reminded myself that the proceeds would – in just five weeks' time – be going to some good causes and when I say *good* causes I don't mean charities. I mean a few friends that I care about, who could use, and would appreciate, the extra money. I wasn't selling everything. There were a few bits and pieces that I was keeping hold of to give to some of my friends, friends who I knew would really appreciate them.

I figured that I would give my iMac to Naomi, my next-door neighbour. Naomi already lived in the house next-door when I moved in ten years ago. I remember the day I moved in, she knocked on my door and asked if she could help with anything, or if I needed anything. Not only was there a problem with the combi-boiler when I moved in but the electrics were dead too. Naomi made me several cups of tea and coffee and even brought me a plate of dinner early in the evening. She was about my age (three years older, I found out later) and single when I moved in. I thought about asking her out on a date, as she definitely seemed my type: sensitive, kind, compassionate, selfless, loving and artsy. But, being a neighbour, I didn't as it could make things awkward if she said no. In the end I didn't have to because Naomi got in there first one day, about two months after I moved in.

'You know, I'd ask you out on a date if men did it for me,' she said.

'Huh?' I said, taken aback.

'I'm a lesbian,' she said, smiling, like it was the most natural thing in the world. Well, I suppose it is, if you're a lesbian. I don't mind admitting I was disappointed. Not that she was a lesbian, but because I felt that we would have worked really well together and she felt the same too, but guys just didn't do it for her.

Maybe Naomi and I got along so well because of those circumstances. Over the years we became really good friends and often had dinner at each other's houses. Admittedly, I preferred having dinner at her place as, being Jamaican, she always cooked up the most amazing Caribbean dishes, unlike the bland English ready meals to which I'd become accustomed. After having dinner at Naomi's house for the first time I never offered her take-out pizza again. Instead I dug my slow cooker out and made an effort.

Naomi would always encourage me to try again after any of my brief relationships didn't work out and I'd be there for her when the same thing happened in reverse, which it did, quite a lot. Naomi seemed to get through more women than I did, not just for sex, she, like me, actually wanted to try and form a long-term meaningful relationship, but, like me, she just seemed to attract the wrong type – she hated cliché lesbians.

She only had a crappy old Windows netbook that crashed all the time and it was slower than a paraplegic tortoise – its broadband connection even slower than that. I also planned to give my two Sonos speakers to Naomi as she only has a crappy little CD Radio that can't have cost more than about £19.95 from Argos. I found this quite incredible, considering how much she liked music. Naomi worked for an estate agent in town and didn't earn a fortune and, being single, she had the rent and all the bills to pay on her own, hence her crappy little CD Radio. Along with my iMac and Sonos speakers I also planned to give Naomi a wad of cash.

I planned to give my fridge-freezer, cooker and washing machine to Oksana, who I dated for about

10 months four years ago. As with all my other post-divorce relationships it hadn't quite work out with Oksana. Close, but no cigar, as the saying goes. Oksana and her 14-year old daughter had come to live in Cambridgeshire from Ukraine a couple of years before I met her. She was a lovely woman and she had all of the qualities that I put high up on my list. She was gallant, loving, caring, compassionate, kind and angelic, and she just had this incredible nurse-like quality about her. She was the most selfless woman I'd ever met and she was a true lady. By lady, I mean she always made me feel comfortable in her presence. She was always asking if I was ok or if I needed anything or wanted anything to eat or drink. But, in the bedroom, there was something missing, something I couldn't quite put my finger on. I just didn't feel the emotional depths that I wanted to feel and I could never reach those dizzy heights that I wanted to reach – it was all rather lacklustre. Bedroom activity with Oksana sat right in the middle of the road and although sometimes it tentatively veered off to the right or left a little, I wanted it to career right off the road and head up into the mountains or some faraway land. I guess you'd say that the sexual connection and chemistry just wasn't there and I wanted, needed, that. I wanted the complete package, the whole ball of wax.

Oksana and I remained good friends after we broke up and although we didn't see each other all that often we did chat on the phone every other week or so. I'd always maintained that I would be there for Oksana and her daughter should they ever need my help with anything, day or night, and I meant it. Oksana had had a terrible life in Ukraine and, from what she'd told me, her ex-husband was a mean drunken son of a bitch who took all his anger and aggression out on both of them. She was so grateful when I helped her with all the forms, red tape and appointments, so she and her daughter could get British passports. She thought I was the second coming and couldn't thank me enough. I remember when she got the passports; she was in tears when she phoned me. She was so happy and I was so happy for her. She still calls me when she gets letters in brown envelopes that she doesn't quite understand. I have all of Oksana's immediate life mapped out in my iCal app on my computer so I can remember and take care of things for her: when her car's MOT and insurance expire, when her broadband contract is up for renewal, that sort of thing.

The letter that I've written for Oksana is by far the longest as I've had to write up a road map for her as well as an extensive set of instructions to do with various things that I typically take care of for her because she finds them too challenging or confusing.

I actually taught Oksana to drive and found her first car for her. I always phone her a few weeks before her MOT is due to remind her to take it in and get it done. I also call her when her car insurance is a few weeks away from renewal, but only after I've searched the comparison sites and found her the best deal, then I simply give her the phone number and reference number so all she has to do is call and pay.

I have to admit, when I thought about Oksana and how she would manage after I'm gone, I did have a painful pang and I felt awful, but I also didn't think that it was fair that I should have to stick around and be the 'king of pain' just so some of my friends would be happy and have an easier life. Sometimes I feel like a sad clown spinning plates for children. While the children laugh and smile the lovelorn clown is deeply sad and emotionally dejected while trying to keep everybody else's happiness spinning away.

As for my beloved Hi-Fi and vinyl record collection, I was going to give those to Timothy, who I'd known for ten years since moving to Cambridge. Timothy worked in a music shop in Cambridge and, like most retail sales assistants, he didn't earn an awful lot and he lived in quite a small rented 1-bed flat. I'd bought a few little bits and pieces from the shop where Timothy worked in the past. We'd got chatting and became quite good friends. He invited me to one of his gigs quite early on – he played drums in a jazz/blues band. I went to his house a few times, and vice versa, and our friendship grew from there.

Like me, Timothy is really into his music and, although he has a system, it's not what I'd call 'real' Hi-Fi. It's made up of a Sony amp, Philips CD player and some small bookshelf Monitor Audio loudspeakers. It's just ok but not quite the first rung on the Hi-Fi ladder; he'd be thrilled with my equipment, and he'd appreciate it.

As for my Sony TV (which was huge and state-of-the-art), I planned to give that to Katarzyna, another woman I dated for a while since moving to Cambridge. I was with Katarzyna for about six months and, unlike Oksana, sex with Katarzyna was amazing: out of this bloody world, in fact. However, she was a little too aloof and distant for me. She didn't show her emotions and she came across more like a corporate businesswoman than a girlfriend. Maybe that was the Aquarius in her. Although she said she loved me and cared for me I just didn't really feel it, at least not on the level that I wanted to feel it. So we broke up, amicably. We remained friends and stayed in touch for a while but the regularity of our contact became less and less over time. Once in a while, I'll still get the occasional 'How are you?' text message from her, but not that often, but it's nice knowing that I'm still in her thoughts – somewhere. Katarzyna had the smallest TV on the planet, some tiny LCD Samsung thing that can't be any bigger than 28-inches. I know she still has it because while I was writing up my 'goodbye' letter to her I had phoned on the pretence of an 'out of the blue' chat, and I'd asked if she still had her 'postage stamp' TV in that general 'chitchat' sort of way. Whenever I was at her house I'd comment that it was like looking at a postage stamp. One time we were watching a Polish movie, one that she said I just had to watch, which I did, but due to the little screen I really struggled to read the subtitles. Katarzyna was strapped, financially, and worked two part-time jobs, neither of which paid well. As well as giving her my TV I also planned to give her some cash too. I figured about half the money I got from the sale of my Audi – if anybody needed it, Katarzyna did. She'd be able to go home on holiday to visit her parents, buy herself some nice things, have some extra cash in the bank and just have a feel-good factor for a while as my cash would help relieve the strain for a while. As for Mathieu and Shari, well, they are pretty affluent and don't need my financial help. It was only a few months back that they'd spent just shy of £3,000 on an American Smeg fridge-freezer from John Lewis.

I saw Gina in my peripheral vision as she came out of her house and walked over to the car.

'Hello,' she said, jumping in and closing the driver's door.

'Hello, Gina, how are you today?' I asked.

'Great!' she said, sounding very excited.

'Oh? Do tell,' I said.

'I went to the children's home and met Kaylen.'

'How did it go?'

'It was amazing! She remembered me. I mean, she was four the last time she saw me and that was nearly two years ago, but she remembered me.'

'That's great, Gina,' I said.

'Isn't it? We spent the whole afternoon together and we had an instant connection. We just bonded. It was amazing! Red, thank you,' she said, leaning over and kissing me on the cheek, which took me somewhat by surprise.

'Oh, come on! I told you, I didn't do anything,' I said.

'Oh yes you did! You have no idea. Anyway, she's coming to my house tomorrow. I can't believe this is actually happening. I've turned a massive corner, Red, and I have you to thank for it. I know you don't think you did anything but just listening to me in the pub that day, letting me get it all out without interrupting – it put things into perspective, hearing myself say it all out loud like that. Then what you said to me back at my house afterwards, it all just got me thinking. It was like my antenna had been hit by some sort of emotional falling tree and it wasn't pointing in the right direction anymore, unable to tune into anything, but then you somehow managed to fix it, align it up again,' she said, smiling.

'Well, I'm glad,' I said, feeling a little awkward for being given so much credit in helping Gina turn a corner in her life.

The two-hour lesson went really well, as I expected it to. Gina was coming on in spades with her manoeuvres and driving in general and she was advancing a lot quicker than any of my previous pupils.

We arrived back at Gina's house and, as previously arranged, we went inside so I could help her with her theory for 30 minutes.

'I see you've brought your laptop?' she said, nodding to the case I'd put down in her hallway.

'Yes, I'm sorry I forgot to bring it last week,' I said.

'That's ok, I'm looking forward to seeing some of your pictures, after we get through this theory stuff,' she said, firing up her iMac and pulling up another chair for me to sit on. She made me a cup of tea and we settled down to the theory.

As with her driving, Gina was steaming ahead with the Highway Code and the theory test practice DVD so I suggested that she put in for her theory test right away, with a view to taking it in a few weeks' time. After we went through the theory stuff we visited the official gov.uk website and booked a date for her theory test.

'Thanks for helping me with that. You really think I'll be ready in two weeks? Well, just under,' she said.

'Yes I do. You've nailed the Highway Code and you're getting pretty much everything right on the theory test DVD now. I think you'll totally nail it,' I said.

'I'm so excited. Right, let me see some of your work,' she said. We moved from her computer into her living room where we sat on her couch under the window. I took out my laptop and opened up a folder that I'd created that contained a load of photographs. I enlarged the first picture on the screen and handed Gina the laptop.

'Ok, just tap that down arrow,' I said, pointing, 'to progress through the pictures.'

'I know,' she said, smiling. Course she knew, she had an iMac and, from what I'd seen, she knew her way around it. Gina sat with my laptop on her knee and tapped through the photos, taking her time, soaking up all the detail in each and every one of them: the subject matter, the composition, the lighting and my artistic input. She was 'really' looking at them, not like those so-called friends who just skim though your photos and say, 'nice' and then turn, immediately, back to their futile conversation. Gina was not like that.

'Oh my god, Red! These are amazing!' she said, in awe. She meant it too. I could see that Gina was emotionally touched by some of them. 'They're incredible. They're all so thought-provoking, emotional. I can see that there's an incredible story behind them. I mean, they just say so much. Never has the saying "A picture paints a thousand words" been more relevant than it is with your pictures.

Strange – that's an expression that I use quite a lot. It hasn't gone unnoticed that Gina and I share a lot of expressions and sayings, and she's even quoted some of my favourite quotes too.

'I can see why these got published,' she said.

'Actually, none of these have been published,' I corrected.

'You're kidding me?'

'Nope,' I said.

'But I thought you said you'd had loads of photos and articles published in magazines and newspapers?' she asked.

'I have, just not these,' I said.

'But why? They're amazing! Honestly, Red, these are some of the most amazing photographs I've ever seen in my life,' she said.

'Thank you, Gina, I appreciate that. Thing is, magazine and newspaper picture editors can be a picky bunch. A number of the magazine editors who've published my stories previously thought that some of my pictures were a little too "artistic", said their readers might not understand them. They want high quality, tack-sharp, perfectly exposed images with stunning subject matter and traditional composition, where the rule-of-thirds is blatantly obvious. That's what they care about, images that look like screensavers or calendar photographs, which I can do of course, but I also like to put my own heart and soul into photographs too.'

'I know what you mean about picture editors, being the ex section editor for BBC Wildlife magazine. All these photographs deserve to be published, Red. You should write a book and put all these pictures in it – kind of a 2-page spread layout, with the photograph on the right hand page and the story behind it on the left. These are just too good to go unseen; that would be sacrilege, they deserve to be out there, Red. The world needs to see these.'

'I don't know, Gina,' I sighed.

Well, what was the point? I wouldn't be around to see it and right now I had more pressing things on my mind than to indulge in some book project. I didn't want this and I didn't need it. I thought Gina would just make a few nice comments about my photographs. I certainly didn't expect her to get all sentimental about them and start planting seeds in my head. Like all the inanimate objects and items in my house, I was trying to get seeds and thoughts out of my head, not introduce new ones to complicate things at this late stage in the proceedings.

'Well, I do know. You're still taking pictures, right?'

she asked.

'Erm, no. Not for a long time. I sold all my camera equipment years ago,' I said.

'My god, why? You've got such an amazing talent, Red,' she said.

'I don't know. I just lost interest,' I said.

And I had, I'd lost interest in photography, the piano, and life. I must have sounded totally dejected because Gina looked at me quite intently, like she was trying to figure something out in her mind, read it even.

'What happened to you, Red?' she asked, tentatively.

'What do you mean?' I said, knowing exactly what she meant.

Gina was intelligent and I sensed from the very beginning that she possessed the kind of passion and intelligence that I required, or at least once required, past tense. And, until I mentally built a brick wall around those thoughts I was drawn to her. She was magnetic, her eyes intense and hypnotic – she was so pure and I could sense that although she'd been in a dark place for the past two years herself, her soul was an untainted delight, just waiting for…

'You have a story, Red,' she said.

'Everybody has a story, Gina,' I said, finishing my now cold tea.

One thing (well, there were many things) that I liked about Gina was that she knew where the line was, when not to cross over it or push something. She knew that now wasn't the time to get into this, but she knew there was something. I'd become aware that Gina had an incredible ability so see right through me, read my thoughts almost. Because of this I felt exposed in her presence, emotionally naked, vulnerable, but strangely, I kind of liked it.

She probably suspected it would not be a quick conversation over another cup of tea, but she did say something.

'Red, I have to tell you something,' she said.

'Oh?' I said, looking at her.

'Yes, I'm really sorry, but after you told me that you used to be a photojournalist I Googled you, in the hope of finding some of your photographs… and, well, I stumbled upon a newspaper article about you, not one of your articles, but one that had been written about you,' she said.

'Oh, that one,' I said, knowing exactly which newspaper article she was referring to.

'Red, it's nothing to be embarrassed about. It was a long time ago, you were just a child. It's who you are now, who you've become, that's what's important. I think you're amazing for achieving what you have, and for turning out the way you have,' she said.

The newspaper article Gina was referring to was published in the Telegraph, shortly after my first Beethoven recording for Decca records came out. I don't recall the exact headline they used, something along the lines of 'FROM ABUSED CHILD TO CONCERT PIANIST'. The article told the story – a seriously abridged one – of a child, (me) who'd lost both his parents in a tragic accident when he was only six, and how he was abused, mentally, physically and sexually, by care home staff and foster parents, yet turned out just fine and became an internationally acclaimed concert pianist: the happy ever after. But, reading it back made me feel incredibly exposed, like my whole miserable childhood was out there for the whole world to see, and now, in the technological age of the internet, it would be around on computer screens for all to see until electricity runs out. Another reason I was looking forward to getting off this boat. Nobody would be able to touch me when I'm dead. They could hang my naked corpse from a lamppost in the middle of Market Square in the city centre for all I cared; I wouldn't be around to see it.

'I know,' I said, cheerily, but she detected my faux tone.

'I'm so sorry about what happened to you, Red, but it just makes you even more remarkable. I think you're amazing!' she said, and she meant it, I could sense that. 'I think you've turned into a selfless, altruistic, caring and loving man because of what happened to you as a child, if that makes sense,' she said. It did. Gina seemed to instinctively know my traits and qualities, emotionally and otherwise.

'Well, none of it'll matter next month,' I said.

Oh shit, I thought, not realising that I just said that out loud. That rarely happens to me, vocalising a thought, a thought that should have stayed in your head. This was one of those rare instances and it could not have come at a worse time, in the presence of Gina.

'What do you mean?' she said, her facial expression

changing to one of great concern.

'Oh, don't worry. I'd better be heading off. I've got somebody coming around to pick up an old Omega watch I sold on Gumtree last night,' I said, getting up.

'You're selling an *Omega* watch?' she said.

'Yeah. I don't need it anymore,' I said, putting my laptop back in its case and heading towards Gina's front door. 'Ok, same time next week?' I said, desperately trying to get out of her house now.

'Yes, of course,' she said. She opened the front door for me but I could sense her concern. Her eyes were fixed on mine – I desperately tried to evade them. I thought she was going to grab me by the arm and sit me back down.

'You have a lovely day with Kaylen tomorrow,' I said.

'Oh, yes, thank you. I'm sure I will,' she said.

'Ok, I'll see you next week then,' I said, turning and heading back to my car.

I could feel Gina's eyes on my back as I crossed the road. I got into my Corsa, started the engine and pulled away. I glanced across and gave Gina a brief wave. The sad and concerned look on her face was engrained in my mind's eye all the way home, and well into the evening. In fact, I didn't sleep that night.

Chapter 22

The days seemed to passing by more rapidly, like I was now on the home straight – downhill and with no more hurdles – to my own terminal finish line. The previous two weeks had shot by and, with just three weeks remaining, I was starting to get a little bit concerned. Not about dying, but all the little things I still had to get in order during that time. Three weeks might sound like a long time to get things organised but when you say it out loud, 'I have just three weeks left to live,' it kind of takes on a new perspective and brings everything sharply into focus. My house was starting to take on the internal appearance of a place where the occupant was about to be moving out. I'd sold over half my household belongings now and all the stuff in the garage like Snap-on tools and other car maintenance equipment.

My freezer was empty. Not that there was ever that much in it anyway as I tend to eat on a day-by-day basis. Otherwise stuff just goes off and I always forget about food items that I have in the freezer. I'd even made a trip to the local recycling centre, twice, to get rid of the last remaining bits and pieces in the loft, stuff that would not really be worth anything to anybody; large empty boxes mainly, due to my keeping boxes for items until the warranties had expired, in case I needed to send it back, then they just sat there. Emptying my house had proved relatively straight forward as I'm not a hoarder and I didn't have rooms stacked, floor to ceiling, with loads of crap. I've always been of the belief that if you don't love, or use, something, get rid of it. I always ask myself that same question if I'm out shopping (not that I find myself out shopping much as I positively hate the experience). 'Will I love this and/or use it on a regular basis?' and if the answer is no, I don't buy it. Also, if I'm in a shop looking at something and I can't quite decide, definitively, within about ten seconds, if I should buy it or not, I don't.

I'd popped into town, as I needed to buy a birthday card for Naomi, whose birthday, as it would turn out, was four days post my date with death. I thought about this, long and hard, and wondered if it was a good idea to send somebody a birthday card from beyond the grave. I planned to give the card to my friend, Timothy, and ask him to post it first class the day before her birthday. I decided I would buy the card as I couldn't depart this world knowing it was her birthday just a few days later and I hadn't got her a card. It wasn't like I was going to be sending birthday cards and Xmas cards well into the future or anything; that would be creepy. I'd already worked out what I would write in the card for Naomi so she would, hopefully, understand and see it from my point of view.

I'd wrestled and struggled with my thoughts

regarding how I'd explain to Naomi, Oksana, Katarzyna and Timothy about the various goods I intended to leave them. I eventually figured it out. I'd go and install the TV in Katarzyna's house and explain to her that I was upgrading and didn't need it anymore. Realistically, upgrading from a 1-year old state-of-the-art 60-inch Sony would be nigh on impossible, no matter how fast technology advances, but I very much doubted that Katarzyna would know that. I'd tell Naomi something along the same lines when I dropped my iMac and Sonos speakers off with her next-door. I could do this sooner, rather than later, as they were only used in the bedroom and kitchen, which was not that often. I use my 'proper' Hi-Fi, which is in the living room for my serious music listening pleasure.

I still had to work out what I was going to tell Oksana regarding my fridge-freezer, cooker and washing machine, why I was giving them to her totally free of charge, but I still had a bit of time to come up with a reasonable explanation. As for Timothy and my 'expensive' Hi-Fi and vinyl record collection, I'd already asked him if I could store it all in his house for a few days while my landlord had builders come in to replace the ceiling in the living room. I'd explained that I had no room anywhere else in the house to store it, as I would have to move other items from the lounge into my bedroom; also I did not want to risk it getting covered in dust. He was fine about it and the day following my suicide he would receive a hand-delivered (I was in the middle of working out the delivery details for this) letter that I'd already written up, explaining why I'd ended my life and left him my Hi-Fi and records. Timothy wasn't what I'd call a 'best friend for life' sort of guy, but he's one of the few people who calls, or texts, me with any sort of regularity to ask if I want to get together.

Once, about a year after I got married, I tossed away my Filofax. Yes, I was using a leather-bound Filofax back then. Apple's iMac G4 had just come out and I couldn't quite trust a computer (not even an Apple) to safely keep all my important contacts, names, addresses, phone numbers et cetera. The reason I threw my Filofax away was a kind of clear out process – like when you clear out your loft, only I was doing it with friends, so-called friends in most cases. It was my way of finding out who my 'real' friends were, or who gave any kind of shit.

Back then I lived in London and had plenty of friends, or so I thought. I had noticed a common pattern with my so-called friends, in that it was always me who phoned them to arrange to go out, visit, catch up, and rarely the other way around. So I figured I would throw my Filofax in the bin and buy a new one and the only people I would enter into it would be those who bothered to contact me first. I took the decision to not call any of them, ever again. I'd wait to hear from them, and wait I did. Out of the forty or so people I had in my Filofax only three of them actually called me within three months of my tossing it out. It seemed to work as a good filtering system, a way of clearing out so-called friends, people who just don't really give a crap about you, dead wood.

Timothy calls me quite a lot – as I do him – to ask how I am, to catch up; hence he's a worthy beneficiary for my Hi-Fi and record collection. Also, he was really into music, like me, and he is always going on about the incredible sound quality of my gear, so I know he'll be over the moon with it, perhaps not so much with my death though, still, he can always dig out Mozart's Requiem, I have two excellent versions on vinyl, or some of my Leonard Cohen LPs and, in time, he can progress onto some of my Cooper Temple Clause and Black Rebel Motorcycle Club LPs.

I spent about twenty minutes choosing a birthday card for Naomi, much longer than I'd usually allocate to such a wearisome imposition, but this was going to be the last birthday card I ever bought anybody so…

WHSmith was quiet. A spotty young lad and a thickset older lady – his boss, I suspected – were standing at the back of the shop discussing the rearrangement of a display. At the till stood a bored-looking teenage girl, examining her nails as if expecting them to magically change colour all by themselves. I walked up to the counter and put my carefully chosen card down in front of her. She looked down at it, picked it up, scanned it and rang it up, all without making any eye contact, no smile and no hello.

'Two ninety five, please,' she said, slipping the card into a little paper bag for me.

'Is this contactless?' I said, nodding down at the

card machine.

'Yeah,' she said, chewing away at whatever it was she was chewing on. She couldn't have been more than eighteen, possibly less.

'If I told you you'd still be working here twenty years from now and by then you still wouldn't own your own home and that you'd be driving a shitty old car and could only afford one really cheap package holiday a year and you would be living on supermarket's own brand beans on toast, would you be happy about it?' I asked her. Now she did look up at me to make eye contact.

'Err... no, obviously,' she said, sarcastically, with a strange snort.

'Ok. I don't usually give people advice, and certainly not when they haven't asked for it, but I'd like to give you some, if I may?' I said.

She looked towards the back of the shop; her boss was still busy with the other young worker.

'Ok,' she said, suspiciously.

'Go and get your coat and leave, right now,' I said.

'What? Why would I want to do that?' she enquired.

'Because I'm old enough to have seen this movie a thousand time over and what I'm looking at now is just another re-run. Trust me on this, right now you're young, and you probably think you're going to live forever. But before you know it you'll be 20, and then the next decade will pass, slowly, but surely; and then you'll be 30. I have this friend - he's older than me, about fifteen years older - and every year he says the same thing to me. You know what he says?'

'What?' she said, all ears.

'Well, he's always complaining about being broke. He says, "Hopefully something will change next year", but it never does. You know why?'

'Why?'

'Because he says, "Hopefully", when what he should have been saying for all those years is, "I'm going to make something change next year." You get where I'm coming from?' I said.

'Erm, no, not really,' she said, with a perplexed expression.

'I've known this guy for fifteen years and he always says that same thing year in, year out, but nothing ever changes in his life. He'll be retiring soon and he's spent almost forty years working in retail, just like you, for minimum wage. He doesn't own a house, he drives a shitty old car and can never afford to buy nice things. Now do you understand where I'm coming from?'

'Well, kind of, but what's that got to do with me?' she asked.

'Like I said, I've seen this movie a thousand times. It's a movie about young people like you who get a shitty job in a place like this and twenty years down the line they're still doing it and wondered how the hell that happened. Thing is, once a couple of years go by you'll be in danger of finding yourself institutionalised in this job. You only get one shot at life and when you get to the end of it, well, that's it. Lights out, an eternal sleep with no dreams. One day you'll find yourself lying on your deathbed, muttering the words, "Oh, was that it? That didn't exactly turn out the way I'd wanted. Can I go back and try again?" And the answer will be a resounding no.'

The manager shouted out from the back of the shop, 'Everything ok, Chloe?' eying me with suspicion.

'Yeah, everything's fine,' she shouted back.

'Anyway, I know you're young and you think you're immortal and will live forever, and you don't think the things that I've just said will ever happen to you, but it could and if you stay here much longer, it probably will,' I said. 'Don't waste your life being stuck in this Groundhog Day retail rut of mediocrity and being broke all your life. Remember, force a change. Don't hope for it, you've gotta make it happen, or it won't. It's that simple' I said. I picked up my card and left.

I'm not sure what made me come out with all that stuff to Chloe, my departing words of wisdom to a young girl just starting out in life. Who knows?

The girl must have seen something in my eyes or heard something in my tone. Maybe there's something in one's look, one's tone, when one knows that one only has a few weeks left to live. Moreover, maybe the look in the eyes and/or tone of voice are different still when those remaining weeks are not given to you by a doctor following some test results, but by your own planning – there must have been a certain sincerity in my voice and eyes. Anyway, I left the shop and stopped forty yards down the street to buy a sausage in a bun from the familiar street vendor on the corner. Just as

I was squirting ketchup and mustard onto it I heard a voice coming up behind me.

'Hey,' she said, out of breath.

I turned around and saw the young girl, Chloe, who'd just served me in WHSmith.

'I did it, I left,' she said, smiling and all happy with herself as she finished putting her coat on.

Her expression was a far cry from the bored one she had in the shop just a few minutes earlier. It was one of relief, exhilaration and liberation.

'You did?' I said.

'Yeah, I hated the job anyway; my boss is a total cow and the money's rubbish,' she said. I must have looked slightly shocked, as she said, 'Don't look so concerned. I was thinking of leaving anyway, you just gave me the push I needed.'

'Oh, ok,' I said; now it was my turn to look perplexed.

'Anyway, I always wanted to do creative writing and now I can. There's a 3-year course at Anglia Ruskin that I looked at before, so I'm going to do it,' she said.

'Well, good for you. It's always best to do something you love, something you're passionate about,' I said.

'Yeah, you're right. See ya,' she said, skipping away with a wave and a smile and a newfound spring in her step.

I got to Shannon's house for my eighth therapy session, in a bit of a pissy mood. Well, what's new? Fact is, it's only ever other people who put me in a pissy mood, make me depressed or induce my occasional volatile nature. It's only ever *people* who effect my emotions, my mental state, my volatility, sending my blood pressure up, making that ulcer in my stomach bleed, pissing my off with their inconsiderate driving and about a zillion other things. If it were just me on this planet – with nobody else stinking up my day and putting me in a foul mood – everything would be just peachy.

'Oh, having to deal with idiotic salespeople in the Apple Store,' I said, by way of explanation for my pissy mood.

'What happened?' she enquired.

'I bought an external hard drive about a year and a half ago to use as a back-up drive. The thing gave up the ghost for no particular reason so I took it back to the shop today. The first thing they said was that I had to contact LaCie directly about it. I argued that my contract was with them, the shop, as they were the ones who sold it to me. I was buggered if I was going to start liaising with LaCie, in France, via email or some bloody ticket system. Fuck that, they sold it to me, they can deal with it. So this guy went to get the manager, who then informed me that the 12-month warranty had expired. To which I had to inform him, that as a manager, he should at the very least be familiar with the consumer rights act 2015, which clearly states that electronic goods should have a minimum working life expectancy of 3-years. Besides, LaCie sell this particular hard drive with a 5-year warranty. Anyway, the manager was umming and ahing about it, so I did what I usually do in those situations.'

'What's that?'

'I start to speak a few decibels louder than usual, so the other customers can hear me. Telling him that, as the manager, he should be familiar with the Consumer Rights Act and explaining that my contract is with the shop, and they were trying to palm me off et cetera. No manager wants an irate customer in their shop, shouting loudly about Consumer Rights acts and other things, it makes them look bad. Most managers will just want you out of the shop, and out of their hair, at their earliest convenience and this guy could tell that the only way he was going to get me to leave quietly would be by giving me what I wanted, what the Consumer Rights Act says I'm entitled to. A replacement hard drive of them to deal with the repair of this one.'

'So did they give you a new one?'

'Damn right they did,' I said, pouring a glass of water.

After I settled down Shannon settled into her usual line of questioning to try and ascertain how I'd turned into the man I was today: depressed, volatile, grumpy, pissed off and full of hate for the world around me. Shannon had taken lots of notes during the two months I'd been 'in treatment' and she was taking more during this session too. I wasn't convinced she'd be able to figure out my life based on her hundreds of questions and our conversations while intermittently scribing away on her pad. I felt like Humpty Dumpty who'd fallen off life's wall – or maybe I'd jumped off, who knows? I very much doubted that Shannon would be able to put me back together again, emotionally or otherwise.

Shannon directed the topic of conversation back to the world that I hated, so much so that I'd stopped giving a crap about it altogether to the point that I sometimes looked up at the sun and willed it to move closer, a lot closer.

'Don't you think it would be nice to leave the world in a better place than you found it, for the younger generation?' she said.

'Christ, I hate it when people come out with all that "save the planet" crap. Were people saying that before I was born? So I could come into a nice shiny new world? Were my grandparents doing anything to make the world a better place for when my parents came along? No, because nobody really gave a shit, they didn't then and they certainly don't now. Well, apart from the last few remaining 60's throwback vegetable-rights-and-peace hippies who are still kicking around the planet. Even they'll give up soon enough, when they realise they're swimming against a very strong and resilient tide. I've said it before and I'll say it again, people are inherently evil and if they can take more or get away with more they generally will. Don't get me wrong, Shannon, if there was a piece of paper that I could sign that I knew for a fact would make a difference, I'd sign it, but there isn't and there never will be. We've been raping mother earth for way too long now and we're going to continue raping her until there's nothing left to take. We'll continue taking until we've used up all her natural resources, covered her surface with toxins and polluted the shit out of her oceans and cut down all her forests until she can barely breathe, and all in the name of greed, profit and disgust. I'm not gonna lift a damn finger or make any sort of attempt to save this godforsaken planet. It was this way when I found it and a hundred years from now it'll be so fucked up it won't be fit for any sort of human habitation anyway.'

Shannon took notes, lots of notes.

Chapter 23

I only had three lessons today, including Gina's, which was the first of the three. The others were later in the afternoon. I'd had a busy couple of weeks with more of my household items things being sold, delivered and collected. I'd sorted the majority of my paperwork and had pretty much everything in order, to the point that I could see the finish line clearly now. Two and a half weeks would be more than enough for me to finalise the remaining things that I still had to attend to.

My phone rang – Shari.

'Hello, Shari,' I said.

'Hi, Red, how are you?' she asked.

'Good. A little busy at the moment.'

'Red, I'm sorry I was so upset with you over the whole charity parachute jump thing, and I don't want it to get in the way of our friendship. I spoke to Matty about it and he said I had to respect how you felt about charities. I guess I just took it personally and I shouldn't have and I'm sorry about it.'

'It's fine, don't give it another thought,' I said.

Great, so Shari didn't come to this conclusion on her own, Mathieu had advised her. I suspect, if it weren't for Mathieu, she wouldn't have called. Shari was nice enough, but I was friends with Mathieu first and foremost, Shari just came along later and ended up being part of the package. Mathieu and I were in Nine Yards Of Dead Cats together and knew each other for a good few years before Shari arrived on the scene. Although I considered her a friend, I could take her or leave her and, with just a few weeks left until my planned suicide, I really didn't care which way it went at this stage of the game.

'No, really, Matty was right. I had no right to kick off the way I did. I took it personally, rather than objectively. Anyway, I just called to say that I respect your reasons for not sponsoring me, or, rather, the charity, and to apologise and ask if we can put this behind us?'

'Course, Shari. It's no big deal.'

'Thanks, Red. So, when are you gonna get down to see us?'

'Well, I've got a few things on over the next couple of weeks,' I said.

'Ok, how about after that?' she asked.

'Let me see how things go,' I said, in a polite tone.

I didn't want to tell Shari that it would be impossible due to my corpse being unavoidably detained in a mortuary fridge somewhere. I didn't want to lie to her either, because if I said yes, she might be upset with me, posthumously, knowing that I knew I wouldn't be able to visit in my decomposing state.

I made my excuses, said I was really busy, and hung up the phone before she tried to pin me down to a date to go visit them. I'd typed up several letters – some quite lengthy – to the small handful of friends that I had, one of which was for Mathieu. All the details would be contained therein, and Shari would learn everything from Mathieu.

I suspect that many people who choose to take their own lives don't bother typing up long letters like I did; many probably didn't even leave a suicide note. I wanted everything to be as neat and tidy as possible, leaving little by way of sorting out or organising for those left behind to have to deal with. I'd even researched and half-organised my own cremation, as much as one can organise such a thing without raising any suspicions. I'd written up specific instructions to Mathieu, specifically about religious talk, as in there must be none whatsoever. No reference to God or Jesus or 'He's in Heaven now', or any of that hocus-pocus. I wasn't a believer. I was an atheist, and I knew that any of my friends, who all knew that I was an atheist, in attendance would be cringing for me if they had to sit and listen to any passages from that work of fiction known as the Bible, or any other such talk. We all have imaginary friends, but most of us leave them behind in childhood.

I'd also written instructions that everybody must come wearing trendy, bright, outrageous or unorthodox clothing. No black suits or polished brogues. If there was to be any black, I'd rather it be some torn Goth jeans with studs and tassels down the outer seams along with a Cure T-shirt.

I arrived at Gina's house for her 2-hour slot – plus an extra 30 minutes for theory – in my usual timely manner. No sooner had I pulled up outside her house, her living room curtain twitched. She looked out and waved, a big smile on her face. She came out straight away, even though I'd arrived five minutes early, and jumped in the driver's side.

'Hi, how are you?' she said, all smiley and happy.

'I'm ok. You obviously are. Something happened?' I asked.

'Yeah, quite a lot actually,' she said, beaming.

'You look like a five-year old on Christmas morning,' I joked.

'Well, I feel like one. I couldn't be any happier. I've been to see Kaylen twice at the children's home and she's been to my house with the social worker, twice, and you'll never guess what?'

'What?' I said.

'All the paperwork's been drawn up and she's moving in with me,' she said, full of the joys of spring. 'Isn't that great!'

'Wow, really? That's amazing, Gina! I'm so happy for you,' I said, and I genuinely was. I hated seeing people in dark places, depressed, unhappy, melancholy or just going through a bad time. 'So when's all this going to happen?'

'Saturday!' she said.

'Wow, that fast?'

'Yes, I couldn't believe it either. She's so amazing, now that I've got to know her more during our visits.

She's just as happy about it as I am; she can't wait to come and live with me.'

'I bet,' I said, knowing how ghastly children's homes can be, especially for younger children who need maternal love and nurturing, not some institution where maternal love and nurturing are seriously lacking.

'She used to call me Aunty Gina, and she remembers too. So I've been really busy sorting out one of the spare bedrooms for her. Well, we did it together during her last visit actually. She loves the room and the view out of the window and we talked about what sort of bed, furniture and other things she wanted to have in there. It was amazing, Red! I still can't believe this is actually happening,' she said, looking at me, intently during the last sentence with that 'thank you so much' look in her eyes again. She didn't have to say it. I could read it, and she knew that I knew that she was thinking it.

'She'll change your life, Gina, in the best way possible, and you'll change hers too,' I said.

I didn't have any personal experience regarding looking after children but people do say that having a child changes you and I'd witnessed it a few times in the past with some of my ex-friends. Well, friends who have kids typically become ex-friends with those who don't have kids. That's how it was in my experience anyway. I had two really good friends, who remained good friends even when they met their girlfriends. But when said girlfriends became pregnant and had their first child their friendship with me became seriously diluted and, within a few months, those friendships had totally evaporated into nothingness. Funny, both these sets of friends had suggested that I'd make a great dad and that I should perhaps look at having a child, or children, myself. When I didn't, for a whole multitude of reasons, they drifted further and further away until they were out of my life altogether. I guess if you don't have one of those family membership 'passes', otherwise known as a child, you're not welcome into their little domesticated family circles.

People with children generally only want to hang around with other people with children. They do all their socialising at kid's birthday parties, while standing around a hired bouncy castle or watching their little ones skate around a community centre for an hour to ABBA records (maybe I'm showing my age, perhaps children listen to Taylor Swift, Little Mix and George Ezra these days) before eating an abundance of jelly and ice cream and cake. I, being single, wasn't going to get invited to any of those hot events of the year and, even if I did, I'd probably decline on the grounds that it would seem a little creepy for a guy with no kids of his own to be at such an event – not to mention the horror of having to listen to hordes of nauseating kids screaming at the top of their voices in a community hall with horribly bright acoustics. Yup, it would be fair to say that that just wouldn't do it for me somehow.

Gina had a lot of love to give; that was obvious. She was full of compassion and understanding, and would love and nurture Kaylen in a way that she needed at the delicate age of six. She had the right kind of soul and Kaylen could do a hell of a lot worse than have Gina bring her up.

'I know, and I can't wait,' she said. 'Anyway, I'm excited about something else too,' she said.

'Oh? How much excitement can one have during the course of a few days?' I joked. 'So what else has been going on?'

'You'll have to wait a few hours. It's a surprise, but I can guarantee you're going to love it,' she said.

I was intrigued to say the least. I just hoped she hadn't bought me a gift. I was trying to clear things out of my house and I didn't want any more inanimate objects finding their way into my new-look minimalistic home. No, she wouldn't have bought me a gift. Why would she?

The two-hour lesson went really well, better than well. If I didn't know Gina better, I'd say she'd been, secretly, getting lots of practice in via one of her friends perhaps, but she assured me she hadn't. Back at her house we had our 30-minute theory session, which was flawless. Just as well because she had her theory test next day.

'Ok, go and have a seat on the sofa in the living room. I have to go and get something,' she said, getting up from her computer desk.

I sat on the sofa, aware that I could not hang around too long as I still had two more lessons to do. A moment later Gina entered the living room holding what were, unmistakably, presents, one of which looked quite large.

'Gina, what's this?' I asked, as she walked over to me, smiling like a cat that got the cream.

'Open them and find out,' she said.

'Gina, I feel a bit uncomfortable with this,' I said, and I did. I hated receiving gifts; I was more a giver than a receiver – not just in the present department either. Besides, people *never* bought me what I wanted. I could probably count on one hand the amount of times in my life that I'd received a gift that I actually liked, loved, wanted or used. The last of which was a pair of high quality black leather driving gloves (that fit to perfection), and that was eight years ago from a pupil after she'd passed her test. People don't seem to think about the person they are buying said gift for; instead, they usually choose something that they themselves would like. If a woman bought another woman a handbag for her birthday, she'd buy one that she liked, not necessarily what the birthday girl would like. I could never understand what that was all about. I'd received some seriously fucked up gifts in the past. One pupil bought me some little wooden carved hands in a praying pose, WTF? I'm an atheist, not that she knew that, but who the hell would buy somebody a silly religious trinket as a gift, unless they themselves were a devout believer, which this young girl was. Personally, when I buy gifts for people they are well thought out. I research and figure out what that person could really use or what they would truly love. I'm the bloody present-buying master, period.

'Don't be, it's just a little thank you present, that's

all. I know you don't think you did much, Red, but, well, you know how I feel about what you did and said. We've spoken quite a lot about things during the past few months that you've been giving me driving lessons. It wasn't just that day in the pub and what you said to me after, but you've said other things too – just little things, here and there, but all these little things were real gems, Red. You're the most intelligent and insightful man I've ever known and you have a beautiful heart and soul – I can sense that in you. You're a good man, Red, and whether you like it or not you've changed my life with your insightfulness and pearls of wisdom. I think you're amazing and I wanted to buy you these as a thank you so I don't want to hear any more nonsense about feeling uncomfortable. Just open them up and accept them,' she said. 'But you have to open this one first,' she said, passing me the larger one.

I looked at her, not really sure what to say or how to handle the situation. 'Go ahead,' she said, smiling.

I took the first gift and slowly peeled away the wrapping paper. She'd done an excellent job of wrapping them. They looked like they'd been professionally gift-wrapped. Then I saw the word 'Manfrotto' on the top of the box and I instantly knew what it was: a photographic tripod. I tore away the remainder of the wrapping paper to reveal the large elongated box. I looked at the picture down the side, with the model number along with the key words Carbon and Professional. I knew, from my knowledge of such things, that this was one of Manfrotto's high-end photographic tripods and Gina had bought a 'kit' version that came with a high-end ball and socket head, my preferred type. Back in my photojournalism heyday I was never a fan of pan and tilt lever heads, too much faffing about.

'Gina, this … this is too much,' I said, knowing how much it must have cost. 'I don't know what to say,' I said.

'Here, open this one,' she said, nudging the second gift on the coffee table, a square box this time.

As I picked the weighty box up I had a fleeting suspicion as to its contents. It wasn't a box of Celebrations that was for sure. No, it couldn't be, the box was too big and if it were what I was starting to suspect it was it would have cost a small fortune.

I started to unwrap it, carefully, while balancing it on my knee. *Oh my god!* It was what I'd suspected and the reason the box was larger was because there were two boxes wrapped up together. The first contained a Nikon D5 professional DSLR camera; the second contained a high-end Nikon 24-70mm f2.8 lens to go with it. This combo must have cost somewhere in the region of six or seven grand.

'Gina, this is too much, I ca—'

'Yes, you can, and you will, Red,' she said, shutting me off.

'Gina, I know how much this sort of gear cost. There's no way on earth I can possibly accept this,' I said, feeling really awkward now.

I could not get my head around why Gina would

want to spend the best part of £7,000 on this high-end professional equipment for me. I mean, a small gift for passing your driving test is one thing – a bottle of wine for example. Hell, I'd have found the situation much less awkward if she'd given me some driving gloves; even some carved wooden praying hands. This was in a different stratosphere altogether, and she hadn't even passed her theory test yet, let alone her driving test.

'Red, I'd like you to listen to me for a moment,' she said, all serious now. 'Your photographs are amazing and you're an amazing photographer. I don't know what the reason was behind your decision to sell all your photographic equipment and pack it all in, but you're too good a photographer not to own a camera – you've got too much talent for it to go to waste and not be used. Knowing that you have that amazing talent sitting dormant inside you is, well, it's sacrilege, that's what it is. It would be awful if you didn't allow your creative genius, your art, to spill out of you via your photographic skills, and I don't use the word "genius" lightly. To say that you have an eye for a great photograph would be a understatement, Red.' Gina was passionate and quite sincere. I found myself lost for words for a moment. I looked down at the box with Nikon written on the side and wrestled with my thoughts briefly before speaking.

'That's really nice of you to say, Gina.'

'No, "really nice" is something I'd say to a friend who'd just asked me what I thought of her new shoes. The photographs that you create are way beyond *really nice*, I mean it, Red. The photographs you showed me on your laptop the other week, along with the ones I found in various publications and articles online, they're something else,' she said.

'I don't know what to say, Gina.'

And I didn't. Not about the fact that she'd just spent about seven grand on this equipment for me, but what she'd said about my photographs. None of the publications I was ever commissioned to take photographs for had ever described them as 'art', or my skills as a photographer as 'genius'. They typically said things along the lines of, 'That one will work' or 'That would make a good cover shot', words to that effect.

'I'm not finished yet. I also have another suggestion,' she said.

'Oh?' I said, at a loss for what could possibly come next.

'Those photographs you showed me on your laptop. When I said they were too good to just sit dormant on your hard drive and that they should be published, I meant it. Anyway, I've been thinking about that. Remember when I said they'd look great in a book with a 2-page spread layout design? Photograph on the right page and the text describing the story behind the photo on the left?'

'Uh huh.'

'Well, I used to do bits of layout design and typesetting for the magazine I worked for so I have the skills to do it. I have Adobe InDesign on my computer. You could give me the high-resolution files of the photographs. I'll do all the typesetting and layout and design work, and you can type up between 400 and 600 words that tell the story behind each picture. When it's finished I'll send it to some agents I still know and we'll see if we can get a publishing deal. The fact that I'll have done all the layout and typesetting will help as the publisher won't have to do any of that. It would be ready to go and with the amazing photographs and accompanying text I think it'll be a winning formula. What do you think?' she said.

I was stunned.

'I don't know, Gina,' I said, thinking about the work involved with such a project and the fact that I wouldn't be around to do it anyway, let alone to see the finished product.

'Red, some of your landscape photographs are the stuff of Ansel Adams. I mean, the subject matter, the composition, the texture, they're beyond breathtaking,' she said.

'You've heard of Ansel Adams?' I said. This woman just keeps on blowing my mind with her knowledge of such things.

'Of course, how do you think I can recognise a good photograph when I see one? – A damn good photograph in your case. Red, you use light in a really unique and unorthodox way. It's like you're manipulating it somehow, in a way that other photographers can't. You don't just take photograph, you make them, by sculpting the light in the most amazing ways. You know just what time of day to take the photo, when the light is low in the sky and the sun's rays have to pass through more of the earth's atmosphere, when the shadows are beautifully soft. You work with light in a way that I've never seen before,' she said. Christ, she certainly knew her stuff. 'Red, we should do this, we have to. I'm convinced we'll get a publishing deal with this. Trust me, I know what I'm talking about. I have experience in this field, remember?' she said.

I was aware that Gina had said 'we' should do this. She wanted to get involved in a project with me. If only I'd met Gina back in the day, way back in the day, before I became the man I am today – the manic depressive who hates the world and has no interest in photographing it anymore, the lonely and tortured soul who is just a few short weeks from stepping off this miserable boat – but I hadn't, so none of this can happen.

'Gina, you don't owe me anything. Why are you doing this?' I said, as I tried to nudge the whole photography and book idea to one side of her brain so it wasn't the main focus anymore. I suspected Gina would not just forget about it entirely so I at least tried to send her off track, even if momentarily until I could get out of her house.

'Why do you have to owe somebody something to get something back?' she asked.

She had a point; I'd done so many things for people over the years, people I didn't owe anything too, just out of the goodness of my heart. I'd always given up lots of time, and money, to help other people, sometimes people I hardly even knew and sometimes even total strangers. Quite often people would raise their eyebrows when I stepped up and offered to help, wondering what the catch was, or what I wanted in return, or why I was being so generous – we live in a cynical world with a distinct lack of trust. For me, it just seemed like the right thing to do and it always saddened me when my generosity was looked upon with suspicion. Gina reminded me of myself in so many ways. I could see myself in her so much it was scary.

'So, what do you say?' she said.

'Can I think about it?' I said, knowing damn well that she would not let this go. The passion in her voice told me that. I didn't intend thinking about anything. My mind had been made up for several months now and I was damned if I was going to stick around just to publish a book, or take more photographs of this stinking world. People don't appreciate stunning images anymore anyway; they just want to spend their time moving things around a little 9.7-inch screen with their forefinger. Great photographs should be viewed in print, poster size, hanging on a wall, not on a bloody iPad for a few brief seconds before swiping to the next one.

'Of course, but you're taking those with you,' she stated, pointing at the camera, lens and tripod she'd bought me. 'And that's not even up for debate, before you think about saying anything,' she added, sternly.

'I knew you'd say that, Gina, but the fact remains that this equipment cost a lot of money. Perhaps you should be thinking about Kaylen and putting that money to better use,' I said.

'Ok, I'm going to tell you something. Well, I've kind of told you already, but I'll tell you again, with a little more detail this time. When my husband got knocked off his bicycle and killed things weren't so straightforward. I told you the lorry driver didn't have a licence due to being on a driving ban for drink-driving and that his employer, the supermarket chain, didn't check his licence details when hiring him. Well, because he was drunk when he hit my husband and it was the company's fault as they were the ones who employed him without doing the proper checks regarding his driving licence, or lack of one.

The payout I received because of the circumstances was substantial, Red, to the point that this bit of equipment hasn't even made a dent. On top of that, my sister and her husband took out life insurance policies after Kaylen was born so I'm taken care of on that front too.'

'I don't know what to say, Gina,' I said. I didn't, I was confused, emotionally and mentally as I struggled with all this.

'You know something, Red,' she said, 'after I read that article about you, how your parents and sister were taken away from you in that tragic accident when you were so young. Well, Kaylen's the same age now that you were when you lost your family. After reading your story in that newspaper article online, well … that was the defining moment, the moment that I decided that I was going to have Kaylen live with me, to bring her up as if she were my own child. I don't want Kaylen to have to suffer the way you did, Red. Don't get me wrong, that's not the main reason I've decided to have her. There are many reasons, but they're mostly down to you, how you've helped me and the things you've said. I don't want you to suffer anymore, Red, and I can see that you're a tortured soul and that you probably have more nightmares than you do pleasant dreams.' She was right. 'I figured if you got back into photography it would take you back to a time when things were good in your life and maybe you could pull some of those good times from the past and insert them into your life today, and the future. *That's* why I bought you this equipment, Red. I thought about it long and hard about it and I just knew I had to do this for you.'

I just looked at her, while picturing, in my mind's eye, a photo shoot I went on in Italy many years ago. I could feel my eyes were about to well up. I fought the tears back, and I'm pretty sure Gina noticed.

'After I read some of your articles and viewed even more of your photographs that I'd found scattered around the web, I got busy and did a lot of research. I know you used to use a Nikon F4 film camera back in the day. I read about your equipment in one of your articles. And after even more research, and asking advice on forums and calling photographic shops, I came to the conclusion that the D5 is a bang up-to-date digital equivalent of your old film camera. I've been informed that it's their top of the range, flagship, professional model – I hope I made the right choice.

I've kept the receipt, so it can be changed if it's not quite what you'd use?' she said.

'No, it's perfect. It's exactly what I'd use if I were a photographer today,' I said.

'Well, as of today, Red, you're a photographer again,' she said, smiling. 'Oh, I bought some of your CDs too. I've been listening to them quite a lot, when I haven't been practicing my theory. You know, I just can't make up my mind if you were a better pianist or a better photographer; I think you're incredibly gifted with both. You know it's rare that somebody can have two incredible talents. I know that you're finger injury ended your career as a concert pianist, Red, but this,' she said, pointing to the Nikon box, 'this you can do again.'

I left, equipment in hand, only because I knew that Gina would insist. She'd given me the receipt along with the equipment so I figured I'd now have to write a letter to Gina too. A letter that would be delivered to her, along with the equipment, which she'd be able to return for a refund, as it would still be within 28-days. I'd explain everything in the letter and apologise.

Chapter 24

Introspection and awareness are qualities that I've always had in spades, but after Gina became my pupil, I've started to question my ability to self-examine, to step outside of myself and take a good look at the man who stood in front of me. To figure out the issues he had, the flaws, the shortcomings, his attitude towards the world and those around him. Sure, I was aware of many of my imperfections, but it was how these imperfections and unorthodox ways of looking at things found their way into the very DNA that made me up – like a cancer reshaping a cell and then spreading – that had got me flummoxed. I'd been this way for so long now it was hard to remember exactly when this anomalous nonconformist transition took place and Shannon – as far as I could tell after the ten sessions we'd had – didn't seem to be any closer to figuring it out either.

One of the things I complained about a lot was the fact that nobody seemed to be really *living* anymore. All I saw around me was 'organised living' with little to no room for spontaneity or improvisation. Everybody's lives were lived with an almost military precision and planning, a regimented routine, all set out for us from a very early age. In America it was even worse and because Britain takes its lead from America that means it was pretty much the same here too. I'd never understood why we looked to the American's for our cultural ways when we should be looking to our European cousins – which, after all, is only 21 miles away – for culture, ways of life and ways of living.

In America a nurse will stick a needle in a babies arse within a few hours of its birth, with some vaccination or another (probably an amalgamation of them) and then in the coming months it'll get stuck a whole bunch more times. If the baby doesn't have all these jabs they won't be allowed into any kindergarten in the country. That's the 'organised living' start line right there. Then as their children go through school the regimented regime continues and intensifies. They have to abide by the rules (some of them pathetic, a lot of them not allowing for originality and most of them killing creativity stone dead) and stay in line. Woe betide anybody who dares to step out of line. If they do there will be some bastard in stars and stripes standing there ready to nudge them back in line again, to make sure that they stay on that narrow little conveyor belt of life where they will remain until, one day when they near the end of the conveyor belt, the grim reaper will be there with a wry smile on his face to greet them as they drop off the end into eternal darkness. Hell, in America, lots of girls start planning their weddings from the age of 14, before the legal age of sexual consent, and a good few years before they actually intend to marry, probably to some guy called Chuck with whom they will have a bunch of kids. Thus, life's conveyer belt just keeps on rolling along and nothing ever changes, just like in the Del Amitri song.

In adult life things don't improve much either. In fact, quite often, things actually get a whole lot worse. We work 9 to 5 jobs, meet somebody, get married, have kids, leave the house at the crack of dawn, sit in rush hour traffic, do a day's work under a boss who's a total wanker, sit in rush hour traffic again at the end of the day, arrive home, hug the kids, eat dinner, take a shower, watch some crap on TV, go to bed where we lie next to our wives, too tired to have sex, or we just can't be bothered anymore because, like life, it's all just lost its appeal and just doesn't feel that good anymore. Then we fall asleep and with any luck we'll have a nice dream, but probably not, before waking up and doing it all over again the next day. Then the weekend arrives and we go to the retail park to spend our hard-earned money on a whole bunch of cheap crap imported from China that we don't even need along with all the other dullards. On Sunday we'll go and visit friends or relatives and talk about our weeks, our work and the futile TV shows we've watched. Eventually, our kids will grow up and have kids of their own and we'll be the old folk that they're visiting and we'll listen to them talk about their shit weeks and the even worse shit TV shows that they've watched. We'll look ahead and realise that there's nobody ahead of us to pass the baton to as we realise that we're all but extinct. We can see life's finish line just 10 metres away. During those last tired steps we ponder on our lives with huge regret for all the missed opportunities and all the things that we should have done, but didn't because we all signed up to a lifetime's subscription for that appealing glossy magazine called 'ORGANISED LIVING'. It wasn't really that glossy after all and, in hindsight, it wasn't very appealing either. It just wasn't worth the money or the read.

The thing is, my 'introspection' antenna had been off kilter for so long that I'd become institutionalised in it. It'd become the norm and if you become a certain way and stay that way for long enough you can't get back, no matter how much therapy you have. I didn't think therapy worked on people like me, maybe not on anybody; in the same way that marriage guidance counselling doesn't work on anybody either. At the end of the day, if two people don't have harmony and are not really compatible, marriage guidance won't fix that; period. People can't change, so these unhappy couples should just separate, get divorced, and find somebody else that does work for them (and vice-versa), somebody they won't have to 'try' with. You shouldn't have to 'try' in a relationship; it should just work naturally with little to no effort.

I'm convinced that the reason behind so many 'seasonal' relationships, at least that's what I call them, relationships that last the duration of a season, was because we are not true to ourselves during that beautiful honeymoon period that we have at the beginning of any new relationship. Admittedly, it's probably guys who are more guilty here than the ladies. At the beginning of a new relationship many guys will be on their best behaviour and they will try to be everything that they think the woman wants him to be. He'll buy her flowers, he won't fart or swear in front of her, he'll pay her nice compliments, he'll take her out and treat her nicely, and so on and so forth. But after a few months the said man can't keep up the façade anymore, it's too unnatural; it's too much like hard bloody work. So what happens? He slips back into his old ways, back to his 'true' self. The woman then turns around and says, 'Hey, what happened to you? You used to be really nice but now you've become a real jerk,' when the truth is, he always was a jerk; he just wasn't being true to himself, or his new partner. Thing is, pretending to be something you're not to please your partner is like making a steel rod for your own back. It will simply fall apart when the real you starts to come to the surface, which it always does. If people were totally honest with each other from the very beginning if they then fall in love they will be falling in love with the real 'farting, swearing, football loving, romantic movie loving, having odd nights out with the girls loving, can you massage my back, honey?' deal, with no surprises to come a few months down the line.

The same thing applies to 'compromises' and 'sacrifices'. I hated it when people say you have to make sacrifices in a relationship. No you bloody don't, and here's why. I could meet a new woman and this woman and I could decide to go to the cinema to watch a movie. Said woman loved cheesy chick-flick romance movies while I preferred something with a bit more muscle, say Vin Diesel or Bruce Willis (I don't, necessarily, but go with me on this one). If I was in love with said lady – I said 'in love' not 'loved' as there is a difference between loving somebody and being *in* love with somebody – I would happily go along and watch the cheesy romance flic because it would make me so happy to sit there and watch my beloved partner smiling and laughing as she watched the film. If you're in love with somebody, then their happiness is your happiness. If it *feels* like a sacrifice or a compromise then you are not in love with your partner, it's that simple, or at least that's how I see it – or at least used to see it before I got all cynical – with my romantic theories and notions.

Me, I don't even work with myself anymore, let alone a partner. But I can't divorce myself, I was stuck in my own miserable relationship and there was no getting away from it. Like many couples who have been in unhappy relationships for so long that they have become institutionalised in their own marriages, I found myself in the same place, only with myself. I couldn't change, not for anything, and with only two more therapy sessions remaining I doubted very much that Shannon would be able to give me the answers that I'd once so desperately sought.

'So, how are things going?' said Shannon.
'In regard to my plan?' I asked.

'Well, in general,' she responded.

'Only you sounded a little anxious when you asked how things were going,' I said.

'Did I? I wasn't aware of that.'

'Well, I'm sure you're aware that we only have one more session after this one,' I said.

'Yes, I'm aware of that, Red,' she said, not needing to refer to her diary.

'How do you feel about that?' I asked.

'It should be about how you feel about it, Red. This is about you,' she said.

'I know, but you must feel something, knowing that it's our last session next week and after that... Well, you know ... So, your thoughts on that?'

'Actually, I'm quietly optimistic, Red,' she said, not taking her eyes off me.

'Well, you cutting it pretty damn fine if you don't mind me saying,' I joked.

'Red, I'm not here to try and stop you from taking your own life. If that's what you've decided and that's what you've got to do, then that's what you've got to do. When we started these sessions you came here to ask me if I could help you untangle all the things that have happened in your life. The things that have made you so depressed and angry with the world. How that big heavy black dog of depression you've talked about came into your life and why it's been such a devoted companion ever since. Why you chose to live in that dark corner of your mind. Why all those demons seem to be right behind you at every turn. Why you have nightmares, not only at night, but during the day too and how you've got to the point that you sit in the corner in the evenings with your head in your hands crying and wanting it all to be over. All that internal pain and loneliness, yours is the worse case I've ever seen, Red, it really is and I can't even begin to tell you how sad it makes me. I'm fully aware that we only have one more session left, Red, but trust me on this; I've been working hard with my observations and analysis. I've studied you closely during our sessions and I've considered and evaluated everything very carefully.'

'And?'

'I'm almost there,' she said.

'Almost,' I sighed.

'I'll be there by next week, Red. I've had a lot to figure out in a relatively short space of time but I still have a couple more stones to look under, and that's what I want to do today, during this session,' she said.

'Ok. Sounds like I'm gonna need a cappuccino,' I said.

'Of course,' she said, getting up to make one on her machine.

'So, what kind of week have you had?' she asked. Shannon didn't like to go too deep into things while she was making coffee, just general chit-chat, soft stuff. The deep stuff came when we were both sitting down, facing each other with unbroken eye contact.

'Paperwork, tons of bloody paperwork. You know something, Shannon? I had one of those eureka moments a couple of days ago. I came to the conclusion that absolutely everything that shows who we are and how we live our lives comes down to little pieces of paper, that's it, and without all those little pieces of paper we simply don't exist.'

'Ok?' she questioned, finishing up my cappuccino.

'No, I'm serious. When we're born we're given a birth certificate, or at least our parents are, and we're entered into a database. Our school grades, diplomas, degrees, wage slips, bank statements, tax returns, P45s, prescriptions, medical files, criminal records, driver's licence, passports, marriage certificates – followed by the inevitable decree nisi and absolute of course – and then, the most important little pieces of paper of all, cash. Ain't nothing quite like the smell of freshly minted bank notes. Hell, even after we die it doesn't stop because somebody ties a tag to your big toe and gives you a death certificate and logs that in another database. So, without all this paperwork that we build up during the course of our lives we'd be nothing. It defines us, it tells everybody else who we are, what we are, what we're worth, how clever we are, well, if you have a Mesa IQ test certificate. Where we've been in the world, who we've been married to and for how long, if we have decent moral fibre and have been good boys and girls or not. Take all that away and what's left?'

'I'd say there's plenty left,' said Shannon, sitting down.

'Yes there is, but people don't see that because people, for the most part, don't really care about the core ingredients that make us up, the stuff that really counts. They only care about the icing and the decoration on top; if we're affluent, if we own a house, a nice car, dress in nice cloths, have a degree, a good job and so on and so forth,' I said.

'It shouldn't be like that, Red.'

'I know, but it is and it's not going to get any better anytime soon and certainly not in my lifetime, even if I were to be here to see it, which I'm glad I won't be.

Shannon turned the conversation in the direction of something a little more pressing as she dug deeper and deeper into me, reaching into those dark far corners of my mind. She pushed our conversations deeper, and harder, to uncomfortable emotional levels. Shannon had managed to figure out the number sequences to the combination locks in those far forgotten dark corners of my mind, where I'd kept things, painful things, entombed and locked away in darkness for such a long long time. Now she was setting them all free and, like mummies disturbed by archaeologists, they were hovering in the air between us like visible apparitions of my past. They were so bright and clear, but dark and disturbing at the same time – an unwelcome homecoming. I didn't want these ghosts, ghouls and demons hovering around out in the open like this. I wanted to force them back through the air lock and into the secure Containment Unit in a distant and disused out-of-reach place, locked away back in that far corner of my mind. That particular session was like something out of Ghostbusters. They ghosts, ghouls and demons were all free and wreaking havoc with both my historical and present-day mental state of mind.

Shannon insisted that if I locked them away again, one day, they could all escape and if she were not there to help me deal with them it would be detrimental — catastrophically — on a huge and irreparable scale. I didn't care anymore; I just wanted to get through the next week and a half in peace and quiet, without all this upheaval. I didn't want it and I certainly didn't need it. I just wanted to get up and run out of the room and leave all those ghastly things behind for Shannon to deal with because I certainly couldn't deal with them. I didn't want to deal with them, I didn't have the mental strength or emotional capacity to deal with them and, let's face it, didn't have to deal with them anymore.

Chapter 25

Emma, one of my pupils, passed her driving test and although I hadn't been taking on any more pupils as I'd been winding down, I still had a handful that I had to pass on to the two other automatic driving instructors that worked locally. They were, for the most part, fully booked up but when I explained that these pupils were close to test ready, after a bit of arm-twisting, they agreed to squeeze them in. The pupils themselves were sad that I was not going to be able to teach them anymore and put them through the test myself but I assured them that their new instructor was excellent. I hadn't arranged a replacement instructor for Gina, for a couple of reasons. Firstly, I knew that I wouldn't be able to palm Gina off with some lame excuse as to why I wouldn't be able to teach her anymore. She was too in tune with things for that and secondly there was a lady instructor who taught automatic but she was away on holiday and not back for a few more days. When this lady got back I'd call her. I was pretty sure she'd be able to take Gina on. The two male instructors would probably be happy to take Gina on, I'm sure, but *I* wouldn't have been happy about it. I'm not sure why, but I just felt that a lady instructor would be better for Gina.

Speaking of Gina, she'd called me, all excited, the second she got out of the building after her theory test. She'd passed and she'd invited me over for dinner to celebrate. She'd insisted. Naturally I didn't want to go for a whole multitude of reasons but she was quite insistent and I knew she would not take no for an answer. She also said there would be somebody else there that she wanted me to meet. By the time she told me this, she'd already twisted my arm into saying yes. I had visions of one of her old magazine editor friends being there, to convince me that I should do the book that Gina had been going on about – a lot – recently.

I got to Gina's house at 5:30 p.m. on the dot, as arranged.

'Hi, thanks for coming,' she said, stepping aside to let me in.

'Thanks for inviting me, and congratulations again, though I knew you'd pass.'

'Come on through,' she said.

Gina led the way through into her living room and, as I entered behind her, she said, 'Red, this is Kaylen. Kaylen, this is my good friend, Red, the man I told you about.'

'Can you teach me how to drive when I'm older?' asked Kaylen.

Gina laughed, so did I. Sat on Gina's sofa was an adorable little girl wearing bright red onesie pyjamas with white stars on. Her hair was very long, very fair, and very wavy, almost to the point that it was in ringlets, but not quite. She had big grey/blue eyes and even though she'd lost two of her baby teeth at the front she had the cutest smile that warmed your heart.

'You'll have to teach me in a red car, though, because red's my favourite colour. Is your car red? Like your name?' she said, all inquisitive in that way that children are.

'Erm, no, I'm afraid it isn't. If you'd asked me the same question two weeks ago I would have been able to say yes, but I don't have my red car anymore,' I said, in a kind, but adult tone. I hate it when I hear adults talk to children who are aged between 5 and 10 like they're only 18-month old babies in those silly child-like faux tones that they often use. Kaylen seemed to appreciate me talking to her in a more adult way.

'What colour's the car you teach Aunty Gina in?' she said.

'It's white,' I said.

'You can see it out of the window,' said Gina, pointing.

Kaylen jumped up and ran across the living room to take a peek.

'That's ok too. White's my second favourite colour,' she said. 'It's not a very big car. Could I drive a car like that when I'm bigger?'

'You could definitely drive a car like that when you're bigger,' I said, which made Kaylen smile from ear to ear.

She skipped back to the sofa and got back to her TV programme.

Just when I was starting to feel at a loose end, Kaylen said, 'You can sit here and watch TV with me if you like.'

Gina smiled, almost as much as the kid.

'Are you ok for a minute while I go and check on the dinner?' said Gina.

'Of course,' I said, sitting on the sofa next to Kaylen.

'Do you like this programme?' she asked. There seemed to be some sort of child-friendly medical programme on featuring an injured little boy and a cartoon animation demonstrating how the accident had happened.

'It looks pretty good to me. What's it called?' I asked.

'Operation Ouch!' she informed me.

'And what's Operation Ouch! about?' I asked, making conversation.

'Well. It's about people that have to go to hospital because they got hurt, but they're always children. Adults aren't allowed, they only help children,' she said.

'Well, I think children need more help,' I said.

'Sometimes, but sometimes adults need help too,' she said.

Gina walked back in and put a couple of plates on the small dining table in the corner of the living room.

'Ok, food's up,' she said, gesturing for me to go over and tuck in. Gina informed me that Kaylen had already eaten earlier. She was really into Operation Ouch! anyway.

'I took a guess that you like your steak done medium. Hope that's ok?'

'Oh, yes, that's perfect, thank you,' I said. 'Wow, it looks amazing.' It did. The fillet steak looked great with perfect griddle lines, so did the interesting looking salad and crispy sauté potatoes. 'Thank you, Gina.'

I picked up my knife and fork, but then paused for a moment.

'Go ahead, you can start,' she said.

But I didn't, I just sat there holding my knife and fork, waiting. Gina cut a small piece off her steak and as she put it in her mouth I followed her lead. I was aware that she was watching me in her peripheral vision.

'I think that's so beautiful,' she said.

'What's that?' I said, trying not to open my mouth too much as I'd already put the tiny piece of steak in my mouth.

'What you just did. My father would approve, he used to do that with my mother,' she said, smiling. 'Come on. You waited for me to start eating first, right?'

'Yeah, ok, you got me,' I said, smiling, 'It's just good manners.'

'There aren't many gentlemen left, Red, and I think you're a real gentleman,' she said.

'Well, that's nice of you to say. So, how long's Kaylen been with you?' I asked, quietly.

'Just a few days.'

'How's it working out?' I asked.

'Amazing,' she said. 'She's settled in really fast and she's made herself quite at home.'

'You happy?' I said.

'Oh yeah, but more than that. I've got my equilibrium back now, a symmetry that I haven't had for quite some time. Everything just feels balanced again and I couldn't be happier,' she said.

'I'm so pleased for you, Gina. To say you deserve it would be the understatement of the century.'

'Thank you.'

'So you sold your Audi?' she asked.

'Oh, yeah.'

'I thought you loved that car?'

'Yes, I did,' I said, putting another small chunk of steak in my mouth, hoping Gina wouldn't press it or ask why I'd sold it. She didn't, but I knew the question was on the tip of her tongue.

'Red, I hope you don't mind but... Well, I don't want you to think I'm stalking you or anything but... Oh god, I feel awful about this, but I can sense that you're in a strange place yourself at the moment. I mean, I know you've only been giving me driving lessons for ten weeks now but I've got quite an acute sixth sense. I'm quite sensitive and I know you're not in a good place, Red. Anyway, I put my detective hat on and looked up Omega watches on Gumtree and searched by area and I found the one you sold recently.'

'Oh, yeah, I forgot to remove the advert,' I said.

'I'm glad you did because it allowed me to view the other items that you're selling. It looks like you've sold, and are in the process of selling, the entire contents of your house, Red. Are you going away or something?' she asked.

'Something like that,' I said, taking another piece of the delicious steak. I could feel Gina's disappointment, or was it concern, at what I'd just said. It just came out. Had I thought about it for a moment longer I might have been able to come up with something else, something that would not invite more questions. I looked down at my plate, aware that Gina was looking at me. I wasn't upset that she'd stalked the items I was selling on Gumtree; I knew she was doing it for all the right reasons.

'A few weeks back, when we spoke, I remember you saying something along the lines of "None of it will matter next month". What did you mean by that, Red?'

I swallowed and took a sip of water. 'Gina, I don't feel comfortable talking about this,' I said, politely, nodding towards Kaylen on the sofa. We were speaking quietly, so Kaylen could not really decipher what was being said, but kids were still sensitive to things. I looked at Gina so she could see my expression and the look in my eyes, to reassure her that I was not upset or angry with her but just to let her know that I felt uncomfortable having this sort of conversation – especially with Kaylen sitting on the couch in such close proximity. I knew she was concentrating on her TV programme and Gina and I were talking quietly, but still.

Gina seemed to accept it and the conversation turned back to her stuff, happy stuff, and Kaylen – for now at least, but something told me she was not going to drop this.

'I didn't only invite you over to celebrate my passing the theory test. I wanted to thank you, properly, for the other ways you've helped me,' she said, looking across at Kaylen on the couch and, I don't really know why, but I wanted you to meet her.

Operation Ouch! finished and Kaylen wanted to talk to me about cars and other things, lots of things, like children usually do, for about an hour until she announced that CBeebies Bedtime Stories was about to start. Gina changed the channel and Kaylen settled on the sofa and focused on the TV again, insisting that Gina and I sit either side of her to watch it too.

When the presenter had finished the story Gina announced that it was bedtime and took Kaylen upstairs to bed.

'Goodnight, Red,' she said, turning at the living room door and waving with a huge smile. She was such an endearing child, so pure, so innocent, so polite, and so smart.

'Goodnight, Kaylen,' I said.

Chapter 26

As I drove over to Shannon's for what would be my final therapy session I was curious to hear what she was going to say. The previous week she'd told me that she'd have answers for me, though I was somewhat sceptical and even if she did, I doubted it would make the slightest dent in my plans. I'd always been a little bit cynical when it came to counsellors and therapists. Quite often the wrong sort of people get into the profession for all the wrong reasons. Having a failed marriage, going through a messy divorce and having to struggle to bring up two children on your own or going through some family tragedy does not qualify a person to become a counsellor or therapist. That's like saying I fell over and cut my knee and needed seven stitches once so that qualifies me to become a surgeon.

I'd researched Shannon and she appeared to be good at what she did. I'd wanted to ask her what made her get into the profession but hadn't got around to it. Anyway, Shannon seemed to be one of the few therapists that actually knew what they were doing – and there are a lot of nutty ones about – but I still wasn't convinced she'd have anything tangible to tell me today.

Up ahead of me a cyclist came out of a side turning onto the main road and collided with the nearside of the Citroen C3 in front of me, buckling his front wheel and bending the car's wing mirror back in the process. The driver pulled over, put his hazard lights on, and got out of the car to go and assess the situation. I watched, unable to overtake due to the narrow street and the constant stream of cars coming in the other direction. The cyclist, whose face I could not clearly see due to his helmet and glasses had to be pushing sixty; going by the unusually large volume of brown corduroy he was wearing – trousers *and* jacket – with elbow patches. His chosen footwear were a pair of brown Velcro things, the kind shops will only sell you if you can prove your age by showing your free bus pass. This guy was probably wearing Old Spice too.

I just had to open my window to hear what the old guy was shouting and screaming about. I'd pulled up right behind them so I could hear the ensuing argument building up. The cyclist was yelling something about the driver not looking where he was going and that he should have seen him come out of the side road and should have let him out to join the main road. Citroen C3 man was yelling back, something about it being a main road and that cycle man should have stopped and waited for a gap in the traffic before just pulling out like that and that he shouldn't have assumed that the driver was going to let him out.

'And look what you did to my mirror, you stupid old fool,' he yelled, gesturing.

'Well look at my front wheel. How am I supposed to continue on my journey now?' the old guy yelled back. 'I thought you were going to slow down and let me out?'

'Well you thought wrong. You know what they say about assumption being the mother of all fuck ups. Did you see me flash my fucking lights or gesture for you to come out?' yelled Citroen man.

'Don't you swear at me,' yelled cycle man, wagging his finger in the face of Citroen man.

'I didn't swear *at* you. I swore *towards* you, and take that fucking finger out of my face before I break it off,' he yelled.

'You see this,' said cycle man, pointing to the device on his helmet. 'This is a camera. I have evidence you know,' he said, with a 'Ha!' at the end.

Citroen man reached forward, grabbed said camera and broke it right off cycle man's helmet. He dropped it on the floor, stamped on it and retrieved the little memory card that had spilled out onto the road as a result of his heavy stamp. He bent the card in half using his teeth and then dropped it down the drain in the gutter, saying, 'Now you don't. Next time watch where you're fucking going,' and went to get in his car. Just then cycle man started kicking his car door with all his might. He wasn't causing much in the way of damage as the Citroen had that weird black rubber bubble wrap stuff running along the doors. Cycle man's foot just seemed to bounce off it, to his annoyance. But this didn't stop Citroen man from getting out of his car again and threatening to break the old guy's foot off if he didn't stop. A crowd had gathered and some of the younger members of the audience were recording the scene on their mobile devices, probably in the hope that a fight would break out, while a couple of grown-ups intervened and tried to help out.

Another fine example of how society had become. The amount of cyclists with helmet cams and motorist with dash-cams was ridiculous, all riding and driving around policing each other then rushing into police stations clutching their little SD cards, grassing each other up for every tiny little misdemeanour they did on camera. It's pathetic. We get punished enough as drivers by corporations and governing bodies – petrol prices, tax, congestion charges, toll roads, insurance, extortionate parking fees, speeding tickets, parking tickets; the list is endless – without the need to punish each other too. We should be looking out for each other, not stabbing each other in the back. Things are no better with coronavirus and the lockdown either, curtain twitchers everywhere watching out for anybody who might have left their house for a second exercise that day, when they should only be having one because the Government said so, so they can pick up the phone and call the police on them, or some twat on Facebook outing a neighbour on a public forum because she didn't come out and clap the NHS with everybody else on her street – these people are pathetic and have too much fucking time on their hands. This little street-monitoring Facebook squealer needs a fucking boyfriend.

Great, I'm gonna be late, I thought. I was tempted to get out and suggest to Citroen man that he pull his car into the side street so they could continue their argument in private while the rest of us continued on our journeys, but I figured it would only add fuel to the fire so I turned the radio on to see what jolly 80s songs Star Radio were pumping out: Kajagoogoo 'Too Shy'. Jesus-fucking-Christ, could this day get any worse?

'Hello, Red. Come on in,' said Shannon.

'Sorry I'm late,' I said.

'Oh, that's fine. You're only a few minutes late,' she said, showing me through to her therapy room. 'Would you like anything to drink? Your usual cappuccino?' she asked.

'Please. I haven't had a coffee today and I could use one,' I said, sitting on the couch.

Shannon didn't make any small talk as she made my cappuccino. She was silent for the entire two minutes it took, like she was gathering her thoughts or checking her mental bullet-point list of the things she wanted to talk to me about.

'There you go,' she said, putting the cappuccino on the coffee table in front of me. She sat down and picked up her note pad and studied it for a moment before speaking.

'Ok. I'm going to discuss several things with you today, kind of a re-cap, so I can lay out a picture that I'm hoping will clarify a lot of things for you,' she said.

'Ok,' I said.

Shannon referred to her notes and then systematically started to go over several key events that had occurred during my life, starting with the death of my parents and sister when I was six, moving through my abusive childhood in care and with foster parents, my late teams, my failed marriage, the severed tendon in my finger which led to the end of my piano playing days, the numerous failed relationships and abundance of brief affairs, pretty much all of which were emotional disasters, and a whole bunch of other stuff too.

After about half an hour of this she got to the all-important part, her conclusion and what she'd managed to deduce from our sessions together.

'Red, all this stuff,' she said, tapping her pad with her pen, 'and all those terrible things that happened to you when you were younger, it's not who you are and it doesn't define you,' she said.

'But it has defined me, Shannon, whether I like it or not.'

'Red, you've been suffering from post-traumatic stress disorder for a very long time, ever since that awful day when you witnessed your family die right in front of you and you've been living in that state ever since.'

'Oh, come on, Shannon. You can't have PTSD for 36 years, a few weeks, or months, perhaps, but not 36 years,' I said.

'Oh yes, you can. There's no set time for these things. You should have got counselling when you were six, to help you adapt, come to terms with it and work through it, but you didn't. So your defences kicked in and you became uncommunicative and just locked yourself away deep inside yourself. On top of that, you were placed with unloving foster parents who proceeded to put you through the most unimaginable abuse, which resulted in a whole new layer of PTSD right on top of the previous one. Then, later on in life you found out your wife had been unfaithful and, as a result, you damaged the tendon in your finger so your career as a concert pianist was cut short, you suffered PTSD yet again, for a third time. So, it's all compounded into thick horrible layers built on a horrific foundation that was put in place the day your family died. Red, you've suffered major PTSD three times in your life: the death of your family, the abuse while in the care of foster parents and then your unfaithful wife and the resulting severed finger and the end of your career as a concert pianist, and over the years it's snowballed. You never got any help or counselling for any of these things when you should have. What's happened to you has been a tragic story, Red, but none of it's your fault.'

'Well, when you put it like that, I guess I'm well and truly fucked then,' I said.

'No, Red, you're not. This can all be reversed,' she said.

'Shannon, I know how this works. Listening to you lay out my whole life like that, well, I'm damaged goods, damaged beyond all repair, I'm a broken man. What was it you said, tortured and tormented hence the content nightmares every night?' I said, sighing at the thought of all the shit that I'd had to endure during my life.

'Red, you just have to get back to the person who you were before all of these terrible things happened. You have to become the man that I know you can be.'

'Like being re-born,' I said.

'Something like that, yes. You're a good man, Red, a decent man. Beneath all that bitterness and hate, which you have every right to be by the way, I can see a beautiful man. You're full of love, compassion, and kindness. In a way, what you had to endure throughout your childhood years has actually turned you into the kind and loving man that you are today. You can't tell me that you're not aware of the pattern you have when it comes to helping others and giving up enormous amounts of time for other people, sometimes people you hardly even know. Why do you think that is, Red? Where do you think that comes from? It's not co-dependency either, only an inexperienced therapist would suggest that, but I can see deeper,' she said. 'But you are a tortured soul, Red. You suffer from anxiety; depression and you have a deep-rooted pain and anguish that even manifests itself as nightmares when you sleep. You don't get any peace or let up, day or night. You're not at rest with yourself, Red, but you can be. I can clear all this out and rid you of your demons, fears and anxieties … but it will take a little time.'

'Ah! And there's the caveat,' I said. 'Shannon, people like me with these sorts of issues are usually in therapy for years, their whole lives, and at the end of it they're still fucked up.'

'Red, we've only had twelve sessions together but I know enough about you and all that's happened in your life to know that I can have you well on the way to a balanced and healthy life inside of six months – if you let me.'

I looked at her, sceptical. Neither of us said anything. I just looked at her, intently, while I pondered on what she'd just laid out for me.

'Red, you're a good man, a very good man, and the world's a much better place with you in it,' she said, almost pleading.

I just sat there on her comfortable couch and paused for a minute before getting up to leave. I took some cash out of my wallet to cover the final session and put it on the coffee table next to the box of tissues.

'Thank you, Shannon,' I said, extending my hand for a farewell handshake.

Chapter 27

I stood in my living room and looked around. Everything had now been sold, except the items that I was going to be giving to Naomi, Oksana, Katarzyna and Timothy. I paced from room-to-room – bedroom, second bedroom (which I used as my office), bathroom and kitchen. My house was all but clear. I didn't even have a sofa to sit on anymore. This was going to be an uncomfortable last three days. I'd booked a transit van from a local van hire company so I could deliver the various white goods and other items to my friend's houses and I'd arranged times with them to do this. I had no more pupils and no more lessons; I'd passed my few remaining pupils on to a couple of other driving instructors in the area. Gina was still expecting me to arrive at her house for her usual two-hour lesson next week but she'd soon learn that it was not going to take place, at least not with me. I'd made arrangements with the lady driving instructor – who'd since returned from holiday – to take Gina on, but I hadn't given her the specifics yet. She'd reserved a two-hour slot for her, for the same day/time that she was used to with me, so I knew she'd be ok about that part of it at least. I didn't want the driving instructor to have Gina's details just yet as I didn't want Gina finding out about it.

I'd only have my Corsa for another two days, then that would be gone too. I'd taken it to a local car dealer who'd offered me a price that was only about £600 lower than I would have got privately and I needed to know, for sure, that this car would be gone in time. I'd arranged to drop it off at his showroom in advance of my suicide, but still leaving enough time to deal with the money the dealer would transfer into my bank account i.e. draw it out to give away and close my account. I already had Oksana's bank details as I'd helped her out with a couple of things in the past that required bank transfers and I had Katarzyna's bank details too as she'd asked me if I could loan her £50 or £100 until she got paid a few times in the past, so I'd be able to transfer money into their banks on *the* day. I planned to give Naomi and Timothy cash, along with the goods I'd set aside for them.

I had a pile of letters on the kitchen worktop that were ready to be delivered to my friends, along with a few other people, and I'd made arrangements for them all to be hand delivered to be sure that none of them would get lost in the post. Most of my friends were within a 30-mile radius anyway, except Mathieu and Shari who were in London.

I made a cup of tea and stood at the kitchen window while I drank it. Well, I had nowhere to sit and I didn't fancy sitting on the cheap inflatable bed that I'd bought for a tenner off Gumtree – I figured that could stay. As I stood there sipping my tea, mentally going over the final details, double-checking yet again, my mobile rang. It was Gina.

'Hello, Gina.'

'Red, hi. How are you?' she asked.

'I'm ok,' I said.

'Are you busy?'

'Not really.' I wasn't. I'd been over every last detail and had double-checked everything. I was good to go – permanently.

'Would you like to come over for coffee?' she asked.

'Erm … well—'

'Kaylen keeps asking about you. I think she wants to talk to you about cars. I know, strange right? I mean, little girls usually want to talk about Peppa Pig and pink fluffy things. What can I tell you? She's so mature for her age. So, would you like to come over, if you're free … please?' she said. She was trying to make it sound casual, but I could hear that she had a pleading tone in her voice, almost desperate even.

I looked around. What the hell! There was nowhere to sit in this place anyway and, although I knew what was coming in just a few days' time, I didn't particularly want to have to look at the rather large and complex contraption that I'd spent a week building in my living room, a contraption that was going to bring my life to an end.

'Sure,' I said. 'What time?'

'Is 5:30 ok?' she said.

'Ok. I'll see you then.'

I hung up the phone and although it was only 3:30

I left the house and went for a drive around rural Cambridgeshire. I'd always felt 'at one' with my car. Well, not necessarily my tiny little Corsa, but I certainly did with my now sold TTS. I'd always been passionate about cars and driving. I just felt at one with my car, in the same way that Julian Bream feels 'at one' with his classical guitar or how James Galway feels at one with his flute. Their instruments are like an extension of their bodies and that's how I felt when driving and the nicer the car the more at one I felt. I found it relaxing, therapeutic even, and it allowed me time for introspection. But best of all I was untouchable when I drove around quiet country B-roads when there weren't many other cars on the road. I was cocooned in my car with all the doors locked and the windows closed. No radio, no CD, no distractions, just me and my thoughts, where I could be at one with myself, away from commerce, people walking up to me with clipboards, people trying to hand me flyers, people calling me about PIP overpayments and other cold callers. I always put my phone on Airplane mode when I went out on these little solitary reflective drives.

The only other thing that I've done in my life, that not only came close to this feeling, but surpassed it, was being in a glider. Once I did a glider aerotow launch at the Cambridge Gliding Club in Little Gransden. Being up in the air like that – gliding and rising on the thermals while looking down at the world below – made me feel untouchable. The only thing that killed that feeling slightly was the pilot sitting behind me. Still, he was a man of few words and he only spoke to say something necessary – why can't everybody be like that in life? I could imagine how amazing it would be up there on my own, gliding higher and higher on the thermals, like an Eagle soaring. I enjoyed the feeling so much I actually looked into taking flying lessons and buying a glider of my own, but, as I suspected, it's a pastime of the wealthy. Most of the cars that drove into the club, with glider in tow, were usually large Range Rovers, BMW X6's and the like – hardly the pastime of a lowly driving instructor on £17,000 a year.

Oh, there was one other experience that fell into the same ballpark and that was the time I spent 60-minutes in an immersion tank on a health spa break that my ex-wife had arranged. Health spa breaks were not really my thing but I did enjoy the floating experience, known as Restricted Environmental Stimulation Therapy (REST) in complete darkness and complete silence: the ultimate sensory deprivation experience.

It was like a bathtub, only egg-shaped and with a large soundproof and lightproof lid that closed across the top. Wearing only swimming shorts I got into the warm salt-water, and when I say salt-water, I mean lots of salt. There was so much salt mixed in with the water that it was impossible not to float. As I lay there in total darkness and complete silence, floating on a bed of warm water, I could practically hear my own organs at work, certainly my heart and the blood in my ears. I'd got into such a deep state of relaxation and so 'into' myself, I could almost tune into my own soul. I remember thinking to myself that this was how I'd like to die.

I arrived at Gina's at 5:30, as arranged, and noticed the long blonde curly locks of Kaylen at the living room window. She waved at me, enthusiastically, and then yelled something to Gina. As I got out of my car and walked towards the door, the living room curtain fell across the window as Kaylen released it and ran to the front door with Gina.

'Hi,' I said, as Gina opened the door.

'Do you like doughnuts?' asked Kaylen, who was peering around Gina's waist.

'I love doughnuts,' I said.

'With pink icing sugar on top?' she said.

'Especially with pink icing sugar on top,' I said.

She smiled her super cute smile, which was even more endearing with her missing front teeth.

Inside, as Gina had predicted, Kaylen wanted to talk about cars, for a little while at least, before she moved the conversation onto other fascinating topics. The little girl seemed to be genuinely happy, euphoric in fact. She was so full of live, the polar opposite to me. It looked like she'd been well looked after these past two years too, unlike my own bleak childhood instructional experiences. Gina told me that she had, and she'd received a lot of love, support and attention from some kind and caring people. I was glad to hear this, as there would be no lasting detrimental or damaging effects later in the child's life.

Kaylen had taken an instant liking to me, just as a few other young children had at various points in my life. Although I'd never really been into kids, kids always seemed to be into me. Whenever I (or my ex-wife and I) had been invited to friend's houses for dinner and those friends had young children, they just seemed to gravitate to me. They found me fascinating, asked me lots of questions, and always wanted me to play games with them. I think they saw me as one of them. They could sense my inner child, my child-like qualities, and the genuine love and compassion that I had deep inside. I've always been convinced that children possess some sort of sixth sense, something they are born with as a protection mechanism to help them out until they get a little bit older and develop the mental maturity to recognise danger without it. Children can sense when a person is kind and loving. On the reverse side, they will typically shy away and stand behind their mothers or fathers in the presence of somebody who is not so kind and loving, or bad, or even evil. I must have oozed a certain quality to attract the attentions of little ones over the years. The parents would usually say something along the lines of, 'I'm sorry. Just let me know if he's bothering you,' or 'Thomas, leave Red alone,' to which I'd always tell them that I didn't mind. So, in those situations, while the adults talked 'kitchen sink' drama, I'd entertain the young ones, or vice-versa – I actually preferred it this way.

With Kaylen, she could see these qualities in me too and she gravitated to me straight away. But there was something else about this little girl; she would sometimes look at me in a certain way, the way a devoted pet dog would sometimes. Although the dogs can't speak, they will sometimes look deep into your eyes and directly into your soul, as if they know something. This was how Kaylen looked at me sometimes. I'd noticed it twice before when I was last here, and again now. Her 'look' only lasted for a fraction of a second, but it was long enough for her to figure me out to my very core. It was like she had some sort of super power, maybe an extension or another layer to that sixth sense I was talking about.

As I sat next to Kaylen, sipping the tea that Gina had made me, watching Operation Ouch!, she seemed to be just as in tune with me – and acutely aware – as she was with the television programme. Gina would occasionally look across at me from her side of the sofa and smile. Not only did I not know what was on Kaylen's inquisitive mind when she gave me one of those brief, but deep, looks, I didn't really know what was on Gina's mind either, but there was something about these two ladies, something I couldn't quite put my finger on. There seemed to be an unusual atmosphere, a vibe. I didn't know what it was but I recognised it from a long lost, but not forgotten, feeling that I had a long long time ago, in the same way that a specific smell lingering in a summer breeze can take you back to a place you'd long since forgotten.

'Mummy, can we have the doughnuts now, please?' she asked, so politely.

'Of course, would you like to get them from the kitchen?'

'Mummy?' I mouthed to Gina as Kaylen headed off to the kitchen.

'Yes, she asked me last night. Just came out with it. Asked if she could call me Mummy from now on. When I said yes she threw her arms around my neck and didn't let go for five minutes,' she said, a few emotional tears welled up in both her eyes while she smiled from ear-to-ear.

'I'm so happy for you, Gina. This is incredible,' I said, smiling at her.

I actually envied Gina, just like how I envied all happy families. I mean *truly* happy families, who love each other and are a rock for each other, a support network. That must be one of the most amazing feelings in the world.

Kaylen returned with a white box containing three doughnuts.

'This one's for me,' she said, pointing to the one with caramel icing on top, 'this one's for Mummy,' she said, pointing to the plain one, 'and this one's for you,' she said, pointing to the one with pink icing on top while smiling like a Cheshire Cat. Gina snorted out a laugh.

We sat and ate our doughnuts and watched the rest of Operation Ouch! And then we played some of Kaylen's favourite board games. *Is this what it feels like to be part of a family?* I pondered, while watching Kaylen take charge of the dice while explaining to Gina that she needed to throw a two.

'Mummy, can Marion come with us tomorrow?' asked Kaylen.

I looked at Gina. 'Marion?' I mouthed.

'Oh yeah, sorry. I was looking at some of your articles online, your journalism and some of your photographs. You're credited as Marion Redwood in most of them. Kaylen showed an interest in some of the pictures. I explained that you'd written them and taken the photographs and she spotted your name under one of them and, well, she can read really well for her age and she's quite clever, aren't you?' said Gina, turning to Kaylen and giving her a friendly nudge. 'Anyway, I'm sorry,' she said, knowing the story behind my hating being called Marion.

'Don't be silly, it's fine,' I said.

And it was. Although I'd always hated my name, from a young age, there was something about the way Kaylen said it that I actually liked.

'So can Marion come with us, Mummy?' she pressed.

'Well, I don't know, sweetie, I'm sure Re— Marion has things to do tomorrow.'

'Actually, I don't, so if you want me to come along, I'd love to,' I said.

Wait! Where the hell did that come from? I'd got swept along in the moment and now that Gina and Kaylen were smiling like a couple of dogs that had just been promised fillet steak and sausages when they got back from their walk in the park, I could hardly backtrack. If there was one thing I knew about children it was that you don't let them down after you've promised them something, or said yes to something, even if it was only a few seconds ago. Kids remember stuff like that and, if you let them down too many times, it can be detrimental to their long-term social development, not to mention the immediate let down feeling and sadness. I just don't think you should ever promise a child something and then to go back on your word. So, it looked like I was off to LEGOLAND in Windsor for the day. I couldn't even begin to imagine how busy a place like that would be, and on a Saturday, it would be teaming with families and kids. I checked myself and tossed the thought right out of my head and, instead, thought about how happy it would make this adorable little girl. I'd mentally checked my dairy of what I still had to do during the little time I had left. I'd still have time to collect the van, that wasn't until Sunday anyway, and deliver the various items to my friends. In fact, I had a large chunk of time free on Saturday and this seemed to be as good a way as any to fill it.

Chapter 28

I wasn't exactly sure why I'd agreed to go to LEGOLAND with Gina and the little girl. In hindsight, it was probably a bad idea, but I'd instinctively opened my mouth and spoken before thinking it through. It was Saturday, and I generally avoided going anywhere at the weekends, preferring, instead, to do my shopping and leisure stuff during the week, during the day, when the masses were at work and their kids were in school. I was usually busy doing driving lessons at the weekends anyway, but during the week I always had spare time. On Sunday I had to pick up the hire van before noon and make a few trips to deliver the various items to four different addresses, all in Cambridgeshire, thank goodness. My next-door but one neighbour's 17-year old son has agreed to help me as there were some white goods that I wouldn't be able to heave on and off the van on my own. When I offered him £50 cash for two hours of his time, he jumped at it.

I'd planned to return the rental van first thing Monday morning, before driving my Corsa (which would be parked in the van rental centre car park) straight to the used car dealer to sell before finally getting a taxi back home, where I'd then deal with bank transfers and a few other few loose ends before strapping myself into my rather elaborate suicide contraption, which was currently taking up about a third of my living room. Since I'd come up with the idea for my suicide machine and had started building it, I'd kept my living room curtains drawn. Although I had net curtains I was still worried that a passer-by might glance in and wonder what the hell it was I had in there, and it did look like something straight from Hell too. I'd hate for somebody to call the police and have them come and investigate – that would take some explaining. Who knew, they'd probably have me sectioned – after seeing the elaborate fail-safe suicide device I'd spent over a week building – and they'd have good reason to.

So, here I was, on a Saturday morning, standing in a ridiculously long queue to get into LEGOLAND with Gina and Kaylen, and I could imagine how long the queue times would be for some of the rides once we were inside. Still, when I looked down at Kaylen – who was standing between Gina and I, holding my right hand and Gina's left, like she was the one looking after us and taking us out for the day – and saw her beaming smile, big bright eyes and how excited she was, the thoughts of queues quickly dissolved away over some distant inconsequential horizon in my mind.

Gina looked at me and mouthed, 'Thank you,' with a smile.

Once inside, Kaylen was as happy as a dog with two tails as she took in the magic of the place. She was in Heaven as we wandered around the park, checking out all it had to offer. After a couple of hours and a few rides Kaylen was starting to flag and get hungry, and so was I. Kaylen chose a place for us to eat and she had her favourite - spaghetti bolognese - while Gina and I shared a large meat feast pizza – a woman after my own heart.

After lunch Kaylen became euphoric and quite animated when she saw the LEGOLAND City Driving School.

'Marion, can I learn to drive here? Please?' she pleaded, tugging away at my hand and dragging Gina and me in the direction of said driving school.

I couldn't say no to anything this little girl asked of me. I hardly knew her but she seemed to have me well and truly wrapped around her little finger. If I had a child, like Kaylen, I'd probably spoil her every chance I got. I'd want her to have all the things and the life that I didn't. Gina, on the other hand, would have to be a bit more considered in what Kaylen could and could not have, or could and could not do, as part of being a responsible parent.

'Look! Can I drive that red one?' she pleaded.

'If there's a red one available,' said Gina. Then she turned to me and whispered, 'I'm not sure how old you have to be to drive these?'

'Let's find out. Some of those kids look quite young,' I said. Turned out that the age range was 6 to 13. Kaylen, being six, made it, just. And, she managed to get a red car too; must have been the way she asked and her endearing smile and missing front teeth. Personally,

I wasn't too keen on the Fiat badge stuck on the front.

'Hope it's not as unreliable as a real Fiat,' I joked to Gina as we watched the overjoyed Kaylen go around the track.

I became aware that Gina had taken my hand in hers as we watched Kaylen having the time of her life in the little red Lego electric car. I wasn't paying that much attention as I was more concerned about Kaylen getting injured. I guess my protective nature kicked in. But then I became aware of that familiar warm electricity that was flowing from Gina's hand, through mine, up my arm and into my chest, where it settled itself. It felt amazing, it felt … right. I turned to face Gina, who was watching me watching Kaylen. She leaned in and kissed me on the cheek. She didn't say anything; she just smiled a beautiful warm smile.

'Look, Marion. I got my driver's licence,' said Kaylen, proudly holding up a plastic laminated driving licence, which resembled a regular adult licence, only with LEGOLAND, Windsor, written on it with pink Lego bricks in the background and a Fiat logo along with the year it was issued and, of course, a photograph of Kaylen, smiling away, with her name on the front. I had no idea why a little six-year old girl would be so into cars and driving. Gina told me that I had something to do with it. When she'd told Kaylen that I was teaching her to drive, she got quite enthusiastic. A petrol head in the making, or probably battery head, or hydrogen head or whatever the norm will be in ten years or so when she's old enough to drive.

Although Kaylen's laminated licence was in a plastic holder fixed to a lanyard around her neck she held onto it like it was a crown jewel. She kept looking at it and then looking up at Gina and me with a big proud smile as wide as the Grand Canyon and as bright as the Sirius star on a clear night. My heart melted, completely.

I don't know where the rest of the afternoon went. It passed so quickly as the three of us stood in queues for the various rides and walked around LEGOLAND holding hands.

Sometimes Kaylen would be on my side (which meant I got to hold Gina's hand, Kaylen insisted), sometimes she'd be in-between us, and sometimes she'd be on Gina's side (which meant I got to hold Gina's hand again), but the three of us were always holding hands in some combination or another and while Kaylen was on a ride Gina and I would hold hands again – with no prompting from Kaylen. Gina gave me a friendly kiss on the cheek and Kaylen had spotted it from her ride and smiled at us.

It wasn't long before we were on the M25 driving back home. Kaylen was still excited from her day out and talked about many things and asked many questions but she soon started to show signs of tiredness. While Kaylen snoozed on her booster seat in the back, Gina and I talked grown up talk.

'Can I get you anything?' asked Gina, after we arrived back at her house.

'A small towel, if you have a spare one. I'd like to

wash my face, if that's ok?'

'Of course, let me get you one,' she said, heading upstairs. She came down a second later. 'The bathroom's the first door on the left at the top of the stairs,' she said, handing me a small towel.

'Thank you,' I said, heading up while Gina went into the living room to tend to Kaylen.

When I came back down Gina was in the kitchen making me a cup of tea. 'All good?' she said.

'Yes, much better, thank you,' I said.

I hadn't been in her kitchen before, or her bathroom upstairs. It all made me feel a little bit strange, but not necessarily uncomfortable; well maybe a little. This was Gina's home, a home she was now making with Kaylen, and I felt a little bit like a fifth wheel. I knew that Gina – and Kaylen – had made me feel incredibly welcome, but something about this didn't sit right with me, but I had no idea what it was exactly. Things had fogged over in my mind during the course of the day at LEGOLAND and now I felt like I was coming round having been under anaesthesia, disoriented, confused. Hard reality was kicking in again.

'Here you go, I've made you a cup of tea,' she said, handing it to me. 'I've had an amazing day. I can't remember the last time I felt this good,' she said.

'Me too,' I said, taking a sip of tea.

'Are you ok?' she asked.

'Yeah, I'm good,' I said.

But Gina could sense my anxiety, that I wasn't totally at ease, I wasn't. My mind had wandered. Now that we were back home, I mean, at Gina's house, my mind was drifting back to other things, pressing things, things that I had to do tomorrow, Sunday, and then … Monday, *the* day.

Kaylen was pretty tired after her day out and there was no way she was going to be in the land of the living by the time Operation Ouch! aired. Not that she'd usually be up at 8 p.m. – even on a Saturday. She only just managed to keep her eyes open for the six-minute duration of CBeebies Bedtime Stories at 6:50.

'Goodnight, Marion,' said a rather sleepy Kaylen as Gina took her upstairs to put her to bed.

'Can I get you anything?' asked Gina, as she re-entered the living room.

'No, thank you,' I said. 'I guess I should be go—'

'Red, thank you for today,' she said, cutting me short and putting her hand on mine as she sat on the couch next to me.

'You're welcome,' I said, in a tone that dismissed it as no big deal.

'No, really, this has been one of the best days of my life,' she said, looking at me, with an all-new kind of intensity. She was looking at me like one of those dogs I was talking about, with the ability to see straight into your soul. One thing was for certain, Gina knew a lot. She knew all about me, and she knew exactly what sort of a man I was.

'Gina, it's no big de—'

She shut me off again, but this time by snapping her upper body, neck and head forward – with the speed and precision of a Heron catching a fish – and planting a kiss right on my lips. I kind of did, and didn't, expect it. I knew Gina liked me but I'd switched my heart off a long time ago, or rather the fuse just blew and I never figured out how to fix it. Or maybe I'd just flicked that biological switch, the one that said 'EMOTIONS ON/ OFF', to the off position, but when, I can't remember. After Gina kissed me she pulled back, but only a few centimetres. I could feel her breath caress my lips and I could see the light and passion in her eyes. She gently brushed my lips with hers while expertly parting them with the tip of her tongue.

'Stay,' she delicately whispered. The way she said that single word, it was loaded with a multitude of emotions, she meant it so much I could feel it to my core.

I couldn't be one hundred per cent certain what she meant: stay, as in stay the night, or stay, as in don't go through with your plan on Monday, or stay with *us*. The way she said it sounded like she meant all three.

Chapter 29

The next morning I was woken by Gina's tender kiss. I opened my eyes and saw her beautiful smiling face a few inches above mine.

'Good morning,' she said, ever so softly. She was dressed in something comfortable and had obviously been up for a little while, fixing Kaylen's breakfast and entertaining her, I'd imagine.

'Hi,' I said. It felt like I was in a dream and last night was the first night in years that I hadn't had a nightmare.

She kissed me again, 'Would you like some breakfast?'

'Er, maybe a cup of tea,' I said, still half asleep and not quite with it.

Just then Kaylen came bundling in. 'Marion, you're lazy, I've been up for ages,' she said. 'Are you going to come downstairs and have breakfast? I've had mine already but I set a place for you at the table.'.

Gina laughed.

'What time is it?' I asked.

'Just after nine,' said Gina, smiling.

'Well, I suppose I'd better get up,' I said to Kaylen, propping myself up on one elbow.

'Yeah, then I'll help mummy make your breakfast,'

she said, darting out of the bedroom and back downstairs.

I looked at Gina, who just couldn't stop smiling. She leaned down and kissed me again, delicately and sensually, then she pulled back and let out her breath, slowly, like I'd taken it away.

'What did you do to me last night?' she exclaimed, rhetorically. 'Is there no end to your talents, Marion Redwood?' She shuddered as she reflected on the night before and smiled. She kissed me and whispered in my ear, 'You're absolutely incredible.'

'Well, it takes two, Gina. I felt it too,' I said.

She kissed me again then headed downstairs to see to Kaylen.

'I got a towel out for you,' she said, smiling and pointing to the towel over the back of the chair. 'You can use the en-suite to take a shower if you like.'

'Thank you,' I said.

Downstairs, Kaylen asked, 'Would you like some Cheerios?' She tapped the box. 'They're honey nut?'

Gina laughed, again. She was laughing and smiling a lot lately.

'I'd love some honey nut Cheerios,' I said, reaching for the box.

Kaylen smiled.

I ate the cereal, which actually tasted pretty damn good, and then I had a couple of slices of toast and a large mug of tea. We all sat at Gina's breakfast table in her kitchen chatting and smiling, when Gina and I noticed that Kaylen had fallen silent and appeared to be deep in thought.

'Marion, I've been thinking about something,' she said.

'What's that, sweetie,' I asked, taking a gulp of tea.

'Well, I'd like to call you something else, if it's ok.'

'Oh, I thought you liked Marion?' I said.

'I do, I really like Marion, but, if you don't mind, from now on can I call you daddy?'

I spluttered and almost choked on my tea, it went everywhere, backfiring from the mug into my face. Gina handed me a tea towel to wipe my face, she was as shocked and speechless as I was. As I held the towel over my mouth I looked at Kaylen, her adorable smile, as she waited in anticipation for my answer. My heart melted and I felt a warm surge of electricity engulf my chest. I could hardly stop the tears from welling up in my eyes; I patted them with the towel.

I looked at Gina, who was struggling to hold back her own tears. She looked at me, smiling, but she had a look that suggested that it was up to me how I answered Kaylen's question. But the anticipation – and hope – in Gina's eyes was even more so than that of Kaylen's. If I said yes, I'd be saying yes to something much bigger than the innocent little question that Kaylen had just asked. I'd be saying yes to something else entirely, something quite beautiful. I didn't hesitate any longer.

'Yes!' I said, 'of course you can.'

Gina exhaled, audibly, tears ran down her face.

Kaylen got up, ran around the kitchen table and flung herself at me, wrapping her arms around my neck tightly. 'Thank you, daddy,' she said, her heart full of joy and sunshine, just like mine.

After we all settled back down from all the excitement I stood up and went over to the kitchen window and looked out across Gina's back garden. There was a bird table right in the middle with some goldfinches, blue tits and sparrows. They seemed so bright, the colours so vibrant and saturated in the morning sun – blues, yellows, reds, tans, blacks and browns. As I looked across the garden and *everything* seemed bright and colourful this morning – more so than usual. Maybe it wasn't coming from the sun, maybe it was coming from within, maybe, just maybe, I was seeing the world in a different way this morning. I turned around and leaned against the sink. The warm sun felt really good on my back through my T-shirt. Gina was making coffee; she looked so beautiful, so angelic. She walked over to me, took my hands in hers and gave me a delicate, sensual, little kiss – so warm, so pure – while Kaylen smiled and kicked her feet in excitement under the table. The warmth of the sun on my back felt amazing but it was nothing compared to the newfound warmth in my heart.

We all spent the day together. I know – I was supposed to be doing something else today, but, somehow, it didn't really seem all that important anymore.

Kaylen was six years old when she found her new family, the same age that I was when I lost mine. But Gina was there for the little girl, and so was I. We were a family now. I guess life has a funny old way of unfolding. I'd gone from having absolutely zero love in my life to having love in abundance via two incredible ladies, be it one quite a lot smaller than the other. Whenever I was around Kaylen my heart lit up and I felt a love that I find quite difficult to put into words. I loved her like she was my own daughter. I cherished her and I instinctively wanted to protect her.

Yup, this endearing little girl with two missing teeth and an incredibly cute smile had me wrapped around her little finger from the very beginning and I liked the way that felt. As for Gina, when we looked into each other's eyes, the way we did, we just knew. When our fingers delicately touched and entwined, we just knew. When we kissed, we just knew and when we made love … well, what can I say, the earth didn't move because we left this planet behind, breached its stratosphere and went on a journey to faraway place.

The little girl taught me how to live, and love again, and Gina taught me how to be 'in' love again. Kaylen fixed my introspection antenna and showed me a new way of viewing the world, a world full of colour and love, while Gina fixed my heart and soul.

Sunday flew by as we enjoyed every minute together. The afternoon came and went and before I knew what had happened the evening had crept up on us. Kaylen watched CBeebies Bedtime Stories and soon after that she went to bed, only this time she wanted both Gina and I to tuck her in, which we did.

Back downstairs in the living room Gina and I snuggled up on the sofa and talked some more. A little later Gina was overcome with a desire to be close to me, very close. She went upstairs to check on Kaylen, who was sound asleep. When she came back down to the living room she wasn't wearing her jeans anymore. She turned the living room light off – leaving just a little light coming in from the under-counter lights in the kitchen – and walked over to me wearing only her knickers and blouse. She straddled me and undid my belt and trousers. I could see the outline of her waist and the shape of her pert breasts through her sheer white blouse.

Nothing was hurried. It was slow. It was sensual. It was out of this world as Gina and I connected in ways I never imagined were possible. Gina took me to an amazing place in my mind, as I did for her, a place that only Gina and I could find when we were that close, entwined, complete … at one.

Then, just as I was enjoying the afterglow in Gina's arms a thought entered my mind. Tomorrow is Monday, correction – I glanced at the digital clock on the DVD player under the TV, 10:35 p.m. – it would be Monday in just 1 hour and 25 minutes. I thought about my suicide contraption in the living room back at my place.

'I have to go!' I said, jumping up off the sofa. Gina looked at me, mouth open, unable to speak, shocked.

'There's something I have to do,' I said.

Chapter 30

8 weeks later

Gina forgave me for rushing out of her house, with no explanation, the way I did that night, especially when I returned 80 minutes later at 11:55 p.m. on the dot. She was so pleased to see me when I returned, but she was very confused. She flung her arms around me and squeezed me tight, relieved.

I just had to go home that night – which wasn't to be my home for long as Gina had since asked me to move in with her, Kaylen had also insisted on it – to disassemble the huge contraption that I'd built. It sat, waiting for me, in the middle of my living room. I'd felt compelled and was overcome with an urge to deal with it. I'd got it into my head that my self-constructed instrument of death had to be out of my house before Monday (midnight on Sunday) so I'd rushed out of Gina's house at 10:35 p.m. that Sunday night, jumped into my Corsa and sped off home to take the thing apart and break it down. I'd put most of the smaller parts in the wheelie bin outside my house and the larger parts in my garage with the intention of taking them to the recycling centre. Once it was broken down it was totally unrecognisable as an instrument of death.

When I got back to Gina's house that night I told her that I had a very large demon that I needed to bury, once and for all. She looked into my eyes but said nothing. She gave me a knowing and understanding look – it was like she knew. Maybe she did, maybe she didn't, but she knew I had something heavy going on, some demon and she could see that it was not gone.

I'd bought another car because my little Corsa just wouldn't do as a *family* car. I didn't regret selling my beloved Audi TTS as it was a two-door coupé that only had tiny back seats that were just about big enough for a brief case, not a six-year old. It certainly wasn't practical enough for the three of us. I had two beloveds to think about now, and it felt amazing. I still wanted a 'nice' car though so after discussing it with Gina and Kaylen I decided to buy a BMW 3 series, with four doors. Of course, Kaylen had insisted it must be red, which I didn't mind and, as it happened, a local dealer had a nice two-year old one with just 12,000 miles on the clock finished in gleaming Melbourne Red metallic – Kaylen approved and during the test-drive she even asked the salesman if daddy could play music from his iPhone through it. I adored her; she was unique in so many ways. She wasn't a typical little child who thinks the world revolves around them; Kaylen was a selfless child, always thinking about other people, that's a damn rare quality for a six-year-old child in today's world.

We all went to pick the car up together on a Saturday morning and the first trip we did in it, as a family, was to the retail park in Cambridge – yup, me, in Cambridge, in a retail park *and* on a Saturday, unheard of.

Kaylen wanted a Nintendo Switch, the Neon version, whatever that was. Gina didn't know what it was either and when Gina saw how much it cost (£279.99) she raised an eyebrow, not because she could not afford it, but out of being a responsible parent. I was aware that you could not just go around buying kids everything they wanted, giving in to their every whim, not unless you wanted to build a steel rod for your own back, but when I saw how excited Kaylen was at the sight of the box on the shelf, 'That one, that's the one!' she'd said, I immediately grabbed the box and headed over to a till to pay for it. However, Gina and I explained to Kaylen that expensive items like this would not be a regular occurrence and that they were typically the things of birthdays and Christmas. But this was the first present that Gina and I had bought for her and, as Kaylen had joked, I'd just spent a lot more money than that on a BMW and it wasn't even my birthday.

I always wanted to spoil Kaylen at every opportunity but Gina would always reel me in, well, *almost* always. Was this organised living? And more to the point, was I subscribing to it? Maybe, who knows? All I knew was that with Gina and Kaylen in my life this kind of living just felt right and I wouldn't change it for the world.

I got back into my photography, thanks to Gina. Not just because of the expensive equipment she'd bought me, though it helped, but because of the things she'd said about my photography and the talent that I had for it. I even managed to get a few commissions quite early on too, after I'd shown my portfolio around a few magazine and newspaper editorial staff. As it happened, my unique 'style' was in demand these days and my style was just what some picture editors were looking for.

Gina did as she promised and got busy with Adobe InDesign and laid out a considered selection of my photographs in the two-page spread design she'd previously talked about, while I wrote up the one-page descriptions to tell the story behind them. Gina even managed to get a publishing deal on it too, though it wouldn't be available to buy in the shops for about another ten months.

I was taking lots of photographs of Gina and Kaylen, as well as professional commissions and some artistic shots for my own pleasure. I took some photographs of the three of us together with the use of the tripod and self-timer. Gina had one of them printed out, framed, and put up in the hallway.

I'd rediscovered, and rekindled, my love of photography and, because of Gina, I'd learned how to express myself again via my photographs. They now spoke louder than ever before because you need a heart and soul to take meaningful images, and Gina had given me that.

I'd spent lord knows how many years thinking that everybody else was missing the point but, maybe, it was me who was missing the point all along. I'd allowed the years to trudge on by as I ambled my way through life up to my knees in a thick miserable sidewalk of treacle, dark treacle that was of my own making. There are decent, kind and loving people in this world, people with pure and organic souls. You just have to open your eyes and heart to be able to see them. My heart had been closed for a very long time but now it had been re-ignited and it was well and truly open.

As for the future and all my predictions of a miserable outlook followed by Armageddon for the entire human race, well, the truth is, nobody knows how long any of us have left – I certainly don't. I learned, through Kaylen, that there's no point in worrying, or trying to predict, when the world is going to come to an end as there's too much to live for in the here and the now. We go through life thinking that we're immortal, that we're going to live forever, but it doesn't work like that. Anything can happen to any of us at any time, totally out of the blue, like it did with my parents and my sister, like it did with Gina's husband and sister. Life's too precious to let it stagnate and waste away so from here on out I was going to enjoy every minute of what time I did have left on this planet, with my beautiful loving family.

Epilogue

1 year later

Gina didn't feel comfortable living in the house where she'd spent many years living with her husband. I must admit, when we sat down and talked about it, it did feel a little bit strange and I could understand why she wanted to move. Gina would never forget her husband and I understood this and I wouldn't want her to. Just because somebody dies it doesn't mean they're gone. She didn't want to move to a different house because of the memories of her husband; she wanted to move so she could build new memories with Kaylen and I. Gina had not been able to move on from her husband's death, but she was well on her way to moving forward now. She wanted us to find a new house together, where we could start afresh. We stayed in Cambridgeshire, as we all liked it here.

Gina went back to work, but only on a part time basis, and she worked from home, for another magazine. She didn't need the money as she'd received a rather large insurance payout after her husband's death and another one from Kaylen's deceased parents' life insurance policies. But she wanted to keep a foot in the world and in the creative camp. As for me, I'd become friends with a couple of magazine editors who'd commissioned photographs and accompanying stories from me and they were doing a really good job of spreading the word about my work. I'd got to the point where I could pick and choose the assignments I was offered. The pay was pretty good, but I'd chosen not to work too many hours because I wanted to spend as much time as I could with Gina and Kaylen.

I'd said goodbye to Shannon, my therapist, for a second time. I'd called her back on the Monday I was supposed to end it all, to her relief, and arranged to go and see her every week. I'd continued to see Shannon for about five months until we got to the point where she felt I didn't need it anymore. She managed to put my childhood, and all the crap that went with it, to bed, along with the mental damage that losing my ability to play the piano, in any virtuosic capacity at least, had done. As for all my failed relationships, it was quite simple really and in the end it didn't require that much analysing. Most of the women I'd had brief relationships with were totally unsuitable for me (and vice-versa) and it was simply a case of waiting – and being patient – for the right woman to come along. Now she has. As a thank you present I'd given Shannon my eight CD recordings, which Decca – having found out about my finger injury – had since released as a box set to celebrate my career. In the booklet that came with the CD there was a section about me, and the injury that brought my career to a sad end, and the composers whose works I'd recorded. Classic FM magazine did a story on me and the box set shot up the classical charts.

Kaylen was now seven and, after she heard a CD of me performing Beethoven's Moonlight sonata, she asked me if I could teach her to play the piano. We bought a nice upright and put it in the study in our new house. Even though my middle finger on my left hand didn't work too well, I could still play, just nothing virtuosic. Liszt's Transcendental Studies and Rachmaninoff's Piano concerto number 2 were out, but the odd Chopin nocturne or slower Beethoven movements didn't pose too much of a problem. I enjoyed teaching Kaylen and, although she was a total beginner, I avoided tuition books with pictures of green frogs and other animals on the pages. She said they had nothing to do with music and that they were silly. I agreed.

Oh yes, I almost forgot. Gina and I got married. I was never that bothered about marriage, having been there and done it once before. I figured that two people didn't need a piece of paper to show that they were in love with each other. Gina was of the same opinion, but it was Kaylen who wanted us to get married – who were we to argue?

About the Author

Nigel Cooper is a British author of fiction. He writes across a diverse range of genres including: contemporary, psychological thrillers, suspense, crime and supernatural. He found his 'voice' as the editor of his own magazine, which he ran for eight years before becoming a full time author of fiction in 2011. He studied screenwriting in London and ran a video production company before becoming a freelance journalist writing articles, reviews and stories for various newspapers and magazines. Nigel also studied to be a private investigator and spent a year working as a PI, the knowledge of which certainly helps with his crime writing today. Having attained a degree in classical piano performance Nigel loves nothing more than to sit and play Beethoven when he isn't writing. Also, being a Hi-Fi nut and a vinyl connoisseur he can often be found in Market Hill in Cambridge browsing through the used vinyl stalls in the hope of picking up a mint condition first pressing of 'Selling England by the Pound'. Nigel also loves a good game of badminton and enjoys walks through the meadows along the river Cam. He lives and writes in Cambridgeshire, UK.

Photo by: John Lawrence

For more info about the author visit:

www.nigelcooperauthor.co.uk

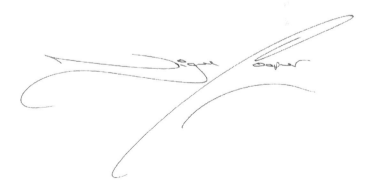

THE 95,000 WORD SUICIDE NOTE

Generic Pool Publishing

ISBN: 978-0-9573307-5-7

Printed in Poland
by Amazon Fulfillment
Poland Sp. z o.o., Wrocław

58546440R00226